Montauk Tango

From The Ashes of 9/11 To The Frying Pan Of A Hampton's Restaurant

Lewis Gross

iUniverse, Inc.
New York   Bloomington

Montauk Tango
From The Ashes of 9/11 To The Frying Pan Of A Hampton's Restaurant

This is a work of fiction. All of the characters, names, incidents, organizations, and dialogue
in this novel are either the products of the author's imagination or are used fictitiously.

iUniverse books may be ordered through booksellers or by contacting:

iUniverse
1663 Liberty Drive
Bloomington, IN 47403
www.iuniverse.com
1-800-Authors (1-800-288-4677)

Because of the dynamic nature of the Internet, any Web addresses or links contained in this book
may have changed since publication and may no longer be valid. The views expressed in this work
are solely those of the author and do not necessarily reflect the views of the publisher, and the
publisher hereby disclaims any responsibility for them.

ISBN: 978-1-4502-1643-2 (sc)
ISBN: 978-1-4502-1645-6 (dj)
ISBN: 978-1-4502-1644-9 (ebk)

Printed in the United States of America

iUniverse rev. date: 4/1/2010

Author's Note

What you are about to read is a fictionalized account of my family's experiences while opening a restaurant in the Hamptons. I have taken some liberties with the duration and sequence of events for simplification, clarification, and most importantly, to get to the truth of it all. Names and locations have been altered and are not based on any one individual or business. I want to thank my family and the Montauk community for playing the unwitting muses. In particular, I want to honor my wife, whose bust has proven the perfect partner for my pedestal.

Chapter 1

Memorial Day

In a spontaneous act of guerilla tango, I tore my wife from her baking cupcakes and forced her into a tightly held dance embrace. Fortunately, no one was watching. Pulling her outside through the back door of our seaside restaurant and into the unoccupied beach parking lot, we aped arms in parallel position.

"Beast!" she cried.

I ripped her apron off and led her through an impromptu tango. Our entire bodies engaged in the complex rhythm—slow, slow, quick, quick, slow. The tango lesson continued. "One, two, left leg back on three, four, cross on five, right leg back on six, seven, close on eight. Good, now repeat."

The poor woman shook like a fallen leaf.

"Opening day jitters?" I asked, face-to-face. "Remember. Eight steps and cross at five." Turning shoulders, I dragged my shoeless left foot slowly through the sand.

"If you have to speak it, you can't lead it." She hesitantly stepped back on her right and made a half-hearted embellished kick. "The cupcakes?" she screamed.

"Screw the cupcakes."

We walked tentatively in an open embrace following an imaginary circle, a solitary couple dancing on an empty stretch of beach. Soon, we picked up the pace and closed the space, intimately attached breast to chest. A few practice exchanges and then we connected cheek-to-cheek, till our foreheads touched at the third eye.

She looked down at her watch. "Scissors. The boys are late?" She stopped dancing and attempted an escape back to her baking.

"I called already."

Their incoming truck roared louder than the crashing waves.

"Now look what you've done, gone and woke the child."

"Sure I called, to see if they lived. Everyone is waiting," I said.

"You're just a fair weather father. Can't you have some blind faith for once?"

Giving up on the tango, we proceeded back to the Shack for last-minute preparations. Opening night was only three hours away and our three coming-of-age sons were already late. Tracey put the apron back on. Fortunately, a black flatbed loaded with wooden fish crates and nets of clams tore into the rear lot and screeched to a halt.

"Oh, look, they've come to play with us," Tracey said.

"Morning?" I rolled my wrist inward to show time.

"Gifts from the sea!" Our oldest son, the fisherman, offered up a freshly caught porgy and kissed it on the lips. As he affectionately squeezed the body, a dark fluid dripped down his arm. "Ah, herring for breakfast?"

"Do we really need to know what's in the anus?" asked the musician, our middle son, as he helped his brother unload the dock produce from the truck.

The youngest, the family chef, came out to assist. "I can't cook a Montaco without the fish. Where were you guys?"

"I had to check out a blitz. Fortunately, it was a false alarm," Arden said.

"Otherwise, we might still be there." Sky dropped the load of clams.

Head chef Scott, his mane of hair held beneath a flour sack cap, confidently strolled past us, canvassing his piece of turf, issuing opening-day directives. We paid him megabucks to whisk the crew of seasonal help into a well-bound kitchen. Gathering the whole staff together in the back prep room for a last-minute pep talk, Scott preached his restaurant rules. "We make the big bucks by buying the best ingredients, preparing it just the way I taught you to, and persuading the customers to try it."

My beautiful wife beamed like a proud parent at her son's graduation.

He looked each one of us in the eye. "I'm confident. You kids are the heart of our community. Just do what I taught you, and the customers will love us. To the Shack!" Scott raised his arm in triumph.

"Gig Shack, Gig Shack!" the troops cheered.

"Young-ins, to your stations!" Scott railed. One for all, and all for one, they high-fisted. Some positioned themselves outside for the first celebrity sighting.

I followed our leader with rapt attention as he inspected the final dinner preparations. "Tell me, Scott, what is it going to be like opening a restaurant in the Hamptons? Will we make any money? Will it make me happy?"

His face cringed as if a failed root canal was calling.

I assumed we would be an immediate hit in this seaside summer retreat. Our new restaurant would be a neighborly affair where local youth could grab a Montaco, the striped bass caught that morning from the shore, or hang for an impromptu jazz gig. We'd create a beachside Bohemian Bistro where surfers and surfcasters could share an espresso with resident artistic dignitaries, such as Paul Simon and Jimmy Buffet, while admiring my son's handmade guitars. Meanwhile, Edward Albee would be entertaining a gaggle of want to-be playwrights, and Ralph Lauren would be rolling up in an antique Rolls Royce. Like the announcer's voice from "Live! It's Saturday Night!" we would play "Live! At the Gig Shack!"

Pots and pans clanged like harbored metal boats, waiters ran to and fro practicing the taking of notes, charred meat emitted barbequed motes, and expectations of a full belly churned my stomach's hopes. Suddenly, the noise from the dozen cooks and counter staff muted. Scott stopped in silence. Silence.

I continued talking. "Everyone always said Tracey and I would be perfect restaurateurs. I'm a natural host and she loves to cook. Do you think Montauk's ready for a change?" Questions I should have asked before opening the door. "My biggest concern is the effect it will have on my marriage."

Slowly, ever so slowly, he stuck a pointed finger into my chest and surgically traced the outlines of my heart, his hand stopping in the center as it played with an open button. With expert deliberation, his hands worked, but his tongue cut like a scalpel. "Doc, you stick to your teeth," he said, referring to my dental practice in New York City, "and leave the restaurant business to me." With that, Scott focused his attention on the inspection and barked more last-minute instructions. Round one went to him and we hadn't even opened yet.

Next on the list was the outside beer and wine bar. We walked through the back kitchen prep area, past the gelato counter and through the indoor dining area, out a side door and into the alley. Under an awning, the bartender assembled the outside wine and beer bar, haphazardly placing the beer bottles. "Man, this is great. We're going to rock Montauk," said the young man.

"What did I say to you? Line the bottles up neatly," ordered Scott, rearranging the beers in size order.

"I thought by nationality," the bartender apologized. "Sorry, I'm a bar back."

Arranging the bottles with stern concentration, Scott said, "Then get out from behind the bar. If you're going to be our full-time bartender, you have to know beer from the customer's point of view, as well as the origin and flavor of every bottle you serve."

"Yeah, man, I'm down on the beers already." He took a deep, satisfying swig of Oregon's Dead Guy Ale and smiled. "That's number thirty-nine on my list."

"Keep up the good work." Scott adjusted the sleeve on his patchwork velvet coat, and we headed back inside to review the twelve flavors of gelato.

"I'm ready, boss," the just-graduated-high-school counter girl said.

"Remember, as soon as a customer places an order, their mouths start to salivate," instructed Scott. "They picture the food before it hits the plate."

"No worries, boss, your Lamburgini's a homerun. Ground Moroccan lamb and secret spices on a whole wheat roll," the girl said, and then sensually licked the length of her lips. Confident she could explain the menu to an incredulous customer, she blushed suddenly with embarrassment. "The spices are Moroccan, not the lamb? I think. Sorry, this is my first real job."

Our food would be substantial, honest fare. Eco-farmed vegetables simmered into a ratatouille and seasoned with my garden's homegrown herbs. Lobster bisque braised in their shells and the bones of hand-caught black fish. A perfectly prepared burger with freshly spaded fries. In our food hall, there would be no simple starch, like they serve Up

Island; there would be no deep-fried, fat-laden, nutritionally devoid spring rolls and high-calorie wontons—mere spoons to mop up alcohol and their patrons' pennies.

Continuing his check-off list, Scott made a virtual tour of the entire restaurant, from rear prep area to the L-shaped front counter to the interior seating for fifty, side alley bar, and additional sidewalk bistro seating for thirty. "That should do it."

In the corner, the food runner was frenching her boyfriend. They were inseparable, like twins joined at the lips. "What's up, boss?" she chimed in an attempt to untangle her boyfriend's tongue from a mouthful of her metal braces. "No worries."

Scott's face twanged as if he had ground down on that same infected tooth that stood above its socket. He looked away in disgust.

Our three sons, aged eighteen through twenty-three, swatted stray flies and shagged odd jobs, this being a family-run, initially low-budget team.

The only employee besides Scott with any experience was a seventy-year-old grandma, whom we had stolen from the Fish Farm for a free agent's salary. She had worked the food business for centuries and was slated to run the food prep.

"The cool slaws a' ready." She spoke in a Bonacker drawl, the unmistakable patois of the Lazy Point locals. She waved a six-inch steel blade like a warm-up bat and added, "You wan' a mango salsa?" That woman had cracked more clamshells than the seagulls' dive-bombing off Gosman's Dock.

"No dancing," replied Scott, rolling his eyes and walking away briskly. He turned back to me and whispered, "I need to teach that woman how to use a food processor. Cutting every cabbage by hand, she'll be here all night."

I was the silent partner, as long as I stayed silent. Otherwise, I was benched.

Tracey had her team raring to go. The fish tacos were jumping, and the Gig Chips, homemade and spiced, were flying out of the fryer as we anxiously awaited the invasion of tourists. Located in Montauk, a seasonally busy pedestrian spot and surrounded by other, long existing restaurants, we were bound to be an immediate hit.

Standing in the street, we admired our handiwork. "It was a steal!" I told Scott the story of how we bought the building that housed the present-day restaurant. "The broker called it a real steal."

"Brokers need to shake the leaves," he said arrogantly, winning round two.

"We were always feeding the local kids anyway," I said, offering yet another reason our restaurant was destined to be a hit. "Our house was their food hall."

Deciding not to comment on that, Scott instead said, "I love Tracey's design, the corrugated steel walls." His eyes searched longingly for our perpetually busy hostess. "Using the local phone exchange, 668, great name."

"The legal name is 668 the Gig Shack, but we refer to it as the Shack, for short."

"Yeah, whatever."

I stuck my hands in my pockets. "Will we ever make a buck?"

"Money, money, money." Scott fingered his unkempt mop.

I ignored his insult and continued with the story. "It was originally a rundown ice cream parlor, but Shaggy, the previous owner, ran it like a regular restaurant. He even had a full liquor bar outside in the alley. He showed me the license one time."

"My menu is going to shake that old timer off his pedestal. You just wait and see—I'm going to put Montauk on the food map," boasted Scott.

"Shaggy is an institution in this town. He was the Grand Marshal once in the St. Patrick's Day Parade. That's bigger than being the mayor of Montauk." I didn't know why I was defending my competitor, who operated another nearby restaurant, but it seemed like the right thing to do at the time.

"Just wait till the Hamptons gets a taste of my Lamburgini and Montacos." With his floral pants, polka-dotted bandana, and tie-dyed sneakers, Scott looked like the Jolly Green Giant perched beside the little table runner. At four foot eleven, she was Lolita-like, with perky breasts and tight-fitted shorts inked with "The End" on her ass. The two made an incongruous couple out on the sidewalk, handing out flyers to passersby.

"I hope you're right," said the runner, surveying the empty dining room.

Scott promised, "By the end of summer, we'll be making money hand over fist."

"How come nobody's coming in?" I asked.

"Aren't you supposed to be the silent partner?" he said, trying to hand me a stack of flyers. "Here, you want something to do?"

I pushed the flyers back. "Not my job."

We circled one another like two male cats spotting new territory. Which of us would get to leave his scent? He knew the business, but I had the bucks. After a three-second eyeball, he retreated into the back prep kitchen. What had I won?

Eventually, an older couple entered from the front sidewalk patio and peeked their faces through the open door. They appeared confused as they searched the corrugated steel walls for a familiar clue. "Wasn't this an ice cream parlor?" they asked. "It looks so clean and new." Their eyes searched the hand-painted and artistically calligraphic blackboard menu. "New ownership?" They looked at each other incredulously, as if the menu were written in Chinese.

"Try the Lamburgini." Before I could explain what a Lamburgini was, they had run out and into Shaggy's restaurant across the street.

The evening continued in much the same way. Customers would look confused and then run to Shaggy for dinner. By the end of the night, not only weren't we an immediate hit, we were completely shut out.

Blame it on the bad weather, the bad economy, or just bad planning, but our opening weekend was a disaster. The locals came. More often they went. They'd peek in but preferred to wait an hour and a half for a table elsewhere. Over our heads, it rained and rained. Another perfect spring day.

That first Sunday night, Tracey and I waited for the Hampton Jitney to arrive. The rising tension was etched into my beautiful wife's brow. Fear had filled the creases the Botox had missed, her face frozen in a deeply pained frown.

"What was I thinking?" Tracey moaned. "I've sunk all our available cash into this folly. We don't know squat about this business. At this pace, we'll never break even."

"Don't fret. The season has just begun." I placed a hand on her shoulder.

"No one came, not even our friends," she fretted.

"It may take a little time for the community to understand your product. I'm confident you and the boys will be a big hit."

"Maybe we should have had a hard opening, hired a few celebrities and invited the local papers for a free bash. What do you think?"

"*Now* you're asking me? You didn't want any press releases. You're still not confident in the staff."

"But look how packed that new Surf Lodge was this weekend. They just opened, and they're already being written up in the *Star*. What did I do wrong?"

"They're just a bunch of drop-in, soft-top surfers! You're the real deal."

"The wave should have been wide enough for us all," she moaned.

"Surfing is a territorial sport. The wave belongs to the cat most willing."

The owners of the Surf Lodge were experienced New York City restaurateurs. Their big-bucks backer had hired party promoters, professional press agents, winners of top-chef contests, and the best looking bus maids and bar boys this side of Shinnicock. They were an instant hit, shipping out supermodels and celebrities in long black limos. They'd already created a new entertainment niche. Overnight, the Manhattan Meat Market had marched into Montauk and chased away the local fish.

"The townies aren't happy their fishnets are being run through with high-heeled stilettos. The High Liners have no respect. They think they can park their Lamborghini anywhere and we're supposed to eat it? A war's coming for the soul of this community, and you're on the front lines," I warned, right before retreating to the safety of the Jitney commuter bus to New York City.

"You're glad to be rid of us, aren't you?" Tracey said as she waved me off.

"Call if I can be of help." I blew my wife a good-bye kiss, and with sadness mixed with a little glee, escaped to the relative saneness of my own professional life as a dentist in New York. She wasn't altogether wrong in her assessment of my motives. I dearly love my family, but this new venture of hers was putting a huge strain on our marriage, not to mention our finances. There wasn't much I could do to help except raise some dough. As Sarah Palin advised, "Drill, baby, drill." We needed an income cushion in case the restaurant failed, though we had projected some initial losses.

The restaurant was such a huge responsibility, and we were getting by only by the skin of our teeth. We might not change the culinary world, but we had a lot of mouths to feed. My wife, our sons, and all their contemporaries were dependent on my largess. In New York City, the mouths, or at least the skin of the teeth, fed me.

I had other reasons to be a little gleeful. In New York City, I lived alone and was responsible only for myself, like a bachelor, washing the dishes and making the bed when I felt like it. Tracey was a neat freak, reworking my bed mess with military precision.

There was another more secretly sinister motive to my decamping. I'd fallen in love. Living alone in NYC since 9/11, I'd needed to fill the hours of loneliness. In my new, empty nest with my alternative adult lifestyle, I'd fallen. I'd fallen head over heels for the Argentine tango. Who would have guessed I was a great dancer?

"I love you," I said to my wife each week as I boarded the Jitney. I spoke without guilt as a recurring image of swirling tangueros waltzed through slivers of infrared shadows, a kaleidoscope of last week's tango milonga. The visual image still hung thick with the scent of dancer's sweat.

"Don't work too hard." Her smile clouded with worry. "We'll be okay. I love you too," she said, waving good-bye to my fleeing Jitney.

"You will always be the only woman whose compliments I crave."

It was the iconic summer of 668.

Chapter 2

The Off-Season Marriage

Looking back at its conception six months earlier, it's amazing that Tracey even delivered this baby. The Gig Shack was the brainchild of my wife, procreated in an epiphany of parentage. Having grown up working summers in Montauk, she had always dreamed of escaping NYC to return to her roots and open her own eatery.

My wife and our three sons had moved to Montauk a few years back, after the debacle of the World Trade Center collapse. The 9/11 epochal had filled our loft in Tribeca with six inches of human dust and chemical debris, so the next morning, in one of those "Ah-ha!" moments the Greek philosophers ruminate and religious fanatics fantasize about, we picked up sticks, made lemonade from lemons, and relocated to our summer home in Montauk. The boys enrolled in East Hampton High School, and although I would gladly garner sympathy, this was no Greek tragedy. Fortunately, my wife and sons made a seamless transition to coastal life after that timeline moment.

"You can go surfing before and after school," we cajoled Gray, the youngest and most resistant son, who pined for his closed school in Lower Manhattan. Images of long boards, short boards, and boogie boards floated though his head.

"You can drive trucks with big wheels and loud engines," we encouraged the middle one, who had just earned a license. Skylar was already fantasizing about owning a Bubby Bus, a fashionably loud pickup truck lifted off the ground on oversized tires.

"You can go fishing every day," we told Arden, the oldest, already pulling out his gear to spend his first night in the waves slaughtering striped bass.

My wife became a yoga teacher at the local spa and developed an enthusiastic following. My wife is a spectacular woman. At fifty-some years, she has the face and body a woman half her age would envy. We suspect she sold her soul to the devil, because as the rest of us age, she seems to get younger. Many clients took yoga class only to witness her perfect Downward Dog or Standing Hand to Big Toe.

I continued to commute to New York City every Monday night, where I am a holistic dentist in Lower Manhattan. A few months post-9/11, we finally reopened the apartment, and I now live there alone three to four nights a week. My Bicoastal Existence (the coasts of Long Island) has been a serviceable enough arrangement, and our Weekend Marriage worked reasonably well until my Off-Season Wife decided to open the restaurant. With some trepidation, I agreed to buy the building, although in the back of my mind I feared that I was buying more than real estate. I'd heard it a hundred times: "Opening a restaurant is the quickest way to get divorced." I wasn't too concerned, not really. We loved each other, and after twenty-five years of marriage, it was her first opportunity to do something on her own.

Fretting in the bank conference room this past February, with pen in my hand, I hesitated putting my name to paper. *If your life is so perfect, why tinker with it?* The commitment contract waited until I'd satisfied my marital due-diligences.

"I love to cook and I always wanted to open my own restaurant!" she joyfully whispered, as we were about to sign. "It will give the boys an opportunity to do something with their lives." Our sons had come home to relax after knocking around colleges for various semesters. "Hello, they're waiting." She pushed the paper toward me.

"Banker's on the clock." I pushed the paper back. "Closing or no closing."

The banker absentmindedly bit at his nails from the far end of the conference table while our lawyer left the room and took a long leak.

"Maybe we should give the kids one more strike at school?" I said.

"Would you wake up? They refuse to step back in a classroom."

"Something close by this time—where we can keep an eye on them?"

"Jesus, are you ever in denial."

I recalled a visit to one of my son's schools; the closet in his dorm was filled with hundreds of empty boxes. Who collects beer boxes? "So, we should buy them a bar?"

"You're not buying it for them," she hissed through teeth I'd once bleached.

"Don't you remember the therapist's message? The family is powerless."

"We're buying it as a family investment," she insisted.

"It seems like a pretty expensive way to get them to work. Can't we just pay someone to employ them?" I pushed the papers away.

"You've been talking about buying real estate here for years. This is your last chance. I want it!" She stamped her delicate but determined Aries foot.

"But they haven't worked the past two summers."

"I know they'll be really good at it. They just need another chance. You're a little late for cold feet." She clawed every gesture like a cornered mother bear.

"Maybe they should work as waiters somewhere else for a while first," I suggested.

"They refuse to work for other people—only their mother. Look, this is the last time. You're constantly shopping for real estate but never buying. Sign or get off the pot." There was no turning back as she bit at my hand that held the pen.

My hand shook, but still, I held out for a better offer. Tracey was both buyer and seller. I played my last card.

The bored banker tallied dust motes.

Our lawyer fidgeted her timepiece and cocked an ear toward our conversation.

"I don't know. I was hoping you'd move back to New York City with me after Gray graduated from high school."

Tracey acted as if she hadn't heard me. "We can finally employ all of their friends, the Lost and Found Boys of Montauk who live in our house half the time anyway. Make them work for their room and board now." Overcome with a sudden wave of brilliance, she continued. "It's the ultimate in community service. If you're a truly rich man, you'll give the local youth jobs and training."

"I'd rather donate to the Red Cross."

"You *are* a rich man?" She winked a challenge through pencil-thin brows. "You're constantly advising people to give back to their community. Here's your chance."

My mind wandered. When the children were young, I had been the founder and president of the Downtown Little League. For ten years, I was the Big Daddy, the mayor of Tribeca, the guardian of over five hundred families. It was only after 9/11, the closure of our home baseball fields, and our relocation that I retired from this voluntary post. Our residence had proven to be medically unhealthy for upwards of one year, but my family's escape from downtown Manhattan is not a moment I'm proud of. Tribeca had been our home, our community. Our children were born on the city streets. Running away to Montauk had appeared cowardly.

"Hello. We're waiting?" Tracey waved a hand in my face.

My guilt resurfaced in the conference room. "I remember the faces of all the Little Leaguers when I told them we were moving. They looked so wounded, so scared to stay and pick up the pieces when their general was running from the battle."

"Did I ever tell you that my father packed up our family during the Cuban Missile Crisis and shipped us to Canada for six months?" Tracey confided. "You have nothing to be ashamed of. You gave your heart to the city."

My mind escaped again to the West Side Highway that morning. Gray and I, a thousand lost souls, shrouds of office workers and Wall Street tycoons, shoeless and covered in contaminated dust, running away, crying into unconnected cell phones. Across the highway, a fireman had commandeered a motorcycle, and with helmet and uniform hosted, headed south, across the path of humanity, into the avalanche of ashes from the second tower. That was true bravery, one man's charge of the Light Brigade.

"Focus on the future, please," Tracey whispered. "Sign the fucking paper."

I daydreamed. I had been a coward. When City Hall called a few days after 9/11, canvassing for trained forensic experts to help with the identification of the victims, I froze at the steps of the medical examiner's office, unable to face the morgue's music.

"Create a new community, here with us," my wife said, alluding to Montauk.

I had also been an active member of Community Board One in New York City. Community service was in my blood, and I bit her bait for local, Montauk activism. Tracey had been the First Lady of Little League. Now the restaurant would be her opportunity to do Little League for twenty-one-year-olds. I would play the first sir.

"Community service? A privately held, not-for-profit?" I asked.

"We're doing this for the family; I don't care if it makes money."

"I'll agree, but only on the condition that this is a seasonal business. I want my wife back when the season's done."

"An off-season marriage!" she confirmed. We shook hands. "A marriage of convenience," she reiterated.

I John Hancocked the declaration, unsure if I'd agreed to marital independence.

The banker gleefully closed his bookings. "Thank you for your patience. I'm in your debt," he said, noting the obvious IOU.

Our lawyer departed to the next big deal. "I'll send you a bill."

With closed eyes, I waited for a special thank-you hug, a long kiss, some sign or even a hint of a well-earned intimacy from my wife. Instead, I got a quick peck on the cheek.

"Work!" She plowed past me with the out-stretched, straight arm of an NFL fullback. "No time for romance. I've got to write my business plan."

The gift I got that day for closing was a hug at Tracey's fleeting shadow and a lifetime of blessed memories. I had invested in real estate and family, tangible assets. Not such a bad business deal, as these things go, but it got me to thinking. Would opening a family restaurant really buy me happiness?

What the modern husband wants is to be a witness to his wife's life, to see her failures and celebrate her accomplishments, to be a witness of fact. But even after twenty-five years of marriage, I'm no expert witness. I haven't a clue what my wife really thinks. Tracey says I'm hard of hearing because I don't understand what she is saying, but I hear her words clearly enough. It's just that her sentences don't make any sense.

Chapter 3

If You Build It, Will They Eat It?

A week after we had signed the commitment letter, as I slept, the whole Montauk house started to shake as if it were the WTC collapse all over again. Sky, the bartender, and the other cook—our local garage band—were laying down a riff from an upstairs room, shaking late winter icicles from the windows. Although their musical talents were quite good, my head was splitting from the volume and a growing anxiety that the restaurant we were about to close on was in much worse shape than we had been told. There were leaks all over, the roof was in need of repairs, and the plumbing wasn't functional. The place probably needed two hundred thousand worth of renovations. I couldn't sit still and do nothing.

"Tell the lawyer we want to reduce the bid." I sat up in bed.

"She'll blow an ovary if we change the bid." Tracey yawned, still half-asleep.

I rolled the wife over. "She's supposed to work for you."

"Are you second-guessing my choice in lawyers?" She was awake now.

"No, I'm not, it's just she's so hormonal. I've never met such an estrogenic attorney. Everything you ask her is such a big problem that you don't even want to ask her advice. I swear she's just being difficult to justify her fee."

"Then you call her," said Tracey, handing me the phone.

The lawyer was a local girl who had once been a barmaid at one of Shaggy's joints. Small-town justice: everyone's either related, employed by, ex-employed by, or in debt to each other. Where did an out-of-town dentist fit into this economy?

I took the phone and called the lawyer. "What's up?" she said when I told her it was me. Getting her help would be like pulling teeth.

15

"The place is a mess." I tightened my forceps.

"You're crazy. Nobody reneges on Shaggy. He's a tough guy," she warned.

"Still and all, the place is a mess." I released the pressure.

"It's take it or leave it, but if you insist, I'll prepare a motion for his attorney."

Every letter cost a thousand dollars. How much would I save? "Can't you just call Shaggy and tell him the place is in shambles?"

"I've got to live in this town; I'm not doing your dirty work. Call your damn broker." She hung up the phone.

"I'm going over to talk to Shaggy directly," I told Tracey. "I want fifty off."

"If you screw up this deal, I'm going to kill you," she said, making a finger pistol.

"We're justified. It would be a new kitchen."

"Just give him the asking price. I hate that game." She pointed at my head.

"Do you know how many teeth I have to drill?" I said, throwing up my arms in frustration. "It's not like money—"

She interrupted, "Yeah, I've heard this a hundred times. Crowns and bridges don't molt like shark's teeth. Now, go see Shaggy, but don't screw up the deal."

With much trepidation, I confronted Shag in front of his bar. A large man with a weather-beaten face, he had succeeded in the local restaurant business for over forty years by beating the starch out of dissenting chefs, uncooperative waitresses, and complaining neighbors. I had heard he'd kicked Killjoy, the owner of the souvenir shop, clear across Route 27 when he complained about the bar noise.

I decided to appeal to his sense of compassion. "Shag, I know you've been a great father, that you built all these restaurants for your family. All I'm trying to do is give my kids a chance too." Shaggy sniffed the air, unsure where I was going. "We're a local family, just trying to do good for the community." Finally, getting up the courage, "I need you to cut the price … a little."

His right hand clenched into an extra-large, tight fist.

"Listen, Shag, the building needs a lot of work, at least fifty grand more than I'd anticipated. I'm going to have to lower my initial bid."

His left hand clenched into a tight fist. His lips were pinched into an angry, tooth-spitting frown, yet, strangely, he didn't utter a sound or throw a punch. Instead, Shaggy looked me hard in the eye. It was a contest of wills.

I swallowed the dried spit of my wife's threat, ready to leave a beaten man.

"Let's split the difference, big guy. Twenty-five?" he offered just as I was about to exit empty handed.

I shook his right hand immediately. "It's a deal, sir."

"Let me know if there's anything you need—a chef, a crepe machine? I won them in a poker game. By the way, I got a cousin down at the liquor board if you run into any problems with the alcohol license. I was running a full bar in that outside alley. It was real popular with the late-night Irish." He flashed me a copy of the liquor license. It looked legit. "With a little love, you should be able to turn the tables hands over fists. A mighty fine little restaurant you got. You won't have any problems if I can help it!"

"That's mighty gracious of you, sir." I exhaled.

The next day, my friend Kevin came by to take a look. He was a professional chef with many years of experience opening restaurants. It was a gray and rainy day that March, and it was hard to muster much enthusiasm since the Shack was unheated. We had hoped Kevin would go partners in running the place, but he had other, more lucrative engagements as a private chef for a wealthy Southampton family. "Easy money, no hassles. You get to keep your life and your wife," he giggled.

He looked around the nearly empty dining room and bit his lip. There was a long counter on one side that held broken ice cream equipment. He inspected the kitchen. From the look in his eyes, I could tell he thought we were crazy. "This stuff's all garbage. You'll need all new ovens and fryers." He wiped the grease from the poorly maintained stove. "When Shaggy left, he obviously wasn't planning on coming back."

"But he swore the kitchen was fully operational," Tracey said.

"Listen, little darling, the first lesson in this business is to not believe anything people tell you. They're all liars and cheats. If they're not lying, it's only because they're too dumb. Take your pick; either way, you'll always lose."

We inspected the stove, which had three inches of crud burnt into it.

"Didn't you read *Kitchen Confidential* by Anthony Bourdain? He warned that dentists should stay out of the restaurant business."

"He didn't say anything about a yogi," countered Tracey.

Kevin laughed. "He didn't have to. They don't have any spare change. I hope you people know what you're getting yourselves into. You'll slave over a hot fire from sunrise to sunset, get burnt every time an employee walks out on your busiest night, and throw every penny you can muster into the joint. If you're lucky, I mean really lucky, you won't lose your entire shirt the first year. The restaurant business is a killer." He laughed louder and slapped his thighs. "But that's what keeps the industry going; there's always another sucker born to burn the doughnuts!"

"You're just jealous," Tracey said, and she meant it.

"How would you like it if I decided to pull teeth? Since I'm an expert at brushing my teeth, that must entitle me to do your next root canal. Or better yet, because I can do a sit up, I'm sure I can teach a class of yoga. Why is it that people think they can blindly open a restaurant, just because they can fry an egg?"

"You wish you were me," she challenged with increased tension.

After thinking for a moment, he conceded, "You're right. I apologize. I've always wanted to run my own place. So, what kind of food are you thinking of serving?"

"Tacos, burritos, simple food that the local kids would like and can afford," she said. "The kind of food my kids already cook at home."

Kevin laughed out loud. "Kids—you can't make any money off the local kids. Well, maybe if you ran a year-round pizzeria, but even that's nickel and dime. You're talking a seasonal business. A hundred days of hell! All the restaurants in Montauk close up tight after the summer. You got maybe a three- to four-month window to make the money for the year. If you want to open a restaurant in the Hamptons, you've got to kill the tourists in the summer. Soak 'em for every penny they got."

"I don't care about the tourists," said Tracey.

"I love you guys, but nobody's going to drive that long stretch from East Hampton for a taco. You need to create a destination menu."

"What's your advice?" I asked.

"A seasonal restaurant is tough. It's like opening a new business every year. You've got to hire new staff and fix all the equipment that broke while you were away. You've got to advertise all over again because people forgot about you as soon as your doors closed. The Hamptons is the worst place to open a restaurant, and Montauk is the end of the Hamptons." Turning toward me, he asked, "So, while she's frying the doughnuts from morning till night, what's your job going to be?"

"I hadn't thought much past buying the place," I said.

"The family's here, and you're out on weekends? Are you prepared to dice carrots?"

"No, Tracey won't let me in the kitchen."

"So, you'll be the bartender?"

"No, the boys want that job."

"Waiter?"

"I can't take orders."

"You need to find a job, or you'll go nuts."

"Okay, I'll crack the nuts. It doesn't really matter as long as I'm around the wife and the boys. I'm their business partner."

"She's made it very clear that this is *her* business!"

I knew he was right, but I couldn't think of a single job I wanted.

"You get to pay for it," he said, laughing to himself.

"I guess that makes me the accounts payable manager," I said.

"Well, buddy, you better manage to drill a few more teeth than normal, 'cause you're going to be paying for it. Through your teeth and nose."

He exited laughing, exposing a full smile that left no tooth unturned.

I ventured timidly to my car, seeking a moment for quiet solace and reflection. I needed to be alone to gather my thoughts and evaluate the implications of our investment. Turning on the stereo, a heavy metal riff blasted at full volume in my ears, tearing my inner meniscus, an unwelcome reminder that one of our sons had recently borrowed these wheels without asking. The band Shadow's Fall was screaming violent lyrics about the end of the world, toppling buildings, electromagnetic mind control, and the light that blinds. I couldn't understand half the words, but their ferocious conspiracy theories made for a melodic witches brew. Why did they have to yell so loud? They were beating a dead horse. I clicked off the burning CD and inserted one of my mellow tango melodies.

Driving directly east, I sought escape from the black hole of responsibility.

A gust of gray light split the sky as pregnant evil clouds charged in from the sea. Flashes of lightning echoed, announcing their arrival before the first tracer even hit land. The air smelled like fetid dune dust warmed in a kettle. Bursting over the town, raindrops machine-gunned the hood of my car. The angry downpour crashing on the roof and cascading across the front window caused a momentary driver's blindness. The sudden spring boil funneled off the feverishly beating wipers, hurling me through the deluge, toward the lighthouse at the end of the road, which had already plunged into almost darkness. Marvelous flashes of electrical bolts speckled the gloom and marked my way.

Parking in the empty lot, I pondered the expectation of a good hangover with a satisfying swig from my private stash. The brown liquor burned my throat. I couldn't think straight. I drank deeper, but the drug went to my belly instead of my brain. There were just too many interwoven people and their divergent needs. I took a walk.

The murmur of the storm disappeared as quickly as it had sounded, the lick heading straight out to sea right in front of me, engulfing Block and Plum Islands. I was left alone with a trailing scent of Black Pine. Torn leaves swirled at my feet and marked the entrance to the state park. Moonlight kissed the outline of the tall colonial era tower from which an incandescent eye circled, endlessly scanning the horizon, Foghorns echoed like spring peepers in Fort Pond and an incoming swell roared a rogue wave.

I followed a trail of leafy decomposition into the unknowable darkness of Turtle Cove. I'd fished this beach with Arden many nights before, but never by myself. That night the dunes held an unearthly presence, as if someone or something was following my steps. I could sense its cold breath on the nape of my neck and the nearby woods smelled from dead deer. Maybe it was an ill effect from the storm, but the trail looked unfamiliar. Unlocking the rusty gate, a shape suddenly flashed in my side view. In the hit and miss moonlight, I couldn't be sure an animal had crossed my path or if the mere passing of an overhead cloud had played shadow games. It was so fleeting, like when a mouse shoots past your feet and under a cabinet. Were my eyes playing a trick? I wasn't sure, but watching me from some distance were another's eyes that shone like two drops beading off a bush. Was it an illusion? Post-storm steam rose from the wet forest floor and convalesced into pearls. Did the vision bear fangs? In the surrounding overgrowth, it was impossible to tell. I called out loudly, "You'll not have me yet." The eyes blinked an alternating reflection from the lighthouse's flickering beam. There was no choice; to get to the beach I had to traverse this shaggy tunnel of ferns.

Step by step I crept toward the hovering reflection never once averting eye contact. Surveying the sandy ground in search of a stick or stone to use in self-defense, I picked up a broken branch a meter long. I could have run back to the safety of the car; instead, I attacked, making big sweeping motions to frighten the intruder. Without thinking, I advanced the steep path through a rocky crag and pounded a tree with all my might, until the weapon snapped, leaving me defenseless against the demon's attack. Either it was a false alarm or my bluff succeeded, because the tears of light evaporated. The unknown beast had fled.

An intense cold invaded me. To my right an oversized spider's web, thick with the sticky remains of fresh victims, blocked a retreat. Chilled to the bone and honestly having second thoughts, I turned meekly, but the road back up the hill appeared even darker then before. My eyesight and courage failed to adjust. Needles of moonlight perforated the forest shroud, and a cutting wind swept like a flying hand pushing me forward and toward the walking dunes just ahead. Taking a deep breath, I plunged in that direction. Finally, as the last fear ran dry, a window of star studded night opened through the head high beach grass. What a vision I beheld.

The pristine Montauk view was free of human pollution, the air uncut with the business of dust. In the clearance of the open beach, the radiant clarity of night sky unfurled with a million, trillion stars and blinking lights, swept clean by the fierce storm—all God's creation exposed in one glance. Out to sea, the Milky Way mirrored its own reflection in the surface ripples of murky water, and to the north, New England cities flickered with activity across the not so distant sound.

I walked to the edge of the now calm surf and noticed that it was littered with the rifled remains of many seas creatures tumbled from their shells and the human flotsam that often follows a storm. Hedges of seaweed marked the high tide, interspersed with plastic bottles, lost leaders, and lobster pots. Drawing back the curtain of darkness, my eyes finally adjusted, and I could pick colored beach glass out from glacial quartz. The bay stretched wide on either side, without another person, not even a solitary surfcaster, in sight. Finally, I was alone. The mighty ocean shimmered, and soon I realized that I was humming as I picked my way through the sand. I don't remember ever humming happiness before. I giggled and for a moment felt a sense of weightlessness and peace that I hoped would never end. I closed my eyes and listened to rocks rolling in the surf. All five senses held the universe as if in a dream. I was so tired, so very, very, tired. I wanted to fall into the sea and wash up on a foreign shore, Portugal or maybe Ireland. A message in a bottle, the current could have carried me powerlessly like a child's paper boat. I just wanted all the monkeys to leave me be.

Not yet, the mind monkeys whispered, *not yet*.

It was the stench of death that first caught my attention. Not even a dentist who deals with dead teeth and rotten root canals on a regular basis gets accustomed to that smell. I followed the vaporous thread of purification to its source. At my feet, a rotten corpse the size of a small child had begun to disintegrate. Possibly it had recently been tossed onto to the beach in the storm. In the gloom, I covered my nostril and put my eye closer, trying to make out the shape and identity of my discovery.

Using a firm stick, I leveraged the frigid body from its sandy coffin.

Already partially unearthed, it wasn't hard to tilt the swollen corpse a little on its side. Uncovered now, fresh odors slapped me in the face, and I reeled backward to let the fetid current pass. I threw up in my mouth. What had I discovered? It wasn't human. Was the creature another Montauk Monster, a cryptologist's wet dream, or Dr. Moreau mutation?

The previous summer, not too far from that same spot, some local girls had also discovered a dead animal. That creature appeared to have the legs of a dog, the body of a pig, and the face of a turtle. They took a photo, but the animal disappeared the next morning. No one could guess what it actually had been. The media got wind of their photo and quickly dubbed their find a genetic experiment from Plum Islands Animal Research Lab, which was entirely possible, since we all know the government was secretly cloning new species, and a Northeaster cross current from that island could easily have pulled an escape onto this beach. Some smart-ass had nicknamed the unidentified creature *The Montauk Monster* and made themselves a killing, blogging, selling T-shirts, and giving tours.

Taphonomic changes from rolling in the surf had waxed the fur completely off my creature. It lay pinkish and naked like a newborn baby, scrubbed clean. Its grotesque hairless body was bloated and also unrecognizable. The defleshed snout anatomically appeared to be a curved beak, but on closer inspection, that was only because the pre-maxillary teeth had been lost post-mortem. The bony brow and convex forehead held hollow sockets. This was no teenage mutant turtle without its shell. Without upper teeth, my creature displayed a pure over bite that would have made an orthodontist proud. Remember, I'm a dentist and I've been around the morgue once or twice.

Unable to abandon my inspection, I probed without really knowing what I was looking for. There was no skin on the front paws, and the hands were held in a very humanlike praying position. The creature had strange, elongated fingers. The eye sockets were empty and face reminded me of an Ewok, almost simian.

I concluded that this tantalizing zoology was no rare zorilla, a cross between a Wolverine and a Tasmanian Devil, no photo-shopped defect or Plum Island reject.

It was a God-damn-it raccoon that had spent a little too much time in the water. Probably the same raccoon I'd chased from my house a few nights previous after it had strewn the yard with the contents from my garbage can. I hated raccoons.

With a quick flip from my stick, I kicked the dried-up devil back into the drink. Let the fish and hermit crabs finish their dinner before some tourist spotted the corpse in the morning and called in the camera crew. Montauk didn't need another media circus, although the motel beds were only half full. I watched the body sink.

On hindsight, maybe I was wrong. It was dark outside and my eyesight isn't what it used to be. Maybe the creature was a mutant from Plum Island, but we already had enough trouble with the town and I wasn't interested in mixing up my story with ET investigators and the guys in plastic suits.

Chapter 4

Cash In or Check Out

In late March, while my wife juggled the endless renovations and the mind-numbing permitting process, Tracey enrolled in a restaurant management course at the French Culinary Institute, hoping to learn *The Secret to Opening a Restaurant*.

"What a waste of good money," she complained after a few weeks. "For the price, I could have bought a new smoker. These chefs are on some ego trip. Micros, spreadsheets, and markdowns have no relevance to my little beach shack."

"Maybe it will make more sense once you're open," I suggested.

After much discussion, Tracey drew up a mission statement using Business Plan Pro Tools. She decided that the restaurant company would be her sole ownership, to limit my legal exposure. The real estate was mutually owned and rented to her, but the market value rental income barely covered the mortgage. The bank required that our Montauk house be used as collateral, even though the commercial property was assessed at near cost. The bank wanted no part of the restaurant business or her optimistic earning projections. "Three out of four restaurants close within three years," they warned.

Her stated business objective was to turn the rundown ice cream parlor into a functional restaurant. She practiced her bank speech out on me: "My hope is to create a more youth driven and operated business in keeping with the very popular surf style, with take-out food and only beer and wine service." After consultation with our alcohol license expeditor, we had decided to go for a seasonal wine and beer license, which was cheaper and easier to get. We were concerned with underage drinking and didn't want to be the last drink in an already sobriety-challenged resort town. Hard alcohol consumption around these parts can get ugly and end in fights and police interventions.

She read aloud. "By creating a more contemporary atmosphere through decor and music, we wish to introduce a more global menu to a sophisticated tourist clientele." Most of our competition was serving commercially prepared frozen foods, fried clams, or fish sticks. Even though Montauk is one of the largest commercial fisheries on the East Coast, the local version of fresh fish was farmed salmon from Maine. Often, the local fish was shipped to the Fulton Fish Market, repurchased, and shipped back to the Montauk restaurants. Unbelievably, it was impossible to find a decent fish stew or bouillabaisse. The few upper-class establishments produced boneless, spineless, cookie-cutter stamps of fillet, deep-fried or Americanized French cuisine, increasing the saturated fat content while removing the slow-cooked essence. With such under-marinated meat, no wonder Americans are overweight.

Her plan continued. "Offering live acoustic music in the evenings ..." Besides Nick's, no other restaurant in town was offering the tourist free entertainment in the afternoon. The music was very important for us because we hoped it would encourage Skylar's talents. I was dancing tango in the city and harbored some fantasy that one day I would host my own milonga, a social dance party, once a week at our Shack. The local tango community was infinitesimal, but I hoped it might draw cliental from Up Island and provide a value-added incentive. If nothing else, we would differentiate ourselves from the other Nick and Toni's. We chose lightweight tables and chairs so we could easily clear the floor for dancing.

She practiced her bank speech. "We'll have superior baked goods, a cappuccino bar in the mornings, and light ethnic-based snack foods throughout the day; we hope to garner a following from the huge pedestrian traffic by offering an atmosphere and a product virtually unavailable at this time." The town had prohibited food chains such as Starbucks, so there was an underserved need for good coffee. Neither our next-door neighbor, the market, which offered sandwiches and prepared food, or the local bakery, offered seating. We would prepare homemade scones and bite-size delicacies to battle the calorie-laden, hormonally inflated muffins that now owned the street.

She stopped to breathe. "Utilizing the patio area for picnic table seating, we hope to invite the families and casual customers frequenting the many hotels and summer resorts along our beaches." Offering the warmth of the northern facing summer sun, we hoped to garner après beach, afternoon pedestrian traffic, like the bistros of Lower Manhattan. The Gig Shack would be the most desirable pedestrian table in town.

"As well, we plan to sell a line of casual clothing, custom printed in proto-psychedelic style to subliminally promote the name of the establishment." Sky designed and ordered a line of Gig Shack T-shirts, which the staff wore.

Tracey's early interest in staff and community was apparent. "Opening in our hometown will allow us to employ many of the young people we've come to admire while raising our three sons. It's their ideas that will influence the menu and décor. With my children and their friends on the cusp of adulthood, I have a wide array of young, local talent ready to come on board." For better or worse, Tracey was dedicated to the youth of Montauk. As she often said, "It's not about the money. I'm doing this for them." Although she had planned to use local vendors, she found the Lavazza Italian brand of coffee to be better quality than that of the local roasters. Jay King, the national conglomerate, was more reliable than the local farmers, who wouldn't deliver. The NYC wholesalers delivered baked-off bread. She purchased keg beer brewed in Southampton.

Of course, the bank couldn't give two shits about her expertly written business plan and made me take a second mortgage on the barn and home. Still, I had unlimited faith in the financial advantages of owning a small business. No accountant will teach you the tricks, but even in a depression, it's not what you make but what you keep.

"I'm not sure what kind of food I want to serve at the Shack," she said in a rare, public moment of self-doubt. She couldn't decide which outfit to wear as we prepared to go out to dinner. First she tried on the blue jeans, then a sexy dress.

"In any business, you have to know your niche. It's quantity or quality. You managed my office once. You're a bookkeeper at heart," I reminded her and pointed out my preference for the low-cut red dress.

"I trust numbers," she said, settling on jeans, "more than people."

"Imagine a graph of an upside down bell. On one side is volume and the bottom is quality. In business, you can't have everything. The owner chooses where to belong on that curve. A high-volume store, such as McDonald's, has high overhead and small profit per sale, while a very fancy establishment has small sales, but expensive markups. The ideal place on the curve is slightly to the right of the median, where you have moderately high volume and decent, hands-on service. That's where you get the most profit for the least amount of energy. I know you'll figure out your place on the curve."

"The Gig Shack is bleeding money," she moaned.

"You're a bean counter; count the beans."

"I don't have the time to check the change. I refuse to count nickels."

"Even if the Shack doesn't make a profit, your loss would be an offset to my gain. My income is large enough to offset your losses, thereby lowering our joint taxable income. In the meantime, we're paying off the mortgage. In one sense, it's the government paying the mortgage. Love the loss. The IRS gives you a free ride for a little while. Anyway, in this recession, it's not just nickels being lost in the stock market."

The renovation expenses were mounting. What at first appeared to be a green-mine was quickly turning into a landmine. "Boy, were we naïve; this place is a bottomless pit. The Shack doesn't even have a proper heating system," said Tracey.

"Good, so you won't be tempted to open all year."

"It has limited sewage and one bathroom."

"Great, we won't be a free urinal for the tourists."

"There's restricted parking in town."

"Fine, let the customers walk to you. It will build an appetite."

"The town is limiting us to disposable plates and no dishwasher. They claim we're too close to the beach and might alter the ecology."

"Go green. Use bamboo plates and recyclables."

"There's another small problem," Tracey confided with a hint of desperation.

"Okay, let's have the really bad news."

"I don't have a legal Certificate of Occupancy to be a restaurant; I can only serve food over the counter, without waitress service to the tables. The Shack is legally a retail store that was granted a variance for food service thirty years ago," she said, swiping a tear welling in her right eye. "I'm preexisting, nonconforming."

"But that doesn't make sense. They're allowing you sixty seats, but you can't serve those seats? East Hampton doesn't differentiate ice cream from cooked food. Shaggy and the previous owners have had table service here for years!"

"Illegally, it appears. Shaggy lied or did whatever he wanted."

"How'd he get away with it?" I asked.

"The same way Cyril's parks hundreds of cars on Route 27. Everyone knows that's a death trap, but he's been doing it for years. He must have the dirt on some official. Well, after forty years in this business, Shaggy must have collected a lot of dirt too. What am I going to do? I don't want to run an illegal establishment," she said.

"Do you have any dirt on anyone?"

She thought for a moment. "Just you and our kids."

"That's probably why we got such a good price. No one else wanted to buy a preexisting restaurant in which it was illegal to serve food," I said.

"Apparently, the way it's done is to put in an application for a change of use, but the paper is usually filed away, and the town never rules on it."

"How much is their filing fee?"

"When in Rome. We'll need to proceed with the renovation and paperwork; otherwise, we won't be open by summer, which would be the kiss of death."

"How can we start demolition if we're not legal?"

"The only one who might complain about the renovations is Shag, and he doesn't want the building back."

"Good point." Quickly, we were learning that you did whatever you had to do to open in time. Skylar and Gray proceeded to demolish the old walls and plumbing. They tore up the ugly linoleum and retiled the whole place in a checkerboard of jewel colored tiles. They covered the walls in corrugated steel and built an outdoor tiki bar, inlaid with the caps of forty brands of beer. The rundown ice cream parlor was taking on a new life as a Gig Shack. The design was perfect for the location—a laid back, surfer shack a block off the beach. All the other places in town were shitty or snooty, over-priced, white cloth or plastic cushioned pizza parlors. The Gig Shack would be a goldmine, the fruition of Carl Fisher's 1920s pre-Depression vision for Montauk, the Miami Beach of the north, a mere train ride from New York. It was amazing that no other restaurant had successfully captured the image of this beach hamlet. Like Balthazar's was to French Bistro, we would be the new face of Surf Cuisine.

Tracey had a point. The physical labor of renovation was proving to have a positive influence on the boys. They had changed noticeably: their lack of motivation for anything but self-medication had turned into a desire for an honest day's work, and they were proud of it. There is no success like success. Maybe the parenting solution is to treat them like adults and stop all the coddling—more responsibility, not less.

To celebrate closing the deed, Shaggy invited us to dinner at his restaurant.

Our attorney joined us for the dinner but wasn't feeling the celebratory mood. "You'll never get away with operating a restaurant. Just because Shag served alcohol and had waitresses doesn't mean the town won't enforce the old rules against you," advised our attorney. "You don't have a clue what you're up against." Her advice would have been more useful before we negotiated the deal, not that she had ever offered.

April Fools, we ignored her warning and celebrated the closing on the property.

A little high after a second bottle of champagne, Ms. Attorney critiqued men as they walked by. "Nice butt," she pronounced as a local fisherman bent over his work boots. "I did him once behind the bar," she referred to another. She obviously had an open eye for the open fly. "How long did you guys say you were married?"

"Twenty-five years," I replied.

"Amazing!" she gushed. "Don't you ever argue?"

"Sure, like every other couple, we argue about sex and money and the cost of sex—" I stopped mid-sentence as Tracey shot me a shut-your-mouth look.

"You must be the longest married couple on the East End. As real estate prices go down, divorce rates go up. My business is booming either way; I'm a jack-of-all-trades, marriage closings and real estate openings. What's your secret?"

"I married the best looking woman I could find and kept her primed with Bulgari. Marriage is a job, you got to work it," I said, and then tenderly kissed my wife's hand.

"Lewis … is larger than life," whispered Tracey, looking lovingly into my eyes.

"That's the sweetest thing you've ever said." I was really touched.

"I don't have much confidence in marriage," countered the divorce lawyer.

"Men always marry someone like their mother," I said.

"Explain this: if men marry their mothers, and woman their fathers, shouldn't we all be exact replicas of the last generation?" Tracey asked. "Closet clones?"

Without waiting for an answer, the lawyer continued, "I only want to marry a wealthy man so I can afford a really expensive divorce. Otherwise, marriage just isn't worth it."

Chapter 5

The Bowery Bums

In mid-April, we made the pilgrimage to the Mecca of used restaurant equipment, the Bowery in Chinatown. We needed seating and kitchen equipment. This stuff can be purchased at auctions, which are advertised in the *New York Times* every Sunday, or through resellers—magicians at refurnishing rusted, broken stainless steel into virtually brand-new, spanking, spit-polished equipment.

After much shopping, Tracey selected an assortment of tables, chairs, and barstools from a Chinese merchant. She took a sample back to the Gig Shack and had second thoughts about the chair's design, but when she tried to return it, they wouldn't refund her credit card. They wanted to charge her a restocking fee, even though they never delivered anything and the order was cancelled the next day. The once helpful sales staff no longer spoke English. It took six months to get a refund from those thugs.

Another supplier sold us an electric smoker for ribs. The piece of equipment never worked, and we are still waiting for a refund. The restaurant business is "buyer beware." Contractors came and went, carrying fly-by-night electricians and lube-free plumbers. It was getting painfully clear by late spring that we would be lucky to open by Memorial Day, the official beginning of summer in Montauk.

The start-up problems continued in the selection of a chef. Although Tracey felt she was a great cook and had new ideas about food service, her only real experience in a professional kitchen had been twenty years ago as a baker in training and running a small catering business. She knew from the get-go that she would need a professional to teach her and her young staff the intricacies of the business.

Her ads for a chef in the *New York Times* and the *East Hampton Star* got an under-whelming response. None of the locals seemed interested in training a totally new staff, and the applicants from the city were more concerned with housing. Eventually we interviewed two candidates over cups of coffee in our backyard.

A soft-spoken, middle-aged fellow offered a four-page resume, listing his work in one capacity or another at every big-name establishment from Park Ave. to Park Place.

"I'll love Montauk in the summer." He slurred his words, slightly.

"You clearly know your way around a restaurant kitchen." Tracey admired his impressive resume during the interview but secretly wondered why he'd changed jobs so often. Job loyalty is usually an indication of character. This guy had turned tricks more often than the working girls in Atlantic City.

"I've cooked with some of the best and the worst," he said, downing a tall glass of water, his hands trembling. Although well dressed, he smelled slightly ketonic, a clear indication of alcoholism, diabetes, or non-detoxified sugars.

"For this job, you've got to like kids," commanded Tracey.

"Kids, goats, lamb, you kill it, I'll cook it," he said through a missing lateral incisor. "I can cook anything that's not still kicking." Maybe he was just nervous.

"No, I mean, have you ever worked with young adults?" she asked.

"You lie." Maybe he'd been in the business too long and was just burnt out. Coming to Montauk would be an escape. "Hue Li! In Chinatown," he said.

"Oh, it's a restaurant?" I said. "So, have you given any thought to payroll? How much are you asking?" I held my breath.

"Money's not important as long as I like the people I'm cooking for."

"That sounds good to us, but if you'll excuse our inexperience, you must have some number in mind. You'll require housing?" I asked.

"I'm single. I can sleep on a couch."

"Ballpark?"

"Okay, I need to clear $1500 a week. You pay all the taxes. I'll want access to a car, preferably something red, and my house should be within walking distance to the beach, but not so close that the sound of the waves wakes me. I'm a very light sleeper."

I swallowed hard on those numbers. We'd have to sell a lot of tacos to pay his overhead, besides all the start-up costs we had already laid out.

"Oh, I'll need a month paid in advance before I'll consider your offer."

"Well, thank you for making the trip," said Tracey. "We'll contact you."

He eventually landed a job cooking in Sag Harbor.

After we had driven him to the train, she commented on the difficulty of finding the right chef. "These New York City guys may be out of our league. We can't afford those kinds of salaries, plus housing."

"The Irish kids that work during the summer will live five in a room, but these professional chefs are real prima donnas," I added.

"Well, I want a professional. I'm not opening naked," said Tracey.

"With your body, if you opened naked, success would be a given."

She rolled her eyes. "Sometimes, I wonder why you bother to speak."

The next interview was more promising. Fabio, a hyper-speaking Italian, greeted us warmly with a kiss on both cheeks. He said he enjoyed working with youth and his menu selection tended toward pasta, which struck a comfortable note. He gesticulated wildly, and every sentence ended with a *"Mama Mia!"* He spoke with an ethnic spiciness, which was quite endearing. Good food was in his family's blood, and even if he couldn't cook, he'd be a lot of fun to work with. He'd brought his young daughter, Tia, along for the interview.

"Ah, the wife and I, we *fini*! She's going back to Jamaica." He made the gesture of slitting his throat with his right hand. "Today my day for Tia. *Mama Mia!*" The daughter, although pretty, was as ADD as her dad, bouncing off the walls and chasing our cat around the garden. "Tia! Leave the little pussy be. Ah, a handful. *Mama Mia!*"

On the whole, we liked Fabio, but we were quite concerned the daughter would present a problem. If the marriage failed, and he was stuck as a single parent, we anticipated problems. He eventually landed a job with a friend, where he worked for the summer. He was wrong about the marriage, and the wife kept the daughter in New York.

We were getting worried that we'd never find anyone when, by chance, a neighbor recommended a chef from Arizona who wanted to move to Montauk. Tracey and Scott spoke on the phone and immediately hit it off. Although his resume was impressive, there were many blanks between employments. Still, she sent him a roundtrip plane ticket, and a day later, we interviewed him in person.

Scott had some unusual, hippy ideas about the restaurant business, but they jived completely with Tracey's vision. It was love at first sight, a common food philosophy. This self-assured "Dr. House" look-alike seemed to embrace us wholeheartedly.

"I love the idea of teaching you all the business," said Scott, feeding us tidbits of his wisdom. "In fact, I consider myself more a teacher than a cook. Anyone can cook. For instance, I want the young people to keep a journal, a diary of their experience. I'll pay them at the end of the summer if they make it through the season and turn in the journal."

Tracey's artistic inspiration was ignited. "I love that."

"And we'll place cameras around the kitchen to create a reality show. I can see the headlines now on how we started a restaurant in the Hamptons."

He knew how to reach our inner literary aspirations. "Cool," I added.

"You see, most people think a restaurant is about food. Well, they're just wrong. There are five essential priorities to creating great service and hospitality. To do that consistently, you've got to focus on your staff. The first priority is to teach the staff and treat them well. If the staff is happy, the customers will know and be attracted to their energy. The second priority is community. In a small town like Montauk, that should be easy. The neighborhood hangout, the local bistro, the coffee shop, the joint."

Tracey was on the edge of her seat now. "I want a joint where the local kids can play music, show their surf movies, or display artwork," she said. "I'm creating this for them. Sky's got a great band."

"Our own private rec center?" I joked. "Tracey's Talk House."

She threw me a sneer. "Ignore him, Scott."

"To create the right atmosphere, you must first focus on your staff and the community. The customer comes last." He spoke with a patrician's disdain.

"Ah, excuse me, Scott, but in most enterprises, the customer comes first," I explained humbly. "I'm a successful dentist. Are you sure?"

"That's your mistake. The customers don't know anything. It's all in the presentation. People are lemmings; that's why you always fill the front first."

"I've been in business thirty years ..."

"Lewis, could you reel it in?" Tracey hooked my reply. They made private eye contact out of my reach. "Scott is the expert in this business."

He continued his lecture. "After your customers, you'll need to invest in good purveyors. A reliable food and alcohol source is an invaluable resource."

"Well, that shouldn't be a problem," I said. "Tracey's very generous. Her favorite activity is to buy food and then throw it out. Our refrigerator's never seen a leftover."

His nose twitched at my offhand comment, but whatever he was thinking was left unspoken. After all, *he* was the one being interviewed for the job. Wasn't that so?

"Fresh, local produce is my brand," she replied, ignoring my comment.

"That's perfect. You can't screw up fresh food," he admitted.

"What's the last priority?" I asked.

"The last priority is your investors."

"I'm her only investor."

They both looked at me with a blank expression, and at that moment, I realized that indeed I would be her last priority.

Chapter 6

The Bone

The genesis of a plan to open a restaurant can be traced back to the previous summer, when Tracey and her friend Leslie were sunbathing at Ditch Beach one afternoon, idly admiring the celebrity surfers and surf cast models. "The food in this town sucks!" they agreed. "We should open our own place."

"We could do this business so much better," Leslie beat her chest like every other novice restaurant owner.

After much shopping, Leslie independently took a lease on a preexisting restaurant in Promised Land. It was a beautiful spot off the beaten path. "Join me in the business," she said to Tracey one day. "We would make great partners. I'm an expert at marketing and management, and you could make the doughnuts." They never consummated the deal, and Leslie opened by herself in May.

We took Scott, our newly hired chef, to check out Leslie's lunch, as we waited for our endless renovation to proceed through the spring.

I hated to admit it, but Leslie was a genius at marketing and self-promotion. With a brash bravado, she hired a professional video crew to give a virtual tour of the place. The video was broadcast on the local TV station. She had planted shill customers to spike the review. I should know because for some reason she chose me to give the fake interview with the reporter. "Best squid in town!" I wiggled a calamari to the camera.

She had only been open a few weeks, but Leslie's place was already busy. Every potential customer that peeked in was seated. The woman knew how to close a deal.

After the camera stopped rolling, we heard her boyfriend, Mark, cursing and slamming a door. "That's it. I'm through with you."

Leslie came over and shrugged her shoulders. "That's the third time he's quit this week. He'll be back. These back-bay boyfriends are just a bunch of born users. Imagine him trying to tell me how to run my business. Loser!" she yelled to him through the closed door. "No guy is going to tell me what to do."

We sampled her excellent fried calamari, lightly breaded in beer.

"The secret to good squid is to get the last catch; otherwise, they could be out there a week," explained Leslie. "As the new kid on the block, the fish mongers will try to unload the crap on you," spoke the veteran of two weeks.

"You've got an in with the locals?" I asked.

"I saw the fisherman fondling his girlfriend. Now I get the freshest catch."

"So?" shrugged Tracey.

"I threatened to tell his wife."

Leslie's place was renovated on a shoestring, almost a month ahead of schedule. "Never pay those damn contractors on time; that's the only thing the bastards understand," she said in a constant harangue of business advice.

Tracey retorted, "I offered my electrician a bribe, but it's been a month."

"He screws in one bulb, promises to be back tomorrow, which becomes a week. Island Time!" I added. "It's ridiculous. If I treated my clients like this, I'd be sued."

"Long Island Time?" Tracey rolled her eyes toward Leslie, her feminist friend. "Are you criticizing my choice in contractors now?"

Looking toward Scott, a fellow male, for some help or marriage counseling, I tossed up my hands in a what-did-I-say-now gesture.

"I had a wonderful electrician, but your job's too small for him," said Leslie. "How are the kids?" She was barely able to hold eye contact long enough for a conversation, bouncing off the walls, running from table to table. "Frank, would you bus their table!" she screamed at the waiter. "Damn, what a moron my bartender is. He's a drunk. Last night I caught him having a beer."

"One beer," I replied. "So what?"

"I know he's stealing from me," Leslie said with a wink, "but I'm going to catch him tonight. I marked the alcohol level on all the bottles in invisible ink."

"Don't you think that's a bit extreme?" remarked Tracey.

"This is a nickel and dime business. Every nickel you don't lose is a dime saved." She ran off to harangue an Irish waitress who spilled a glass of water.

"That woman is clueless," said Scott. "Without professional help, she'll lose her shirt, or worse, her mind. I've witnessed owner implosions on more than one occasion."

I wondered whether he had merely witnessed or caused the implosion.

Tracey rolled her eyes lovingly toward her star chef. "Promise me, Scott, if I turn into a mad woman, you'll either shoot me or shoot him," she hissed while pointing her pistol finger at my head.

I was tempted to shoot Tracey, who was already showing early signs of FRS—First Restaurant Syndrome, a previously unknown disorder I'd recently diagnosed. The disease occurs in owners lacking the essential business acumen of conflict resolution. The main principle of business conflict is to first communicate with your adversary to determine what they really want and then actively find a solution to fix the problem.

Leslie dumped a computer on our table. "Look what I got here," she said, proudly showing the latest laptop. "It's a high-tech touch system. It'll track every french fry and T-bone. No one's stealing from me. You must get one."

"The old paper and pen system works fine," said Scott with an arrogant authority, "if you know what you're doing."

"You're such a Bohemian, Scott," she replied coldly.

"Just because I have no use for all this razz-a-ma-taz?" he laughed.

"Whatever." She flipped him the bird and walked off.

Mac Cool, Leslie's sixteen-year-old son, delivered our fried food. He dressed for La Belle Époque, a nostalgic Edwardian-era frock of gray railroad pants held by silver button suspenders, a ruffled white cravat, and hand-painted sneakers. The faint shadow of facial graffiti grew as want-to-be sideburns, just past his ears. His eyes were covered in steel, tinted glass goggles. The child was the woman's true work of art.

"Toothsome, pliant meat. Done to a turn." Mac flashed us an angelic smile. "The little nippers, mere babes out of water." His hands played with the words as if he were practicing for an off-Broadway production. "A quick turn in the bed and straight to your plate." In a puzzling Irish-tinged voice, he asked, "Do tell, how goes your *Patris et Filii et Spititus Sancti?*" He bowed in an overly theatric adieu.

"My heavenly pastry shop? You can come work for me any time," Tracey purred.

"The honor is mine, my lady." Mac had such a sweet face as he pondered the possibilities. He was home for the summer from a private high school, where he'd made the honor roll in graffiti art. "I'm off to paint the White House," he explained, but he wasn't planning on running for office. "Art and the streets await the master's stroke. Tootles. I'll put beef to my heels. Enjoy your stir-about."

"Why does he talk like that?" asked Scott, impressed by Mac's stylized manner.

"He's from New Joyce-sey," I said. "He recently read James Joyce's *A Portrait of the Artist as a Young Man* and is reliving the role in real time. Characters in a novel are often based on real people, so why not the reverse? It's a youthful affectation."

Leslie noticed a table of four getting up to leave before their dinner was served. She ran over to the errant table. "Is there a problem, miss?"

"Are you the owner? We've been sitting here for at least half an hour, and no one has even brought us bread!" The woman tossed her napkin to the ground.

"We don't give out bread, miss, until you order first." Leslie picked the napkin off the ground, refolded it neatly, and placed it on the table. She took a deep, calming yoga breath. "Can I take your order now?"

"Well, we can't wait any longer. We're meeting people at the dock." The woman moved to leave and threw the folded napkin again to the floor.

"You've been sitting at my table for half an hour. You think we're a public park?"

"Are you kidding me? We've been waiting for your staff to take our order. All they did was bring over a glass of water," she said, stomping out the cloth napkin like a lit cigarette.

"Sit down!" Leslie yelled. "I'll send the waiter right over. Mac, get over here!"

"No. Please, we're leaving." All four customers headed toward the door.

"Without paying?" screamed Leslie, her right palm open.

"All we had was a glass of water!" the woman replied.

"Nevertheless, you used one of my tables. I could have served other people, my regular customers, who appreciate good food and this fine view."

"Here!" The wife slammed a ten-dollar bill on the table.

"Relax, lady! You're on vacation!" Leslie yelled at their fleeing backs. "Tourists!"

Chapter 7

Family Dramas

"Thank God I hired Scott," said Tracey, staring at our empty restaurant tables. "Every time I flip out, he calms me down; he's better than drugs."

Finally, it was Memorial Day weekend, the beginning of this story. The staff—including my three sons—raved about Chef Scott's creativity. He had quickly wormed his way into becoming my family's hero.

"He can cook anything. Today he made the best ribs." Tracey made a fluttering wrist motion. "I couldn't go on without him."

"Everyone loves the ceiling he designed," concurred Sky, referring to the soundproofed panels of canvas, stretched into Jackson Pollack's explosions of paint. "That was such a blast, everyone throwing paint in the wind down at the beach." He pumped his fist into the air. "Scott's so down. He's created Beach Art."

"That belongs in the book," I agreed. "His ceiling is a work of art."

"He's the real Montauk," my wife purred lovingly, eyes rolled skyward.

"Scott's the dope. He's really taught me a lot about cooking," added Morgan, Sky's best friend and fellow cook. "I had a little talent, but he knows how to bring it out. He spends all day showing me and Sky the exact way to plate a dish. Man, the guy's an artist when it comes to food."

"Scott's down on the music jam too. He agreed to be in our band." Sky lip-synched the words to a surfing song he'd written, "Head-high."

"He's like the father I never had," exclaimed Morgan. "All the other men in my life have been such letdowns. They pretended to support me at night, but by morning they forgot my name. I really trust Scott; he'd do anything for me."

"Me too," Skylar agreed, right in front of me. "I've never felt such unconditional support from a man." He blushed as his eyes met mine— his filled with embarrassment, mine with anger. After twenty years of Little League biological fathering, this Bohemian chef/artist/musician/ want-to-be male role model had replaced me. Just like that. There's no justice in fatherhood these days.

After overcoming a hike in blood pressure, I wanted to concur with my family's idolization of Scott, but something about the guy disturbed me. First, he had really pissed me off a few days earlier when I tried to get a customer to come in and try the food. All I did was explain the ingredients in the fish taco. It wasn't as if I'd dragged people off the street, but Scott dropped a nasty comment. "What do you think this is? Little Italy?" It was an offhand reference to the aggressive marketing of the cheap Italian eateries of the Lower East Side. Then he complained to Tracey that I was interfering in his management of the kitchen.

During our first dinner out alone in two months, Tracey laid down the gauntlet. "You need to let Scott and me manage the staff. It's my business, damn it!"

"So, what do you want me to do? Just come and eat the food?"

"That would be a start. Just act like one of the customers."

"Don't worry. When my friends come in to critique the place, I tell them it's not my restaurant. Talking to me is like talking to the wall."

"Can't you just be a fixture?"

"Yeah, I'm already the family wall fixture. That's some role model for my sons."

"Can't you play the elegant owner, holding court in a corner?"

"You could hire a dummy dad for that role. It would be cheaper, you know. One of those stuffed police dummies they put in speed traps, or a mannequin with a sign around his neck saying Silent Partner."

"Whatever!" she replied with my least favorite phrase. "All you want to do is complain. You're never happy. It's not in your nature. You just can't express happiness. Whatever I do is never good enough. My choice in lawyers, in electricians, in chefs, nothing's right. Would you prefer I spent my day in the mall?"

What could I say to her? There was no point in arguing further. The primary goal of the modern married man is survival. The primary weapon is to shut up and listen. So I let her do whatever she wanted, but it didn't make me like her choice in chefs any better.

"Why did Scott write the word *disrupt* spelled backward on the menu?" I asked Tracey the next morning as we waited for the Tuesday morning bus back to New York. "That's just evil. I don't trust the guy."

"It's a joke. You're being suburban."

"I can't wait for his wife to finally show up." Scott's wife, Erin, was traveling with a band from Arizona. She was a professional music groupie and was waiting for the weather to warm on the East Coast. "He must be getting lonely."

"You aren't internalizing Scott's magic."

"Well, I caught him smoking a joint with our sons. That magic?"

"You're overreacting. It's all under control. He was just bonding."

One night, one of my boys had more to drink than the customers. He was stumble down drunk. When I complained to Scott that underage drinking could be a problem for his young staff, he just shrugged his shoulders and took a deep drag on his hand-rolled cigarette. "I'm not their father," he replied.

It was my responsibility to deal with their drinking, but I felt so out of touch, and every time I intervened, Tracey complained that I was interfering.

"His car is broken," I said. "I'm not paying for it to be repaired." The bus was late, and our going away conversation was quickly going downhill.

"You think your money is going to get them to toe the line? You're just trying to manipulate the situation. This isn't your dental staff; they are your damn children." She impatiently checked her watch. Time stood still.

My mind wandered. I knew she was right, but the lines were a bit muddled. As a weekend parent, I was disconnected. Every time I sat one down for a father-son conversation, it became a lecture. I'd nag them about appropriate behavior for young men and family obligations. It reminded me of what happened the previous summer, when I broke the Buddha's neck. I had purchased a large, stone Buddha and had asked that they build a stone platform so we could place it in the garden. Weeks went by, and although they never actually refused to do it, the Buddha lay in its original spot. Rapt with anger, I eventually moved the statue by myself. Blinded by rage at my sons, I accidentally snapped the stone neck when I laid the statue down. I was going to throw the statue out, but when I returned the following weekend, they had expertly repaired the Buddha's neck, tiled the platform, and placed the votive in a new bed. Ironic, but this Buddha, which normally evokes a sense of peace, still reminds me of my rage.

"You can't chase a monkey," she said. The Jitney pulled behind and honked.

"You read that from a fortune cookie. So what do you suggest?"

"You need to engage them. Find some common interest, small steps that you have in common. Maybe a father and son camping trip," she advised and revved the car.

"So, we should go out for a drink together?"

"Okay. Make a joke of it, but kids are like old pennies."

"My parents used the carrot and stick. It worked on me."

"Now you're delegating again. Remember what the family therapist told you?" She knocked me gently on the head. "No triangulating!" she said and pointed a perfectly manicured nail aggressively in my face. "I'm not doing your dirty work for you. Be the father, damn it. No triangulating."

"*Triangulation* and *whatever* should be struck from your vocabulary."

"Whatever. The Jitney is waiting." She gave me a quick peck on the check, as I departed for the 6:30 AM bus and my usual, year-round schedule of work. We had been doing this Transition Dance for seven years, but now the transitions from living alone to weekend marriage were becoming increasingly harder. It seemed like we needed to get ugly with each other to lubricate the separation, she pushing me out the door, and I jumping away from the nest. The transitions were thoroughly unromantic.

Three hours later in New York, I called Arden, who was in his ninth semester of college. "When will you start working at the restaurant?"

"I've got a small problem, Dad," he said. "I need to take summer school in order to graduate next year."

"But you agreed to work. We need you. It's a family business."

"The situation has changed. You do want me to graduate on time, don't you?"

"That was your responsibility. You shouldn't have dropped so many courses."

"If I need a fifth year of college, it'll cost more than I could possibly earn."

I could see his financial point, but I had hoped his return might sway the power of family dynamics. "I need you," I pleaded, hoping to garner some sympathy.

"I think the Gig Shack is a dumb idea."

"Thank you for the support," I said, my voice dropping two octaves.

"Okay, okay, I'll come, but I could earn more working here at school, and still graduate on time," he said.

"Tell the school you're doing community service—or better, a family service!"

"Okay, maybe it'll be fun in the end. Running a bar, I'll probably meet a lot of hot chicks. I want the Friday and Saturday night shift."

Not feeling particularly satisfied with the outcome of that call, a few hours later I called Gray, a senior at East Hampton High School.

"What are you doing today?" I nagged.

"My homework. What are you doing today, Dad?"

"I'm working. How's your mother?"

"She's taking a lunch nap between shifts. She needs to relax."

"Yeah, she's out of control."

"Maybe you need a chill pill too, Dad," prescribed Gray, the family doctor.

"You think so?" I respected his advice. He was the calm mediator in the family, the only member we would all listen to, and the one who spoke with unconditional love.

After three solid days of fixing NYC decay, I returned to our Montauk home hungry and exhausted. The weekend marriage transition started innocently enough.

"How was your week?" I searched the home refrigerator for a morsel of food, but the cupboard was bare. The Shack had sucked up my private stock of condiments.

"Are you asking if I made any money?" Tracey frowned.

Swallowing stale bread, I said, "What do you think of those Mets?"

Later that night, as the wife and I worked through the transition the old-fashioned way, I wondered where the marriage was going. A gorgeous female specimen, my lust for her was stronger than the day we'd met. The mother of three healthy, model-featured sons, we really liked each other. When we weren't trying to kill each other, we were actually buddies. Where would I ever find anyone else who could fill that job description? It's amazing how much pain we bear in a good marriage. Bottom line, I would shut up and suck it up for the hundred days.

Later, as she lay sleeping, intertwined in my arms, she suddenly started crying out. "Shant" or "Shanti" or "Shanty," I thought I heard her say. Her face twisted into a painful nightmare, brows twitching, lips pinched. Her arms swung wildly back and forth. "Sky, Sky, Sky!" she yelled.

I shook her awake, but it was a few seconds before she could open her eyes. "Wow, that was horrible," is all she said.

"Was it something you ate? The Indian food?"

Twisting her face, she responded, "I can still taste my stomach in my throat."

"Cumin gives me nightmares too." I was trying to make a joke. "Do you remember anything?" I gently kneaded her neck.

She thought for a moment. "We were driving up a hill. I was in the passenger seat, and you were behind me. There was a priest on the corner, smoking a cigarette, watching us drive by. The higher up the hill we went, the tighter my seatbelt got, until it started to hurt, and then I realized it wasn't the belt, but you. You were strangling me! It really hurt. You were trying to strangle me. I called out for Skylar's help, but then you woke me up."

Momentarily guilty, I recalled that my arm had lain across her chest. "I was strangling you?" I withdrew. "What the hell does that mean?"

"I don't know," she said with a shiver. "I thought the driver was a woman, but she had no face and she may have been a he. I don't really remember." She offered a prudent smile, but it wasn't particularly satisfying.

"Oh, come on—you *must* remember." I prowled her psyche.

"If I did, don't you suppose I'd tell you?" she answered provocatively.

I wondered whether this was a trick question to which there was no right answer. She had always advised that if either one of us had an affair, there would be no point in telling the other. I wasn't so sure and the thought was too painful, so I changed the subject. "The tightening seatbelt must have some significance. Maybe I'm not strangling, but protecting you, like in an accident?" I pleaded with an open heart.

"I don't remember any accident, but maybe you woke me up too soon."

"Now it's my fault 'cause I woke you. The priest? Life and death?" I proposed a face-saving solution. "The seatbelt's an analogy about your insecurity?"

Poisoning my plan, she responded curtly, "Or about the state of our marriage?"

"What's that supposed to mean? Was or wasn't there an accident?"

"I told you I don't remember. It was only a dream."

"I don't believe you. You had an accident in your dream, and you're now refusing to tell me about it. That's so typical! Like kinky sex, you're withholding your dreams."

Taking my face gently in her hands, she peered with a quizzical grin. The stress crowfeet crowded her brown eyes in sadness. Above, accented by the rays of the moon, dust molts danced in moon shadow. The molts were laughing at me.

My heart missed a rapt beat, and my breath cockled in my chest. I waited for the ugly, untold confession. It was about Scott, I thought. I could kill that bastard.

"There's no accident and there's no other man," she whispered softly. "I've told you everything, except what I should have spoken a long time ago."

There it was, the Dear John, You're Toast speech.

"I haven't been entirely fair to you," she said in a whisper. Not for the first time, I had trouble hearing her words. "I want to thank you for allowing me to do the Gig Shack. I know it's a sacrifice and you have to work very hard to support me. I really appreciate you. I love you, husband. More then you'll ever know." She kissed me hard.

"I love you too, wife. I'm honored to be your husband."

We made love as only people married many years, with investments of estate, children, trust, and common goals—the physical and psychological possibility of a life breathed through another's life, willing lips interlocked in a delicate embrace, the provenience of eternal pleasure. One-on-one made a tribe. It was just as son number three, the fortune cookie, and the Dalai Lama had prescribed.

Screw the transitions. If Tracey hadn't fed me so much happiness, then maybe I just didn't know what real happiness tasted like.

Barn fire on the beach,
Neolithic Surf Haiku,
True tango takes two.

Chapter 8

Live! At the Gig Shack

I'd finally found a job at the Gig Shack that no one else wanted and which Tracey was willing to allow me to do. The joint's most undesirable job wasn't dishwasher, fish skinner, or toilet bowl scrubber. It was being their press agent. I figured, I'm already the king of self-promotion in my dental practice; now I would write advertising copy and e-mail the local papers a description of upcoming events and menu specials.

"Young and trendy, the new 668, the Gig Shack, is a quick favorite with local artists, foodies, and surfers. Located on Main Street, Montauk (a.k.a. the End), the atmosphere is East Village Boite. The chef, Scott, is offering finger-sucking ribs, Montacos (fresh fish taco), burritos, and much more. For the Après Surf crowd, there's an outdoor wine and beer bar, espresso, and homemade ice cream sandwiches. This Saturday at 9 PM, come listen to Live Delta Blues. There's never a cover."

My public relations coup appeared in the *East Hampton Star*. This would get the customers in to try the food. Proudly, I tacked the newspaper piece over the front door.

Initially, I had assumed Tracey or Skylar would be the face of our show, *Montauk Mother and Son Team Create Global Surf Cuisine*. But they flatly refused to cooperate. Displaying a shared genetic trait, neither wanted their picture or name ever mentioned as the owners, chefs, or hosts. In fact, Tracey aspired to be the princess of anti-self-promotion. The mere thought of outright commercialism made her skin cringe. Her older brother had been an excellent artist but refused to sign his name to his artwork, under the banner of anti-commercialism. Such arrogance might fly in an artist, but for a new, public service business, it was pure self-destruction.

Tracey's hesitancy about advertising, fearful that her young staff wasn't ready, eventually led to Scott being the public face of the joint.

He had no problem having his face plastered over every newspaper in town, even offering to have professional headshots, as long as I paid the photographer. Promoting this arrogant bastard made me cringe, but that was my family's choice.

We had discussed many advertising/naming concepts, from Bohemian Barbeque, to Beach Bistro, to Surf Shack, before settling on the local exchange 668. Anyone who was from Montauk or was in with the locals would know this designation. There had been contention about whether to use the numerals 668 or spell out the numbers, six, six, eight, but in the end we decided to use both. This would present a problem later, because customers had difficulty creating a visible memory of the signage, which was now spelled two different ways. Using the 668 had a big advantage when advertising because numerals are listed first in alphabetical lists. Later we added a suffix to the number because the online domain was already taken. The vague name Shack was chosen over other descriptions because it seemed to fit the look, but Café would have been a clearer food designation. Skylar decided to add the Gig to the Shack to designate it as a place for music. For better or worse, 668 the Gig Shack became the restaurant's name, but signage and a simple explanation of the product was always a problem; there were just too many words to pronounce in one breath. "Welcome to six, six, eight, the Gig Shack," was a mouthful.

Erin, Scott's wife, finally arrived with the band from Arizona. They had driven across the country, gotten lost crossing the Mississippi, and disappeared into the depths of Manhattan before finally resurfacing two days late for our Memorial Day opening bash. Their caravan of broken down cars screeched into the back parking lot.

"You must be Erin?" I greeted her with open arms. I was the only family member around. "Welcome home," may have sounded a bit corny as the words escaped my lips, but it was well intended.

"Where the fuck is Scott?" she demanded.

"Off buying food for tonight's dinner," I apologized.

"Figures the bastard wouldn't be here to greet me." With hands on hips, she looked up at the rear sign of the Gig Shack. "Duh," she mouthed, tongue out, and shook her head back and forth in disbelief. "We came halfway across the country for this? I need refreshment. You got any Maker's in this joint?"

"Bourbon? Sorry, only wine or beer."

"What kind of fuckin' bar doesn't serve Maker's Mark?" She was clearly sloshed already. "It's so fuckin' cold in this country!" She shivered, holding her unclothed arms aloof, exposing a snake-like tattoo. The tattoo slinked up her right arm and across her chest before plunging the small cleft of partially exposed cleavage. "What country is this anyway?" Drunkenly, Erin slumped down against the car door. The handle clawed her dress, exposing the snake's head planted deep between her thighs, its slimy tongue flickering toward her panty-less quiver. The whole show was but an instant, and I very well might have imagined the snake's and Erin's entire anatomy, but written along the tattoo was the same word Scott had used: DISRUPT.

"How was the trip?" My eyes were still fixated on her maidenhead and her nicely proportioned inner thighs. Our eyes met ninety degrees above her crotch.

"Who the fuck are you?" She wavered, her eyes wild and unfocused.

"I'm Scott's boss."

"That bum-slinger! He said his boss was a babe."

The driver of the other car helped Erin to her feet. "No fuss, no muss. Ignore her, man; she's a little over-lubricated from our long journey." He wiped some sand off her bare legs, her arm draped helplessly across his neck. He offered me a handshake. "I'm Tom. We're playing at your Shack tonight, I believe."

"Welcome," I said, extending my hand to his firm musician's shake. "You people were expected days ago. Your arrival was anticipated by the whole town."

"Sorry about that, old chap. A little car trouble along the way." Looking at the assorted rundown scraps of automobiles, that was entirely believable. "What day is it? Didn't Scotty inform you of the delay?"

"He did mention a previous club engagement in the city."

Tom pulled the slumping Erin back to her feet. Her eyes rolled back in her head, and she emitted a loud snort. "The girls want to take a short dip in the water. Fella, which way to the pool?"

I pointed to the sand dunes, a short block away. "But, Tom, your band is set to play in three hours! I've plastered flyers all over town."

The rest of the band, a guy and two babes, stumbled out of the two vehicles in various stages of undress. With unkempt hair, dark lines under their eyes, and foam creeping from their lips, they appeared more Dead on Arrival. "No problem, man, we're professionals!" roared the rabid band members.

"Do I need a suit?" asked the suddenly sober Erin, as she unzipped and pulled off a tight-fitting skirt. "I've never swum in my bum, but I guess the birthday suit will do," she giggled. "Euan, euan, eu-oi-oioi!" she cried and ran half-naked into the sea.

As they stumbled along the beach, I wondered how long it would take EMS to pull their drowned, drunken bodies out of the crashing waves. The surf was up that day.

A few minutes later, Tracey and Scott pulled up with a trunk full of food. He recognized the cars immediately. "Where did she go?"

"Taking a dip in the pool." I pointed toward the loud echo of crashing surf.

"She can't swim! She's never been out of the desert. How could you?" he cried.

"Tom assured me the show would go on."

Scott took off toward the ocean at a run as I helped unload the car.

"So what does the wife look like?" Tracey asked, more than a little curious.

"Think *Snakes on a Plane* meets *The Chronicles of Narnia.*"

"Scott says she's a great bartender, a real male magnet." Did I detect a hint of jealousy in my wife's voice?

"Bipolar male magnet, if you ask me. She'll reject as many customers as she attracts. She's a complete lush, a professional groupie, a Maker's Mark."

"Now there you go being negative again. How long did you talk to her—five minutes? You think that entitles you to make judgments? Scott loves her."

"If someone loves her, that's good enough for me." I offered a gentleman's bow. "Maybe he'll stop chasing after you like a mutt in heat."

"Would you please stop the negativity for a little while?" She put her hands to her head to withhold a brain explosion.

Reversing course and psychology, I said, "Please hire her. I indulge bartenders with biblical affectations, and Erin definitely lives out that good or evil drama."

"Lawyer, contractor, chef, and now bartender. I can't stand this second-guessing every business decision I make."

"I said hire her. Scott loves her and she has great inner thighs."

"No matter," came Tracey's all too common refrain. At least she was expanding her vocabulary from the typical *whatever*.

Later, the band appeared on schedule at 9:00 PM. Decked out in vampish party gear, the women wore crowns of ivy and wild garlic that they had handpicked in the woods. The men wore black leather and silver chains. Montauk hadn't seen so much leather since the Rolling Stones knocked the "Memory Motel" and the Rough Riders humped their saddles.

The band mesmerized the audience with their pagan, New Orleans inspired rituals. Led by Tom's husky, raw voice and chorused by the ladies satanic verses, it was as much theatre as musical. Beach Boys beware, the music was changing.

In the shadows, reunited, Scott and Erin danced seductively, framed by torchlight, a waning moon, and my over-heated insecurity.

Dozens of tourists were drawn to this pop landscape, littered now with passersby and poseurs, a gloriously raunchy scene, the real deal, suffused with an erotic glow. The heart-stopping décolletage was lead by Erin, raven-headed, coquettish, and sultry with red Kewpie Doll lips and agent provocateur attire.

"Raise some ruckus!" The band finished a tune. "Euoi, euoi, euoi," Erin screamed wildly into the air as she slithered across the floor.

"Good party," is all I could add.

Sky and Morgan jammed with the band, playing in tune with the professional musicians. Tracey's Talk House was just as we had pictured it, only louder.

An audience gathered in front of the restaurant, enjoying the free music. People started dancing in the streets. Cars honked appreciation as they passed by. Location, location, location indeed worked.

"Party, party, party," Erin cheered with a flapper's, hot-to-trot smile.

"Maybe you could turn it down a little?" I asked. "The music's kind of loud."

"Fuck that." Tom riffed a glass-shattering electric reply.

"There are noise regulations." I spoke, but no one listened.

"Fuck them." Erin motioned toward the rest of the world.

"Tonight's our first real musical performance. You're too loud!" I pleaded.

"Out of gas already, old man!" she replied. Erin was Old Hollywood glam, a Jazz Age throwback, and sexpot alpha female. "Damn you, people! Party!"

"Montauk may not be ready for this ..." were my last words as a police officer strolled through the front door. "What's the problem, sir?" I inquired, trying to cut the gunslinger off at the path.

"Noise complaints." He fingered his weapon, his words triggered by an angry disposition. "You the owner? I'll need some identification."

"But it's only ten o'clock. Who complained?"

"Kill the music or I'll have to shut you down," he explained.

"But everyone's having such a good time."

"Are you the owner?" He took out his book and protested like only the police can.

I looked around. Tracey wasn't in sight, so I made an executive, spur-of-the-moment, decision. "Okay, everybody, party's over." I motioned to the band to slit their throats. "Kill the music, now!" I hoped Tracey would support my fast thinking.

The band continued to play, indifferent to the policeman's presence and my command, so I grabbed Tom's shoulder and hollered into his ear. "Please stop playing, there's been a complaint. The music's too loud!" I yelled over his amplified riff.

He laughed and in a higher octave added a new chorus, "The Gig Shack don't give a damn about the man. We play our music for our fans."

The cop wrote a novel in his little black book. The title had my name.

"You musicians don't give a damn about anybody!" I yelled and pulled the electric plug. There was a sudden explosion of silence, followed by a general moan in the crowd, blaming me as the party crasher.

"Sorry," I announced to no one in particular. "Noise complaint." I took the officer aside. "If you let them continue, I promise they'll play quieter," I whispered in his ear.

"No." Then he sized up the angry mood of the crowd, who were booing and yelling. Reconsidering, he relented. "If I have to come back for another complaint, I'm hauling your ass back to East Hampton. You'll take full responsibility for the volume?"

"Yes, sir." I handed him my card but withheld the Ben Franklins. "Please call if there are any problems." Why did I get myself in this position?

"This says you're a dentist in New York City. How'd you get involved in a joint out here?" He laughed to himself.

"Family business, long story."

Not completely satisfied, the police officer started to leave, but halfway out the door, Erin grabbed the back of his shirt. "You can't shut us down; the party has just begun!" she screamed at him. "It's not even dark."

"Miss, please remove your hand from my uniform," he snarled.

"This is complete bullshit. This band came all the way from Arizona just to play in Montauk. What kind of hillbilly town turns the music off before midnight?"

"Miss, I don't write the laws." He neatened his shirt.

I frantically waved at her to back off.

"Back in Tucson, the bands play all night. What's wrong with this fucking town?" The snakehead rose to strike.

"Miss, you're in East Hampton now." He turned to me. "Thank the little lady here, because there will be no more music tonight." Pointing his book at me. "You understand?" He turned to leave. "No music. This is your last warning."

"Hillbilly," she grumbled to his back.

If the officer had heard her nasty remark, I'm sure he would have thrown us all in the can. Fortunately, he didn't, but Scott did, and when his eyes met mine, he smirked his evil "Doctor House" grin. You know that scene where the arrogant, overly patronizing, all-knowing HBO doctor pops another Vicodin and tells his hospital bosses to take a hike because only he knows how to cure this patient's terminal *Restaurantitis.*

I recalled his previous warning, "Stick to the teeth, Doc, and leave the restaurant business to me." The recollection sent a wave of stomach acid burning down my esophagus along with the poorly digested Lamburgini I'd had for dinner.

Chapter 9

Chicken Fights

We gushed a veritable fountain of creative catering ideas, always thinking outside the box, observing underserved openings in the local market, and trying to fit jobs to match the personalities of our staff. Our motto was "Think global—eat and drink local."

Morgan's family had emigrated from Nova Scotia in the early 1900s to work the fishing fleets off Promised Land, processing oil from the once abundant bunker into all kinds of useful products. Throughout Montauk, there are racial remnants of this emigration, scattered up and down the aisles of the IGA, the local supermarket. Many continue to man commercial boats, the life vest for the year-round community, but their genealogy is particularly apparent in the women, who are blonde, big-boned, and tough as nails, spending the winters womanning both sides of the local bars. Sandra, his seventy-year-old grandmother, was six feet and had hands that could crush a clam. She had been a fishmonger for the best of her seventy-odd years. She breathed cockles, oysters, and mussels, and could fry a fish sandwich with the best of them. Her hand-me-down flatbed had more miles than a cross-Atlantic captain and stickers that read: "Montauk, a drinking town with a fishing problem," and "Kiss my Bass," and "Our fishnets aren't stockings."

"We should do a raw bar on the street, sort of like Coney Island," I suggested.

"Morgan could crack local clams and oysters; the tourists would love it."

Cracking up at the suggestion, Morgan said, "Yeah, baby, there's big money in that. I could dress like a pirate. It's in my blood. Hello, mates! Fresh Montauk clams and oysters on the half shell!"

"How close to the sidewalk can we take the raw bar? How come no one delivers food to the beach?" I asked. "In South Beach Miami, there are food shacks right in the sand and vendors going up and down the beach."

"Probably some town ordinance, but the Ditch Witch has a stand."

"Preexisting conditions?"

"The Pizzeria delivers to the beach," said Gray, his independent, entrepreneurial spirit kicking in. "I could hire all the local kids, have them cover the surfer beaches, hand out menus and take orders by cell phone. There's nothing wrong with it if you don't park there. We'd make big bucks."

"Dial 668-food. We'll deliver," I suggested.

We all agreed that the street-side clam bar and the beach delivery were a no-brainer, but our head chef had yet another, really clever marketing idea. Scott walked into the walk-in refrigerator and came out wearing a raw, whole chicken on each hand. "Guess?" He banged the two chickens together, spraying himself with bits of gizzard.

The rest of us buzzed about his apparent charade.

"A new marinating technique?" quizzed Tracey. "You're such a genius. Here we come, *Gourmet* magazine."

"A Cuban specialty?" I wondered. What a retard.

Playing this messy game of charades, using a raw chicken as a boxing glove, Scott silently hit himself in the face with an upper cut and then held the chicken fist aloof as the bird's blood dripped down his naked arms and onto the floor.

Referring to the local butcher's long-standing ad, I yelled out, "Nobody can beat what's his name's meat!"

Sky added, "We'll beat his meat and his lousy chickens too."

"Chicken tenders?" asked Tracey.

Scott shook his head no. "Haven't you damn Yankees ever heard of Chicken Fights?" He punched the air in a fake right cross and left jab to the wishbone. "It's a popular sport back in God's country, but instead of boxing gloves, we wear chickens."

"Got a particular recipe?" Sky inquired. "Before you beat them, which comes first, the chicken or the egg?"

"I'm serious," he said.

"In a domestic disturbance, do they beat their chicks with a chicken, or vice versa?" I added for an extra level of annoyance.

"Come back after midnight," he replied. "You'll see."

So, later that night, Tom the musician and Morgan, dressed as professional boxers, with USA Grade A gloves, naked, oiled, muscular chests, and complete disdain for personal injury or affront, fought 668 rounds of Chicken Fight. It was a bloody, ugly affair, each vying for the belt, body punching the wishbones out of one another until they both fell exhausted in a bloody heap. Gizzards, torn hearts, and broken necks littered the floor. The battle for best chef was a draw. Forget those forged cook-offs played out on late night TV by gentleman chefs. This was real sousing chafing.

The whole episode was photographed and modeled for some future publication. Nicole, the tiny food runner, dressed in a scrimpy bikini, was the round girl. Prancing around the room in high heels (with a five-inch heel, she still only stood five feet), she cheered each time Morgan landed a solid blow.

Sky, as the referee, called a clean fight, overlooking the broken ribs and torn appendages. Exhausted and covered in chicken blood, they fought to a draw.

Holding a long-term contract, I played Morgan's manager. Fortunately for me, the contract caught fire and ended Morgan's chances to be the champion of chicken fighting.

We considered using the photograph with the round 668, spelled out as an ad, but the negative publicity value might not work for a family establishment.

"Montauk Association for Cruelty to Animals," added Tracey. "After all, they're already flying banners protesting the Shark Tournaments. Wait till PETA hears what torture we performed on their poultry dinner."

It made great photo-food journalism, but for now, Ruth Reichl beware; you can only guess how your dinner was prepared.

Chapter 10

Tango and the Married Man

This story is really for all you metro, middle-aged men with working wives, weekend marriages, and wayward children, or at least two out of three. We are the Rapt Generation of husbands. It is no longer sufficient for men to bring home the bacon, mow the lawn, and slap the ball. Now we have to cook the bacon and slap the sausage, as the women are busy making the bread. Wake up, guys, and smell the doughnuts. The world is still round, but we're no longer the center. We've become the hole in the doughnut.

"What do you want, pies or paychecks?" Tracey quizzed me, referring to the working wife's lot in life. "Now you've got a wife who not only bakes the pie but gets paid for it." She plated a perfect key lime with velvet frosting on the front counter and stood back to admire her creation. "It's a new world. Can you handle it, big boy?" Tracey flipped a flirtatious smile and heeled a faux flamenco.

God, my wife was gorgeous. Dressed in a blue and white checkered, self-designed and sewn shirtdress, she made a picture-perfect Donna Reed, slaving away, smiling, in her own professional kitchen over a fresh batch of chocolate chip cookies. She was living every mother's dream and getting paid for it.

Watching her perform pastry magic forced me to review my own, self-created job description. I had no real job title or responsibility at the Gig Shack other than the silent, invisible partner. I'd tried my hand at press relations, but Tracey wasn't confident enough in the kitchen. I had booked some of the music acts, but we hoped Skylar would eventually be the music promoter. I thought the most supportive role I could offer Tracey and the kids would be to complete the domestic chores. The family's attendant entourage and half of the homeless kitchen crew had turned my castle into a hostel. Our living quarters quickly became an unmitigated mess, requiring constant pick-me-ups. Returning on Thursday night, I discovered that the dishes were still stacked in the dishwasher, where I had placed them on Monday night, before taking the bus to New York. Letters were bubbling over the edge of the mailbox. A volcano of dirty towels erupted from the Maytag machine. Tracey had quit all domestic chores, and the once-a-week Salvadoran cleaning lady was obviously overwhelmed.

When I got back to the Shack, Tracey frantically ran from table to table, taking food orders and directing the staff. We hadn't been together since the previous Monday and it was proving mighty difficult to get her attention, but eventually she sat down with me at an outside table and we shared an espresso and pastry. "Did you make this croissant?" I asked with sincere admiration for her pastry skill. "This is the best croissant I've had since that morning in Paris. It's better than Balthazar's."

"I proofed before closing. Do you think the crust is too flaky?"

"Are you kidding? They're a work of art. Most croissants are just glorified bread, rolled into a crescent. This is the real thing. You haven't forgotten your baking."

Her eyes rolled toward an under-served table and the inattentive, distracted wait staff. Half of the tables needed busing.

"Uh, hello? I'm still here." I waved a hand in front of her.

"I'm not sure about that Tim. He may be a little green, but he's a smart boy and his family are good customers. I'll need to spend some more time with him." Sipping her espresso, she finally remembered I was there. "You were saying?"

"Now I've forgotten. Oh, look, there's Leslie driving by." Leslie crammed her head out of the car window as she sped by. Her eyes seemed to be counting heads of our customers. "She better look where's she going, or she might run over a tourist."

Tracey commented ruefully, "Mac Cool just got arrested for graffiti on the Metropolitan Museum."

"What's the sentence? A slap on the paintbrush?"

"Beats me, but she's pretty upset," she said, jumping up to police a table, even though some staff stood at the door sharing a smoke. They only moved once Tracey picked up the customers' glasses and never missed a drag. Coming back to my table, she said, "So how's New York? Am I missing all the action?"

"I can't believe that after 9/11, they still allow planes to fly so low over the city. It's creepy when a plane roars past the Woolworth Building," I said.

"Well, you were right there that morning."

"It's the sound that sticks with me, sort of an avalanche sensation."

"You'll probably never forget." Again, she jumped up to clean a table. It was virtually impossible to hold a conversation with her. Returning once again, she asked, "How's the office?"

"I think I'm finally ready to fire my orthodontist. She's gotten wackier than ever. She drives the staff nuts. Why do some people demand so much attention? Why can't people just take care of their own business?"

"What's that supposed to mean?" Our eyes met for a moment. She blushed and looked downward. "The squeaky wheel," she started to say, but another under-served table grabbed her attention. "I'll be right back."

But she wasn't. There was always another table, another customer, or another employee vying for her attention. The night before, a group of six French men came for dinner. They ordered bottle after bottle of wine and everything on the menu. Tracey was glamorous and flirtatious as she personally serviced their orders. They loved it, and they loved her. What a beautiful woman. They stayed open way past the normal closing time.

Sitting with Skylar at the bar, I silently watched her. Inwardly, the rapt attention was eating me alive. I felt helpless and—yes—jealous. I wanted to explain to my son that I was becoming insanely jealous of all the male attention his mother was receiving, but how does one say that to one's son? After all, on one level, this restaurant was his opportunity to advance himself. My jealousy could only block his ability to thrive. I couldn't blame Tracey for trying to throw everything into making her business work. The whole family was suddenly changing before my eyes, and I had no way to control it. My life was a runaway train headed for that hole in the doughnut.

The wife eventually came over to the bar. "The Frenchmen want more wine." She looked guiltily toward me. "I'm going to stay open another hour. You look bored; why don't you take the car and go home. Sky can give me a ride."

"Awesome!" Sky said. "Those guys are going to break the bank. Whatever you're doing, Mom, keep up the good work. This could be our best day ever."

"Great," I mumbled to myself. "Since you obviously don't need me here, I'll go home and do the laundry."

"Please, whatever you do, don't iron the clothes!" she pleaded. "Dear, you're a great husband but a lousy ironer."

"I'm out of here!" I yelled. I went home and cracked open a bottle of wine, then drank by myself while watching a rerun of *The Sopranos*. Tony was about to crack his big-mouthed mafia wife in the kisser. I felt like doing the same to mine. She had nerve. I killed myself all week to make enough money to cover her loss, I tried to help with the Shack, and I cleaned the house. What else could a woman want from a man? All she could say was that she doesn't like the way I fold the sheets. Who gives a flying fuck how the sheets are folded as long as that mountain of wash gets climbed? I was not going to touch another one of her dirty dishes, even if it killed me!

I couldn't wait to escape to my secret city life. Not the dentistry, the dancing. In the city, I danced the Argentine tango. I had taken lessons for the past three years, private and group, to learn the most difficult step of all ballroom dancing. The tango is magical, the dancer's dance. It's great exercise for the mind, body, and soul. Living alone, the other dancers had become my community. Each night in New York City, at least two or three nightclubs hold a milonga, a tango dance party. For twelve bucks, you get two hours of lessons, a performance by a world-class couple, usually from the home of tango, Argentina, and the chance to dance with dozens of willing women. I'm telling you, married people, the tango is the salvation of many troubled marriages. You get the flirtation without the risk of exchanging any body fluids other than a little sweat.

Tracey's a great dancer, but she's not that into the tango. When she dances, she's just doing it for me. She doesn't like that part about exchanging sweat with total strangers, and some people need more personal space. Also, she only visits New York City about once a month, and never when the Shack is in season.

I harbor a faint hope that one day she'll dump the Gig Shack on the boys and run off with me to Argentina, but when I'm really angry, I silently scheme to run off by myself. After all, we have but one life to live.

Later that night, the bed wasn't big enough to bridge the distance between us.

"I have one special favor to ask." I rolled to the edge of the bed.

"As long as it doesn't involve cameras and mirrors." She showed shoulders.

I proceeded to list all the things I had done to support her restaurant, until I had exhausted all my fingers. "It's not as if you're in my debt, but this is important to me." I swallowed hard at my request and reached out across the divide.

"You're a great husband. Which body part do you want in return? Please leave me my right hand so I can still bake." Her hand reached out to touch my back.

"It's nothing like that."

"Sounds like I'm in real trouble. I'm really scared. At least if payback involved more sex or kinky sex, it would be a devil I knew." She gently rubbed my neck.

"Well, that would be welcome, but that isn't what I had in mind."

"Okay, hit me, but not too hard or someplace I can't have surgically repaired."

"I want to hold a weekly tango milonga at the Gig Shack. I know this young couple from Argentina; they're great teachers and they want to come to Montauk for the summer. They'll need room and board, but they won't charge to give lessons. We could pull up the tables, maybe on a Sunday night, that's usually the slow night."

Tracey didn't speak for a few seconds, but then she blurted out, "I'm not sure. It might interfere with dinner service, and our customers might not be into it."

"Who cares what they want. I want it."

"Dancers don't buy any food or alcohol. It would be a money loser."

"Tapas and tango, a perfect combo."

"We don't make any tapas."

"Special menu?"

"I'm not making a special menu just for the tango."

"Okay, but think value-added-ness. How many other beach shacks in town have their own dance space? You would be one of a kind. It's a natural fit into the Gig mentality. Imagine, my own Montauk milonga."

"I would have to ask Scott first."

"Scott? Scott? Who gives a shit about what he thinks?"

"He's the manager. If he thinks it works."

"So, I have to beg Scott now?"

"You don't have to beg. If he thinks it's a good fit, them I'm okay with it."

"Why the prejudice against the tango?"

"That's an aggressive thing to say." Her back-up defense is to attack. "I'm not against the tango. I just don't think it fits with the Shack's philosophy."

"Everyone else in the family is being given carte blanche to express their creative juices. I'm totally supportive of that, but why is it okay for everyone to be creative but me?" If I rolled any further away, I would have landed on the floor.

"They're not always telling me what to do."

"I'm not telling you what to do; I'm asking if it would be all right if I held a milonga at your restaurant."

"And if I said no?" She slammed her right hand on the pillow, expressing two feathers that hovered conspiratorially over my face for a few seconds. The feathers bobbed and weaved around each other, as if participating in an acrobatic winged tango, until an updraft sucked them into the overhead fan.

I hadn't considered that possibility. "Well, I guess I'd just have to find another artistic venue." It wasn't a particularly good or satisfying response, but I suddenly realized I was out of options. Not used to lacking control over my own destiny, the hole in the doughnut, the black hole in our marriage, widened.

"Let me think about it first, but don't promise your tango people anything yet." Tracey rolled over, offering a glimpse of back and shoulders.

Her resistance was caused by an information overload. She had so many daily decisions, but for me, this was an issue worth fighting for. All the other small miscommunications aside, this would be my line in the sand, my little tango fantasy.

Chapter 11

The Beach Billy

Once Tom and his band escaped town, Erin, our resident groupie, grew increasingly despondent. She covered the tattoo in multiple layers of clothing, claiming she was cold, and was more interested in sampling the beer than bartending.

"What's wrong with Erin?" I asked Scott one slow afternoon.

He looked her way for a moment and rolled his eyes. "Ignore her; she's useless."

"I'm concerned with the welfare of all our employees. She doesn't appear content." I slipped him forty bucks. "Buy her some flowers."

He turned the cash over disdainfully but slipped it into his pocket. "Thanks, but a couple of roses isn't going to sweeten her mood."

"You never know; women are women."

"Not in her case," he said, walking off in an angry huff.

Jay, our town's ex-supervisor, and his band, Jayakari, offered to play next. Jay's family ran a local motel, and he had been the East Hampton mayor for two terms. East Hampton owns the hamlet of Montauk. Due to the mandatory term limits, he had graduated to an Up Island position. Although once a popular politician, as a Republican, he was presently on the outs with the heavily Democratic new administration.

"What a stroke of genius," I complimented my wife. "Jay's connected. He could be the house band. The new supervisor wouldn't dare bother us now."

The band consisted of Jay, a box drummer; Ed, a barefooted, bass-playing lawyer; and Paulie, a tall black flutist with a shaved head. Jayakari cut the rug, the flute, the saxophone, and a string of assorted instruments. Their jazzy style was spontaneous, quasi Latin, and fortunately, not overly amplified.

Being celebrities, their first concert brought out a large local following. Situated in the back indoor corner, Jayakari was an immediate hit. This was our busiest night to date, and although many of the patrons were complimentary or friends of the band, I could see the Gig Shack's potential for business. The entertainment-starved tourists, trolled by the hook of live music, were boarded for alcohol, ice cream, and coffee.

Jayakari started playing around eight that evening, and after an hour, just as the crowd was getting going, a policeman showed up and ordered the music turned off.

Erin started waving a baseball bat from behind the bar, but before she hit the cop, I quickly intervened. "I'm sorry, officer, we'll turn down the volume," I promised, waving to the band to lower the noise, which wasn't really all that loud anyway.

"It's too late for that," he ordered.

"Come on, please give us another chance."

He approached the band, knocking over a microphone by accident. The fallen mic boomed an errant echo, sending shivers through the crowd. Suddenly, the cop recognized Jay as his one-time boss. "Oh, I apologize, sir. I didn't know you worked here, but there's been another noise complaint." He gently picked up the microphone stand and dusted it. The cop wasn't much older than my own kids.

"You know who I am? Keep your hands off of that."

"Yes, sir. I'm really sorry," the police officer apologized to Jay.

"That's so anti-business. We're in a downtown commercial resort district. No one lives within half a mile. Why would anyone complain? We weren't playing loud."

"Sir, I apologize," the cop said, backing away. "Orders."

In a small town, it pays to have someone connected. The old boy network was alive and well, and our drummer stood empowered and against the new administration's ridiculous, anti-resort, anti-Montauk business law. "Who made the complaint?" Jay demanded. "I bet it was the new supervisor. He's so paranoid. He heard I was playing music in Montauk and is trying to screw with me any way he can."

The politics in East Hampton were upside down. The Democrats were the wealthy landowners who were anti-development. They were Nimbi's (Not in My Back Yard), ultra-conservatives. Don't pave over paradise. Their answer to every request was no. They didn't want the blue-collar tourists driving SUVs and campers through their big, glass houses to reach Montauk, but there's only one road into our town.

"He blames me for the budget shortfalls, but it's just a matter of time before he'll get caught with hands in the cookie jar. The present supervisor will self-destruct."

Hiring Jay as the house band turned out to be a political double-edged sword. He had more powerful enemies than friends. Was the present supervisor punishing us because his competitor played music here—guilt by association—or because Jay wrote incriminating letters to the local papers? We were caught in a power struggle.

"As you know, sir," the cop said to Jay, "anyone can file a noise complaint anonymously." In a gesture of goodwill, the officer ricocheted both eyeballs in the direction of our neighbor, Killjoy's souvenir shop. So Killjoy was our chronic complainer? The plot, like ripe lobster bait, was thickening. I should have known. Since the moment we'd bought the building, Killjoy had been a thorn in Tracey's side, yelling at her contractors, threatening the staff. He lived above his store with a wife and son. Killjoy was born in that back room and had lived there for sixty years. If anyone represented the Old Montauk, the town that time tried to forget, it was he. He threw paying customers out of his store simply because the tourists didn't know a hook from jig. I'd bought some stuff from him twenty years ago and swore I'd never return. It was time for a showdown with the squeaky wheel across the street.

I strolled over to see if Killjoy was home. His store was locked shut, but as I returned to the Shack, I noticed a face flash across an upstairs attic window. It was Killjoy, sneering at me from behind a curtain, his middle finger held high. He pumped the bird twice in my direction.

While I dreamed of revenge, Jayakari finished their set. There was a loud cheer of joy from all the happy customers for the excellent music. Everyone agreed that live music was a real asset to our resort town. Why should one chronically grouchy guy be able to spoil the party for the rest of the community?

The next day, I vowed to do a little conflict resolution with our neighbor. As a dentist, I specialize in that sort of thing, gaining intimate access to other people's bodies and getting paid for the pleasure. Resolution is about effective communication, listening to another's chief complaint, and resolving to cure the defect. I consider myself something of an expert on solving problems. The key to climbing any mountain is just one small step, followed by another and another.

"The secret to conflict resolution is to blame the problem on a third person," I lectured Tracey as we sat at an outside table sharing an espresso and pastry. "This way, you and your adversary don't get into that in-your-face ego thing. In the end, you chastise a third party. I'll blame it on the musicians; it's no big deal. I'll just ask Killjoy what his comfortable music volume level is."

"Boy, are you naïve. You don't know who you're dealing with," warned Tracey.

"Everyone has a need for resolution. We can't live in a constant state of warfare."

"Okay, wise guy, be my guest, but don't be getting in any fistfights. Your hands are too valuable. Offer him some money to move."

"I'll beat him with my brains."

Killjoy's family habit was standing in front of their shop. Carrying a peace offering, it wouldn't be a problem buying his attention, so I crossed the street to his store. I brought a big plate of ice cream, Venezuelan chocolate gelato. Killjoy spied me from a distance, whispered to his wife, and ducked inside his store.

"My treat." I offered the plate of desserts to his family. The kid eyed the desserts hungrily, but the wife ordered, "We can't accept that." She turned her back on me. "Anyway, we don't like ice cream."

"Oh, sorry to hear that. Can I offer you guys a free dinner some night?"

"We never eat out."

"You're right across the street; it's not traveling." This was going to be more difficult than I'd imagined. "Or we could deliver." I peeked into their store.

Killjoy stole into a back room as if he were expecting a violent confrontation. With thick fisherwoman's arms crossed at her muscular chest, his bodyguard blocked my access. "Are you through?" she demanded.

"I grow my own flowers. Can I bring you a bouquet of roses?" I offered. What woman doesn't like flowers? It always worked on my wife.

"I'm allergic," she said.

What could I offer as a peace sign? What would break through their feigned anger? "I could give you both tango dance lessons? I teach beginner tango."

Mrs. Killjoy stared at me as if I were an invader from a foreign planet. "We hate dancing, don't we?" The kid grunted, although he still eyed the ice cream.

"Well, to be honest, I came here to talk about the music. I'm on your side. These musicians are so difficult; they won't perform at a reasonable level. I tell them to lower the volume, but as soon as I walk away, they up it. What do you suggest I do with these musicians? How can I be a good neighbor?"

"We open our store by 6:00 AM. We're early to bed. We don't want any noise."

In hindsight, I should have paid more attention to her reply. It would have saved us a lot of grief, but the musicians were the problem. They never showed up on time and always played too loud. "I agree with you. Musicians are like giving a mouse a cookie; every time you add a member, they want more. What would make you comfortable?"

"No live music." She puffed out her chest.

"Maybe I could move them to another corner—"

She grabbed my shirt. "Read my lips, you noisy tango freak."

The son, a nice boy, piped in. "We hate live music?"

"Come on. Work with me. What if they played earlier?" I pleaded.

Pulling her son in after her, she slammed the glass door in my face, and the lock clicked tight. Killjoy poked his face from behind the interior counter and snickered. That was the only time I'd ever seen him smile.

"So you want war?" I vowed and returned to my side of the street.

In my absence, Killjoy regained his perch in front of his store. Spying my flanking motion, he jumped back inside. When I left, he'd step back out front, and when I approached, he'd jump back inside his store, as if he were comically challenging me in a game of cat and mouse. "He's like a hermit crab, hiding in its hole at the beach. You know those ghost crabs—as soon as someone approaches, they hide back into their hole."

Tracey assessed the situation. "There's nothing we can do but ignore him. I have more important battles. The best revenge is our success."

"The whole community is being cheated of live entertainment just because one Beach Billy doesn't like music."

"What did you call Killjoy?"

"A Beach Billy. He's tumbleweed-white-trash hillbilly. The furthest west he's traveled is the Napeague Stretch, and even that's a stretch. It's a peninsular way of thinking. The End, that says it all. Some of these townies think they can keep the world beyond the Great Wall of Route 27. They want to keep Montauk from ever changing."

"Beach Billy?" lamented Tracey. "We weren't born here; the townies will never support us. They only want the tourists' dollars."

"Montauk's made from glacial runoff. The ocean pulverizing this very stone and carrying the sand westward formed Manhattan Island. We're the beginning."

"So, what does that make us?"

"Tocals!"

"What's a tocal?"

"Tocals are tourist locals. We're seasonal business owners with second homes in Rincon, Tribeca, or Breckenridge."

"You're right. Our best customers are the tourists. Forget about the locals."

"That big boulder on Cemetery Hill is going to roll west no matter how hard Killjoy and his kind try to pull it back," I warned.

Chapter 12

Take a Night Off?

"Why are you yelling at me?" Tracey cried. It was Friday night, the witching hour, our weekly bicoastal reunion. We'd spent a nice afternoon together, a movie and lunch at Rowdy Hall, but now the separation anxiety from her baby, the Gig Shack, was getting the best of her. "I can't just sit around the house doing nothing." She fidgeted. "They might need me down at the Shack."

I had purchased a filet mignon from Ray, the butcher at Citarella, the fancy food store in East Hampton, and goat cheese for a quiche from Larry, the cheese merchant. I'd handpicked the garden salad and chilled the French champagne, but for some reason, I'd delayed in setting the romance and the table. If I couldn't have her mind and hunger, I didn't want her body. "Go back to work. Please!" I waved to emphasize the level of my frustration. "You're obviously uncomfortable leaving the Shack on a Friday night."

"Fool!" she threatened.

"No, you're the fool."

"A woman can't be a fool; it's a male term. Only men are fools."

"Oh, well, *whatever*," I added for ill effect.

"Whatever? Whatever is a female word; men aren't allowed to use it." Then she threw down this week's addition of the *East Hampton Star* in my lap. "When is the *Star* going to print a review of the Gig Shack? They're purposely dishing us because we didn't buy an ad in the restaurant section. All they do is specialize in advertising obituaries and DUI's. I can't read any more of this trash."

"Go back to work. You'll be happier in a world you can control."

"You constantly complain that I don't pay enough attention to you, but when we're together, all you do is complain about my lack of attention!" She mashed her foot into the cover of the food section of the

Star, as if she were putting out a fire. "You're a self-fulfilling prophecy. Nothing is ever good enough."

On one level, I knew she was right, but I continued to attack. "Tracey, you whine when you've had too much wine." It was meant to be a joke, a double irony, but it was an aggressive response. I'd felt justified. I'd planned a romantic dinner for two, but this was like romancing a stone, Tracey Stones. She was a ghost of her usually effervescent self. Getting her to take a break from work was my most important and most difficult job. To date, I'd been a failure. It was a thankless job. I was willing to show patience, but I just didn't want to be the whipping post. I pointed at the door. "I'm a big boy. Go baby-sit someone else. I can take care of myself." The line in the sand had shifted, but the rock was unmoved.

"Mr. Drama Queen." She sat down and picked the paper back up. "More champagne, please." She handed me her empty flute as a peace offering.

Marital and martial are spelled with the same letters. The fine art of verbal jiu-jitsu, the bickering battle of the sexes, is the real art of marriage maintenance. A good marriage isn't rocket science, but it sure is more convoluted than bad plumbing.

"I'm serious. If you're uncomfortable being home, go back to work." I changed tactics to take the offensive, against my usual stance of self-protection. I usually undercook the conflict. That night, I turned up the heat, knowingly playing with fire.

"It's not like one of my customers swallowed a three-inch nail. It's raining, and the restaurant's pretty quiet tonight." She sipped her champagne quietly. "Maybe you're right. I should take a night off." She kicked off her shoes and put her feet lazily up on the sofa. "I've worked for two weeks straight. Sky will just have to run the show alone." A calming breeze whispered through the wind chimes, a change of season and tune.

"Brilliant."

"You're a saint, Lewis. I don't know how you put up with me. I must be acting horrible, but it's like an addiction; I can't get enough of the action."

Rubbing her toes gently. "Saint Lewis says you need to pace yourself." I carefully applied more pressure to her trigger points. "You're doing a spectacular job. Opening a new business was a good family plan, to diversify our financial risks."

"Thank you for getting me out of there, for showing me that the Gig Shack can function without me, for learning that even I am not essential."

Wavering toward the proper response, I felt like a male praying mantis stooping for romance with an eye toward decapitation. One wrong gesture and I would be dinner. "My greatest fear is that you'll find me non-essential." I held my breath.

"Yes, dear." She studied her wedding band-less left hand. She had plenty of wedding rings—a gold one and borrowed and blue ones—but she claimed they all gave her a rash. A solitary giggle escaped her, and for a brief moment, she didn't take herself so seriously. She spoke in a playful, flirty tone. "That's a fear I've entertained too." She laughed quietly, showing a flicker of her Doctor Gross laminated smile.

Suddenly, the home phone rang. The robot voiced the omnipresent Big Brother ring, "668 the Gig Shack." The melody sang a bad backdrop for romance.

Tracey picked up the call, and her blossoming erotic demeanor shrank into abstinence as she listened with raw concern. "The kid did what?" Her eyes turned accusingly toward me. "The mother is still there?" She twisted her lips angrily in my direction. "Yeah, I'll tell him. Scott, in the meantime, buy them dinner on me." Tracey looked down at her watch, which read 9:00 PM. "I'll be right over." She frowned.

Being a restaurant mistress is like riding a rodeo bronco. The horse doesn't hate her rider. It just doesn't want to be rid. If our marriage were to survive the "One Hundred Days of Restaurant Hell," I'd have to hang on to that horse for dear life. I'd grab throat, rope, or tail with my bare knuckles, rather than get thrown from that horse. I wasn't trying to break her. I was just trying to hang on long enough to score some points.

She hung up with a loud click and proceeded to tie her boots.

"Can I come with you?" I asked but already knew the answer.

Looking away from me, she shook her head negatively. "No."

"What happened?" I couldn't resist a little drama.

"I'd rather not say." She got up to leave.

"Oh, come on, you can't leave without telling me something. That's just not fair."

She relented. "Some tourist's kid choked on a peanut. Scott intervened. The kid's all right. Thank God for Scott, he's my life savior. I told you the peanuts were a bad idea, but you had to insist!"

"Customers need something to snack on while they wait for the food."

"The shells make a mess, and someone might be allergic. That's all we need, some kid swallows a nut and goes into convulsions. Ana … phi … lack … tic … shock?"

"Shouldn't the risk-adverse parent prevent their kid from eating the nut?"

"I can't be in the Shack watching every nut!" she screamed. A tear welled angrily in her right eye. "I can't control the fucking world." Spoken like a true Aries.

"The kitchen's still too slow. People need a chip or something to nosh on."

"Stay out of my fucking kitchen and leave the fucking noshing to the professionals, damn it!" She slammed the door and went back to work, leaving me an empty house, an empty bottle of champagne, and some uncooked meat.

I threw the steak in the freezer and went out for a drink. Trying to get as far away from the Shack as possible, I ended up driving around. Leslie was out front, rifling through her menus, looking for one that was up-to-date. "Morons, I have to do everything myself." She looked up toward me. "Oh, hi, what do you want?"

"I just needed a break from the Shack. Can I have a drink?"

"I fired my chef this week, and I'm having him arrested." She rolled up the sleeves of her shirt and showed a lot of little muscle. "All the males think they can fuck with me? Screw them. I am woman!" She ripped the old chef's menu out of the holder and replaced it with a new copy. "The bastard forged my name on his check."

"Did you owe him any money?"

"That's beside the point. He forged my name, and he left my house and the car I lent him a complete mess. I hate him."

"Left a mess, huh? So who'd you hire?"

"I met this wonderful Italian man. He specializes in Mediterranean fare. Everything will be all right now. He's wonderful! He starts tomorrow."

"What's his name?"

"Fabio. He's gorgeous and he speaks so cutely. He's from the city and everything he says ends in *Mama Mia*."

"Does he have any children?"

"He didn't say so. Do you know him?"

"No, it must have been someone else I met. So how's Mark?"

"We're finally done; I kicked him out too. He acted like this place was his brainchild. He was using me." I took a seat at the bar while she angrily re-stuffed menus. Mac Cool made me a martini. He dressed in turn of the century garb.

"So how's life for you, little man?" I asked Mac. "Stoli, please."

He looked over his shoulder to see if Leslie was watching, but she was off screaming at one of the Irish waitresses. "I'm getting worried about her; this place is killing her. She broke up with Mark, too." He spun his board like a top.

"That relationship was doomed from the get-go," I noted.

"Maybe so, but at least he provided some stability. I'm worried she's going to throw herself or one of the Irish girls into the brink. They can't swim."

"Ah, your mom's a lot of hot air. She's harmless."

"Before she opened a restaurant, I thought so too, but now she's under such pressure, such a short fuse, any moment she could explode. And believe me, you don't want to be anywhere near that kitchen when she goes ballistic. The plates will fly."

"Another plate smasher? You could have helped by staying out of trouble."

"Yeah, she's freaking about my getting arrested, but art belongs to the people, not some stuck-up museum that charges for the pleasure. Art should be free."

"Did you have to spray paint the steps of the Metropolitan?"

"Who would have guessed the police were on the lookout. Anyway, it's not graffiti but a political statement. People should be able to use any canvas for art."

"So, what happens now?"

"Mom hired some big-ass attorney, but if I get busted again, my school will suspend me." He performed an acrobatic skateboard maneuver behind the bar.

"Well, stick to bathroom stalls and out-of-work phone booths in the future."

"Yeah, man. Mom needs my support," he said, balancing on one wheel.

I liked Mac Cool. He was a hip-cat kid, a great artist, and the best skateboarder in town, but I worried about him. He was an insecure cat climbing the big life tree. I hoped he didn't climb so far out on a limb that he couldn't find his way back. In his family, there was no fireman, no father to rescue him from that limb.

"Mac Cool, if you ever need a dad to talk to, I mean, if you ever need help—"

"Back to work, Mac!" Leslie stormed between us. "Just because you're the boss's son doesn't give you the right to goof off."

I thanked them for the drink and guiltily drove back to the Gig Shack. I understood Tracey's addiction to this work and ached to get back into the action and help, but when I got there, the place was half-empty. Scott was sitting at an outside table, nursing a glass of wine and his hand-rolled cigarette. Instead of unsuccessfully triangulating through Tracey, I figured I'd take the bull directly by his horns.

"So how's business?" I asked cheerfully.

Scott seemed to take my comment as a criticism of the empty dining room. He frowned and said, "My business is fine. How's yours?"

I sat down next to him. "Brilliant. I just can't get enough of that tooth decay."

An old couple walked up to the entrance and studied the hand-drawn chalkboard menu. The blackboards had been hand painted by Scott in one of his artistically manic moments. "What's this *ceviche* stuff?" the wife asked with a Long Guy-land accent.

The husband acted confused too. "It's a Mexican beer, honey-bunny."

"What's this lamb-bur-dini?" she asked in a Tweedy Pie falsetto.

"This must be one of those immigrant Latino places." His nose pinched with disapproval. "Doll face, I could sure go for some good-old American beach food."

I was about to play host and explain the menu, when Scott jumped up and arrogantly confronted the couple. "For your information, you bird-brains, *ceviche* is uncooked fresh fish, marinated in citric acid, lime, lemon, and special herbs."

The couple jumped back, surprised by his aggressiveness. "Are you the owner? You mean sushi? My wife can't eat raw fish. Do you know where we can get some real food—a hamburger or hot dog?"

"I'd just love some local clam chowder," exclaimed the wife.

"You want McDonald's cat food, go back to Brooklyn," Scott scolded them.

The couple walked off in a huff and ended up at Shaggy's. Scott returned to our table, but his eyes couldn't hold mine. "Maybe the menu needs a little tweaking," I suggested in the kindest tone I could muster. "Something more plebian, a good quality cheeseburger and some *kiddy* food, in addition to your famous fare."

"Tracey didn't persuade me to travel all the way here to prepare *kitty* food."

"I support your gourmet aspirations. Tracey considers you a genius, but until we get some cash in the *kitty*, maybe you could add a chicken finger or dog for the bank."

"How many restaurants have you opened?"

I admitted the obvious to my inquisitor. "This is my first."

"Well, if you checked out my resume, you'd know that I've opened almost ten. It takes time for the public to appreciate a new place."

"I was meaning to ask about your resume. Why have you moved around so much?" Before he could answer, a young couple with three children asked for a table outside. They also looked confused by the hand-painted, calligraphic blackboard, so I quickly handed them a regular menu. "Can I offer you a table inside or out, madam?" I asked, half-hoping to demonstrate to Scott proper customer relations.

"You're very sweet," the wife replied. "Is this your place?"

"I'm just the silent partner. It's really the wife and son's place."

"How wonderful, a real local family business."

I handed them the extensive wine list. "We have wine and beer from around the world. We're also the only restaurant serving Montauk Light, a local draft beer."

Smiling with digestive anticipation, she asked, "What kind of pasta do you serve? My kids only eat pasta, but they're not too choosey. A little butter and cheese will be fine for them, and I would love some fresh fish."

"I'm sorry, we don't do pasta. Would they like some fresh chips?"

"We've been coming to Montauk for twenty years. Every restaurant serves pasta; that's what children eat. Could you ask the chef to make an exception?"

"I'm sorry, our chef doesn't make pasta, or serve exceptions."

"You seem like a nice guy, so I'm going to give you a word of advice. If this moron of a chef doesn't serve pasta, you aren't going to last a year. My motel doesn't have a kitchen or I'd cook myself. This is a family town. I'll buy the pasta and boil it for you." She headed toward the kitchen.

"Our chef doesn't allow strangers in his kitchen; in fact, he won't even allow me."

"Good luck in the restaurant business, buddy! You're going to need it." They went across the street to Shaggy for a plate of his plain primavera.

When I turned back, Scott had shrunk back into a hole in his kitchen.

In the meantime, Tracey sat with me. "Have you had dinner? I'm going to have a Caesar salad and some ribs. You want to join me?"

"What kind of ribs you got?"

"Scott's experimenting with three types, but the beef is way too fatty. The smoker's on the fritz, so it's all done in the oven, but my favorite's the short rib."

"I'll just pick."

"Come on, honey, you know you can't just pick; you'll devour all my food. Please order a real meal." She looked drop-dead gorgeous in her red Calypso halter.

"Okay, I'll have the fish and chips. So, how was your evening?"

"Unfortunately, the kid survived and the parents ordered everything on the menu. I think we were taken. The kid's a professional peanut choker."

"The restaurant hustlers, if you could only see them coming."

Tracey walked past the bar, where Erin was flirting with two middle-age male customers. "Erin, if you get a moment?" Tracey frowned disdainfully toward the lustful men playing with Scott's wife. "Could you bring me a glass of Merlot, please?"

Erin rolled her eyes at Tracey's back and continued her flirtation with the men without any acknowledgment of the request. Erin and the men laughed to themselves.

"I think she hates me." Tracey sat down heavily.

"Erin? Why? She's only worked for you for a few days."

"She gives me the evil eye," she said, demonstrating the female art of eye rolling.

"Who's being paranoid now?"

"What could she have against me?" Tracey shot an evil eye back to Erin.

"Let's play devil's advocate."

"I've given her and Scott a healthy paycheck. She has the nerve, the little bitch," Tracey sneered in Erin's direction. "Did you see her roll her eyes at me again?"

Our oldest son Arden strolled into the bar. Erin broke off her conversation with the men, ran over, and gave him an intimate hug, followed by a wet kiss on the lips.

"Wow, did you see that?" I asked. "Fast work in twenty-four hours."

"Now she's seducing our son?" Tracey cried.

Who's seducing whom? I wondered. Son number one had recently moved back.

Arden flashed his famous girl-slayer, post-buck-tail, Doctor Gross's lumineers.

"I hope Scott doesn't see them. That's all I need," Tracey confessed. "Another *Kitchen Confidential*."

"Maybe that was her intention," I wondered out loud.

"And why would she want to make Scott jealous?"

"I'll give you one guess. Women know these things. Tit for tat?"

She rolled her eyes at me and added, "Dear, I have to go back to work now. I don't have time for your make-believe dramas, tit for tats, eye rolling, or whatever."

Maybe I was wrong about Erin's intentions, or maybe it was just a case of old-fashioned, female rage, but more than a good cup of coffee was brewing in that kitchen. The drama smelled of fermented fish left too long in a barrel. Lobster bait you find down at the docks, a trap set for scavengers and their lovers.

Chapter 13

Blessings of the Fleet

Tracey offered to throw a party for my fifty-fifth birthday, but I just wanted to spend the day alone with her doing nothing. Owning a restaurant is a constant job in entertaining, and even though we'd been opened only a few weeks, I was getting tired of this constant chore. I can handle the obligation when I'm greeting friends or meeting strangers at the Shack—that was a necessary part of being the owner—but the idea of buying, cooking, and cleaning at our own home, even though we'd hosted hundreds of wonderful parties in the past, was more than I wished to handle. Entertaining as a business took all the fun out of it. I said, "Maybe we'll have a party in the off-season."

Her birthday present was to take the afternoon off, and we just lay about in the backyard under the blossoming white apple and pink cherry trees, reading to one another, telling funny stories, and making love. We were both too tired to even go to the beach. Later, I picked fresh herbs and greens from my garden and created a perfect homemade, homegrown salad. "Thank you for the gift," we lip-synched to each other.

The next day, Sunday, June 8th, was a major holiday in Montauk. The Blessing of the Fleet and St. Patrick's Day are local traditions, almost religious rituals, as the whole town prepares for this season's "Deadliest Catch." The commercial fleet hosted catered parties, each ship a lavish smorgasbord of pigs in blankets and buckets of beer, as expensively laid out as a Further Lane, red velvet wedding.

At the jetty leading to the harbor, a priest, a rabbi, and a monk stood hand-in-hand, blessing the draggers and long liners, as they paid homage to those lost at sea and prayed for a good catch of squid, whiting, and cod. With due pomp and circumstance, the Catechism of Monkfish, Jewfish, and Jesus fish came off without a hitch.

Once out on the ocean, the professional bay-men mercilessly blasted one another with water cannons, wet balloons, and twice-used condoms. Sea turtle and breached whale, beware. It's a fight to the death, or at least until everyone was so drunk that they're hacking through the portholes. The big battleships were peppered by small private cruisers, as pesky as a hornet's nest, which scooted beneath the bow and between the gunnery of the slower long liners and draggers. It was a wonder no one ever got killed.

After the battle, drenched and thoroughly inebriated, everyone in town retired to the Liar's Saloon, an infamous beer joint on the harbor. We escorted Scott and Erin to the party, hoping to introduce them to some local color.

"Now this is a party," claimed Erin, knocking back two fists of Maker's Mark. She was dressed in a red striped miniskirt and fishnet stockings: a real fish out of water amid the loosely hung, blue jeaned, or otherwise over-alled lady. Not that the fishermen minded as they ogled her shapely legs. "Damn, what is it with the women in this town," Erin sneered. "They're the worst dressers. They dress more masculine than the men."

"It's the same in East Hampton; the pink and green cashmere crowd that does lunch dresses like a bunch of old ladies," added Tracey.

I have to hand it to Erin. She had her own style, throwback provocateur. After Tracey, she was the best-dressed dame in Montauk. "It's a fashion-challenged community," I said, admiring her coquettish, fish-netted legs and four-inch stilettos.

"Erin, your skirt's even shorter than normal," said Scott, with an obvious hint of annoyance. "You're giving these Bonackers a free hard-on," he snorted.

For all her in-your-face flirtation, Erin didn't seem to garner much romance from Scott. At times, it appeared they hardly knew each other. There was no touching of hands or any other outright sign of affection. "When's the last time you noticed?" she retorted and went off to buy another drink. "More Maker's Mark!"

From a short distance, I studied Tracey and Scott, lurking side by side, wondering if there was some secret affection hovering between them, something Erin as an outside observer was aware of, but I, wearing marital glasses, was blind to. After all, they were spending twelve hours a day together, and I was only in Montauk a few days a week. How was I to know if I was being cuckolded by this Bohemian? He had no obvious affection for his own wife. "Opening restaurant equals divorce?" Would my sons watch their father's interest? They were already under this chef's satanic spell.

As I spied on my wife and her head chef, considering self-destructive, dangerously jealous comments, a young man with a wavy mop of hair and soft feminine features strolled a few feet in front of Scott. The boy winked at Scott, and to my complete surprise, the chef smiled back an acceptance. Had an illicit romance just blossomed before me? Astonished, I turned to Tracey, but she had already followed Erin to the bar and completely missed this carnal interchange. When I turned back, Scott was wagging the dog, walking away from me to the left, behind the young man. He was gone long enough for Erin to knock back another three Maker's Mark.

Tracey came back after one beer and asked if I'd seen Scott. I didn't have the heart to tell her my new secret, but when the chef finally came back, his eyes couldn't meet mine. If I had something to hold over the chef, I didn't know what to do with that knowledge, but I felt better believing it.

The next day, Monday, rainy weather changed our string of good atmospheric fortune, as a frightful fog engulfed the End, obscuring the tide line and white sand. You could taste the salt air close on your lips, and the foghorns from the commercial draggers, not more than a half mile off the main beach, bellowed as if in one's bedroom. The tourists stayed inside their rooms, waiting for a reprieve. It rained all day and night, but not as much as my fiftieth birthday, a few years back, when we'd set up a tent in the backyard. That monsoon blasted the tent with at least two barrels full of runoff.

"I'm going to take the bus back tonight," I told Tracey. "The weather sucks, and the early morning trips are killing me. Tuesday is always a tough day—dental emergencies and a pile of paperwork." Silently, we drove to the bus station.

"You need to take better care of yourself," she warned. "You should always go back on Monday night." Is she getting rid of me to be alone with her chef? "The expense of opening this place has put a serious dent in our savings." She kissed me gently on the cheek and added, "You need to get out of here and make me some money too." She sang the words from that 1930s flapper song.

"My little concubine," I said playfully, as I unfolded a roll of Hamiltons into her hand, fulfilling my end of the sex game we played each weekend. If we made love every other day, I handed her cash before I left. If we didn't, I still paid her the cash. "My only function in this family is to pay your rent and seed your eggs. Once stem cells catch on, women won't need men." Why did I say that? Kicked myself right out of the nest.

She refused my usual payroll. "Well, now that the Gig Shack has caught on, I might not need a sugar daddy." She tried to take the words back. "I'm sorry, I was joking." She kissed me on the cheek and handed back my stash of tens. "I've had a good week." She offered me a pile of her own twenties. "No one can stop me now." She neatly folded a Jackson and pinned it to my pocket. "Buy yourself a glass of champagne."

I pulled away, momentarily speechless. The world was topsy-turvy; our usual song and dance played a different number. If she refused my cash, what was I good for?

"It was a joke." She realized she had hit me below some unspoken belt. "You're the best husband any girl could wish for."

"Famous last words." The tango that night was looking more attractive.

She grabbed at my arm as I attempted a Shakespearean escape into the out-stretched arms of the Jitney, the chariot to my other life. "Lewis, I love you." Act one.

Stage left, the uniformed escort driver called out, "All aboard."

"Don't leave like this. I'll always need you," she cried. Act two.

I remembered the male praying mantis, so I chose my words carefully: "Tracey, you're a regular god-damn-it!" I pictured my decapitated head rolling down Route 27.

The driver and passengers waited with bated breath for her reaction.

Clamshells rained over our head from the sky, smashing into the sidewalk.

Tracey stood frozen by my words. A seagull scavenged at her feet.

The engine roared, and the line in the sand smelled of spent diesel and salt.

Suddenly, Tracey's face broke into the widest beaming smile she could manage. Her eyes sparkled with delight, and she threw her arms passionately around my shoulders. She kissed me hard and square.

"That's the nicest thing you've ever said to me!" Act three.

We kissed magically as the other Jitney passengers and driver watched. Open-lipped, we breathed one another's breath, a scene from a silent movie; the husband dressed for battle, the little woman wishing his safe return. There was happiness, too, in leaving, as long as one planned to return.

Chapter 14

My Three Sons

"What job would you like?" Tracey and I interviewed Arden.

"I really don't care. Wherever you need me is fine, as long as I can go fishing. Anyway, I'm not planning on staying past the summer."

Ignoring his lousy attitude, I said, "You've got great people skills; you're a real charmer. Since you're twenty-three, how would you like to be the new bartender?"

"Whatever," he replied, echoing his mother. "It'll cost a fifth year of college."

"We want you to be happy, to make the most of the experience."

"It's all good, as long as you both understand I'm only doing this for the family."

Tracey angrily slammed her hand down on the kitchen table. "That's really nice! After all we've done for you? We paid your college tuition, and you're going to grace us with your presence. Go back to school or get a real job. We don't need you."

"I'm sorry, but between the local kids and your Bohemian chef, I don't see how I can help. What do you want me to do?" He threw up his hands in frustration.

"You can help by just being there. A family member to watch the cash register."

"Okay, I'm in." He got up to leave. "Can I go fishing now? The bass are blitzing."

Although he and Tracey had a push-and-pull relationship, I was all right with a certain degree of his reticence. He acted as a buffer, an extra pair of eyes to watch my back. There's no better way to prevent thievery in this business than a family member holding the chastity register, the cash belt, and the keys to the alcohol closet.

Gray, on the other hand, immediately took to cooking, studying Scott's technique and scientifically developing new recipes. He had just graduated East Hampton High School and was planning to attend college in the fall. "Try this," he said, offering me an overstuffed, golden fried wrap he'd just invented. "Is this not the perfect chicken burrito?" He fed me.

The multilayered ingredients tasted fresh and crisp, with the slightest hint of Worchester sauce. "Wow, this is a hit. How about chicken fried bison burger?"

"Dad, I really love cooking here. Scott's a great teacher, and all my friends from school are coming to eat. The Shack's going to be the hot hangout this summer."

It was inspiring to witness such enthusiasm. They say the third child is usually the comedian in a family because that's the only way he can get a word in at the dinner table, but in our household, the youngest son was the staff psychiatrist. He was our muse and meditative spirit and maybe, if we'd given it a moment's pause, our true pedestal.

To this point, Sky was the mainstay of the kitchen, preparing Scott's menu to perfection. Over an order of Lamburgini and fries, I asked if he liked the work.

"What's your favorite meal to cook?"

"Chicken. I have a thing for chicken breasts," Sky confessed.

"You know, your grandmother credits your chicken Parmesan recipe for being the inspiration of our opening a restaurant. She says it's the best dish she ever ate."

"Really?" He raised an eyebrow.

"They say the best chefs are under twenty-five. You did a great job with the renovation. I anticipate that one day you'll be very successful."

"Really?" he beamed.

Tracey intervened in my parenting and put her two cents in. "I think we've reached a new plateau. Opening a real restaurant in the Hamptons with my three sons once seemed like just a dream; now I can taste the reality. With a professional chef to run the place and teach them the business, I'm so blessed. Let's entertain like the rich restaurant owners tonight instead of the poor want to be's."

"Who should we invite?" I asked.

"I don't know. Who would you like?"

"It's your restaurant—you decide."

"No, you decide."

"No, you," I demanded. "You hate all my friends."

Sky looked at Gray. They both looked toward the gray sky and shook their heads.

"Well, how about the hotel owners?" Tracey offered.

"He can't leave the kitchen."

"The yogi?"

"And listen to her describe every woman as a goddess?"

"Okay, how about the local dentist and wife?"

"Are you kidding? I didn't come out here to discuss decay!"

"Well, give me a hint. Who should be our first dinner guest?"

"I don't really care," I bantered back.

Sky and Gray's eyes and heads ping-ponged through the conversation.

"You're so superficial. You just want good-looking babes in short skirts."

"That would be a beginning," I said. "Or the end."

"Do you know any? Because I don't."

"How about your parents?" I suggested.

"Grandma in a miniskirt?" She called her mother. "Yes, they're available."

Tracey's parents became our usual guests at the owner's table. It was a kind of payback—the family barter system—and to be honest, it was easier than entertaining free dinner guests who were obligated to spend the whole night and drink themselves silly. The owner's table was real work and my least favorite job. At least her parents had the decency to leave the waitress a large tip.

Tracey was "god-damn-it-gorgeous," an involved mother, a good wife, and a real go-getter. She was four wives in one, or in the local fishing vocabulary, a keeper. She had taken this rundown ice cream shack, and with a little spit and polish, had in a few months turned it into a functioning business. She'd systemically reviewed all the issues and found creative solutions. Faced with the ban on real silverware and dishes due to water issues so close to a beach, she ordered fancy plastic forks and knives that appeared metallic. She found bamboo plates that could stand up to a fish stew. Tracey wasn't willing to push the envelope by operating a full waitress service, but the staff did run the food to your table. Slowly she was overcoming her rookie fears.

The whole extended family stood by and listened. "This is the first moment since we bought the building that I feel safe. I have a good feeling that everything's finally going to be all right." Tracey called out to Margo, a waitress, "Tell Scott that I want to try everything on his menu. I'm really hungry. Let's all eat."

Our friend Kevin and the food writer Anthony Bourdain were wrong. It wasn't impossible for a yogi and a dentist to open a brilliant restaurant in the Hamptons. Really, what was the big deal?

Chapter 15

It Rained Clamshells

Sky, Gray, and some of their friends joined the men's softball league, which played in Lion's Field. These high school seniors and college dropouts called themselves the Gig Shackers, but they were half-pint rookies compared to the more experienced teams, such as the Memory Motel and Pioneer Bar, staffed by six-foot-five bouncers who could tear the seams off a softball or a drunken patron's scalp if they ever got their paws on one. We made up for our lack of experience and power with youthful enthusiasm and speed. The youth could run circles around the thirty-year-olds who had consumed too many burgers and beers in a few short years.

The other team was dressed in perfectly laundered jerseys while our team had mismatched outfits, hand-me-down mitts, and badly battered bats.

Our coach chain-smoked unfiltered Camels in the dugout. With a loud and raspy voice, he ordered our team though their first rookie game against the more experienced behemoths from the Memory Motel.

Our starting pitcher walked their first four batters for an easy score.

"Way to go!" yelled our coach through a cloud of Camels.

From behind the dugout, I advised, "He can't hit the plate."

Our coach just shrugged and continued to yell blind encouragement. "Keep it up!"

Our pitcher walked the next two batters across the plate. We were down 3–0 and he hadn't pitched one strike. The other team was laughing it up.

A nice guy, but the coach wasn't concerned with wining. "He has a history of epilepsy," he explained to me. "When he throws a strike, he gets too excited, so I told him to throw balls and let the other team swing away."

His plan didn't work. The next batter connected with a ball two feet outside and cleared the fence for a grand-slam homerun. We were down 7–0 before Sky came in to pitch and eventually got us out of the inning.

Gray was our leadoff hitter. "Open stance, pull the ball over third base!" I yelled, relying on my ten years of Little League commissioner experience.

"Sit down and leave him alone," said Tracey. She knew how often I'd complained about fathers vicariously hitting through their children.

Gray ignored my advice, went the other way, grounding meekly to first base.

We couldn't hit the ball out of the infield. In between innings, as the ump dusted the plates, half our team was out back smoking or drinking beer. Final score was 25–2.

A few days later, we lost to the Ravens by a score of 30–3. It was obvious a change needed to be made, so Sky fired our coach. He had been our best customer at the restaurant. It wasn't an easy decision, but baseball took precedence over business. Sky became the new player/manager and in a wise coaching move, made Margo the starting pitcher. He also outlawed smoking and drinking in the dugout between innings.

Our next game was against the Fire Department, one of the more polished but aged teams. Margo was the only female in the league. In addition to tossing a mean underhanded curve, she had a well-developed torso. The opposing batters' eyes were more focused on her figure than their own balls, or so it seemed, and struck out. In the following innings, our speedy outfielders caught their deep, hanging flies. The low-scoring game was broken open in the third when Gray hit a grand slam to the opposite field and Sky doubled over third. It was our first win, 10–5. All those years of my Little League tutelage were finally paying off. With Margo pitching, the young Gig Shackers had proven to be a force in a league that was slow to change.

Tracey and I invited the team back to the Shack for a free dinner. When Tracey went into the kitchen to see what she could help with, Scott was waiting with hands on hips and an angry sneer.

"Why do you hate Erin?" Scott was filleting a large striped bass.

"Did she tell you that?" Tracey nervously swiped at the dirty counter.

"Erin thinks you don't like her," he said, his hands tearing fish's flesh.

"I don't dislike her. We're not touchy-feely," she answered, squeezing the sponge. She rolled her eyes toward a spot on the ceiling.

"Could you make an effort to appease her, please? Something special, for me?"

"Appease her? Is she complaining about me?" Tracey threw a pot into the sink.

"Erin can be a bit moody."

"Moody isn't the word, she's just rude. Where's the pink elephant now?"

"Pink elephant? She doesn't do LSD. Why did you say that?"

"The pink elephant in the room—the person we're arguing about?"

"She says you're being abusive." He slapped the fish filet pieces into a big bowl.

"Abusive? Why would I be abusive to my chef's wife? It doesn't make sense, but if appeasing her will make this go away, whatever." She tore off her apron strings.

"Thanks, Tracey. I knew you would be the adult in this."

After Scott left, Tracey sat down with me. The steam was still rising from her forehead. "That little bitch, I can't believe she ratted me out. As if I don't already have enough on my plate." She bit at her lip.

"Your plate just got some dirty dishes."

"Scott's making me out to be the bad guy. I've bent over backward to make Erin at home. I've wined and dined her and have given her a job and a home. Is it my responsibility as boss to be her fucking therapist?"

"She's obviously uncomfortable being around you."

"What did I do to her? We've spoken twice in the two weeks and she has the nerve to be disrespectful, even arrogant. Who does she think she is?"

"Speak to her directly; otherwise you're triangulating through Scott."

"Triangulating, huh? Well, if Scott's unhappy, I guess I have more to lose."

"That's my girl. Be the queen, be gracious. You own the world. Erin is a want-to-be-you. Now she wants your love and attention."

"Yeah, yeah, yeah. I'll show her my love, through the back door."

I proceeded to lecture Tracey on how the owner of a business needs to protect their investment. "It's dangerous to get emotional with unhappy customers or employees. You need to be defensive. The owner has to suck it up because you have more to lose."

Tracey made every attempt to envelop her staff in the heavy quilt of our family's love. Pleasure being the main course at our table, the staff ate till their eyes glassed over, but sometimes all those ripe eggs in one basket brought the snakes out of the grass. Some evil, lonely snakes envied our apparent abundance of eggs.

A new band played that night. The music was a huge success. Customers came in off the street and ordered dinner. The Gig Shack was packed, but the police came, like clockwork at nine o'clock, and ordered the music turned off. Opening a restaurant was supposed to be about food. I was getting sick of waiting for the police. A little drunk, I went across the street in preparation for a confrontation with our chronic complainer.

"Get your ass out here and fight like a man!" I screamed up to Killjoy's window.

From the attic window, a solitary hand stuck out a middle finger.

"Beach Billy! I'll get revenge!" I returned his bird. When I got back into the Gig Shack, I told Tracey, "We've got to do something about that moron. It's harassment, his constantly calling the police." I was so angry I could have exploded.

"Get an order of protection?"

"Can you do that? Get an order of protection from the police so someone won't call the police? It seems like an oxymoron," I wondered.

Which brings up another story. A few days later, I was drinking alone at City Hall Bar when the fellow sitting at the adjacent stool started to moan, "I'm going to kill myself." His face fell into his martini. "Maria, I loved you," he moaned.

"You okay, buddy?" I asked, pulling him out before he drowned in his drink. I picked the olive and its skewer from between his lips.

"Thanks man," he said, "but I'm ready to die."

"It can't be all that bad."

"She's left me. After thirty years of perfect marriage, she's off to manage some hotel in Paris. *It's my big opportunity,*" he paraphrased his wife's singsong voice.

"That doesn't sound so bad; you could always visit her in Paris."

"That's what she said, but it's not fair. I have to stay here and work. I've been the perfect husband and father. How could she choose a career over me? I gave her everything a woman could ask for. What do modern wives want?"

The drunk on the other side of me had overheard the conversation and piped in, "That's the same thing that happened to me, fellow. The wife opened a new store. Now I only see her on weekends. It's a weekend marriage," the enraptured hulk moaned.

"I'm stuck in a cross-Atlantic marriage," cried the first drunk.

"And I have bicoastal, off-season relationship."

"We guys did everything right. What do these women want?" said the first drunk, as he knocked back the dregs of vodka truth, the rapt of fermented potato.

"My comrades!" I pronounced. "Modern marriage is like chasing a monkey. The faster we chase after these women, the faster they run away." Throwing up my hands, I said, "Do any of you apes know how to catch a monkey?" I was drunk too.

"You stand very still and hold out a banana?" ventured the first drunk.

"Exactly!" I waved to the female bartender. "A round of bananas and martinis, on me." The three lonely apes, like musketeers, clicked glasses.

The bartender looked confused. "Stoli and banana? Is that a new drink, a banana twist? Do you want them peeled? You American guys are pathetic," said the young barmaid. "I'm from Poland. Polish guys don't want their babushkas after thirty years. You're cute; forget the old ladies and find some babe half your age. I get off at two."

Holding the bananas aloof like swords, we clicked fruit. "To all the lonely married men—one for all and all for one." For the remainder of the evening, we sat around the bar with an unpeeled fruit in one hand and a stream of cocktails in the other, until the image blurred into a drunken circle jerk. Three apes sitting in a bar moaning the fate of their marriages, holding their own bananas. Rapt, the state of the modern man.

Chapter 16

The Compost Hits the Fan

Our next game, on a Monday night, was against the Liar's Saloon, a younger and more powerful team than the Fire Department. Coaching first base, I stood next to the opposing team's first baseman, who towered over me and must have weighed close to 270 pounds. He was a mean-looking, disheveled fellow, a Beach Billy bouncer who preferred to clothesline the heads off our speedy runners approaching his base rather than actually catching the third baseman's throw. When Sky legged out a ground rule single, he had to dive under the thug's high-stick check of a forearm.

"Hey, buddy!" I yelled. "You can't do that. Are you playing softball or hockey?"

If looks could kill, I would have been tuna tartar, because he came over to me and growled in my face. "Who the fuck are you?" he hissed through missing lateral incisors.

"I'm their mascot tocal. Are you bouncing a bar or a baseball?"

"We're going to teach you city slickers a lesson," the townie threatened.

Our whole team had graduated from the East Hampton High School, so it was ironic that this big palooka considered us outsiders, but maybe it was just me he was referring to. Anyway, he wasn't a very good first baseman, and an inning later, a screaming line drive hit by one our lefthanders caught him straight inside his unprotected balls, sending his testicles into his throat. He had to sit out a few innings, and when he returned, his growl had grown two octaves higher.

Going into the last inning, we were down 10–9 to the first-place team. Margo had pitched one of her best games, overcoming the catcalls and obscene remarks of these Bonackers, but our fielders couldn't catch flies that didn't land to earth and the bouncers had some hitters who could powder the ball clear across the left-field fence. Two of their guys got lucky and went all the way on Margo, but that's a different story.

Sky had reached second on a fielder's choice, and Gray was up with two outs.

"Pull the ball over third base!" I called. "Open stance." Ten years of Little League had taught me that pulling the ball was a more powerful alternative than going the opposite way. We were down to our last out.

Gray looked at me. He smiled. From his open foot stance, I knew he had other ideas. On the next pitch, he hit the ball far into right field, but unfortunately it was a lazy fly and was easily caught. We had lost another game.

Maybe if I had practiced more with him or moved my dental business to Montauk after 9/11, things would have turned out differently, but at that moment I felt all the pangs of being the peripheral parent. Feeling rapt, I escaped to the Jitney.

When I returned to the NYC apartment that night, there was a frantic message from Tracey. "He's gone. He's gone," was all I could make out of the message. I attempted to reach her, but no one answered any of the phones at the Shack. The home phone responded with a usual robotic answer, and it was useless cold-calling the kids' cell phones. Assuming something awful had occurred to one of our sons, I had a fitful night's sleep, the kind of nightmares only a peripheral parent would appreciate, FADD—Fathers Against Drunken Driving, another form of rapt thinking.

Finally, Tracey answered the restaurant phone at 8:00 AM the next morning. "Six-six-eight the Gig Shack," she said in a sad, weak whisper, barely all the syllables in one breath.

"What happened?" I asked nervously, thinking terrible thoughts about one of the kids. "Are the boys all right?" My heart was in my throat.

"Scott quit!" she cried.

"Oh, is that all? I was worried about the boys."

"Is that all? Are you crazy? This is the worst thing that could happen to me!"

"He just quit? He can't quit. You paid him for two months to get the restaurant open. You finally get open and he quits right before July 4th? That's unethical."

"He left me a note. He said it was for the sake of his marriage," she moaned.

"His marriage, that's a joke. If it was too cold in Montauk for Erin, why didn't she wear more clothes? What else did he say?"

"It was a cryptic note apologizing to me and the boys."

"Talk to him. Maybe you can change his mind," I begged.

"I can't. He disappeared. All I found was a note taped to the kitchen window. He didn't even have the decency to tell me in person."

"The bastard! After all you've done for him, that's criminal."

"I feel violated, like I was dumped after a one-night stand," she moaned.

"Did you go by their room? Maybe there's still a chance."

"Completely empty. I have to hang up and put all the pieces back together."

"Did you check the restaurant? Did he steal anything?"

She screamed into the receiver, "That doesn't matter!" Then she hung up.

I came out as early as I could on Thursday, but the Jitney Bus got stuck in rush-hour traffic. It was 10:00 PM and Tracey had already closed the joint for the night.

"What are you going to do now?" I surveyed the loose pile of invoices.

"I haven't a clue," she cried. "I let myself get totally dependent on Scott. He left no recipes or records. I don't even know where he ordered the milk from."

"The bastard. Okay, okay, just calm down. Check all the invoices. You can recreate the trail of purveyors, and Sky and Morgan know how to cook the food."

"I hope so," she sighed, "because I never watched him make a fish taco. There's a lot more to running a professional kitchen. How do you manage the inventory?"

"Let's start with a walk through the walk-ins. Pull all the produce out of the refrigerator and the freezer. It's not rocket science."

"Don't lecture me about rocket science. You're a dentist."

"I know it's a huge job, but what choice do we have?"

So we closed the restaurant for a day, and the entire staff counted eggs, lettuce heads, and pounds of lamb. We made up lists, practiced recipes, and cut the menu to items our under-trained cooks could manage.

"I still don't know how to run the kitchen," she complained. "I need to find a professional chef or I'll go out of my mind."

"Look on the positive side."

"I can't go on. This is a money pit," she spoke sadly. "What have I done?"

"At least you're rid of Erin," I explored the obvious.

"The Gig Shack is a recipe for disaster."

"Let's put out the word, run an ad. There must be more unaccounted-for, out-of-work chefs in the Hamptons. The season's still young. Leslie already fired two."

"Scott was one of a kind."

"He sure was, but what kind?"

"Don't go blabbing all over town. I don't want everyone to know, and there's no time to run an ad. It's a short season. Let's face it," she cried, "we're finished. Who wants a restaurant without a chef? We're back to ground zero."

"We started this project at ground zero. The beginning, the end, it's all the same thing. I've been reading from the Dalai Lama's book, *The Secret to Happiness*. Life is about the passage. Finding a new chef will be my quest."

Somewhere in there, I must have said the magic word, because a ray of hope shined though my beautiful wife's eyes. She rubbed a tear-soaked chin against my rough five-o'clock shadow. "You're the best pedestal any girl could stand on. Thank you, my wonderful husband. You're my hero."

Calmer now, she read me the letter Scott had left under the door.

> *Dear, dear Tracey. I owe you so much. I leave you a situation so undeserved. It drives a burning iron through my heart's intent. I love you all so much. Believe this if nothing else. I share your current feelings and cry and cry. I can't help you. I can't help the youth. I am so unable.*

Unforeseen forces will help you. I believe in all of you. Please be strong. The sun sets only to rise again. I loved the Gig Shack, all the kids, and yourself. Don't entertain any malison on my part. My decision to leave before August occupied the two most difficult days of my life. I have made the correct one. Your love, trust, and devotion mustn't surrender, as mine shouldn't either. I will talk to you face-to-face someday. I hope your smile will be as beautiful as I remember. It is chaos now; your focus and mine are opposite. I apologize. You are in my prayers. You are in my thoughts—the youth—the Gig Shack—forever. I wish, I wish ... you will be able ... you will be able.

"I still don't understand why he left," I said. "Nice letter though, you bastard."

"I have another letter he sent to our mutual friend, which might explain." She read from Scott's handwritten note.

Thank you. We are saddened to leave. The situation I am leaving behind is undeserved. You both are Tracey's true friends. Love her. The sense of abandonment will fade. I gave my heart to the Gig Shack and nearly lost my love. I made the choice to seek counsel with my wife upstate. My other choice would have doubled my failure. The choice to save my marriage was the right choice. Doing the right thing is sometimes very unfortunate. Your hospitality is a gift.

Tracey read with tears running down her cheeks, like a bride stood up at the hoopa. Raindrops falling on a red velvet wedding cake.

"What a bunch of baloney. Doing the right thing? That's a joke. Scott's marriage will never last anyway," I said.

"So, where do we begin?" she spoke softly. "My head's about to explode."

I filled a plastic bag with ice and placed it gently on her head. "This should help, but you've got to leave it on for at least a half hour."

"Thanks, but if it doesn't work, I'm running home for a little mother's helper."

"So, have you considered hiring a restaurant manager, someone to control the inventory and staff, instead of some hyper-ego-inflated chef? After all, you have the line cooks, and you could create the menu."

The ice started to melt as the condensation dripped down her forehead, adding running mascara to her tears. "There are such people? Wow, that would be perfect, but where to find him?" She cried to herself.

"Reopen the doors and put the kids back to work. I'll go talk to some of the other owners," I said and kissed her wetted cheek.

A ray of sunshine poked through the kitchen window.

She threw me a wide, toothy grin edged by a wad of gummy gum line, thin-lipped, but not lacking definition. That first lousy lateral incisor laminate I'd constructed showed poorly in the light, the tooth-maker's wife.

I left Tracey standing on Main Street, a cook's cap of crushed ice melting on her forehead. I was on another chef quest.

The first restaurant owner I pleaded with was Shaggy, who had sold us the Shack. I'd heard rumors that he was going around town making fun of us, calling our staff a bunch of losers and insisting we wouldn't survive one season. I swallowed my pride.

"I heard you lost your chef?" he laughed to himself. "I didn't like the guy, with his floppy hat and flossy wife. He had a big mouth for an outsider."

"Bad news travels fast in a small town," I said.

"I've been in this business for forty years. When you operate seasonally, you're hiring from the same chef pool, or as I like to say, cesspool." He laughed louder at his joke. "I should have warned you, but then I'd be stuck with the mortgage."

"Is that why you operate a cesspool company on the side?" I asked.

"One good hurricane and this town will be swamped in sewage. We need a central system, but it's cheaper to do my own pumping." He sniffed the wind for a hint of blowback. "The restaurants that stay open year-round only do it to keep their staff employed. The winters are money losers. Otherwise, you have to go down to the docks each spring and pick the drunks and stoners out of the dumps. It's a dirty business."

"Well, when I bought the place, you promised if I ever needed anything."

"Yeah, but I was referring to pots and pans, not people; you should have asked in the spring. My staff's already accounted for. Come to think of it, there was this Guatemalan fellow used to work for me. I think he got divorced and moved upstate, but I'll put out the word, you never know."

"Thank you, sir." I hated being in his debt, but what choice did I have.

The next place I visited was Aqua Terre, an upscale restaurant around the corner. The head chef, Chris, had served as a paid consultant in planning the kitchen renovation.

"I heard you lost your chef already," chorused Chris with more small-town gossip. "It's for the best. Scott's ego was so big you could drive a truck through it."

"That's the good part of my working in New York City, the anonymity. In Montauk, everyone knows everyone's business before it happens."

"Yeah, but in a small town, people take care of each other. I've already contacted an acquaintance, a local surfer, Larry, who's between jobs. He might be a good fit, a food manager for your little hippie joint."

"That's mighty gracious of you."

"No problem. You and Tracey have always been supportive of me. I'm only repaying a favor. Look, he's already parked at the Gig Shack."

Larry's olive-green truck had two ten-foot surfboards hanging out the back, a common site in a surfing/surfcasting addicted town. He was already shaking hands with Tracey when I arrived. She introduced me to her new food manager.

"Larry's going to start today," said Tracey with a hint of relief.

"That's fantastic. Chris had the highest compliments," I said, but noticed with surprise that she still had the bag of ice on her head, albeit completely melted. I motioned to her over Larry's shoulder that there was a bag on her head, but she didn't understand.

"I'm the chef. I'll get the kitchen in order, but don't ask me to cook," Larry said.

"Larry will be the kitchen manager; the kids can cook," said Tracey.

"She's all yours." I pointed to the kitchen door, and when the chef turned away, I frantically pointed to Tracey's head again to get her attention. I grabbed the bag of melted ice water off, but the Ziploc broke open and all the water poured over her face.

Her introduction to her new chef was inauspicious. Completely water logged, she let out a small scream and ran out back to the car. I offered him a good-bye.

"Yeah, man," he frowned. He was a man of few words. "Nice job."

Tracey and I took a much-needed break, immediately falling asleep to the sounds of the pounding surf. Montauk has the most beautiful beach in the world—wide swaths of crystal white sand, protected by multicolored wild rose and beach plumed dunes, deeply eroded glacial cliffs, and Gulf Stream feed, tropical water that is warm enough to swim in from June through October. Arm in arm, we dozed beneath the Walking Dunes.

We sneaked back to our empty nest house, showered, made love, and dressed for the owner's dinner. In her new Pucci dress, the one I'd bought on sale that week in the city, she looked like a million dollars. Dressed in high heels and a tight-fitted skirt, she couldn't slink off to be the bottle opener, soda pop jerk girl, or dishwasher tonight.

Larry, who wasn't much older than our boys, immediately bonded with them. The kitchen was developing an extended family enthusiasm. Tracey's mom brought homemade tarts and pies, and my mom sent her famous pound cake, which we had lovingly dusted with confectioner's sugar and served warm with ice cream. Morgan's grandmother, still prepping in the kitchen, had cooked swordfish stew. Neal, Tracey's stepfather, was recycling the hundreds of glass bottles we produced each day and collecting a pretty penny from the IGA supermarket. Our dinner, professionally cooked and served by our own three sons and their friends, was a complete success.

The town had taken notice. The tourists quickly filled the place to capacity.

Tracey smiled proudly, but noticing an under-served table, quickly escaped. "I'll be right back," she promised, leaving me alone to finish a perfect salad, hamburger, and freshly cut fries—new, family friendly, post-Scott additions to the menu.

"Careful, you're wearing three-inch heels and that kitchen is a slippery mess."

"I have the balance of a ballerina," she sang her swan song.

The table of Italian male tourists, each strikingly handsome, thirty something, Marcello Martini types, worshiped my god-damn-it beautiful wife with her always ready, Doctor Gross, perfectly lumineered smile. "Tracicita, our gorgeous hostess!" A swarthy ringleader proudly introduced her to his avaricious, lustful entourage.

"Paolo! How are you?" Tracey kissed him on the cheeks, Italian style.

Butterflies fluttered in my stomach, nesting indigestibly with the sodden fries.

Taking turns kissing her hand, they chorused, "*Bellissima*, more wine."

The entire meal congealed into a gluttonous mass lodged in my esophagus.

"Tracicita, what would you recommend?" Paolo purred. She leaned over him, and they studied the menu, cheek to cheek. "You make the best espresso and croissants."

I felt like the voyeuristic husband, hidden behind the louvered closet door, watching his wife make love to other men, yet somehow enjoying the act.

Suddenly, a small bird flew right past my nose. A lost feather nestled in my right nostril. The swallow was chasing its dinner—a large, multi-winged butterfly. The two creatures locked into a tight, high-speed aerial performance that the WWI fighters would have been proud of. The rapt bird chased the slender-bodied insect up and down Main Street, Montauk, past the round gazebo, under the awning of White's liquor store, over the roof of the Corner store, back around the bistro tables of the Gig Shack, and if there had been a traffic light in town, which there isn't, they would have encircled it. In a flight of fearful anticipation, the butterfly carved precise right angles, spectacular dippy doodles, and reverse spins. For at least fifteen minutes, the bird stayed within two feet of its prey, hoping for butterflies in its stomach.

The butterflies in my stomach were slowly ascending to my throat. No matter how I tried, I couldn't catch Tracey, and the harder I tried, the faster she seemed to run away. I knew I was being insanely jealous, but I couldn't help myself. The Shack had become her new lover. If the competition had been a man or woman, I could handle it, but how does a husband compete with the wife's creation? That's what I mean by being rapt.

There was a sudden crash, like someone falling off a horse. A loud curse, "God-damn-it!" Followed by a cry of bone-breaking pain from somewhere deep within the depths of that slippery kitchen.

Chapter 17

Accidents Will Happen

This was one of the perks of owning your own restaurant in the Hamptons. A hot babe in a red striped bikini and high heels was flirting with me in front of the Gig Shack. We'd exchanged mugs of foamy espresso, coffee as cuisine. The Playboy Bunny look-alike warmed her buns in the afternoon sun as she crossed one tanned, firm thigh over the other and explained why she was wearing a bandage on her wrist. "Broke the fifth meta-tarsal," she said, admiring the medical cast, already artistically autographed. "That's it. Our relationship is over! I'm breaking it off. I'll never be hurt again. A girl's got to do what a girl's got to do." I'd not fixed her teeth, yet. She had a hard, asymmetric smile.

"He did that to you?" I asked. "The bastard?"

"Yes, that bastard. I'm through with him."

"Some women are gluttons for punishment."

"I gave him everything. I groomed him. I fed him only the best that money could buy. I took him for long walks on the beach. I loved him."

"The first time I met him, I knew he couldn't be trusted," I said. "It was that wild look in his eyes, and he had bad teeth." I couldn't hold her cold gaze.

"But he was so hot. What a body, those long legs and thick mane of hair. I nicknamed him Scrod the Bod, but he was way too fast for me. Almost broke my heart."

"Did you try the whip?" I felt his pain.

"The whip, my heel, I'd swear he was into S&M."

"I've heard you've been around the track."

"I'll admit I'm no virgin when it comes to animals, but I can't go on with him. It's self-destructive. I'm going to sell him tomorrow."

"You sure looked good together in the saddle." The image burned my brain.

"You saw us? Were you spying? Is there no privacy in the Hamptons? What happens between the hedges should stay between the hedges. Damn it, the first time I'm tossed, the whole town knows. Don't tell me it was in *Dan's Papers*. I thought at least you were my friend. I'm done with the four-legged beasts for now."

"Isn't that what got you in this trouble in the first place?"

"Why? You know any eligible men?" She tore up Scrod's picture.

"I was half-hoping to keep you for myself."

"You're a married man; at least that's the rumor. Don't let it go to your head. Look, there's my girlfriend, Tracey. Why is she wearing a cast too? What happened?"

"She fell off her horse too? No, just kidding. She slipped last night, nearly broke her wrist. She might have been a ballerina once, but not on ice. That kitchen floor is so slippery, sometimes I need to take baby steps, even in sneakers, and she was wearing three-inch Jimmy Cho's."

"If anyone could wear high-tops on a tight rope, it's your wife; she's the real deal. Is she all right?"

"It will be awhile before she rolls the dough or does a Downward Dog. Customers don't appreciate how dangerous the restaurant business is—fireproof ovens, boiling caldrons, knives in all the wrong places. Why just this morning, we had to take Tim for stitches; put a broken glass through his hand."

"Oh, how horrible."

"Tracey took him to the doctor and paid the bill, even though he deserved to be fired. He was having a food fight with one of the customers, the epileptic. What do you expect from a bunch of kids?"

Suddenly, a very thin, young woman strolled past us. She walked through the open door of the Shack. She turned once to the left, looked twice to the right, and passed out cold on the floor. She lay in a heap in the middle of the busy dining room.

"Lewis! Lewis! Come quick!" Tracey screamed from inside.

I picked the unconscious girl off the floor and carried her to a bench. Barely breathing, her eyes had rolled back in her head. I've seen people die before—remember, I'm a doctor, well, a dentist, but I did assist the medical examiner's office once.

The Gig Shack had been open three weeks, and now we had our first fatality; I was really scared. We would finally get some copy in the *East Hampton Star*, which to date had thoroughly ignored us, but not for the quality of our food. I turned away briefly to get a wet towel, and her limp body slithered off the bench, her head making a heavy thump on the hard, tiled floor. If she wasn't dead already from some drug overdose, that thump must have killed her. I washed her face. She started to moan. EMS came within minutes and took her away in an ambulance. She was okay in the end, other than a headache from when I dropped her. I learned later that she hadn't taken her anorexia medicine that day. Just think what might have happened if she'd actually eaten our food.

"Thank you for being the only doctor in the house." Tracey kissed me.

"I probably made it worse. In the future, if someone faints on your floor, leave him or her there. Make sure their airway is clear and wait for EMS."

"Famous last words. She can't sue me if she didn't eat the food, can she?"

"I doubt it, but anytime an ambulance is parked in front of your restaurant, it can't be good for business," I added.

"Well, we got through it okay. Lightning never strikes twice."

A few days later, lightning did strike again. Our ex-starting pitcher strolled into the bar area and suffered a grand mal seizure. Maybe he'd thrown one too many strikes or maybe he'd been drinking. He was too large to pick up, so I watched as the poor soul flailed his arms and legs for a good fifteen minutes. EMS and his mother took him away, but the episode cleared the bar, and my appetite, for the night.

The next night, a large opossum dropped from the overhead awning into the middle of the outside bar. The patrons screamed and ran faster than if someone had yelled "Fire!" Who knows what a blind, nocturnal beast the size of a dog would want from a noisy, crowded bar. Maybe he just wanted a Bud. Sky eventually cornered the creature under the Montauk Light keg and forced it into a garbage can. Holistically, he deposited our visitor at a faraway beach. He left the possum an open can of Bud.

Although the kitchen was finally running smoothly under Larry's direction, it seemed as though he had brought a curse with him. He'd been with us less than a week, and the accidents were mounting. Arden, an experienced fish cleaner, cut his hand filleting a striped bass, and

Gray burnt himself. We were so desperate at the time, no one had checked Larry's resume.

"Have you ever heard of a dead-chef curse?" I asked Tracey.

"Now you're complaining about my new chef?"

"I'm not complaining. It's just, there's something funny about him."

She mouthed a fake smile. "I'm not laughing."

Suddenly, a police car screamed down Main Street so fast you could smell his tires burning. Headed east toward the point, it was soon followed by another, lights blaring at full attention. Our EMS friends in the ambulance weren't far behind.

"This looks bad," I said. "It's more than the usual drowning tourist."

"How can the cops drive so fast through town? They're going to kill somebody on their way to save a life," Tracey said.

Larry and the kitchen crew came out to see what all the commotion was about. "Damn, it looks bad," he laughed. Why was he laughing?

Overhead, a Medivac helicopter buzzed the town as it headed east in the direction of the accident. "That can only mean one thing." I pointed toward the ambulance in the sky. "You know, Larry, this is like the fifth accident this week."

Larry guiltily stared at me with an open mouth, and his face turned purple. He started to fidget nervously. "Yeah, man, shit happens." His eyes darted up and down and couldn't hold my stare. "Why are you looking at me? It's not my fault shit happens."

"I never said it was your fault. Accidents happen."

He turned quickly and ran back to the kitchen.

He was right, compost did happen. Elani, our other waitress, and Margo had been crosschecked by a pickup truck as they'd turned onto Flamingo Road. Their car was totaled, and they barely escaped with their lives. Both suffered multiple broken bones and had to be airlifted to Southampton Hospital. Just like that, the entire front waitress staff was out for the season, but the worst part was that the Gigs Shackers softball team had lost their starting pitcher.

Chapter 18

Surf's Up

After only a few days of work, Larry left a cryptic message on our home phone, "Surf's up!" For the local business owner, that's the indigenous signal—you might call it Code Montauk—to designate that the employee will not be coming to work today due to an incoming surf swell. For many local employees, the perfect wave is an accepted rite of unemployment. When the surf is up, the tribe is out; contractors drop houses, high school seniors drop English, and the local doctor drops dead.

I'm just kidding. The doctor's a nice guy, and the lucky bastard never has to write medical-absence excuse slips. The townies, when they are actually sick or truant, would rather blame it on the high tides than bronchitis, cancer, or another hangover.

Larry's non-appearance excuse lasted two days, and since we didn't even have a phone number for him or know where he lived, I drove down to Ditch Plains, a popular surf break, and asked around. Thor, one of the want-to-be Montauk locals, said he saw Larry earlier but that he wasn't out on the waves now. Lee said that I just missed Larry, but if I waited, he was sure he would return, as the surf was improving. John and Woody, visitors from Hawaii, swore they'd just crossed him in the lineup. Borrowing a pair of binoculars, I searched the lineup, but the break was way off shore.

After an hour wasted searching for our lost chef of the sea, I returned to the Shack. "No luck." I gestured the empty-handed sign to my disappointed wife.

Tracey, with bandaged wrist, was flipping burgers. "I gave Sky and Morgan the night off. They're exhausted, but Heavy D has offered to help."

Heavy D, one of Sky's friends, was a part-time house painter and occasional cook, but in an emergency, he could flip the fries with the best of them.

Nico, one of Arden's fishing buddies, had called a month ago asking for a job, but still hadn't shown his face at the Shack. "The fish were biting," was his excuse.

"All we can do is wait for the weather to change. Larry's bound to return. None of these other little Indians wants to be the chief anyway," I complained.

"I heard a rumor that Scott is still in town. Sandra thought she saw him and Erin in East Hampton this morning," Tracey marveled.

"You're kidding? Well, even if that was true, you wouldn't bring the bastard back, not after what he did to you."

"Well, why is Scott's sudden departure any worse than this local 'surf's up' nonsense? In the end, whoever shows up for work should get the job."

"Come on, Tracey. Scott? He nearly broke everyone's heart."

"Nevertheless, it's my restaurant, and if I want him back, I'll hire him!"

The clouds on Venus must have been pretty thick, because from where I stood, in the Martian Red Crater of Marital Rapture, rehiring Scott was more foreign than traveling to another planet. What did my wife want? Should I listen to what she said and not what she did? What planet was Tracey on? Maybe she was just scared. As she approached July 4th weekend, a third of the journey through the Hundred Days of Hampton Restaurant Hell, she'd lost one and maybe now two captains of her ship. Where were the professional chefs-for-hire in the Hamptons?

After aimlessly putting in more hours up and down the back roads and dark alleys of Montauk Highway than local law enforcement, I too abandoned ship and went over to the Bones for a drink. Mac Cool bought me a martini while Leslie wasn't watching. Cool and I hovered conspiratorially over the free drink.

"How's the Bones?" I tipped the zucchini martini to my young host.

"Frickin insane!" he said, pointing to his head wound. "Fabio, the chef, pan-cocked me. Creamed by a spaghetti pot. He's one fucking crazy Italian."

"Cooking is a dangerous business."

"Bloody endless summer. Someone's got to die!" He rubbed the swollen welt, and the reddened mass blistered. "My mother and Fabio are like oil and water. I swear, they're going to hurt someone before the season ends." His whole body shook with fright.

"The Shack's got its own compost," I said.

Mac shifted his hand to his forehead, striking a soothsayer's thoughtful pose. "Lost chef? Stinking mean thing, that's what it is." He peered to the right and left.

"Word travels fast."

"Meddler." He affected an Irish Brogue from the nineteenth century.

"Right again, oh swami one."

He crossed his chest. "Center cut. Forgive you, Father, for you have sinned."

My work had always been the center of my family's attention. "The Shack's like another lover," I complained. "Renaissance child, skateboarder, graffitist, and now astrologer. In Boarder's Paradise, what does my future hold? Speak now, mighty rabbi."

"I ask you now to repeat after me the acts of contrition. She calls to you. You are hers. She who made you out of nothing. She loved you as only a god can love." Theatrically, he knelt onto his skateboard and prayed. "Be not afraid. Lie with her in green pastures, so that you may once again be as one."

"A psalmist? I'm not a big believer, but if it will help me to get laid."

The scent of burnt weed fouled the remainder of conversation. "*E publics* union."

"Don't get me wrong, Tracey's done an amazing job. Single-handedly, she's Hellenized that Montauk Rock a little further west, but at what cost? I understand in here," I said, pointing to my head, "that the only way she can do the job is to be a racehorse, put blinders on, and forge straight ahead." Pointing to my heart, I said, "But there's a funny hole here. It's crazy; I have everything a man could want, yet that hole's always hungry."

"Mercury rising. You need a fling." He struck the match.

"A fling?"

"A fling! Outside your normal comfort zone." He sucked the reddened embers of tufted weed and blew the dregs of swish in my direction. "Take you to the edge. A quest to fill the hole in your heart." He offered me a hit.

"You don't know me very well. I'm afraid of heights. A friend of mine recently fell off his roof; now he's fucked for life. The owner of the Jitney, you heard what happened to him? He and an employee were moving a telephone pole. The pole fell and crushed out his innards. A rich guy; he didn't need to die doing manual labor."

"One of these days, I'm going to take myself to the edge, just to see if I can touch heaven and return." His eyes dimmed, parboiled by the blanket of mental mist and reeking smoke. As he puffed, he wept for the innocence he longed to lose.

"Here comes Mother. I'm going to make my escape." I slipped out the back door before she saw me. "Thanks for the drink and religion, kid." I laid him a ten spot.

The whole argument with Tracey had become a moot point. I can't say that I preferred Larry—he was unreliable and carried a curse—but we knew for sure he was somewhere in town. The surf would change; he couldn't stay in the water forever.

I spent the rest of the afternoon driving around town, looking for Scott too. I checked all the bars, assuming that Erin would eventually need her fix of Maker's Mark, but their whereabouts were unknown. If I found him, what would I say? He had acted criminally; even if he hadn't stolen monetary value, he'd stolen my family's confidence. I brought along a baseball bat, just in case he had any balls.

Scott never contacted Tracey, and we never learned if Sandra, who had failing eyesight, had imagined the whole thing. Larry, on the other hand, left an un-addressed note under the door. Tracey read it angrily out loud.

> *I don't feel comfortable putting my name on the product you're serving. There are a lot of hands touching the food along the way. You have a good opportunity for someone willing to work within your frame of thinking and guidelines. Finding that person may be difficult. I will continue to assist with the ordering. I don't know if anything else I'm doing is effective. This is damage control.*

I will help you in this capacity at least until Sept. 10th. (I have a catering function for 25 persons at $25/hr on Sept. 9th) If you choose to look for someone else, let me know. If you wish to schedule time for training of specific tasks to specific employees, let me know. There's too many people coming and going creating many loose ends which I feel leads to a chaotic environment that's not very enjoyable. I feel bad that you're losing money but don't know how to stop that and work within your parameters. My suggestion is to just keep doing the best you can, which you have been doing. Thanks in advance.

She crumbled his letter in her fist.

"Nice guy," I noted, facetiously, "but Scott was a better writer."

"That's my second chef-quitting letter and I've only been open a few weeks," Tracey cried miserably. "He'll never return. He wants nothing to do with a bunch of restaurant losers who are accident prone and destined to fail in the business. Now what do I do? It's almost July 4th and I'm chef-less again."

"At least he's not asking for a letter of recommendation."

"This is serious. Do you always have to make a joke out of my failures?"

"Okay, I'm sorry. We do have a problem here," I admitted.

"Our restaurant is going under and we've only been open a month," she cried into the skirt of her apron, the salty tears mixing dregs of coffee into her mascara.

"What is it with these supposed professional chefs?"

"What a bunch of lowlifes," she complained.

"You think this book is about you, don't you?" I sang to her. For a brief moment, the bloom of a smile blossomed from the nourishment of tears. No matter what the world threw at her, her beautiful bust would always make the perfect partner for my pedestal. "I can't speak for the other male lowlifes," I warned, "but at least you'll always have me."

"All a woman really needs in life is one good rock. Okay, okay, I'll put my smiley face back on."

And just like that, she did. What a woman.

Chapter 19

Drink It In

Upon learning that Larry, the "I'm a chef, I don't cook," had dumped us without a paddle, Sky disappeared. Without saying a word, he drove off alone in the direction of the beach. When he didn't return that night, we got worried.

"Maybe we should call the police," Tracey cried over his empty bed. "He looked depressed. I'm worried. I've never seen him like that."

"You're speaking like his mother. No, we don't need the police. Sky's friends are all out looking for him. They know this town and our son better than the law."

Eventually, Morgan found him asleep in his car at the lighthouse.

Morgan helped Sky into his room and put him to bed. "He'll be all right now."

"Thank you, Morgan. Sky's lucky to have a friend like you," I said. "You know, it's ironic, but with all the adult chefs flaking out on us, I expected that you'd crash too. I never realized how emotionally stable you are."

Morgan smiled. "I never had a father stick around long enough in my life to develop confidence in the institution, so I wasn't particularly hurt when Scott and Larry left. You spoiled Sky. Previously, you were his only role model for trust. Now he's seen how the other half of the adult male population really behaves. Nothing but heart rapists."

"Thanks for the compliment," I said. "I think?"

The kitchen staff now consisted of Arden, Gray, Morgan, Sandra, Heavy D., and any day, we hoped, Nico. Saint Nico's name, as we like to refer to him, was bantered about like the 7th Cavalry. Our would-be savior was the most experienced of the bunch. He had cooked at the Yacht Club in Antigua, the Caribbean, that previous winter. He was trained at the Culinary Institute of America, but like Arden, his best friend, he preferred fishing over a regular job. "I'm just a kid; you need a man for this job," he had told Tracey when she asked over the phone if he would be interested in managing the kitchen.

Between the high school dropout house painters and the "I'd rather be fishing" crew, the Gig Shack's kitchen possessed about six months of actual cooking experience. Arden, although displaying excellent customer service skills, was not temperamentally suited for the kitchen. When the orders got backed up, he'd lose his cool and start cursing and throwing pans, and he wasn't Italian. He couldn't handle the kitchen heat.

Gray made fun of his older brother. "Arden, you're being a moron. Just calm down." Gray was like a good gin and tonic. He had my Teflon skin. No matter the heat, he handled the backlog with a calculated plan. "Take a chill pill, big brother."

Sandra continued to do prep work, but she was as slow as molasses.

"For what I pay that lady, I could have two people," Tracey complained, referring to the new Spanish dishwasher. "What does she actually do all day?"

Tracey distilled the menu even further to accommodate the untrained staff.

"If I shrink it any further," she warned, "all we'll be serving is toast and hot water, a Polish diet. I need to find a real chef—and fast." She made a praying sign with her hands and looked toward the sky. "Otherwise, I'm closing the door and turning the Gig Shack into a yoga studio. I'll throw the kitchen down the drain with the boy's bath water."

"Don't do that. The Bible says providence smiles on those that provide."

"If only Nico would step up to the plate," she pleaded. "He would be perfect, but I've never met such a reluctant hitter. He would be my first choice."

"He refuses to work more than twenty hours a week, and he doesn't want the responsibility of running a kitchen. He's a twenty-three-year-old kid; keep looking."

Things in the kitchen had gotten so bad that finally, Tracey allowed little me to help. Suddenly, I was artfully filling ketchup, mustard, and mayo cups to their brim and neatly arranging the condiments so that the staff could more efficiently service customers. I tossed the Gig chips in their rectangular plastic bins so that the deep-fried potatoes wouldn't stick to one another. I neatly stacked the water, Coke, ginger ale, and root beer bottles in the takeout fridge. My floating job description expanded as the season progressed and Tracey wore out. I bused tables, expertly swiping water cup marks before they dried. I placed wooded shills under the tables so that they wouldn't tilt when a customer leaned on one. I inexpertly played barista and hosted parties, but my most necessary function was even more menial. I'd lug produce and fish from local farms and mongers. Finally, I had my foot in the door.

I had become the house mule.

Chapter 20

The New Employees

According to the famous food writer Calvin Trillion, "The owner of a restaurant gets to name the place, create the mission statement, and choose a couple of recipes." In addition, the owner selects the location and design, signs the lease, and interviews the staff. Trillion's theory on restaurants was that "the quality of food a place offers is often in inverse proportion to the splendors of its scenery. In a beautiful place, the cooks are often outside drinking in nature's wonderments, instead of standing in front of a hot stove, where they belong." He must have been referring to the Gig Shack; between surfing, body boarding, and surfcasting, it was impossible to keep the cooks in the kitchen. He also warned against allowing each new itinerant chef to redesign the menu. No matter who the final head chef was, we would continue to serve "international surf cuisine" based on memorable meals from our travels.

If the menu had been up to me, I would have served Serrano ham baguettes like the ones offered in the Madrid train station, bouillabaisse from Marseilles, Moroccan chicken stew, *pizza del mar* from Naples, eggs Benedict ala Balthazar's, baby birds barbequed in Kyoto, or the tiny clams of Venice, but "it" was Tracey's quarter and she had the final say on the food.

"I feel like a deer in headlights. What am I going to do?" Tracey struggled to wake up and make the doughnuts. It was 7:30 AM on a Saturday morning. Between getting dressed and unlocking the door for the prep staff, there wasn't time for getting reacquainted and figuring out the universe.

Remembering the 15 percent rule of marriage consulting, I contemplated how to act as the muse without telling her what to do. In other words, where was the unknowable marital line in the sand being drawn this morning? I chose the safest response, which was to pose a question: "What am I, a mind reader?"

It was the wrong answer.

We unlocked the doors for the prep staff at around eight the next morning. Tracey took out a tray of croissants she'd prepared the day before, allowing them to rise before baking. Immediately, she made tarts, cookies, and red velvet cake, her new specialty. It was a triple-layered, moist, red-colored cake with a creamy white icing.

I swept cigarette butts and assorted trash that had collected overnight and reset the bistro tables and chairs, which were stored inside. Noticing me clean the public street, Bill from the hardware store called out, "Hey, Doc, you got a PhD in street cleaning? What a town, we got the most pedigreed garbage men in East Hampton." He laughed out loud. "A doctorate in street cleaning. I hope Tracey appreciates it, because I wouldn't do that for my wife if you paid me."

"It's a dirty business; somebody's got to do it. It might as well be me."

"When you're done with your side of the street …" He pointed to his curb.

After I'd finished sweeping, Killjoy came out with an air blower, sending dust and leaves into the street. He kept his storefront immaculately clean. When I wasn't looking, he blew some of the leaves in front of our Shack. When he went back inside, I swept the leaves back in front of his shop. When I came back later, the stack of leaves had been blown back in front of our restaurant.

I considered my rightful revenge. I could stand in front of his window all day, so he would be stuck staying inside his shop, but what a waste of time. The hermit crab was playing with my head. I was mixing it up with the locals, the local grouches. I left the leaves to Mother Nature and returned to watch Tracey bake.

Wearing another checkered shirtdress and a pleated wide skirt, which Tracey designed and sewed, she appeared the perfect embodiment of a 1940s French chocolatier. She was gorgeous as she gently whisked the fruit and sliced the lush flesh by hand. Alice Waters wrote, "The senses are the pathway into the mind, and cooking fine tunes them." Tracey put so much love into her creations that one bite of her cake sent men and women into a moaning ecstasy. It was my prognosis that one day her red velvet wedding cake would birth a Babette's Feast.

"If we are what we eat, Montauk is lucky to have your food. Tracey, you've done a spectacular job with this place. Everyone in town is talking about how awesome the food is and how the Gig Shack has such special karma. You've created a salon for all these youngsters. You are the queen of the salon."

"Thank you, dear. You've always had a way with words."

"Is there anything I can do to help?"

"Could you wake your children and tell them to come to work?"

I looked at my watch. Between fishing and surfing, you never knew.

"Please. Don't go home and start screaming at them!"

"Screaming? It's twelve o'clock. Time for all good little boys to be up working or playing, but not sleeping." An early riser, I have little patience for other people's clock.

"They're my employees; let me deal with them. They just need a little time."

"They're my three sons."

"Well, they're my employees and sons."

"Another chance to garner Mother's attention, a swift kick of the boot would do."

"Please, leave it alone, you'll only chase them further away. You aren't appreciating how hurt they were when Scott left. They're a lot more emotionally invested in the success of the Gig Shack than you credit them. I know you need to play the father—"

"Play the father? Okay, I'm out of here. I'll go home and prune a few dead limbs off the trees, and if that doesn't work, I'll do the ironing."

"I didn't mean it like that!" she called to my fleeing back, but she *did*, and she was probably right. To date, my attempts at high-handed parenting had always resulted in failure. Tracey had engaged the boys, giving them a platform to perform. The theory that "success breeds more success" made a lot more sense to me than the Al-Anon's "do nothing" approach. My rapt intervention could only screw it all up.

Meanwhile, her reputation for fine food and service was spreading via word of mouth. He told three friends and she told three friends, and before we knew it, the foodies were blogging her fame. Tracey avoided advertising and press relations because she lacked confidence in the quality of the kitchen staff, but the public was attracted to her because of location and visibility. We were reaching that critical mass of a customer base, which attracts the uninitiated strictly because a place looks popular. Tourists always avoid the empty restaurant and flock to the full house, even if they have to wait in line. Humans are lemmings on two legs. Why else would hundreds of supposedly educated thirtysomethings flock to the bar at Cyril's, where they're as likely to be roadkill, or drink a twenty-dollar cocktail at the Surf Lodge?

Tracey's ongoing renovations were slowly improving her business. Once that Bohemian Scott left, she initiated a computerized management system, Adobe, with printed menus, daily specials, and inventory and cash controls. She placed colored neon Beer signs in the windows, wrapped the awning with chili pepper lights, cushioned the long wooden banquette on the back wall, and covered the outside picnic tables in blue vinyl, which kept them more serviceable in inclement weather. The overall effect was to make the Shack warmer and cozier.

In the outside bar area, a small flat-screen TV occupied the eyes of the beer-swigging sports fans, and inside, a larger projector ran surfing and snowboarding films, which warmed the hearts of many a parent whose previously screaming child was mesmerized by the crazy humans swallowed by the giant waves and seamless, senseless jumps. The surf films were a stroke of genius. One day, we hoped to hold our own film festival at the Shack, where locals could play their home movies.

Two college-aged, blonde Polish girls took over the front after the car accident. They were skinny, fair skinned, and as cold as frozen potato vodka. On multiple occasions, middle-aged men offered me money to be introduced, but the girls' consistent response to any request was, *"Nyet."*

I watched them take orders and run the food from behind the counter to the tables. It was noon on a Saturday and the bartender was late, as a group of five adults requested a table for lunch and some beers.

"No beer," replied one of the waitresses, with a firm Eastern European attitude.

The party of five retreated to Shaggy for lunch. Another group came with the same request and was sent away with the same response. "No beer," she said to their fleeing backs. Having grown up in a communist country with nothing to sell and long lines for material goods, she seemed to take satisfaction in turning customers away.

"We have beer, forty kinds of beer," I said, incredulously. "Why are you telling all the customers that we don't have any beer? We have plenty of beer. You're sending all our business next door."

Wide-eyed and open-mouthed, she looked at me as if I was from outer space and the answer was self-evident. "No beer? The beer cabinet is locked. No bartender?"

I showed her the keys on the ring. "Well, all you need to do is open the lock." I opened the simple lock. "The bar is now open. Beer is served."

Later, a couple came in and requested fish and chips. Rather than offer a similar alternative, like the fish taco and a separate order of fries, she answered, "No fish and chips." Another group wanted an egg sandwich. Of course, Anna replied, *"Nyet,"* even though we did offer an egg quesadilla.

I explained in my most gentle tone, "You need to find creative solutions to customer requests. You need to find yet, I mean yes, instead of always answering *nyet*. I understand that it's easier to say no, but if you apply your thinking cap, you can put a positive spin on any situation. Try it, just say yes!"

She looked at me as if I were speaking in a foreign tongue. Maybe her English wasn't really that good or a positive response was alien to an Eastern European. "Yes?" The syllable broke awkwardly off her tongue and she looked repulsed.

"Come on. Try it again. Yessss!"

"Yesss? No! The bar was closed and we don't serve fish and chips. You want me to lie? I will not lie for Yankee dollar. Never. I not want your money."

"You're not lying. You're searching for creative solutions to provide customers satisfaction. For instance, a woman attempts to bring her dog into the restaurant. The dog isn't allowed to sit inside, but you can offer to bring water in a bowl over there. What would you say if a customer asks for waitress service?"

"No, we don't do waitress service," she answered distrustfully.

"That's exactly the kind of response I'm referring to. Forget that word, no. Permanently strike it from your vocabulary, that's the only way. Try this out. *Yes, I will be happy to take your order now. Take a table, and I'll bring over your food. Would you like some complimentary chips while you wait?"*

"I'm confused. Do we offer waitress service?" she asked.

"Once they place their order at the counter, we bring over food and beverages and we clean the table. It's virtually the same thing, without the negative preface. Okay, another example—a customer asks if we take reservations?"

She had to think about that one for a while, searching in her mind for the correct response. With furrowed brows, she answered. "Yes," she said proudly.

"Wrong, we don't take reservations," I explained.

"I thought I was supposed to always say yes? I'm confused."

"Try this response: *we offer tables on a first-come, first-served basis.* You see, I never said no. Instead, I spun the question so the customer was welcomed."

"Okay, boss, I have an example for you. One of your old, fat American friends asks me for a date. I say yes, then go back into the kitchen refrigerator and bring him a plate of date fruit. How's dot spin?" she angrily pronounced.

Overhearing this conversation, Tracey asked me, "What are you doing?"

"I'm teaching the Polish girls how to say yes."

"Why?" she inquired.

"Because it's a foreign language. Saying yes is better for business than no."

"Are you criticizing my management skills now?"

"No, I mean yes, I mean, maybe it's for your own good."

"Well, which is it going to be?" asked my goddess wife.

"I'm going to go home and put a positive spin on the wash cycle. I noticed you were running out of towels and aprons, and there won't be a delivery until tomorrow." So I went home and bleached those towels and chef's aprons till they were snow white, but no one taught me that you must first tie together the apron strings before doing the laundry. Imagine two pounds of cotton spaghetti straps washed and spun through a high-speed spinning cycle. It took me nearly two hours of mind-blowing concentration to untie the Gordian Apron Knot I'd just created.

Chapter 21

That Bitch Goddess—Happiness

The only reason a wealthy man would want to open a restaurant in the Hamptons is the need to have a business in a town that you have no business being in.

Some Further Lane fools have wrongly implied that Montauk isn't the Hamptons. You might know the type—never worked an honest hour, East Hampton artists, who bought farmed land in the fifties that has exponentially risen in value. Their acre is worth a lot more now than when they painted a picture of it. Real estate is the quickest path to material wealth. Modest Montauk motels were being converted into expensive condos, and 20,000-square foot homes were popping through the Pine Barrens like weeds.

According to the chamber of commerce, Montauk is a modestly priced, convenient destination, popular with families, surfers, and fishermen. "All Aboard!" rang the conductor. "That's the end of that line!" Montauk Highway and the Montauk train track span the entire length of Long Island, the beginning of New York City and the end. Visualize Montauk as the epicenter of the metropolitan weather map. Every morning and night, New York City weathermen flash her name in front of your screen. Montauk sits as a spit in the ocean, the point of the peninsula you run to when the world self-destructs or in case of another 9/11, a magical escape in the minds of the inhabitants of the metropolis, which happens to be the largest metropolitan population in the fifty states.

If you aren't born here, the best way to become a Montauket is to open a business, but that doesn't explain my identity crisis. My family is considered local, but I'm the tourist investor; call me a tocal. "You need to hang out with the other dads more. I'll invite you to their next pig roast," Sky advised me.

The other restaurant owners weren't filling ketchup bottles or cleaning toilets like I was. Was I doing something wrong? Over cocktails at his restaurant in Amagansett, I asked a wealthy investor why he got into the business.

"It's a deduction and an investment in real estate, a place to hang with friends where I'll always get a good table. I own a professional sports team and other businesses around the world, but when I'm here, I want to feel I belong."

Another owner said, "I have my special seat at the bar."

"The owner's stool?"

"Yeah, something like that. This stool's the real shit."

Sometimes, while I watched Tracey baking herself to the bone, I wondered why I'd mortgaged my marriage to this investment. I wanted the real estate, sure, but these other owners and their wives weren't slaving in the kitchen. Their sons weren't emptying kegs. They were out front dining with their friends, if they were in the place at all. The other owners hired professional promoters, managers, and chefs to run their business.

Maybe I wasn't rich enough, but I was blessed with many assets that didn't tally in the stock and bond score, the strength of family and community. According to the Dalai Lama's *The Art of Happiness*, "The true antidote of greed is contentment. The four factors of fulfillment, or happiness, are wealth, worldly satisfaction, spirituality, and enlightenment. If you possess this inner quality, a calmness of mind, a degree of stability within, then even if you lack various external facilities that you would normally consider necessary for happiness, it is still possible to live a happy and joyful life." I would will myself to happiness.

Henry Thoreau said that a man who spends half his day walking through the woods is wealthier than the man who cleared the forest for a profit. Living on the beach was my walk in the woods. I decided to practice the Art of Happiness.

"Hello, Papi chulo," called the new Dominican dishwasher, as I entered the back kitchen door. *"Esta bien, Senor?"*

"Que es, this Papi chulo?" I replied in my pig Spanish.

Trying to find the proper English translation, he said, "El Grande Cabeza." He bowed respectfully. He mimed a quick motion of a bank teller handling a wad of cash.

"Oh, you mean the man with the big hat. We call him The Godfather. The rich man who takes care of all the little people. I like that description. Thank you."

"*Si, Senor Luis.* You are El Grande Padre."

"That's the big guy, I understand, but I'm more like the patron."

"*Si,* El Patron, very good tequila, the sugar daddy."

I was honored that the Hispanic dishwasher thought so highly of me. Soon, many employees started to refer to me as "Papi chulo." I always wore a Panama hat. Tracey considered it a joke, but she was honored as well. Interestingly, there wasn't a Spanish translation for Mommy chulo, the woman with the big hat. In the traditional Hispanic, male-dominated society, there's no historical precedent for the female boss.

A few weeks later, I learned a different definition of the Papi chulo moniker, which is the gigolo, or the guy who gets all the girls. I'm down on that too.

A toast to that bitch goddess I called Happiness. I've been chasing after her my whole life. Finally, I'd found a job I loved and was an expert at. When the Shack got slow, I came over and acted the "shill." That's a Yiddish term for a fake customer, or in an auction, a fake bidder to raise the price. I sat outside at a bistro table and read, ate, or gave free holistic dental advice. People seemed to be attracted to me. I was a human magnet. Usually, we reached critical mass in about an hour and I could leave. That bitch, the restaurant, was fully fed. It was another successful day at the office.

With practice, I'd become extremely adept at playing the shill game with potential customers. If they were an attractive couple or an interesting group, I'd close my eyes and will them to come in off the street and check out our menu. If they were a good-looking group of single girls in bikinis and high heels, I made the extra psychic effort to draw them into my lair. In my mind, I paved a path to an outside table, where they would be modeled to the rest of the world as bait. On the other hand, if they were an unruly, fat family from mid-Island, with four noisy and obnoxious kids, I willed them across the street to our competition. I was a very selective shill.

The Café across the street opened at about the same time as us. They and Shaggy were our main competition in town. The previous owners mandated that a Greek family own the Café. They served three meals a day and had a full bar. The morning sun shone on their four outside tables, but around noon, the sun shifted to our side of the street. It was in that witching window, when the sun crossed the street, that I did my best shill work. Potential customers strolled both sides of the street, checking the menu and décor of our competition. Shaggy had history, the Café played soccer games on their wide-screen TV, but the Shack had my positive state of mind.

The Buddha says, "If you maintain a feeling of compassion, loving kindness, then something automatically opens your inner door. Through that, you can communicate much more easily with other people." I practiced that mental discipline too.

Chapter 22

The Hurricane Party

We awoke to an unseasonably stiff, northeastern wind. The weather was changing. Normally, Montauk's weather is a temperate microclimate; horticultural zone seven, more similar to the coast of Georgia than New York City. Protected by the sea, the once-a-year snow is soon melted by the salt air. In summer, a cool breeze prohibits the need for air conditioning. But that morning, the winds had angrily spun in the opposite direction, pulling moisture and tides from the mighty Atlantic Ocean toward the shore. Storm clouds gathered over the famous colonial lighthouse at Montauk Point, enticing surfers from around the globe to the uprising swell.

A horizontal rain struck the Shack from the east, seeping through the rafters and flooding the side of our building. Three inches of incoming water soon surrounded the Coke machine, threatening to short circuit the adjacent computerized music center Sky had set up to record the bands.

"You're constantly offering to go on a quest for me," said Tracey. "Well I want you to go to Shaggy and demand that he get his damned roofer in here and repair these leaks. It was agreed to in the purchase contract."

"A quest? I love it when you give me a quest. That's so sexy."

"Don't be so dramatic. It's only a leak, dear." Tracey smiled mercifully.

"In this town, getting a leak fixed is a quest. I've called him numerous times, but I'll get in his face. If I don't come back alive, set up a plaque in my honor."

"In the meantime, I'll get Sky to clean up the mess."

Sky had returned to duty a few days earlier but made it clear that he would no longer be cooking. He'd agreed to be the sound engineer and to run the bar. I had reservations about his being the bartender, but once again I followed Tracey's advice to be positive and allow him to fight his own demons. He had been recording the live music all summer with the intent to burn his own album, *Live at the Gig Shack*, which we would eventually sell at the store. That was his quest.

Sky moved his expensive music recording system to a safer place and pumped the flooding water out the back door. After an hour of hard labor mopping the mess, serious damage to the sound system was avoided.

The afternoon's business was a washout, as the tourists chose to stay dry indoors in their motel rooms. Instead of closing the place and going back to bed, I cleared the floor of tables and chairs, setting up a dance space.

"You gave me a quest." I bit a corner of my lip and slowly released it. "The roofer will be here tomorrow. Now I have a quest for you." I played tango music and offered her my hand. "Let's stir up this tumbleweed town and make some lemonade."

"Women don't do quests, that a boy thing." She turned down my offer with an if-looks-could-kill-you'd-be-dead expression. "You're embarrassing me in front of my whole staff. I'll dance some other time, when we're alone." She blushed a social smile.

I ignored her warning and forcibly placed her in my studied tango embrace, an open stance, my left hand holding her right in a horizontal out-stretched position, my right hand in the small of her back, the steering wheel, balanced in a parallel position. Our bodies were perfectly erect with the slightest inward tilt. "Damn, you've got good posture," I flattered her. "Close your eyes, just like riding a bicycle."

An almost imperceptible recoil of her shoulders demonstrated that she didn't want to do this tango performance, let alone be touched, in front of her staff. She was unsure where to place her hands. It occurred to me that if I said anything the least bit critical or sentimental, she would bolt through that fire-exit door.

"Just don't talk." Her eyes flashed a reproach. She posed self-consciously in the footlights, paralyzed in a public formal smile.

"You look wonderful." I had planned to bend down and kiss the back of her hand, a dramatic beginning, but realized my window for dancing could shut tight with the slightest breeze. Tightening my embrace and my masseter muscles, I turned my head to the side to display a more commanding, macho look. Wavering at the precipice, I moved stiff-legged to the left, steered to the right, and shifted gears. Following the tango rhythm, we walked the tango walk in a counter-clockwise circle around the room. "You haven't forgotten a step." An Argentine tune beat with the blood in my eardrums.

"We can stop, please, anytime you want."

After ten minutes of dancing, I'd found that the curve in her back rode more neatly in my hand, and her breathing had miraculously slowed to an even hysteria.

Dancing with my wife had always been magical, but because she had so much upper-body strength from teaching yoga, at times it would turn into a wrestling match for the lead. She is more adept at going forward in life than at retreating.

"I'm going to kill you later." She displayed a poor replica of her curtain-call smile.

"At least honor me with another dance before my decapitation."

"My scissors at the ready."

"Listen, we can do this. You can do this."

"Is that a threat or a promise?" She wobbled on three-inch heels.

Awestruck, the staff of young people gathered to watch. Having never witnessed an actual tango performance, a welcome smile of anticipation crossed their hungry faces. This was a taste of a different world outside their limited, safe, ocean-surfer nest. Their eyes were filled with wonder, and they started to clap. "Go, Tracey, go," they chorused in unison. "There you go, girl. Dance like you live."

We progressed from a simple walk into "cruzado" crosses and then "corte" cuts, which we had learned in Buenos Aires the year before. I had to be attentive to her fragile follow, not showing more than she was comfortable. It had been a long time since we danced together, and her tango was rusty, but what must have been ten minutes seemed to last a lifetime. Sweat pebbled on my forehead as I tentatively led her into a more complicated step, but the cheering staff brought down the house.

Pressed close and sweating in my arms, her jaw locked numbly in a brave smile. "Slower. Easy, boy." She carried her head high and followed my lead. If at first she had accepted the dance in a state of shock, there was now no more anger or blame. Composed, she lifted her chin, tossed back a loose strand of hair, and willed herself into a *Dancing with the Stars* smile. She looked straight into my eyes. "Ah hell, go for broke."

It was magical. Henry Thoreau was wrong about one thing—the walk in the woods. This was true wealth, dancing a tango with my wife in my own restaurant.

We bowed to the cheering staff. "So, do any of you youngsters want a tango dance lesson?" I asked. "Come on, don't be shy. I don't bite."

They looked toward one another and shyly ran back to their odd jobs.

By now, the weather had cleared enough for a few of the more ambitious tourists to take to the streets. The leaks had stopped, and crowds of passersby gathered at the window, poking their faces in. Tracey and I continued our dance.

A police car stopped in front to see what the commotion was about. He flashed a red light, tapped on the window, and frowned a parody of displeasure.

I turned down the volume. "Can I help you, officer?" I asked politely.

"Let me see your dance permit," he ordered, tapping his nightstick on his thigh, out of beat to the music. He had the facial disdain of an officer not to be trifled with.

"Dance permit? It's a rainy day. I'm dancing with my wife. Is there a law against that? Why do I need a permit?" I should have spoken with honey, but I was fed up.

"My boss, the supervisor, requires commercial establishments to post a license for dancing. It must be posted at all times."

"Okay, so I'll get a license tomorrow." I gave him an arrogant shrug. "What's the big fucking deal? Dancing while intoxicated, not your usual DWI?"

"He's not issuing any more licenses." He smacked the nightstick aggressively against his thigh. "That's the big fucking deal, smart mouth!"

"Wait, I just remembered," said Tracey, trying to diffuse the tension. She rummaged through her paperwork and produced a ten-year-old, faded dance permit.

The officer sniffed at the paper to detect the scent of a forgery. "I'll let you off this time, but don't let me catch you dancing again."

After the policeman left, we opened the doors and moved the tables back. A head-high wave of hungry customers barreled in and ordered food. By late afternoon, the weather appeared ominous. Once again, the sky blackened fiercely, interrupted by crackles of lightning, thunder, and torrents of rain. The leak returned with a vengeance.

"It is unconstitutional that we can't ballroom dance or play live music in our own place! It's absolute bullshit! The supervisor is a hypocrite who is anti-development and anti-business. Montauk is a resort town. Ninety percent of the population makes their income off the tourists. Tourists crave entertainment. Now I understand why the commercial business in town tried to incorporate. The only way Montauk can gain self-rule is to secede from East Hampton. Give me liberty or give me dance. It is un-American that we don't even have a local representative on the town board. Somebody's got to do something about it!" I yelled at the top of my lungs to the world or anyone listening. "The supervisor is an anti-artistic, tango-hating fascist!"

Tracey stared at my public tirade in disbelief, and a slight tear welled. "Dear, if anyone in this damn town had the balls to tell that old geezer off, it would be you, my dancing dentist." She kissed me gently on the cheek.

God, the FBI, or the supervisor's informants must have been listening to my wanton, ill-advised threat, because the electricity immediately clicked off and the Shack's lights blackened. The oven hood stopped sucking smoke, and the exhaust fan ceased blowing. The Gig Shack stood silent, so silent in fact, that you could hear the click of the plastic knives dropping on bamboo plates. A whiff of burnt, barbequed meat floated on grease moats and landed on my tongue, leaving an acrid, bitter aftertaste. I bit at my lip.

"Oh my God!" cried Tracey. "You've done it now. They are really pissed off. I told you we can't dance, but you … had … to have … your fucking tango!"

I was overcome with guilt that I had thought only of my needs, worrying that I had played the public official for a fool and fearing that the kitchen might explode at any moment. The hint of smoke grew more urgent. "Where are the fire extinguishers?" I wondered out loud.

The insistent siren of a racing fire truck echoed down Montauk Highway. From far beyond the train station and Flamingo Road, a yearning panic sped toward our little Gig Shack. The customers and staff murmured, concerned for their own well being. Did someone yell, "Fire!"? That hint of smoke burned in intensity.

The fire truck sped past our Shack, its siren doing a Doppler down Main Street. The echo headed toward us and away in the same breath.

I ran outside. The whole town was dark as night. The blackout had spread virally. Being so isolated in a small town on the end of a peninsula, really only a spit from the sea, it's hard to know when a power outage is a local event or the end of the world. For all we knew, it could have been another 9/11.

"Everyone, relax!" yelled Tracey. "The smoke's just feedback from the hood. As soon as the power comes back on, your dinner will be served."

The lights briefly flickered back on, and the customers cheered. The light went back off, and they moaned. The light flickered back on and seemed to want to stay this time. We all cheered and returned to cooking. The staff put candles on the tables.

A woman and her ten-year-old son, who were sitting in the corner, called me over. "Sir, excuse me, do you work here? Do you know how long it will be before our food is ready? We've been waiting over an hour," she complained.

"Miss, in case you haven't noticed, the whole town is down. There's no place else to go. Your motel will be dark, too." I shook my head in utter disbelief.

"My son is scared," she pleaded like a wounded goat.

The kid didn't look scared; in fact, he seemed to find the power outage to be a fun game. His mother was just another self-obsessed customer, intent on demanding my undivided attention. "I'll bring him a complimentary ice cream. The kitchen is back open, it won't be long," I consoled her and winked at the smiling child.

This time, the power stayed on. In fact, our block was the only lit place in town for hours. Wet, hungry, and scared customers faded in from other restaurants. We were suddenly the hottest spot in town. There's nothing like a hurricane to bring out the party in people. They ate and drank like it was the end of the world, a waiting line halfway down the block. It was our best sales to date. We finally closed the kitchen about midnight. Tracey and I went back to say good-bye to the boys, who had earlier promised to clean and shut the place down. There was a mountain of unwashed dishes and nobody there to service them. Troubled, she twisted her fingers in her mouth.

"Javier had to go home early because of the storm. Where are all our boys?" Tracey demanded, obviously upset by the disgusting trash. "Arden promised."

"Arden said he was going fishing and would come back in the morning to clean up. I don't know where anyone else went." I called Sky and Gray's cell phones, but there was no answer. There was no stemming the tide of her displeasure.

"I don't care which one of them is right or wrong. Can't they just act like human beings for once instead of spoiled men?" She threw down her raincoat.

"You're being unfair to them. We all worked our butts off tonight."

"Until the next time? You men, it's all about your ego." She wept with anger at her spoiled eggs. Fumbling a sharp knife, she was capable of anything at a time like that.

I removed the weapon from her grasp. "Can't it wait till the morning crew arrives?" I wiped the tool clean and placed it on the rack, out of sight.

"No, it can't wait. Tomorrow is Sunday. That's just fucking great." She angrily wrenched on plastic gloves and attacked the pile straight on.

Quivering, I picked up some dirty dishes. "I'll help."

Her eyes raked me up and down. "Go home!" In the whisk of a breath, a fight was on about more than dirty dishes. "I don't want your help." She scrubbed the dried grease like scabs from old wounds, scratching and clawing nasty remarks until she'd found the weakness in my Teflon. "You've already made it perfectly clear that you don't want to be here, that you hate this place." The words convulsed off her chest. "Go home!"

I tried to swallow, but my throat was dry. "If you leave the dirty dishes long enough, they'll have to eventually clean them. They can't cook in a burnt pot." Switching tactics to make the phrase ring true. "I'm on your side." A mealy-mouthed attempt at conflict resolution. Blame it on the third party.

She took hold of a soiled pot and burrowed both elbows in a sink full of suds. "Have you seen their rooms? They just drop their wet towels on the floor and expect that it'll be magically cleaned," she moaned. "You poor, poor self-deluded man."

After a long silence of faulty concentration, I dropped the dish. For some reason, it didn't break. I was the family enabler, washing their underwear, hanging the wet towels, and when they were babies, wiping their little asses. I didn't know what else to do. I just wanted to help, but she was so insistent that she just wanted to be alone. When Tracey got herself in one of these rages, I'd found it best to leave her be, so she could expend her negative energy on the pots—maybe even destroy a few—rather than cursing out my offspring and me. I froze, paralyzed as to the proper course. There was just so much cleanup for her to do by herself.

Arden showed up from fishing and offered to finish the job, but she was just as nasty to him. "You're all useless. I'll wash the damn dishes."

I motioned for him to meet me outside. We sat on the fender of his truck.

"Mother has to learn how to delegate to us," Arden complained. "She told me I could go fishing this afternoon. A typical woman, she says 'yes' but she means 'no.'"

I frowned conspiratorially. "If you had been here a half hour ago, when you were supposed to be, then none of this would have happened."

"Now it's my fault? I offered to help." With all his strength, he swung an ugly kick against the hood of his fender. He punched the roof three times for effect. It reminded me of when he was a little boy and things didn't go his way. I'm still re-plastering those toe holes in the walls.

Inspecting the slight dent in the hood, I said, "Are you through?"

"Why is she spazzing out?"

"All three of you only give 85 percent. Javier had left already. Sky and Gray could have been washing dishes as they went. We wouldn't be stuck with this pile."

"I can't believe she's blaming me. I offered to help. Mom's a psycho."

Tracey threw a pot out the back door, which ricocheted off the dumpster in the general direction of his car. "I hate you all!" she yelled over the sounds of his engine.

She eventually came home at three in the morning, beaten and exhausted from her kitchen-cleaning-and-making-a-point tirade.

Chapter 23

Beef

We were a little café with a big secret. Our kitchen was being run by a bunch of kids who had no idea what they were doing. A few were certified in food handling, so they weren't going to kill anyone, but if the health department came for an inspection, we would be in trouble. Tracey had more experience, but between the morning baking, playing the hostess, and balancing the books, she was totally overextended. Nico had finally shown up, but he only wanted to work two shifts. He'd made it clear that he had come to Montauk to go fishing, and we were already deep into the July 4th holiday rush.

"I heard the health department is in town," Tracey cried. Another chef had called to warn her. "If he inspects us today, we're fried."

"Do you know what he looks like? Maybe he can be bought off."

"Scott took care of everything, getting the place open and all those permits. He did the original walk through. I have no idea what to do. Please, do me a favor, dear, if the health inspector walks in right now, don't try to bribe him. You don't know shit from Shinola when it comes to bribery." Her face froze as she turned toward the kitchen.

When it rained, it poured. A large man in a cheap suit walked though the back door and straight into the kitchen. He had dark, angry, searching eyes. He wiped his finger on the greasy prep area and frowned with a look of complete disgust.

I reached into my pocket to check the size of my cash wad.

Tracey ran to the kitchen. "Can I help you?" Her hands were shaking.

"Are you the owner?" he asked in an official, disdainful manner.

"Yes. I am. If you could come back in an hour, I'll have this all cleaned up. I'm sorry. I'm new to this. What am I supposed to do?" Tracey shivered.

Surprised by her naivety, his face clouded. We'd finally hit the abyss. How could we ever think that a dentist and a yoga teacher could open a restaurant in the Hamptons? The health department was going to shut us down for our stupidity. Our friend Kevin and the food writer Anthony Bourdain were right. Just because we were good restaurant patrons didn't entitle us to cross the divide. You wouldn't want Bouley doing your next root canal or Keller teaching a Downward Dog.

"I'm Beef," he spoke with a Spanish accent. He searched around the kitchen, as if there was something missing. Had we posted all our paperwork correctly? That's the inspector's favorite, first infraction: poor paperwork.

"Yeah, and we're chopped liver." Tracey didn't laugh at my joke.

"Mr. Shaggy sent me."

"Shaggy?" I asked. Why would our competition send the health inspector, unless he was trying to screw us? Professional jealousy? "We only sold out last night because of the storm; normally we're completely empty." I nervously reached for the cash. Should I wait for him to ask for a bribe, or should I make some gesture, like accidentally dropping a few hundred on the floor and saying, "Oh, I'm sorry, is this yours?" What was the protocol for bribing the health department? I'd read bribery was standard business.

"Who are you?" He offered me his hand.

As I pulled my right hand out of my pocket, the cash accidentally jumped out and fell to the floor. A wad of a few hundred lay unattended in a pile. None of us bent over to pick up the dirty money. He looked at me and tilted his head. I couldn't tell from his poker face what he'd planned to do next. Tracey had murder in her eyes. My murder.

The man bent down and picked up the cash. "Five-second rule." He handed the dirty money back to me. "I heard you need a chef." Beef was the Guatemalan that Shaggy had mentioned. The 7th Cavalry had arrived in the nick of time. He was a seasoned cook, having run Shaggy's kitchen on and off for ten years. He was about thirty years old, broad shouldered, and plain speaking. "My kitchen will be the best in Montauk," he boasted. "I taught Shag and his son everything they know."

"So where've you been the past year?" I inquired.

"I cooked upstate; please call them for references. My wife and I, we have some problems, but I want to be in Montauk with my children. I love my children. I promise you both, on my children's heads, that I will stay through the season, or as long as you would have me. Thank you for the opportunity to cook in Montauk."

"If your resume checks out? Maybe?" We hired him on the spot.

"You will not be sorry. I will work fifty, sixty hours a week. I will make your place a big success. I swear." Beef went right to work rearranging the location of the kitchen equipment so it was more ergometrically efficient. He moved a fryer and the food pass through, shrinking the space so two cooks could handle more orders. He placed the small refrigerator, which held the condiments, to the other side so it wouldn't act as a bottleneck and shifted the location of the central food service bar to allow better traffic. He built a locked cabinet in the back to hold the wine so it wouldn't be stored in the thermally challenged outside storage, and he taught the boys how to properly maintain a clean kitchen, so when the inspector finally came, we would pass with flying colors.

These little changes went a long way to creating consistent food quality.

He tweaked the fries, crisped the ribs, and whipped the staff. Beef's taking over the kitchen allowed Tracey to focus on baking and banking, her favorite passions.

We were now deep into the Hundred Days of Hampton Restaurant Hell, and the kitchen was finally putting out a consistent, quality product. Each day was busier than the last, and we were tripling our early-season income. At that rate, the Shack might actually have covered its expenses, but Tracey was too far behind in the paperwork to have a clear notion of the profit and loss.

"You're a Big Restaurant Macha now," I flattered her.

"So, why do I feel like a sham macha?"

"A Shixza Macha. It's an oxymoron for the wife of a Jewish Papi chulo. Don't you get it?" I threw up my hands at the weak joke.

She obviously didn't. "Just don't go calling me the Ditch Witch," the name of another local female caterer. "I hate monikers, like Shack Witch."

I made the surrender sign of the male praying mantis.

"So, what do you think of Beef?" Tracey asked after a few days.

"He's the real deal. He's already improved efficiency, and the kitchen's cranking out the orders. You're a big success."

"I'm not so sure," she whined. "He's such a Latino machismo."

"Are you questioning my choice in chefs again?" I complained.

"Funny," she frowned. "He wants to add pork chops to the menu."

"So, what's the problem?"

"The problem is that I hated the food at Shaggy. In my opinion, who wants to eat an overcooked slab of beef on the beach? His public isn't my public. We're the youth of Montauk. He doesn't understand that my public wants light, cheap beach faire. He's trying to change the menu to be a Shaggy mini-me. I'm disgusted."

"It's worked for Shaggy for forty years."

"I don't want Shaggy's drunks and leftover litter. I'd rather close the Shack than serve that kind of food. Beef just doesn't comprehend what I'm trying to do. Who would want to eat a pork chop or a steak on a paper plate?"

"At some point, you need to sit down with him and have a heart to heart."

"I can't. He doesn't respect me. I'm a woman, and in his world, the professional restaurant kitchen is a tough place filled with thugs and drunks."

"He's been in the business a long time; maybe he knows your previous chefs. Would you mind if I spoke to him? He and I seem to get along."

"Would you? No, on second thought, leave it alone. He can cook whatever he wants. I don't care anymore, as long as I'm not responsible."

"But it's your establishment. He's working for you!"

"I know that all too well," she warned and walked off in a huff.

I left my wife to her pots and pans. In the end, it wasn't really that hard. I'd been recalled to a hot tooth and the hope for a flush of new faces, a flip of the cards, a new milonga, an escape to the mid-week husband, which was much simpler.

While I was away, the inspector from the health department visited the Shack. It was a full military dress down, including the horn and ten-gun salutation.

"Her name's Pearl and she'd just lost her dog," Tracey murmured into the telephone receiver. "She's single and depressed."

"Wait. I didn't hear that correctly." I checked the connection. "Who's depressed? Oh my God, the health inspector finally came?"

"Pearl and I are touchy-feely now. I told her the whole story, how we escaped the flames and ashes of 9/11 and raised the kids out here, how this is my opportunity as a fellow woman to create my own business. She was very moved. She owned a restaurant once. It was spectacular bullshit, if I may say so myself."

"That's great. Who's depressed?" We had a bad cell phone connection.

"Depressed? I'm ecstatic! Are you depressed, dear?"

"Me? I just called to congratulate you. I'm not depressed."

"Pearl gave me all kinds of advice on how to make the kitchen work better. She likes me. I have a buddy in the health department now," Tracey sang. "I'm in the money. I'm in the money, and I've got a chef, too. Ha, ha, ha."

"Great," I said. Maybe I was depressed. The depressed person is the last to know.

"Are you happy now?" she asked, but hung up before I could answer.

"That's just great," I whispered into the silence. I didn't call the rest of the week. It was an awkward moment in the marriage, maybe the Waterloo Week.

Getting off the Jitney the following Thursday at 10:00 PM, after a four-hour delay, I didn't know what to expect. No one was home or available to meet me. No one answered my calls. I walked from the bus stop over to the Shack. The Gig Shack was packed with customers for coffee, ice cream, and Tracey's famous homemade desserts. The family was up to its ears with business. I just wanted to help! Without being asked, I threw off my business suit and jumped into the fray. I filled a few dozen ice-cream cones and orders for espresso. Everyone was smiling at me, finally part of the team. I was happy!

"This is hard work," I admitted, stamping the brew, playing the barista.

"More foam, less milk," Tracey instructed in a harsh tone.

"I never understood the difference between a latte and a cappuccino." I sloppily filled the order somewhere in between. Maybe my foam wasn't properly boiled, but it was good enough and I really didn't want to learn. I presented her with a "Cappalatte."

"Dear, coffee-making is an art. Your patients wouldn't want me to fill their teeth with a crown, Cap-pa-latte? Would you? Please," she gently pushed me away from the machine. She was still wearing an ace bandage where she'd damaged her wrist. "We need a consistent product. It's my reputation! Stick to your molars. Please."

"Okay, I'll scoop ice cream. That can't be so hard, and it'll save your wrist." I wet the rounded scoop in its water wash, just the way she'd previously taught me, and attacked the frozen container. The ice cream was hard as a rock, and it took some sweat and a lot of perseverance to fill the cup. Like a little boy showing his mother his first poop, I presented Tracey with my first filled ice-cream cone. "Lookie."

"What's that?" she asked with a look of complete disgust. "You can't scoop ice cream without wearing a rubber glove. It's a health code violation. You're a doctor; you should know better." She grabbed the scoop out of my naked hand. "Away."

"But? But? That was an experiment. I'll eat it." I went around the front of the counter and crossed past the two twelve-year-olds who were waiting for me to fill their ice cream order. "Sorry, kid. You'll just have to get a job here and fill your own cone." Angrily, I licked the cone in his face and snorted. "Hmm, good."

"What a bozo," he murmured to my back. "Mister, you ate my cone?"

I licked the cone again and offered it back. "Here, you still want it?"

"Ignore him, boys. One Venezuelan vanilla and a coco chocolate cone, coming right up." Tracey handed them their dessert. "Lewis, I'll be done in a minute. I know you must be exhausted from the bus ride," she called to my fleeing back.

She packed up her bags and we drove home together, mutually holding back voices in a painful, biting silence. My marriage was unraveling right before my eyes. There was no "Welcome Home, Dad" sign on the door. Instead, there was the same pile of dirty linen I'd left unwashed the week before. This laundry lesson—leave it until they have to wear it—obviously wasn't working. Or perhaps they had too many clothes.

The scent of reefer floated from an upstairs room, and the empty beer bottles lay scattered on the floor, a litter of dead soldiers. My blood pressure rose violently.

"Nothing's changed," I complained in a low growl. "I know you worked all week, but the kids could have lifted a hand." My ears blushed bloody red. Wounded by the way she'd greeted me at the restaurant, I decided to attack. I kicked the washing machine. I wanted to fight, about the ice cream, about the laundry, about all the kinky sexual favors I deserved for being such a supportive husband, but knew I'd never receive.

"You're triangulating, father like sons," she replied coldly.

"I don't get you. One minute you complain if I do the wash, the next minute the opposite. I work my ass off for you all week. I'm the only one who ever makes this trip back and forth to NYC. What the fuck do you want from me?"

"Why are you yelling?" We heard footsteps and an outside door slam close. "You see, you're back five minutes, and you're already chasing us all away," she claimed.

"I'm chasing you away?" I wanted to get right back on that bus, but then the bronco would have won, and I'd be sitting on my ass in the dust, waiting for some divorce lawyer to kick in my teeth. It's cheaper to keep her. I changed my tone. "Sorry."

"Why are you wearing that ridiculous coat? I hate that coat; it reminds me of an old man," she counterattacked. "I'm sure you just wear it to piss me off." The fight was back on. She was itching for an opening. "What do you want from me?"

"All I want is a little tenderness." I placed my hand gently on her shoulder.

She shuddered and jumped away, as if she'd been infected with fish poisoning, and all her nerve endings mistook my warmth for coldness. "Tenderness? That's a joke. You just want to get laid." Our weekly transition was off to a bad start.

I visually inspected the curves of my gorgeous wife's breast, and as the carnal image of her spectacular body, naked, reappeared in my memory bank, the testosterone flew south and my anger disappeared. She was right; she didn't owe me anything from that favor bank. She had worked equally hard for me, but after a week living alone, getting laid was suddenly my only imperative. Woof, woof. "Feed me to your young. Is my account still in the black?" The male mantis pulled down his collar and showed neck.

The predatory wife accepted my surrender. She refolded her front claws. "Let's go to the bedroom, dear, before they all return." She took my hand and led me astray.

We hungrily joined bodies. If this wasn't tenderness, it sure was the next best thing. Satiated, we laid naked in soft repose after a stupendous lovemaking session. The phone rang. "Arden forgot to lock up. I'll go over," I offered.

Tracey thanked me, rolled over, and promptly fell asleep.

I drove around to the back door of the Shack to lock up. The two Polish girls froze like deer in headlights, caught sneaking out with stuffed duffel bags. The bags look heavier than their hundred and ten pounds. "What's this?" I asked, blocking their escape.

They attempted to spin a positive answer. "Growing up in Poland, there's no food. We're always so hungry."

"I understand, but that doesn't give you the right to steal." I grabbed the bags from their hands and inspected the contents. The bags were overflowing with meat, potatoes, and every imaginable vegetable from the walk-in refrigerator.

They couldn't eat that much by themselves; it looked like they could have fed the Red Army. "My boyfriend works at ranch. He's hungry too."

"If you had just asked me, I would have been happy to offer, but this is stealing. Pick up your checks in the morning. You're both fired!"

They shrugged and walked off. Two good-looking, English-speaking girls wouldn't have trouble finding employment, but who would we find to replace them?

I locked the doors and returned home to Tracey and my safe bed. I lay beside her sleeping body and wondered if she was dreaming of my death. Filled with a sudden wave of anxiety, I couldn't breathe.

I wanted to throw up. There was a burning in my esophagus, throat cancer I'd presumed, but probably acid reflux. The acid was fluxing up my throat with each thought of the Polish girls. I wanted to sleep, but it seemed that if I ever fell asleep, I'd stop breathing. After hours of tossing and turning, I decided that my knee-jerk decision was correct. Food pilferage was the hole in the watering can, the place the profits leaked. A precedent needed to be set. I swallowed a throat load of acid and ten milligrams of blue pill.

The next morning, when I told Tracey about the Polish Girl Incident, I fully expected I'd crossed her line in the sand and would be exiled to Siberia, "668 the Gulag." My winter clothes were already packed. I'd spent a good deal of the night, sleepless, plotting the conversation. I had no right to fire her staff. The female mantis would be justified if she bit off my head. I'd probably never get laid again. After playing out all the scenarios, I'd decided to lie. In my mind, I'd concocted a fraudulent story that the Polish girls quit when confronted with their thievery.

Stretching her arms to release the sleep, Tracey yawned, "I've got to get to work early to let the Polish girls in." As she dressed, my mind spun possible explanations. If I didn't say anything and the Poles didn't come to work, maybe Tracey would fire them herself. That would be too easy, and they were bound to have a conversation eventually. About to confess my treachery, Tracey confided, "I wish I had the guts to fire those girls. They're cold and completely useless. Beef and I have decided to go to full waitress service, and he introduced me to these smart, young Irish kids who are awesome."

God works in mysterious ways. "Well! That's ironic. They quit last night. I caught them stealing. They quit. The Irish kids sound wonderful."

Tracey stared at me with her eyes shut and her mouth wide open. It was a quizzical expression, the kind you save for really bad news, like when the dentist says you need a post, crown, and root canal. "So, when were you going to tell me this news?"

"Duh?" was the best I could muster. "We just woke up. I'm telling you now." I hadn't considered the possibility that she would shoot the messenger, no matter what the news. Once again, I was wrong.

Chapter 24

The Long Island Louie

Jayakari, composed of Jay and Ed, had become our resident band. Being fledgling musicians, they had successful independent careers and were willing to work cheaply for food, drink, and tips.

That weekend, they invited an old black musician to accompany them. He was ninety, if a day, and played a soulful, hand-carved guitar. He had elegant hands and long, delicate fingers that waltzed through the chords.

His beautiful wife of fifty years sat serenely throughout the impromptu jam. After he finished each song, she blew her husband an adoring kiss. After he had played a few sets and finished the complimentary dinner, I joined them for a brief conversation. They held each other's hands throughout the conversation.

"You make such a wonderful couple," I complimented them. "After fifty years of marriage, how do you do it? This business is killing my marriage."

He smiled demurely through a perfect set of ivory teeth and winked at his wife. "The secret to a long, successful marriage, doc, is how you hold it." He balled his long fingers into a huge, fierce fist, which he parlayed to my face. "You can hold your marriage like this, or you can hold it like this," he said, slowly uncurling the corkscrewed fist to display an open-faced, upward palm. The lifelines in his palm were intricate trifurcated deltas that spoke a generous story of unselfish support and nurtured love.

How was I really holding my marriage? I thought I'd been totally supportive of Tracey's efforts to date, but her perceived thanklessness was making me more and more angry. With each nonverbal shrug of her perfectly carved shoulders or failed attempts at communication, my open palm was self-destructively curling into a fist. I might as well have punched the wall for all the good it did me. I was scathing with inattention, but each furtive attempt pushed her further away. We had made this decision together, and if we were in over our heads, there was nothing to be done until the restaurant closed and my off-season wife returned to her loving ways. Divorces are a lot like earrings: you lose diamonds and find rhinestones.

Tracey returned from a particularly frustrating night, pounded the door, and squeezed her head in frustration. "What am I going to do now?"

I'd finally learned the correct response to that question, the hard way. She wasn't really asking my opinion or advice about what to do. I bit my lip and shut up. She just needed me to listen and support her decision. "You'll figure it out, dear. You always do."

In the meantime, I cut fresh flowers from my garden: pink long-stemmed roses I'd composted with espresso dregs, multicolored snapdragons I'd reared from seed, purple butterfly bushes without the fly, and huge, white, fragrant peonies that I'd debugged ant by ant. I arranged the flowers in large glass jars and gloriously displayed them on her outside tables and front counter. I also planted and maintained seasonal window boxes of impatient and hanging pansies. My acts of love wordlessly attracted the pedestrians.

I shopped for dress sales in Soho and the Lower East Side, walking store to store on slow, summer weekday mornings in New York City, when I really should have been drilling teeth. Instead, I investigated the downstairs sale racks from Prada and Wolford for that perfect baker's shirtdress, polka dot pleated cotton, like the madam from a French food movie, *Chocolat*. When all else failed, I checked announcement e-mails from Daily Candy and the *Post*. I really enjoyed dressing my beautiful wife.

Tracey was a perfect size six. I knew her body and taste well, having spent so much time arm in arm. After twenty-five years of monogamous marriage, my fingertips could serve as a blind tape measure of her waist. I had a Major League batting average for purchasing her clothes, hitting .333, which I faithfully delivered to her bedroom door. The Prada skirt was always a hit, the too skimpy Tracey Feith more often a strike, and the Calypso a bunt, usually returned for store credit. How's that for an open palm?

We had anticipated that I'd make weekly runs to Di Paolo's in Little Italy, where Louie would personally cut half a wheel of spring Parmesan cheese, as well as honoring our inside connection with wholesale prices. Sometimes, I'd visit Despana for Spanish olives and Chinatown for frozen shrimp. The plan was to tightly pack and deliver the imported supplies regularly in the sidecar luggage rack of the Jitney.

I was their New York fetcher. When the music receiver blew, I bought them a new unit from J&R. Skylar actually referred to me as his hero.

Once a week, I harvested fresh lettuce and radicchio from my Montauk garden, which the chef claimed he'd melded with the commercial iceberg salad, but for all I knew, he might have thrown it away or turned it into compost and just humored me into thinking I was of help. I never trusted that any of our chefs actually used the herbs and garden offerings I'd brought. According to Tracey, it was because I did a lousy job with the laundry. I'd washed that salad through a five-spin cycle and still she'd invariably find one grain of sand. Imagine her nasty comments if I'd actually tried to iron the lettuce! At last, Beef took pity on me and taught me not to wash the salad at home and deliver it wilted and wet in a big plastic bag. Instead, he taught George, the dishwasher, the correct way to wash the lettuce so it had some shelf life. I trusted George with my lettuce; what choice did I really have?

Beef and I understood each other, or at least we had some common ground when it came to marriage. He'd been away from his family for a while and was now trying to reconnect. It wasn't easy. He spent a whole lot of time in the walk-in-refrigerator screaming into his cell phone at his wife. Traccey considered his husbandly behavior disgraceful and abusive, because he communicated with a closed fist.

One day, when short-staffed, Beef taught me how to make real french fries from a bag of Idaho potatoes. I learned the correct technique for pealing, removing the eyes, squashing three hundred spuds through the Madeline, salting, and twice frying. It was fun, and as I practiced that afternoon with military precision, I could have manufactured enough fries to feed the Polish Army. I am a doctor, after all.

Next, I attacked a pail of avocados, skinning, pitting, and mashing the green flesh into a Mexican guacamole. I was a Viking cooking machine.

My favorite kitchen prep work was decapitating the soft-shell crabs. After so many close calls at being nearly decapitated by my long-legged, elegant praying mantis wife, I finally got the opportunity to pick out the gills and tail, and cut off the head of a creature smaller than myself. I was in heaven as I wholeheartedly attacked the boxes of two-dozen living, helpless critters. Finally, I was an indispensable member of the team, a professional crab slacker. This was the happiness I quested. It was short-lived though, as the wife requested my attendance out front to greet her guests.

My least favorite job was commandeering the head of the owner's table. Every Sunday night, Tracey would invite a group of artistic brush-ups and neighborhood ne'er-do-wells to be our free guests at the long picnic table out front. Comping food and beverages is a common practice in the business, and since the Gig Shack had such a public, exposed location on Main Street, it was important that the place looked busy early in the evening as the tourist spied out their dinner reservation. I completely understood and supported this marketing strategy. I didn't even mind feeding the hordes of malnourished Long Island landowners who ate like ladybugs alit a plate of aphids; it was a business deduction. But why did I have to spend the evening talking too? I guess I wasn't a very good captain of this ship, whose job entailed navigating the dangerous waters of the South Fork and wining and dining the first class cabins.

To make matters worse, Tracey would seat her friends, open a bottle of her best champagne, and suddenly be called inside to put out a fire or make small talk with another table. I was abandoned to the awkward, agonizing job of entertaining her guests the whole evening. My wife/hostess would pop back for a quick sip, nibble, or laugh, but it was clearly my responsibility to keep the conversations going. As the dead soldier's pile progressed and my holding court tolerance waned, I feigned interest but secretly wondered how to excuse myself from this ship of fools.

Sensing my unhappiness, Tracey suggested that I invite all the guests to the next week's table, but even my oldest friends suddenly seemed selfish and unattractive when I pictured them seated at arm's length. Was the honor of being seated at the owner's table mine or merely theirs?

Ironically, I was the third dentist to own the building that housed the present-day Gig Shack. These other dentists, and even Shaggy, had used the ice cream parlor as an early introduction into their own son's entrepreneurial careers. Maybe the building was haunted by their previous failed attempts at father/son enterprise. I remember spotting one of these dentists pounding the pavement in front of the Shack. Although normally a happy-go-lucky kind of guy, he looked kind of pissed.

Please do me a favor. If you read this memoir, don't blog or invite Anthony Bourdain to Montauk. His *Gourmet* magazine lambasting of a celebrity dentist's upscale health food restaurant in Miami a couple of years ago still sends shivers through my wallet. Even if Anthony calls, he'll get no reservations from me.

Anyway, I was bartender one Saturday afternoon, and Jayakari was jazzing their tunes when it started to rain. Not a hard rain, more of an early morning mist that's typical in July, but it still kept the customers away. The thick fog swallowed downtown. You couldn't see the flashing neon Open sign across the street. We were in the soup. Jay raised the volume on his drums, but still no one came, not even the police. "What do you think we should do?" asked the guys in the band.

Ed came up with the brilliant rain dance song, "Gigggg Shackkk," which we all hummed as they jazzed up an impromptu but consistent chord. I sang along and created lyrics, praying for customers. We repeated the chant over and over. It finally worked! After twenty minutes of chanting, the customers appeared and the tables were filled. Whenever business got slow, Jayakari would play that tune, and indirectly, I'd found another job—Rainmaker (or wet shill who sings badly).

I'll admit it. I made a lousy bartender. If you could call our little beer-capped covered counter an outside bar. I was judgmental of the heavy drinkers, ungracious to the underage, and gave away free drinks to the babes. I was the only bartender who supported sobriety, which leads to the story of the "Long Island Louie."

For various, previously mentioned reasons, we had decided to apply for only a wine and beer license, and that in a fishing town with a drinking problem, or as the locals like to say, a drinking town with a fishing problem. In the beginning, Josh had few customers, but once Skylar took over, his friends started filling the place. Drinking mainly beer, they gave the joint an early evening buzz, which soon sucked in the tourists. Although our bar never reached the volume of the established, hardcore liquor mills within five hundred feet, it fit our space and temperament. Even Skylar couldn't work that bar for fifteen straight hours, so I sat in on the slow afternoons, reading my newspaper and topping off the occasional customer's foam.

Getting bored and, to be honest, overly concerned with the lack of business, I created beer-tail competitions. Customers were invited to create their own beer drinks—cocktails such as Bloody Mary mix and Red Rogue, martini mix and Bud light, and orange juice with whatever. I offered twenty-five dollars to the drink voted best beer-tail. It wasn't a very popular game with the youth, who preferred their Buds clean, natural, and in multiple numbers, but some of the adults considered it. The next category was the best sangria. I had concocted my own formula using inexpensive Long Island white wine with fruit, pineapple, melon, and peach, marinated for fifteen minutes in the smoker. Unfortunately, when added to the wine, the residue from the ribs created an oily mess. Eventually, I settled on marinating the fruit overnight with rosemary, savory, and thyme. Sold by the pitcher with ice, it was my signature drink at the Shack. The real Long Island Louie was a zucchini martini, which I served at home using pickled squash instead of olives. I added a half shot of green chartreuse to one of Stoli.

Skylar hated beer-tails and seemed to continually undermine my attempts to change his bar. Those ten feet of dark, buggy space at the rear of the outside dining area were his turf. I was an unwelcome intruder. Every night, he erased the blackboard's descriptions of the beer-tail competition and my sangria recipe, and every morning I redid the sign. Eventually, I escalated the war by using permanent markers. He just threw out the blackboard altogether. At that point, we hardly spoke more than a polite hello.

The experiment with Arden in the kitchen had been a failure too. He had a poor relationship with Beef, and when the orders got backed up and they were "in the weeds," he often resorted to profanity, pot throwing, and walking out the back door.

Gray, on the other hand, was a natural behind the stove. He cherished the action, the long line of tickets, the intense heat, and boiling cauldrons of soup. He and Beef quickly developed a strong teacher/student relationship based on mutual respect. He made an excellent line cook, but it would take years of schooling to understand the duties of head chef, which included food inventory, preparation, and portion control.

With Sky behind the bar and Gray in front of the stove, two out of three essential jobs were now manned by family. Beef advised us that when Shaggy owned the Shack, he had a full alcohol bar on the outside and waitress service throughout. To date, Tracey had been the conservative, hesitant leader, always choosing the most legal interpretation of the law. The orders were taken at the counter, and the runners delivered the food on trays to the table. But now, under Beef's prodding, she finally agreed to go for broke and implement full waitress service. Arden was elected front of house.

Arden was a natural-born waiter, using his college education, good looks, and people skills to charm the customers into "buying up" off the menu. Families intent on just a snack or ice cream were trolled into a full-course meal. No one left without first trying dessert. Using his fishing skills, customers who had poked in for a peek were hooked into a table. His tips always topped 20 percent. Having previous experience and table vision, he expertly directed the front of house.

The perennial invasion of seasonal Irish college students rounded out the waitress staff and filled the void left by the injured local girls, Elani and Margo, and the caught red-handed in the cookie jar Polish girls. Beef did the dirty work of firing Morgan and his grandmother, because he wanted his own crew. He replaced them with Nico and a young Jamaican. The new staff was complete. Our sons were finally running the ship.

"How did Beef get rid of Morgan and Sandra?" I asked Tracey as we took our first swim in the ocean. It was mid-July and the water temperature took our breath away at first, but soon we got used to it. "They're almost family."

"Beef wanted new blood."

"Every new baseball manager wants his own coaching staff. It works the same in the kitchen. The dynamics are so delicate."

"Honestly, I think they felt sorry for me. It's my first season and third chef. Morgan will make more money building boats, and Sandra should retire already. I approved her unemployment application."

"That's kind of you."

"She did her best. She was just too slow hand-slicing out the slaw."

"You didn't owe her anything," I said.

"Business has been really good, and the music is finally a hit. New bands are calling us every day wanting to play at the Shack. I love my new Irish kids; they're always smiling, not like those sad-sack Polish blondes. The Irish make me laugh. With all three boys solid and Beef running the kitchen, this is the first time I feel confident enough to close my eyes and take a break." Back on the beach, kicking off her sandals, she continued, "I'm hoping the bad guys have run out of shoes to drop, because my fishnets all have holes."

I rubbed the cleavage between her toes. "Are you happy yet, wife?" I gleaned.

"Please. Don't look at my legs." She withdrew.

"But I love your legs."

"They're so pale. I need to spend more time at the beach."

"But are you happy?"

"Yes, husband. You are my hero." Said through her anti-aging, timelessly beautiful smile. "You are the best husband any girl could want."

"That's what I wanted to hear."

"Now, what can I do for you? Are *you* happy?" she asked.

It was a glorious Montauk beach day. The sand beneath correctly cushioned every curve of spine, and the sun caressed our skin without burning beyond a fifteen. Like music, the surf exhaled in tandem with each breath. Our sons were finally a team—in softball, in business, in family, all working as one. On the blanket beside me lay the most gorgeous woman on the East End and she loved me. What could any man ask for? It was as good as I would get a time to pop the question.

"Why are you looking at me so strangely?" Her brows embroiled the question.

I hadn't realized that my face was showing what was in my mind, but after this many years of marriage, it's no surprise she could read my eyes too. I took a deep breath, forced my brows to disengage, and plunged into the pool.

"The Argentine tango teachers need a commitment. I told them to come out in August and teach dancing at the Shack." I swallowed at my dried spit.

"We don't have a cabaret license."

"Actually, the rules in this town are so screwy, at present, the only establishment allowed to hold ballroom dancing events is a church."

Tracey did not respond for a few moments, but lay face-up, eyes shut, soaking up the rays. Her silence reminded me of the moment when I'd first asked her to marry me, a short twenty-five years before. She didn't reply then for a really long time. She knew that whatever she said would be held against her.

I drew a neat line in the sand and held my breath. The mound of sand looked like our bed. "This is important to me." I padded the sand into place.

Silent, she watched me draw the line through the corner of her eye before she injected herself into the covers of my conversation. I had made my bed. "Okay, as long as it'll make you happy." She turned back the bedding and folded the sheets the way she liked them.

Chapter 25

Rose Petal Droppings

My usual routine before my weekend 9:30 doubles tennis match was to cut a glorious bouquet of pink and yellow roses, delicately removing thorns and side branches, wrap the bunch in grass lashings, and place them safely in the basket of my Yamaha moped. Tracey preferred taking the car we shared so she wouldn't be stranded at the Shack, and often she needed to make runs for food supplies. As long as I stayed in Montauk, I tooled around town on the moped or walked. It was fun and saved gas.

I parked in the back of the Shack. Beef was pacing and screaming in Spanish into his cell phone. From the little I could translate, he seemed to be yelling at his wife. He looked depressed, disheveled, and unshaven, as if he'd spent the night sleeping in his car. Our eyes met briefly before he looked away.

Tracey was in her apron, baking cookies and cake, when I presented her with the arm full of beautiful flowers. "What's up with him?" I inquired.

She showed a sour face. "The flowers are gorgeous, dear, but they make such a mess. The rose petals drop all over the tables and floor." She pointed to yesterday's haul, which had laid a delicate halo of spent petals around a table. "It looks like litter."

"Your customers can't tell the difference?"

"I'm afraid not. Someone complained, and the staff hates to clean up."

"It must have been the same customer who thought ceviche was a Mexican beer." I put the flowers in a bucket of water and placed them out front anyway.

I played tennis poorly. Finding it difficult to forget her hateful comments about my rose petals being litter, I played aggressively and over hit the ball.

When I got back to the Shack, Tracey was in a heated argument with Beef. He did most of the talking. The only words I could understand were "specials" and "king of the kitchen." He pounded his chest for effect.

Should I have interfered? He was such a macho Latino and could be intimidating when provoked, but Tracey seemed to be holding her own. I was torn about the proper response. Should I protect my wife or let her fight her own battles?

Our eyes met and he rolled his, shaking his head and gritting his teeth, the facial masseter muscle throbbing, as if he nonverbally communicated, "There's no way I can talk to this white woman." He stormed off to the back of the kitchen.

Tracey and I took a table out front, and she explained her side of the story.

"The nerve of that man. Imagine him telling me how to run my own business."

"What's the problem?" I asked.

"I want Nico to choose and prepare the specials on the menu. Nico is going to be a star chef one day. He just needs the chance. The Shack is about giving the young an opportunity to shine, and frankly, I don't like Beef's style."

"Have you asked Nico how he feels about this? He made it clear he doesn't want to be the head chef." No Jesus I tread carefully through delicate waters.

"No, but he's intimidated by Beef. I know Nico can do it."

"Offering Nico the specials is a real slap in Beef's face." I'd said too much. "I can understand why he would be pissed."

"Are you agreeing with him now?"

"No, of course not. It's your decision, but it's dangerous to back a crazy macho chef into a corner. I was worried about you." Time and marriage stood still.

"That's sweet, dear. I almost wish he'd quit." She smiled as before.

"Yeah, be careful what you wish for. I'm going to go home and do the laundry." Instead, I took the long road home, seeking solace at the Bones. When I got there, Leslie and her new chef were in a yelling match. She spied me and took their argument inside where I was not a witness. Leslie and Tracey were so competitive.

"What's up here, Mac Cool?" I took a slow sip of beer. "Kitchen warfare seems endemic to this town. Maybe the ladies should trade chefs, you know, like that TV show where the moms trade families, husbands, and careers."

"*Super spottum. Pax totum sanguinarium globum.*" He craned his neck in a jerky motion to see if his mom was about. "Are you happy yet, old man?"

"My accountant called yesterday and asked how much money I was willing to lose on the Gig Shack. I always figured it was a write-off, her loss counted against my gain and paid the mortgage, but he explained I had to make that money in order to lose it. Let that serve as a lesson in life. What's my horoscope reading today?"

With an artistic flurry, he read from *Hampton's* magazine, the one with the hot celebrity babes. "Bloody good riddles," he said in an Irish dialect. "Gemini. You're amazing, graceful under the direst circumstances, and extremely seductive with words, so why aren't you getting exactly what you want?" With an angelic expression, he said, "Tell me about the Montauk Monster, the Montauk Project, and the Lost Boys. I've heard rumors that these boys time traveled to another dimension. I want to do that."

"The monster's an escaped experiment in animal cross cloning from Plum Island, the Project was a super-secret WWII experiment at Camp Hero, and the boys occasionally hang out in my house. There are books written about this supernatural stuff, but you can't believe your ears. You be careful, Mac. Some of the townies still follow this cult stuff." I finished the dregs of my beer and made my escape before Leslie showed. When I got back to the Shack, Tracey was fidgeting nervously out front.

"That bastard!" she complained, looking over her shoulder to see if he heard. "Can you believe it? Beef claims he was offered another cooking job for $1500 a week. He'll only stay if I meet that price. He wants it all in cash."

"What does he make now?"

"A grand on the books."

"Yikes. That's a lot of hot tamales. What are you going to do?"

"Especially for a chef who's depressed. I hate him. Now he's telling everyone that the only reason we're successful is because of his cooking."

"Leslie hates her chef. Why don't you trade for Fabio?"

"Are you kidding? Don't you know girls? She doesn't want him, but not at the cost of losing him to me. She'd rather screw a guy she hates than see him dating me."

"I get the analogy. Well, we'll have to sit Nico down and have a heart to heart. I'll call his parents if I have to."

"Call all the boys. We need to powwow. If Nico won't take this job, tell him I'll shut the sucker down. Enough is enough," she claimed.

Chapter 26

The First Tango in Montauk

Back in the old days, Alfonso was my second tango teacher. My first fired me after two months. I never did understand why. I paid my bills promptly, was courteous, and tried hard to learn the dance. Maybe she was just a bitch. She did describe Alfonso's school as being "old school" and "out of touch."

I proceeded to take group lessons at the tango academy in New York. There were about forty members in my class, split equally along gender lines, but 50 percent of the female dancers wanted to learn the lead, which left me dancing with other men. Three months into my tango career, I had been fired by my first teacher and forced to follow other men. A lesser man would have quit the pilgrimage.

This rough beginning motivated me to excel in the dance. Tracey and I finally hired Alfonso, the local South Fork ballroom expert, to teach a class. We danced beautifully together and our early tango blossomed. At that time, she was teaching yoga at a local hotel and the tango/yoga connection was a natural, "Yo-tango." She rarely traveled into New York, so I advanced in the dance, alone.

Unfortunately, the hotel was not supportive of our ballroom dancing. After class on Friday nights, we all went to the main ballroom to practice, but the local DJ wouldn't play more than one song. He preferred the classics and oldies, which wouldn't frighten the children off the floor, or maybe he only had one tango song in his repertoire.

Alfonso moved our venue to the wedding hall at the Montauk Downs. He hired big bands, taxi dancers, and filmed the dance party for channel 20. He spent his school's entire budget trying to develop ballroom dance in Montauk. It was a complete failure: no one showed. Alfonso swore he would never hold another event in Montauk as long as he lived. "The surfers have two left feet, and the fishermen are more roll than rock."

"Please, make another attempt. You can hold the party at our Shack. We'll move all the furniture. I'll give your people free food and drink."

"Okay, but if no one comes, I swear this will be the last tango in Montauk."

He was right. No one came, and those dancers who made an appearance hated the floor in the Shack. Being mainly older swingers and hustlers from Up Island, they preferred a smooth wooden floor for fast spinning. We had large tiles, which were okay for tango but not serviceable for regular ballroom.

In the meantime, I hosted some successful milongas in my New York loft. I created a mailing list and spread the word that tango was coming to Montauk, no matter how poor the odds. The fisherwomen would have to hang their nets into hosiery.

"Why do you want to bother holding tango at the Shack?" Sky asked. "Dancers are cheap. They don't drink alcohol or eat much."

"Value added. It makes the Shack unique, and I've always dreamed of dancing with your mother in a bikini and high heels."

"Can't you do that at home? We're can't afford to remove the tables."

"It's my contribution, and your mother has agreed."

It wasn't much of a conversation, as these father/son conversations go, but those were the most words he and I had spoken to one another in weeks, as we were still conflicted about the Long Island Louie, beer-tails, and past grievances.

The Shack was taking over my life, every day morphing into a monstrous suck-you bus, consuming longer hours, more expense, more stress. Tracey was virtually living at the Shack, and secretly I blamed the entire venture on our sons. I was sacrificing my marriage to their career, and they weren't showing much appreciation.

They asked me to buy friends some beer for a party at our house. I'd purchased two six-packs for about eight guys. Unbeknown to me, some ladies sneaked in the back of the house loaded with bottles of gin and rum they had stolen from their parents. One of these ladies drank too much, and while she was inebriated, one of their friends drafted her torso with a pornographic road map of the essential anatomy, like the tunnel entrance. Amazingly, all this happened right under our noses as the family was downstairs having dinner. Her girlfriends brought the drunken lass downstairs where I washed her face and made sure she was conscious and not in immediate medical danger. The girlfriends assured me that they would bring her home safely. Instead, they deposited her semi-comatose body on the front lawn and ran away. When her parents arrived, she was taken to the hospital and her stomach was pumped. She was fine. She had too much to drink. I was unaware of the fleshy graffiti, but the image made headlines in the local paper. I'm not blaming the law because I should have been a more responsible parental host.

Yes, I am blaming the laws and the lawyers. The parenting situation in this country sucks. Everyone is constantly looking to assign blame, but no other parents are accepting responsibility. I considered myself a guardian, a teacher, and leader of the youth. I screwed up that time and deserved to be punished, but why can't some other parents get involved? Why do they punish the good parents?

Anyway, getting back to this story, the next morning, I was home alone gardening peacefully, when a police cruiser pulled up in front and flashed his lights. I investigated. The cop pointed to his rear seat. In the back lay a young man, clearly unconscious. It was dark and I couldn't identify the face immediately. Oh my God. One of my boys was injured or under arrest? I searched my memory bank to recall if everyone came safely home last night. My eyes cruised the parking lot for a car accounting.

"Is this one of yours?" he inquired in a non-threatening, almost comical tone.

I stuck my face fully into the rear seat to get a better view.

The young man rolled to his side and moaned. He smelled of stale beer and vomit. Blood or vomit stained the front of his shirt.

"We found him in the bushes down by Kirk Park, sleeping it off."

The young man raised his head from the seat. "Wow, where am I?"

"It's my neighbor's son," I told the cop. I sure was glad this young man wasn't one of my own. "I'll take him off your hands and get him home safe." I helped the boy out of the police car and walked him home. I waved to the officer as he drove off. It was curious that he assumed every drunken young man in the neighborhood lived in my house. We were obviously getting a reputation with local law enforcement.

There were police everywhere in Montauk that year. One afternoon, a young officer swaggered up to the counter at the Shack and demanded to talk to the owner. I offered him a coffee while he waited for me to dislodge Tracey from a plate of baking cookies. She wasn't happy to be taken away from her oven.

"What does he want? I'm busy. Let Skylar deal with him," she suggested.

"Sky's not around and he wants the owner. He wouldn't say why."

Throwing down her apron, she confronted the young man. The policeman radiated confidence, although he appeared to have started shaving only the day before.

"Where are your occupancy signs?" he asked, looking around for trouble.

Tracey pointed to the three white and red laminated signs, one of which was hung sideways. Fortunately, it was early in the evening and we were well within the allotted number of customers, but I was already getting that sick feeling in my stomach.

"That sign is crooked." He pulled out his pad as if to write a ticket.

"What are you, an art critic?" Tracey mocked him. "Is there a complaint?"

I wished she had acted more consolatory. You get more sugar from honey.

"What's your name and date of birth, miss?" he requested, puffing out his chest.

"My date of birth? I'm old enough to be your mother. Didn't your mother ever teach you not to ask a lady her age?" Tracey shook her head with disbelief.

The cop started to back step. He wasn't expecting such an aggressive response.

"Now if you're done, I need to get back to my cookies before they burn." She turned her back to him and retreated to her kitchen. "Would you like a cookie?"

The officer looked angry when he left. What was that about? It was a clear attempt at intimidation. Why were the local cops acting like code enforcers?

While we were barely surviving our first season, the Surf Lodge was making waves, pulling in the big bucks, and quickly surpassing Cyril's for cars double-parked on the curb and high-heeled patrons double-parked at the bar. In one month, their professional promotion team had landed front covers in the *New York Times*, *Newsday*, and assorted issues of travel and leisure. Change was surging into town like a Northeaster. Already, they had a two-hour wait for a table, countless celebrity sightings, and beautiful Brazilian models busing. Their well-heeled customers were ferried to the local favorite surf spots in a caravan of antique six-wheeled Jeeps.

"A bunch of sidewalk surfers!" I overheard one old time surfer grousing in the hardware store about the invasion of their private break. "I hate them Surf Lodge soft tops, bulldozing our paradise. It's about time they got a lesson."

"They don't know the rules!" chimed another gray-haired, pony-tailed surfer. "It's getting out of control. The posers will be turning the hardware store into a monogram shop next. That'll be the end of the end."

"Yeah, man, them city slickers should stay in the Hamptons," added the other fellow. "They want to come here and have fun. It isn't the same for us."

"The break isn't big enough for us and them city surfers, with their pork-pie hats, three-piece suits, and skinny broads. Why can't they just let Montauk be? We don't want to become another homogenized Hampton, with Tiffany's and Jay Crew taking over every mom and pop shop."

"If you ask me, that Lodge is a mistake on the lake." They gathered their turf.

"It's a damn invasion. The next one cuts my wave, I'm going to run him down."

"You working today? Let's call in sick and go surfing." They high-fived.

The supervisor took notice of this potential change too, this westernization, and sent in reinforcements. Police cruisers stalked in the dark, pouncing on borderline DUI's as they exited the Surf Lodge. Patrons' parked cars were liberally ticketed, and the club was slammed with a series of legal actions. The Lodge sought a compromise by renting the unused lumberyard lot in the evening to park the overflow and hiring local unemployed youth to valet the cars. The town escalated the battle by prohibiting off-premises valet parking. The Lodge hired big-name bands to bring new money and business into the recessed local economy, so the administration counterattacked with building code and noise violations. Even in the middle of a near depression, the supervisor flaunted his anti-business venom. He wasn't a bad guy; in fact, when spoken to privately, he was quite cordial, but he'd spent the previous twenty-five years in civil service and couldn't contemplate the needs of small business and balancing a budget. His solution to financing hard times was handcuffs.

"I wish them well," said Tracey of the Surf Lodge. "The owners and staff eat at my Shack a lot. They love us. They've invited me to cater their morning buffet with fresh scones and croissants. I'm really honored to be appreciated by such professionals."

"I'm worried the old-timers are going to try to stem the tide." I told her of the anti-gentrification and anti-Surf Lodge rumors I'd overheard. "Montauk is a small town."

"The cars can park illegally to go to church on Sunday, but they can't park on the street on Saturday night? It's all petty jealousy. They hate it when anyone succeeds."

What is it about the sport of surfing that's so territorial? You don't have the same conflicts in skiing or in tango. There's plenty of room for all on the mountain or the dance floor, but there's a narrow window for the long boarders in the surf lineup. When the local surfers aren't fighting with each other over a wave, they're fighting with the fishermen or the tourists. What a waste of time.

Tracey thumped. "The old-timers never supported us. If it's a war the old boys want, it's a war they'll get. I'm calling all the ladies—Screaming Mimi, Calypso, B. J., and those French and Brazilian broads."

I hopelessly searched my mind for a conflict resolution solution.

She took off her high-heeled shoe and tapped the pointed stiletto into the lifelines of her palm. The self-abuse left a red tattoo. "Let them just bring their fish on."

Unfortunately, she got more than she'd bargained for.

Chapter 27

A Recipe for Disaster

"If you elect a general, he'll build you a war." I think I said that first.

The scenic drive into town was a gauntlet for the unsuspecting tourist. Welcome to your vacation; here's a speeding ticket, and isn't your inspection one day old? That's $250. Now we can afford more parking-meter men who'll slash the tourists' tires with a two-hour limit. The supervisor was making money the only way he knew how. In the next election, we need an administration with a pro-business vision.

"What do you expect when you elect code enforcers to run the country?" Jay and I were sitting in front of the Gig Shack, watching the world pass by. "The new supervisor has doubled the police force since taking over your office. Was there more crime in East Hampton? No wonder he can't meet the budget," I concluded.

Right in front of the Shack, two cars gently kissed over a parking spot, breaking a ten-dollar piece of plastic. Within seconds, a police cruiser rushed to the scene of the crime. Emergency lights beaming, more police soon accompanied him. They blocked traffic in both directions. From a distance, another cop siren echoed fiercely from the east. Within five minutes of this minor accident, three fully loaded police had descended on the two fender benders. They checked inspections and licenses. For the same preservation price, they could have returned the Andy Warhol estate to pasture.

He arrested that famous art gallery owner for serving free wine and cheese at one of her openings. She told the arresting officer that she'd been serving wine in her gallery for longer than he'd been alive. They took her away in cuffs anyway.

"There's big bucks in parking tickets and speeding, but it's unfortunate that there's no one we can talk to in this administration.

When Jayakari plays tonight, could you keep the volume down so you-know-who doesn't call them?"

"Yeah, yeah," Jay said. "No problema."

The band had just finished with the first number when the cops arrived, egged on by another complaint from our chronically complaining, old boy neighbor, or, more scarily, a political vendetta by the present administration against Jay's public accusations. Jay had been writing frequent letters in the local press accusing the town supervisor of evil indiscretions. The war was escalating. This time, the cops came prepared with high-tech weapons, noise meters that they barely knew how to use. One cop stood in the middle of the street, trying to assess a background noise reading, but the machine didn't seem to work. Jay and I stood next to him, actively interfering, talking as loudly as we could. "So what do you think of those Mets?" I screamed into the mike.

"It's my professional advice that the restaurant owners gather forces and approach the town board to legalize live music," Jay yelled as loud as he could.

"How do we do that?" I screamed back, straining a vocal cord.

"I'll make sure it's on the calendar, but you and Tracey need to speak your peace. This is ridiculous. There's no system for sound levels. It's completely discretionary."

So a week later, we found ourselves in an East Hampton courthouse, launching a full-scale assault on the anti-entertainment, reactionary forces. Our proposal was that music permits should be issued for restaurants. It was not a battle we were particularly prepared to lead. Tracey and Skylar both stood before the board and pleaded the case for live music. Nick's, Surfside, and other restaurants quietly supported us. Live musicians testified that the town was taking the food from their babies' mouths. Of course, none of these out-of-work musicians were well known for their child support.

On the opposing side of the public meeting was the anti-music contingent, private citizens who couldn't sleep and a private coalition of wealthy landowners, who like their brethren in East Hampton, were anti-any-development. This group had a long history of preventing Montauk's incorporation into an independently administered town. It was their belief that self-government and secession from the autocratic rule of East Hampton would lead to skyscrapers and the Miami of the beach. Their defiance was framed as an environmental issue.

Watching Sky publicly debating the live music issue with the town board swelled my pride. The politicians treated him respectfully. In general, the town seemed supportive, as they realized the present rules were unpopular and unenforceable. When my family finished their moment on the podium, Tracey and Sky wiped the sweat from their brows and ran back to our bench. "Wow, I'm glad that's over," they both confessed.

After an old woman complained about the singing of a neighbor's dog, it was my chance to take the podium. Tracey had expected that I'd just say a few quick words of support and retreat, but I had a different agenda in mind. The tango. I wanted to move the line in the sand and have the town legalize ballroom dancing.

The present rule prohibited any organized dancing unless the establishment had a designated dance space, which couldn't then be used for other purposes. The only location that fit that bill was the Hotel, which hosted weddings, but even they often stretched it. The purpose of this rule was to prevent restaurants from removing their tables at night and morphing into, God forbid, a discothèque.

"Tango and other ballroom dancing require a certain amount of space." I attempted to educate the town board on the real-life consequences of their rule. "No restaurant could ever afford to designate this unused dance space. It would kill them."

The supervisor treated my request as a joke. "I have nothing against a few people moving their hips as they listen to live music. It would be impossible to stop that anyway." He turned to his compatriots on the board and joked. "Could you imagine arresting someone for shaking their booty?" His friends all laughed.

I broke through their laughter. "Excuse me, but you just don't understand!

"People can shake their hips anywhere, but ballroom dancing is presently only legal in a church or community center. Organized couple dancing is being prohibited by your rules. East Hampton supposedly has a history of artistic expression, so why the sudden prejudice against ballroom dance? These rules don't prevent rowdiness. Tango dancers are generally good citizens. You're preventing the full enjoyment of their First Amendment rights. Please rescind the rules on removal of tables."

Finally the council took my complaint seriously, gathering their five heads for a powwow. After a few minutes of quiet arguing, the supervisor spoke into his microphone. "My rule stands! The only way you will ever dance tango in Montauk is on top of a table." He slammed his gavel down. "This will be the last tango in Montauk."

As I retreated in defeat to my seat, I was met by the glaring, disapproving stares of my family. "Why did you have to bring up the tango?" Tracey demanded.

"Now you pissed them off," said Skylar. "Thanks a lot, Dad."

Chapter 28

King of the Kitchen

Later that night, our family sat Nico down on the living room couch and attempted to twist his right arm, left leg, big toe, or any body part that was still exposed. Gangland style, we hoped that if each of us made him an offer he couldn't refuse, the weight of numbers would force him to acquiesce and assume his rightful title as king of our kitchen. "Take the job or sleep with the fish!" I threatened the pesca-sexual, fish-loving young man as he wiggled like a red herring through my grasp.

"I'd like that reference, but I don't want the job," he replied sheepishly.

"Come on, Nico, work with us," I pleaded.

"No," he stated flatly. "I don't want the job. I love you guys, you've been like a second family, but I can't do it. I won't take the job from Beef."

We attempted the carrot and the stick, yet still, he refused. He didn't care about money. He just wanted to go fishing, so we used the rod and reel.

"Beef doesn't even want the job," I explained.

With tears in his eyes, Nico shook his head. "I can't do it."

"This is a rare opportunity to run your own kitchen. Why did you go to culinary school? Can't you at least give it a try?" I entreated.

"I don't want to work fifty hours a week. I want to fish."

"You can fish in the off-season. Please, we need you," I begged.

"I don't want the responsibility of running the kitchen. I'll cook, but I don't want to be in charge. What if I fail? I've only been a line cook for two years."

"You won't fail. We'll all be in there with you," I improvised.

"No, I can't do it." He got up to leave, but his knees buckled before the boss.

"Okay, enough of this bullshit!" Tracey grabbed the kid's collar. "You're taking the job whether you like it or not. I didn't open the Shack so some foreigner could claim our success. The Shack is about you and the boys. I'm firing Beef tonight. If you don't show up with a smile on your face and your apron tied tight tomorrow, I'll close the Shack forever!" She spoke like a mother to a wayward son, a mixture of parental anger and unconditional love. "It's you or no one."

Ten eyes focused on Nico. Would he call her bluff? "Come on, Tracey. You wouldn't shut the Shack. The kids in town would revolt if they couldn't get one of your fish tacos. The whole town would blame me."

"You want to bet? Nico, you will run my kitchen!" she ordered.

He could hardly hold our gaze. "Well, maybe, I could do it for a while." His shoulders dropped to his knees as his resolve weakened under our relentless torture.

"You're a superstar. I have complete faith in your ability." Tracey's tourniquet tightened, constricting the fears and growing pains he'd harbored to a back burner.

Would she really have shut the Shack if he had refused?

"I would like to try some new fish recipes. Arden and I could fish between shifts."

"You'll start tomorrow. It's settled!" Tracey commanded.

"Okay." He smiled broadly. "I'll do it." He shook all our hands.

With a sigh of relief, the head-chef issue was finally settled. Who knows, maybe Nico had secretly wanted the job all along but was too shy to ask.

Beef accepted his firing well. He'd already quit. Tracey bamboozled us.

Other personal changes were also afloat. Emily arrived from Portland to help run the front of house. She and Tracey had worked together in my dental office years ago and developed a strong friendship. Emily had been managing a hotel and had extensive experience in the hospitality business. She became the general manager.

"Mom needs some estrogen to balance all of us young men," Arden confided.

"Emily? She's got some talents, but as an employee, I found she caused more trouble than she was worth," I recalled. "She can be a very negative person."

"Now you're second-guessing Mom's choice in managers? Don't you ever learn?"

"Apparently not. This is definitely a no-win situation, but the choice is hers."

"Emily's cool. Remember, she and I were friends. It will be just like old times, when you guys used to work together in NYC."

"Except for one big difference. I used to be her boss."

"The world's a changing. Better get used to it, big guy," advised Arden.

"Where is she going to live? Is there more room over at the apartment we rented originally for Scott and Erin? That's where Nico will be staying. The hard part about working in the Hamptons isn't finding a job but a place to live."

"Mom didn't tell you? Emily will live in my room. I'll bunk with Gray."

"I have to live with her too?"

"Do you have a problem with her?" Arden asked.

"No, it's just that I'd finally come to terms with life at the Gig Shack, but I hadn't expected that the Gig Shack would live here. I need a break. I'm off to NYC."

Which brings up another story. A neighbor came to the Shack and asked me to hire his grandson for the summer. The kid was supposed to have had experience in kitchens, and we were looking for someone with knife skills. It sounded like a perfect combination. The grandfather finally got the kid to show up for an interview. The kid was shaking, he could barely stand still, and it was obvious he was on drugs. Tracey offered him a job as a courtesy to his frustrated grandparents. He never showed. Maybe he did have knife skills, but from what I later learned, it wasn't in a kitchen.

While I was back in New York playing dentist that week, Nico blossomed as head chef, devising a new fish-oriented menu. He concocted clam chowders and a fabulous fish stew. He smoked pork ribs like a Shixza-dasha son. He jerked chickens the Antiguan way. The food was getting a top-chef following, and the joint was constantly jumping. Foodies were blogging us from London, Paris, and the west.

Nico also started dating Elani, who had fully recovered from her car accident. They made an attractive couple. She knew that he had a girlfriend named Emma, who still lived in Antigua, but as Crosby and Stills suggested, "Love the one you are with."

The other young men in the kitchen stretched their cooking comfort zone too. Gray and his friends were the chefs, artistically finishing fish sauces, dressing the bass and flounder with a vibrantly colored palette. Each plate arrived as a tastefully designed work of art. The youthful energy erupted, just the way my wife had planned. As parents and bosses, we were astounded and amazed.

Upon returning to Montauk that Thursday night, I closed one mental compartment and reopened my Gig Shack state of mind. The softball team was playing the Memory Motel again and one of the umpires fell ill, so I was elected to that job.

"Please be careful, dear," Tracey pleaded. "The other team looks awfully large."

"I'm only calling outs. I'm not planning on fighting them," I teased.

"Well you be careful out there. The Gig Shack is still operating as a non-for-profit. If you got injured, we'd be in a serious hole." She adjusted the lapels of my tailored city suit. "We'd just go bust without your pedestal."

Just like my old Little League days, I confidently strolled out to the playing field and introduced myself to the other team. The shortest player on their team immediately got in my face. "Who are you?" He spat his syllables on my polished Oxfords.

"I'm the new ump," I responded, wiping my shoe on the grass. They say a man should dress for the job he wants and not the one he has, in which case, I was just wrong for this role. The player's eyes raked my Italian, tailored, city-slicker outfit.

"You just come from a DWI in court?" In his limited attire experience, that was the only reason a real man would wear a suit. "I hope you last longer than the last ump. A few bad calls and he accidentally got bulldozed off second base. He's still in the hospital with a broken wrist. You be careful now." He winked.

"Play ball!" I adjusted my linen lapel and positioned behind second base.

The game got off to a quick start. Our first player hit a double, and the next drove him home. Our best player hit an inside the park home run. We weren't as powerful as those big palookas, but our kids sure could run the bases.

When it was their turn, that same short guy hit a mean line drive over third base. It was a clean single, but he was so aggressive that he tried to turn it into a double. He bore down on Sky, our second baseman. The runner's expression was a deep-seated desire for punishment and pain. We waited for the long thrown from Gray in the outfield. Sky's back was turned away from the pint-sized bulldozer. My first reaction was to yell to Sky to watch out for the collision. I held my breath and any warning. As umpire, I was torn; should I protect my son from this bully or wait out the call on the play? Time stood still as clouds of moths and flies gathered under the glaring overhead lights of Lion's Field. The runner drove feet-first through the air into second base, his sharpened cleats intent on striking my son's naked calf. The baseball shot toward the heart of Sky's outstretched glove, the seams spinning counterclockwise as if in molecular motion, the Big Bang, E=Mc squared, the energy, matter and time stopping equilibrium.

How did I get myself in this position? What would the Dalai Lama say? It was a lose-lose situation. If I called the runner safe, our team would lose. If I called him out, the big bouncers on the other team would kill me.

The ball popped into Sky's mitt, and with an elegant sweep behind his back, he caught the pointed toe, right before the guy hit him and the base. They both tumbled in a dusty cloud to the ground, and it was seconds before the air cleared and I could determine that he'd held onto the ball. "Out!"

"What? Are you fucking blind?" The runner jumped up and down, pulling a Lou Piniella. He cursed, grabbed the base, and threw it into the outfield. His eyes glared like a wild man as he ran right up to me. "You're fucking blind, old man!"

"I may be blind, but you're still out." I strolled back to my position.

"Good call, ump," Sky and the rest of the team chorused, acting as if they'd just met me and I was an impartial observer. Who knows, maybe the guy was safe.

The game continued much the same way. The guys from the Memory Motel heckled my every call. I wondered if they'd treated Mick Jagger the same way when he'd slept there. Eventually, I got fed up with their abuse.

In the bottom of the ninth, that same runner, who was half my height but twice my weight, hit another liner over third base. With a man already on, I was positioned behind second base. As the runner neared, I wandered closer to the bag. The runner took a wide swath, intent on inflicting vengeance. I inched closer to the bag, itching for the fight. As he raced across the base, I stuck out my leg. He tripped and flew head over heels. Sky tagged him out, and we won the game. He got up swinging, and the fight was on.

Actually, that's not what happened. Remembering Tracey's warning, I backed off the bag and protected our family assets. It was only a game.

"I'm a failure as a shill umpire," I said, dusting off my suit.

"That guy was safe at second base, Dad," Gray said, "but thanks for trying."

"You think so? Well, I gave one for the team." Fortunately, that was the last time I was asked to umpire a game. I did enough for these kids. Let some other dad do it.

I was always doing something to help Tracey and the boys, but was I really making myself happy? What does the pedestal need? Is the only goal to support more weight, take on more responsibility, or add more mouths to shoulder? My life was certainly grounded, but I always seemed to be reaching skyward toward some wispy, weightless cloud, an epiphany of real happiness. My pedestal couldn't move. If I stayed quiet and strong, hopefully the light would eventually shine on me.

Tracey and I drove home and shared a bottle of wine. After two glasses, she broke down and cried. "What am I doing?" She'd spent the whole afternoon bookkeeping and now realized the restaurant was losing thousands of dollars a week. Even though we were busy, the expenses far exceeded income. "The Shack is a money pit. Every time I take one step forward, I seem to take two steps back. If it isn't the

Internet breaking down, it's the defroster for the ice cream, or the oven overheats. I can never get ahead. I spend half my day just making appointments for repairs. I never get to bake or hang with my friends. I can't leave the place for a minute without something going wrong. I can't do any more than I'm doing, but the job never gets done."

From past experience, I'd learned that this "what am I doing" was not a question but a statement. She wasn't actually asking me my opinion or for business advice, as in, "What should I do?" The correct response was for me to say nothing, listen to her rant, and maybe close the conversation with a, "You'll figure it out. You always do." I bit my upper lip and held back my words, but the spittle of an opinion throbbed in my throat. If I was going to be the family pedestal, I needed to remain strong, firm, and quiet.

"What am I doing?" She clutched at her collarbone and then, gasping for breath, pounded her temples. She held her head tightly as if to prevent a cerebral explosion, as tears flowed down her face. The weight of so many responsibilities crushed her. She was weakening and in serious need of emotional support.

My comforting column sensed an opening and inched toward my toppling wife. I knew I was falling into her trap. It didn't take three trips to our fancy Sag Harbor headshrinker for me to understand that this predatory praying mantis was baiting me, waiting for me to upchuck some kind word of advice, which was presently stuck in my throat. Feinting a tongued-tied silence, I listened to the frogs mating down in Fort Pond Bay and stood as still as a statue.

"What am I doing?" She spoke those words for a third time as she held her head in her hands and sobbed. Black streaks of mascara egged her face.

Seething with frustration, I wanted to hold her tight in my arms, and yes, I wanted very badly to make love to her. That's what pedestals do; we're not very complicated, but we are always phallic. Form follows function.

Her tears shed like tender drooping branches, willows to water.

An inconsolable anger at the beach bullies who were terrorizing my beautiful wife surged in my chest. She had given so much and the dumbasses just didn't get it, or more truthfully, they didn't want it.

On hearing her hook a third time, I swallowed the bait. I broke down and told my thin-skinned wife my opinion. For the next hour, I lectured her about the "will."

"The will is the ability to survive in business, no matter what they toss at you or how many doors they close. Nietzsche's 'the will' encompasses creative energy, delegation of duty, and hard work. You lead by example. The will requires a psychic strength of character and clear direction. It's much easier to create a business than maintain it. You must have the will to carry your staff and business through adversity. You're the general who must lead to win. Willpower is persistence and perseverance."

Thoughtful, she leaned against the coffee table and received my words attentively, but her willingness to act independently overcame her business sense of self-preservation. Tracey may be thin skinned, but she surely was sharp toothed. "Thank you for the advice, but I could have used 49 percent less of it." She shook her forefinger in my face.

I won't bore you with the ugly details. The praying mantis wife handed back the other 51 percent of my head on a silver platter. Let me give you Montauk boys a piece of Man-talk, a little legal logic, maybe a marriage moral: never advise your wife about the will until you are already dead.

Chapter 29

The Neighbors

Darwin and I have the same evolutionary theory, which in a nutshell, boils down to survival of the happiest. People do what will make them most happy. So when an individual complains all the time about their shitty existence, it's because it makes them happy to complain. They can complain all they want; we just don't have to listen.

Our neighbor loved to complain, so I must assume it made him happy. He complained about the live music, the location of our heater system, the benches we placed on the sidewalk for the public to sit on. The problem was, he never complained directly to me. The stoolie loved to call the building department behind my back.

He was getting on my nerves. I should have ignored his complaining, but I'll admit I was listening. I needed some conflict resolution, so I decided to confront my chronically complaining neighbor to determine what was really bothering him. My secret to conflict resolution is conciliation. Ask your adversary what's bothering them, and when you know what it is, you can attempt to fix it.

I knew if I approached from the front, like the hermit crabs at the beach, he would have seen me coming and dashed inside his shop, so I decided to surprise him from the rear. Sneaking up from the side street, I caught him facing west. I stood in front of the door to his shop, blocking the entrance into his hole.

"Hey, Killer, how goes it, neighbor? Brilliant day, isn't it?"

The hermit crab quickly caught his breath. His jowls pinched, and behind his oversized glasses, his beady eyes searched for a way out of this uncomfortable confrontation. He sniffed the air to figure my drift. "What do you want?"

"I'm just saying hello, passing through. How are the kids? Your son's a nice boy. Is he planning to go to college?" I looked inside to see if there were witnesses.

The conversation was entirely too personal. "Fuck you!" he spat.

"Ah, come on, Killer. Why you got to be cursing like that?"

"I hate your fucking guts." His nose purpled with anger.

"I just got off the Jitney." I was taken aback by the intensity. He made a sudden feint to the left, but I continued to block his escape. His only outlet was toward the Gig Shack, a direction I knew he'd never retreat to. "What did I do to you?"

"Fuck you. You burnt my fucking grass, you bastard." He made a fist.

He had me at crosshairs. I didn't approve of his cursing and I definitely wanted to punch him in his face, but that would have inflamed the situation. My primary objective was to help my wife, not satisfy my male ego, so I changed tactics. I blamed it on a third party, the employees. "Show me what happened. I promise I'll get to the bottom of it and reprimand the culprit, if my employees truly did this."

His stance softened, but the expectant body blow still came. "Ah, fuck you. I hate your fucking family." He dove back into his hole.

I let him pass. "I'm in good company. You hate everybody." I retreated to the Gig Shack feeling unsatisfied. Maybe he'd gotten the last swing, the final verbal punch. He wasn't such a dummy after all. Next time, I'd come prepared with a better retort.

Nico showed me the patch of grass he'd accidentally damaged the previous night. It wasn't really burnt and would re-grow in a few days. I made a mental note to buy Killer a bag of seed. It was merely a mental note. I never actually did it.

To be fair to Killjoy and his family, they had grounds for being angry. They lived above their store and had to be awake by 6:00 AM to service insomniac souvenir shoppers, but they had chosen to reside in a downtown business district and should have accepted some noise. Initially, his son and wife were cordial to our arrival, but when they realized we would have live music, their upper lips stiffened. She actually lobbied the other businesses to have us shut down, but most of the neighbors loved us and hated them. Satisfying these people would be a true test of my resolution skills.

I asked the mayor of Montauk, the hardware store owner, to intervene.

"There's nothing you can do with those people," he advised.

I asked the prince of Montauk, the owner of the liquor store, for advice.

"Good luck," he smiled knowingly.

When we'd purchased the building, we had some insight into the complicated permits, which was never legalized as a change of use, a zoning designation, from the preexisting retail/ice cream parlor to restaurant. This would come to haunt us later, but had we flown under the radar as a quiet café, we probably would have gotten away with it. The code enforcers are a reactionary force responding to complaints; they're not out there looking for extra work. Killer kept complaining to them about the noise.

In hindsight, we should have done a better job of policing the musicians and reaching out to the neighbors to determine if there was an acceptable time and place.

I'd mentioned this proactive concept to Tracey, but by then it was probably too late.

"You're wasting your spit trying to make peace with him," she argued. "He hates everybody, and there's nothing you can do."

In the meantime, Tracey was having troubles with other neighbors. The women who ran the deli kept complaining that our staff was parking in their designated spaces. Since our building had been defunct for an extensive period of time, they'd become accustomed to the notion that the whole rear parking lot belonged to them. Although it was a public right of way, which no one owned, they felt so entitled that they didn't even want our staff parked behind our own building.

I sweet talked the deli girls and promised that the staff would move their cars. All the employees obliged, except for Skylar, who continued to park his big blue Ford pickup, which had been tattooed with our logo, behind the Shack.

"Sky, could you please move your truck? I promised the ladies."

"What did they ever do for us?"

"You're right, but we have enough problems already. We don't need to piss off the whole neighborhood. It's not about right or wrong."

"I'm not moving my car. I have as much right to park behind my store as they do." He thumped back to unloading beer cases.

I went behind his back and complained to Tracey, who was unsympathetic. "What did they ever do for us? All they do is complain."

"I'm just trying to make peace with your neighbors."

"Who asked you to make peace?" She stomped back to her baking.

My profitless attempts as "shill peacekeeper" came to naught. So I went back to my other job, afternoon bartender. After restocking the wine and beer, Sky often went surfing. The bar didn't get busy till later, so I stepped in for a few hours.

Though a poor admiral to Sunday's captain's dinner, I enjoyed hosting strangers at the bar. There were short bursts of noncommittal conversations: "Where are you from?" followed with my own elaborated explanations and job descriptions—"We moved here after 9/11. It's my wife and sons' restaurant. I'm just the silent partner." Having exhausted myself on myself, I offered free holistic dental advice. For the price of a beer, I tended a cure for all ails of oral issues.

That afternoon, the son from another restaurant came into my little outside bar. He introduced me to his new girlfriend.

"You got any O'Doul's? I've got to stop drinking; I got a DUI last night," he said.

His girlfriend held his arm tightly and appeared scared. "No beer for him, please."

"Two O'Doul's on the house. Welcome, neighbors," I said.

"Thanks." He took a deep, unsatisfied swig of the low-alcohol beer and wiped his lips. "It's impossible staying sober in this town. Every restaurant pushes alcohol."

"Well, I'll support your sobriety. I'll never sell you a beer. Don't even ask."

"You're kidding, right?" He frowned. "How will you make any money?"

"No, I'm completely serious. I support your sobriety."

The notion seemed to make him uncomfortable. He put down the dregs of his drink, but as they were leaving, his girlfriend turned and blew me a "thank you."

The afternoon sun sizzled and the customers baked on the beach, so there wasn't much business in "shill bartending." You never heard of a shill bartender? In the old days of prohibition, Montauk was a popular port for the offshore still. I could uncork a bottle or pop the head off a can, but God forbid they wanted a real drink.

The restaurant business has more titles than the U.S. Army. Looking for another unofficial job, I went out front for a walk, where I ran into Shaggy, taking a smoke.

"I'm surprised, you guys are getting busy," he tossed us the off-hand compliment. Maybe he was getting a little annoyed we were stealing all his business, but we were bringing a New York work effort to the table. These other established restaurants just threw the food at the customers. "This is the easy part of the hundred days of hell. There are more mouths in Montauk than there are plates to feed them. All you got to do is be open." He inhaled deeply on the cigar. "Wait till the Dog Days of November."

There was more to good service than merely being open, but he'd been in the business for forty years; if anyone knew the secret to the hundred days, it was he. "The wife's is working her ass off. I hardly get to see her," I complained.

"Get used to it or get a mistress," he advised.

"I'm getting fed up with Killer's harassment too. He keeps calling the police."

"That crazy bastard. When I owned your place, he came in once, complaining of the noise. I kicked his ass onto the street. That's the only thing he respects. He's been fighting for thirty years with the owners of your building. You would think by now he'd be tired of the game. He's got to have something to lose."

"So what does he have to lose?" I asked.

"I heard he was into ..." and he whispered the rumor in my ear. Blushing, the troublemaker retreated back to his bar.

I went back to work too, but none of my family was there. Tracey drove by the Shack on my scooter, having gone home to change. God, my wife was hot. She looked ravishing in her blue dress, the wind uplifting the hem in a Marilyn Monroe moment. The yoga girls referred to her as Motorcycle Mama, but her more commonly used nickname was the Montauk Madonna. Arden confided in me once that it was hard having a mother that all your friends wanted to do.

Being an inexperienced moped rider, she brought the bike around the front, crossing the sidewalk illegally in front of Killer's store. As she passed, Killjoy jumped out from his doorway, raised his hairy arms, stuck out his oversized belly, and yelled like a mean old bear, "Ahhhhhh!"

Frightened by his sudden appearance, the bike skidded off the sidewalk. She almost crashed in front of the Shack.

I ran out and helped her off the moped.

"Did you see what he just did?" She was shaking from the near accident.

"It's time that beach bully got a licking." I rolled up the sleeves of my signature all-white outfit—Lands' End loose collarless cotton shirt overhanging belt-less pants. Probably not the best outfit for a fistfight, but what the hell, my actions weren't premeditated. Anyway, what would be the proper attire to match the occasion?

"What are you doing?" she asked, having calmed down.

"Should I go home and change for the fight? Shaggy said it worked for him."

"Shaggy is your new role model? Husband, thank you for playing my white knight, but you are a lover and not a fighter. When was the last time you hit anybody?"

I thought for a few minutes. "Arden, when he was eight and broke the window."

She giggled. "You're the only man who has ever made me laugh out loud. Forget about Killer; he's not worth the spit. Our best revenge will be our success. I'm not injured. He just scared me. I probably shouldn't have been driving on the sidewalk."

The rest of the afternoon was spent playing mental mind games, plotting my nonviolent revenge. Should I run with Shaggy's rumor? What was the weak link in the souvenir business? Self-cast lead weights, worn plastic worms, or personal indiscretions?

Chapter 30

The Mango in Montauk

The famous Polish actress, Veronica, joined me on a quest to find Jimmy Buffet. She came armed with a camera and the limited knowledge that he lived in a surfer shack.

"My love. You must help search for this Jimmy Buffet. My dearest Bobby is in fan with him and I must get picture for our little Love Shack." She spoke in the overly exaggerated style of the European stage, each gesture an artistically relevant movement. "Please, my love, you know where he live? Some shack here in Montauk."

"I guess he'd have a place down by the surfer beach in Ditch, maybe the trailer park? Shall we go?" I chauffeured the famous actress to the beach. Now I had a new job, celebrity spotter. It didn't pay well, but it passed the time.

"You think Tracey would want to come?" our New York City houseguest asked.

"That's okay, she has to work." Our guest had overstayed her visit and was starting to smell like old fish.

We drove to the trailer park and attempted to sneak in the gated community from the beach, but it required walking over wet rocks and through some surf. Veronica couldn't swim and was afraid of the ocean. What would you expect from the Polish?

Instead, we jumped the fence, landing in a time-warp town of little fixer-uppers, trailers moored onto foundations with well-kept gardens and cable TV. Like little Stepford families, groups of neatly dressed and well-behaved children ran between the bushes. The mighty ocean licked the near slope of the protective dune. That ocean was one good storm away from reclaiming this shill community for its shell collection.

"My love. There are so many tiny houses. Which way should we walk?"

Not having a plan, I pointed east. We walked past about a dozen houses before spotting a sign, "Jimmy lives here."

"You are genius. You found him already."

"I'm not so sure." The house was in disrepair, a half-assembled swing in the yard.

"Okay, we try more. I think his house is red," she claimed.

"Well now we have something to work with." We kept walking. Closer to the beach, we found a bigger, more modern version. It was painted red. The sign on the mailbox read, Jimmy's. There were assorted surfboards parked on the fence. "This looks more like it." A guitar lay unused against the bench. As I spoke, a fifty-year-old man exited the back door and started waxing a board.

"You are a genius," she whispered. "That's him!"

"Are you sure? That guy looks older than I'd expect."

"I don't know. I thought you would have recognized Jimmy."

The man appeared about the right body type, but I'd never met Jimmy in person.

"There's only one way." I walked over to his board. "Sir, excuse me, sir."

He turned toward us, uncertain what two tourist voyeurs wanted.

"My friend here is supposed to have a meeting with a Mr. Jimmy Buffet. Do you know where he lives?" Veronica came up behind and waved shyly.

"I am famous Polish actress," she pronounced in her best English.

The man laughed. "You think he lives here?"

"I wouldn't recognize Jimmy Buffet, even if I ran into him," I admitted.

The man retorted, "He wouldn't recognize you either."

"We are getting warmer." She waved.

Veronica and I walked the long way back to the exit. The once-mobile bungalows had each been decorated in their own style. We counted at least five more "Jimmy lives here," signs along the way. "This guy got around more than old George Washington." I added, "Maybe this isn't the Montauk Project but Margaritaville."

We gave up the search, drove by the Bones, and ran into Mac in the parking lot. "Hey Mac, Mac Cool, this is Veronica."

"Hello, I am famous Polish actress."

"Sure and I'm one of the Montauk Lost Boys."

"You wouldn't know where Jimmy Buffet lives?" I asked.

"He's in here all the time. You want to meet him?"

"You get celebrities in here and no one called me. Your mother is so damn competitive. She's probably worried I'd steal one."

Leslie heard my comment and shot me a dirty look. "Did you see my write-up in the *East Hampton Star*?" She proudly pulled out this week's restaurant review. "I guess they only review real restaurants," she said, an obvious reference to our non-stellar status. She read the article out loud so we could all hear. In summary, the review tended toward the negative, sighting the lovely location but inadequate food. "For some strange reason, the chef had disappeared the day the reviewer came for lunch."

"That sucks. Where was Fabio?" I asked.

"He took his daughter to the train station and stayed for lunch. I think your place."

"These reviewers don't give you any warning, do they?" I tried to put a positive spin. "At least you got in the *Star*. They've completely ignored our Shack so far."

Veronica and I walked down to the dock and snapped a picture of her sitting in the back of Jimmy's boat, *The Last Mango*. He wasn't there, but she was happy. Later that day, our ex-bartender had a fender bender with Jimmy over at the cottages. I'm not going to tell where he lives, but I'm available for hire. Job number thirty on my checklist, shill celebrity tour guide.

That evening, we closed the Shack and hosted a staff party at our house. The boys invited a lot of friends. There were more cars parked in front of our house than at Cyril's and the Surf Lodge combined. Hot pepper and Christmas lights were adorned across the backyard, giving our home a festive air. Three kegs were parked up in the woods, and Nico manned the barbeque pit, cooking a whole pig stuffed with a huge striped bass holding a porgy in its mouth—a Porgie the Pig roast.

Sky and his band of unknowns jammed, Tracey and I gave a tango performance, and a new employee from Vermont demonstrated belly dancing. Most of the boys were shirtless, showing off their manly tans, and the young ladies wore short skirts without heels. Two beer pong tables fought tunes late into the night. It was the party of the summer. Even the Irish said so, "Brilliant!"

Steve, the head Irish, slapped me on the back and congratulated me on raising such a fine family. "In Ireland, we never party with our dads. You are legend."

"I am legend?" I asked.

"That's this year's brilliant. Next year, gross will be the new brilliant?"

If I'd been a better father, I might have caught the party on videotape, but that would be evidence. With paparazzi around, it's dangerous to be a legend nowadays.

I'd knocked back a couple of Buds with the boys, when Tracey grabbed the beer bottle out of my hand and emptied the contents down her throat.

"Hey, what's up, that's my beer," I whined.

She shot a disapproving glance at my waistline. "In my twisted world, I'm doing you a favor." She went back outside.

One young lady had a little too much to drink. She was throwing up into the kitchen sink. There wasn't too much vomit, as she couldn't stomach more than one beer.

I handed her a clean towel.

"You know, all the girls think you are the hottest dad in town." She chuckled.

Clearing my throat, I answered carefully. "Thanks for the compliment, but you're drunk." I searched the room to see if we were alone. Everyone was singing outside.

Hiccupping, she covered her mouth to suppress a burp. "Maybe a little." She giggled and said, "But I'd still do you." Playacting, she held the throw up back with one hand and mimicked her oral technique with the other.

"Sorry, I'm not into vomit blow jobs. Anyway, I'm happily married. I've been monogamous through my whole marriage, although no one believes me."

"I want to be like Tracey when I grow up."

"Don't grow up; it's not what it's cracked up to be." I ran out of there.

Tracey was out back and ready to retire. "These kids can go all night." Her laughter was not quite genuine. "We probably won't have a staff till noon. I'm shot. There's a full moon over Montauk—isn't it romantic? To bed, my dear?" We snuck off and got into bed. Tracey fell asleep five minutes later, without even removing her clothes.

Keyed up by the conversation with the young lady, I read an old copy of the *Star*. After getting through the three pages of obituaries, the headlines were all about Christie Brinkley's divorce. Imagine her poor husband. He'd spent his entire life building a nest egg, the perfect family, and blew it on a quickie with a girl half his age. How would my sons have felt if I'd gone through with the proposition by their drunken friend? Excommunicated. Maintenance was the most difficult part of marriage.

That V-sign Christie flashed outside of court made me sick. What did she win?

All she did was drag her family through the muck. If she had nurtured his intimacy when they were married, she wouldn't be alone nurturing herself with the disunity finger.

You never heard of the unity finger sign? Wrap the full length of the middle finger over the pointer. Tip to tip. Either hand. The two fingers represent happiness, male to female togetherness, unity of purpose and design.

Shaking my own wife awake, I held up my left hand and demonstrated the sign, attempting to have Tracey cross her fingers so that we could high-two them. Her hand withdrew once she realized what was up.

"We aren't teenagers from the ghetto who need special kisses and handshakes. Grow up or save it for the locker room."

"So I should flash you the middle, disunity finger?"

"I need escape from your words. Give me sleep. We don't need to be on top of one another all the time." She rolled over, sighed deeply, and faked sleep. "You're playing the forlorn husband role again."

Regretting that I woke her, I said, "And you are just a grass widow at heart. Send me a surrogate wife. Christie, where are you?"

The next morning at 7:00 AM, I drove over to the Shack to take out two trays of pre-prepared croissants so they could rise and proof. It was my morning routine. Tracey would come around 8:00 AM to bake them off. When I opened the back door, a river of water flowed over my feet and outside. I stepped over the surging water and followed the mighty Nile to its source, the toilet. I turned off the water and plunged the beast with all my might. Obviously, she'd swallowed something that didn't agree with her delicate tubes and was now deep in regurgitation of the contents. My shill plumbing effort failed, so after consultation with the boss, I contacted a professional.

The plumber shook his head. "You got a problem here, burnt out the pump. A new one will cost you $1500." He held up a piece of thin rubber, which was partially torn. "It appears one of your patrons tossed some feminine products and used condoms down your toilet last night. This system is designed with a shredder, but it won't cut condoms. I suggest you put up a sign for the men."

That made sense, but where does one read Man-talk? There are signs prohibiting tossing towels in a toilet, but I'd never seen a sign detailing the correct method to compost a condom, or for that manner, a no sex in our beach toilet poster.

Later that morning, I displayed the evidence of my latest occupation. The job advertisement sounded like a casting call for a superhero. "Wanted: Someone with a strong sense of sewage and willing to oppose the forces of evil."

"Thank you for taking care of the sewage problem. I just couldn't face any more shit," Tracey noted. "Where is waste management when you need them?"

"I got your compost covered."

"Is there anything I can offer in return?"

"Do I have your final permission to hold a tango at the Shack?"

"If you ask me again, I'll change my mind."

"Okay, okay, I just wanted to be sure we were together with this."

"I'm not happy to risk further aggravation and shit from the supervisor. He already told you that dancing tango was illegal. We don't have a dance permit."

"Dance permits don't exist in this town. No one is going to give us permission to dance tango, except on top of a table. I think it's worth the risk and I accept full responsibility. I want it."

"Well then, since you want it so badly, that is the end of this discussion."

Chapter 31

Moon Over Montauk

We had survived the first half of the one hundred days, and now, the Gig Shack was developing a consistent winning formula. With Nico and Gray in the kitchen, Arden and Emily out front, Sky behind the wine and beer bar, Tracey baking and playing hostess, and the Irish handling relief, we were jamming.

The Web site was finally up and running, featuring the music schedule and food specials, and positive food bloggers were rating us four stars.

Setting aside the fact that I have no idea what a Gig Shack is in common parlance, this place is completely awesome. I had the fish tacos, and my girlfriend had the lobster roll. Being from California, I don't expect any fish taco on the East Coast to stand up to those in Mexico. I still believe a traditional fish taco cannot be found in NY State. However, the tacos were fantastic and nontraditional, with a hard taco shell, yummy mango salsa, and perfectly fried fish. The lobster roll was a bunch of fresh lobster on a bed of lettuce on a beautifully spongy brioche roll. The lobster tasted fresh and clean and salty goodness. Imagine this: the next night, we have just finished dinner at another restaurant (where my girlfriend had really bad-inedible-BBQ ribs with sauce that smelled like ammonia) and we had just walked half a mile through one of the most intense rainstorms of our lives. We are totally soaked and freezing. She is hungry. I am tired. We head straight to 668 The Gig Shack to get her some right proper ribs. We sit outside on a miraculously dry park bench-table thingy. I order a cup of homemade white chocolate raspberry gelato and a cupcake. The ribs are fantabulous, smokey, slightly sweet, greasy and thick, and almost completely without sauce. The gelato is equally good … raspberries mixed in with white chocolate, with little white chocolate bonus chunks. Puts Magnolia (and Buttercup) to shame. They have Red Velvet cake too, but it's an awfully long way from Manhattan and I don't think they deliver that far. The other best part: everything was appropriately sweet/salt/greasy, but it all tasted remarkably clean and light. I don't know how they do that—maybe it's some sort of magical power. Now, there's only one question left. What the hell is a gig shack?

The answer to his question was a place to have excellent food at reasonable prices, where customers and staff are encouraged to play music or display their creative process, a modern-day salon. Tracey had infused her food with love, and even though the townies ignored us, the world's hunger was finally taking notice. The Gig Shack had become our Love Shack. She was creating culinary magic, seven days a week.

Surf Lodge's Web site had taken off virally. Initially seeded by professional press agents and marketing gurus, they were in every travel and leisure blog, but their immediate success had drawn the attention of unhappy neighbors. Their site was bombarded by the anti-Surf Lodge locals who were peppering their blog with lousy food reviews and excessive prices and under-performing service complaints, and there was even a billboard plastered as you enter town: Surf Lodge, Go Back to Where You Came From.

The war between the old boys and the new gals was escalating.

In the meantime, we were getting some good press releases. *Newsday's* exploreLI.com mentioned us one day:

Worth checking out is this offbeat little café and bar which features acoustic guitar and jazz musicians on weekends. Tracey owns the informal place, a mom whose three surfer sons, Sky, Arden, and Gray, help out at the Shack. Chef Nico offers what he calls global surf cuisine: quesadilias, ribs, lamburginis (Moroccan spiced lamb sliders), fajitas, *and even paella. Mom does all the baking. Both the carrot cake and the red velvet cake were moist and lush. Lemon meringue pie had a flaky crisp crust, its filling a fine balance of sweet and tart. Chocolate bundt cake was homey and fudgy. The Shack also serves ice cream and gelato, and at breakfast, house-made scones and frittatas. As asset to the town, for sure. Cuisine: Eclectic, Mexican/Spanish, and Luncheonette. Price range: inexpensive (under $15), moderate ($15–$25)*

I showed Tracey the article. "Congratulations," I said.

She didn't seem overly impressed. "I didn't even make the carrot cake that they liked," she said, biting her lip badly. "They're calling us an inexpensive luncheonette."

"They did say you were an asset."

"The *Montauk Sun* published a very positive review." Tracey read the excerpt:

Having dinner around sunset on the outdoor patio at the Gig Shack, I overheard guests at the next table ask one another an honest question about the eatery. So what do you think 668 means? The time has come when the phone number 668 is no longer the only exchange in Montauk. A place like the Gig Shack is a rare gem huddled in the midst of a town on the brink of mushrooming into the full-blown Hamptons.

Paying homage to the surf culture, the boys heed the calling for top-notch dishes that are fun, inventive, and satisfying the craving for a nourishing meal. With a passion for fishing and a penchant for bringing the freshest seafood to the table, Nico has cultivated a menu that mingles South America and Montauk. 668 has become our sanctuary after a long day catching waves.

As the End continues to evolve, the Shack brings us back to the local lineage that holds the key to the real Montauk.

This family has created a much-needed establishment built on a sense of community and dedication to quality, with a commitment to the purest ingredients and the best tasting dishes. It has become a well-known fixture on Main Street with its live music and charm. It's the true sense of family that is the core of 668. A real asset to the community.

The article was typeset with assorted pictures of the staff and food. The genesis of a future plan for a Montauk Music Festival.

When Tracey read the article, tears of joy licked her lips. "Finally, I'm getting a little recognition for all my hard work."

I admitted, "The article was very supportive, and the writer captured the mission statement that you professed. From a literary stand point, I found the writing a bit wordy and repetitive." I tried to retrieve my comment as it escaped my lips.

"If you can't say something nice—"

"I apologize. I always knew you would be a success."

"It's not the *Star*, but it's a start." Tracey, the ever-positive Aries, accepted my apology. Quick apologies are a secret to long marriages.

"I'm going to call them," I said. "You're finally ready for some professional promotion. I've withheld to date, at your request. Can I contact the *Star* now?"

Tracey shrugged her shoulders. She desired their review but secretly feared she would be called a failure. "You can't just call and beg for a review, can you?"

I contacted the head editor of the *Star*, who admitted they'd been lax in getting to us. She said they'd recently hired a new restaurant reviewer.

My many jobs now completed for the day, I went over to Leslie's place for a real drink, as we only served wine and beer, and I needed something stronger. She was playing bartender. "I only serve Absolute," she said.

"That will do. Where's Mac?"

She poured my martini. "Damned if I know. He hasn't been to work in days. Have you tried the skate park?"

I showed Leslie our lengthy review in the *Montauk Sun*. She read the article from cover to cover, but closed it with a frown. "This little rag must like you. How much did it cost? It's not a real newspaper like the *Star*," she professed.

"I haven't had any success getting them to print any of my releases. I think I'm going to drop into their office and make them an offer they can't refuse."

"You might try advertising in their paper. I hear they review their own first."

There was some commotion in the rear kitchen. Leslie rolled her eyes. "These male chefs, I'd swear they're all drug addicts or drunks. Next year, I'm hiring a female chef." She yelled back toward her kitchen: "Drop dead, asshole!"

"Sounds promising. An all-female staff, an Absolute Amazon."

She rolled her eyes, now at me. "If you'll excuse me, I have work to do. This drink's on me, and thanks for looking in on my boy. He could use a man in his life."

I downed the dregs of my drink and went looking for Mac, who was kicking back with some young babes along the outside bank of the skate park. He was dressed in a striped one-piece, turn of the century bathing suit, and wore museum quality sneakers, signed by the famous graffiti artist, Snow.

I waved to him from my car, but he ignored me, intent on chatting up the chicks. Why would a sixteen-year-old kid want to be seen talking to some old guy? I wasn't his parent. Finally, he excused himself from the gang and waved me over.

"How's it going, Mac? I hear you're not working at mom's restaurant anymore."

"Like them Lost Boys of Wexford, I'm loyal to lost causes."

"You're my guru. What's my Hampton Horoscope say today?"

He smiled broadly at that reference and pulled out this week's magazine. "Oley, Gemini. Tis a good one," he said in a false brogue. "If you've had writer's block, it's officially ended. Get going! You have two books in you. Publishers will paw all over you, and you love the attention. Remember, the magic number for Gemini's is two (two of each: books, spouses, pets, houses, cars, lovers, phones, sets of friends)."

"The full moon really brings out the heat, but I'm not ready for a second spouse. I took your advice, though. I'm stretching my limits. I'm writing a memoir about my family's experience opening a restaurant in the Hamptons. It's a silly folly, but the writing has been a cathartic experience. She never offered me a job that I wanted, and writing gives me something to do all day while Tracey and the boys are working."

"What does the old lady say?"

"She refuses to read it."

"Well, well, aren't you the chump. The unfair sex?"

"She's afraid and I'm afraid. I've tried to be honest and courageous with my comments, but I think if she reads her caricature, she'll want a divorce."

"And your seed?"

"Also refuse. I read Sky and Morgan one chapter, but when I mentioned Sandra's patois, they got up and left the room. Arden wants to know if a son can sue his father for slander. Gray generally ignores me."

"That bad, huh? Well, I'd be your rapt reader."

"Brilliant, I'll send you pages. Tell me about Tracey's horoscope this week."

"Being a bit personal, like checking the old girl's e-mail?"

"Been there, done that, nothing interesting to tell."

He leaned into his Irish accent. "Riddle me this. Will the year of our lord read two thousand and ten, two ten, or will it be called twenty ten?"

"Two thousand and ten sounds right to me; after all, you only get to play the first century once in each millennium."

"Mine thoughts exactly."

"Screw the skate park, that's a waste of your creativity; you should play a gig at the Shack reading palms. I have the perfect table in mind."

"Gig, jig, fig. It's all artistic creation to me. We Joycians confuse Genesis with Guinness a lot. I'm off to study in that Donnybrook of Debauchery, Shaggy's Saloon. Only he offers my drug of choice. Any guess what condition my condition will be?"

There was something different in his complexion that day. A pallid lifelessness haloed his eyes, the telltale grassy sign of liver toxicity. "You be careful, there are some bad people hanging around there." He didn't look well and smelled even worse.

"You forget, I know my way around a bar, and if I got lost, Shaggy has enough signs plastered on the street to lead even a good boy astray."

"The restaurant business isn't for everyone. You're an artist by nature."

"Fair rebel, I am happier than you shall ever be. I'll not dicker Montauk's motley crew, the canteens' wreak, white lines of snuff and stuff, and the little lies from thirsty fishermen. If Humpty Dumpty I should be, then so shall I be. It's not up to you," he giggled for a moment, "or to me."

Chapter 32

The Man-talk in Montauk

In *The Art of Happiness*, a psychiatrist asks the Dalai Lama the diagnosis of a middle-aged man who is good-looking, wealthy, healthy, and has a loving wife and children, but is still depressed. The man has everything but perceived happiness. The wise man thought for a while and then shrugged his shoulders. "Beats me," he confessed.

The newly found success of the Gig Shack created fresh stresses on my marriage. Just as I'd feared, Tracey was virtually living at the Shack. We didn't have much private time together. She was working from breakfast through dinner, baking scones and muffins for delivery to the Surf Lodge in the morning and hosting at night.

On my return Thursday night, the joint was already packed. Pretty young things were milling about, snacking on tacos or sipping beer, a seven-day bacchanal. The suck-you-bus Shack had taken over my wife, my family, and my life. It was really "Big!"

"I need to find a young baker. This is ridiculous," she confessed. We shared espresso and croissants at an outside booth. It was a magical morning in Montauk.

"Has the Lodge paid you yet for the delivery?" I asked.

"No, I figure by the end of summer, I can barter my whole bill for dinner and a bottle of champagne. At their prices, I'll probably end up owing them money."

"Maybe you should raise your prices." Oops, I've said too much again. Why couldn't I ever learn to just shut up and listen?

Her face pinched into a why-don't-you-mind-your-own-business frown. The conversation would have turned downhill if I didn't find a quick way out. I chose self-pity. "I feel as if I'm constantly in your way." I lowered the critical octaves. My words had a softening effect. She was smiling.

"Nonsense, you are the way." She held my calloused hand in her own. "We must be more patient with one another. Cheers!" We clinked espresso cups. "To thicker skin."

"I'll drink to that, but if yours doesn't toughen, I'll rub you down with Teflon."

Tracey retreated to her kitchen, and I sat out front, soaking up the morning sun.

A local guy sat down nearby and ordered a coffee. We exchanged pleasantries: "How are the kids?" and "How's business?" and "How's the wife?"

"I'm getting divorced!" he said. "I'm sick of the bitch."

"You've been married twenty years. What happened?" I asked.

"She just doesn't make me happy anymore."

He came back later for dinner accompanied by his new girlfriend. He wasn't being very discreet, courting a new gal in the same town as the old. If it were a divorce he sought, this would be a self-fulfilling prophecy.

As the summer progressed, it seemed to me that more and more long-married couples were getting separated. Maybe it was the bad economy or a bad run of luck, but marriages in Montauk were falling quicker than the value of our savings.

Amid this epidemic of marital strife, Nico's girlfriend, Emma, arrived, blown like a cross-Atlantic sailboat, off-course and in need of a good rudder.

We had met Emma the previous winter while scurrying for cover on a remote, treeless beach, in a torrential thunderstorm in Antigua. The Caribbean waves washed warmer than the hailing rain, and while we waited at least two hours, sitting in the sea for the sky to clear, Emma produced a campfire from nothing more than rescued coconut husks and rubbed wood—the barely there, string bikini, her only cover from the elements. The girl was persistent, cooking Nico's hand-caught lobsters and rockfish over the objections of the less adventurous.

We had gone to Antigua to kidnap Nico and bring him back as the chef.

He preferred the simple life of Caribbean fisherman and declined our request.

The managerial gender mix was now screwed toward the estrogenic. Emma shared front of house duties with Emily. They also shared a love for complaining.

"Nico works too many hours," complained Emma. "I never see him."

"There aren't any good looking, single men in Montauk," Emily lamented.

"Fire Elani, or I quit." Emma had already gotten wind of that quick affair. The head chef working with his two girlfriends was a recipe for disaster.

Tracey did her best to accommodate the two young ladies, hiring more cooks so Nico could take time off and be with Emma, and introducing Emily to cute surfer dudes. She paid them more than the other employees and more than they were worth.

"What else can I do to make them happy?" Tracey worried.

"Don't listen. They're both negative people who love to complain," I advised.

"I don't want Emma to leave and take Nico with her, like our first chef. Actually, I wish she would leave. I don't really like her, but Nico does."

Elani played the professional and offered to move on to another restaurant. "Nico is more important to the success of the Shack than I am." What a girl.

Tracey hired a young lady, Tim's sixteen-year-old cousin, to help with the baking. She had restaurants in her blood and immediately picked up Tracey's recipes for pastries and desserts. Watching her develop under my wife's wings, it was obvious that one day this kid would be a kitchen star. It was a pleasure observing their student/teacher relationship blossom. I wondered what would have happened had we a daughter instead of three sons.

Tim had changed from that floppy-haired, clumsy runner who'd cut his hands in a food fight with a customer earlier in the season. Now he had a self-assured waiter attitude and would often cover shifts by himself.

Nico was maturing right before our eyes. The once hesitant "I can't do the job" boy had become a man, running the kitchen staff as if he'd been doing it for years, with unlimited energy and enthusiasm. It's often said that the best chefs are less than twenty-five years of age.

Our sons were growing up too quickly and finally realized the empowerment of owning a restaurant in the Hamptons. Gorgeous, ravenous, young ladies were circling them like bluefish to a black hole of bait, dashing in for dates, hoping to gobble up the little princes. We had the best-looking staff and customers in town.

Their commitment to the restaurant business was clearly growing; there would be no future dentists from this seed. Sky had a definite desire to stay in town and manage the place, although he had no plans for the off-season. Gray enrolled for the winter semester in the French Culinary Institute to learn the art of artesian bread baking. Arden had made it clear from the get-go that he would only help for this one season and then wanted to take a job in NYC in marketing. He had bigger fish to fry than our little joint, and there wasn't enough here long-term for all three of them.

Tracey and I had found some homeostasis too. Her skin had thickened to my perceived criticism, and I had retreated from offering so much advice. With the staff stable, we were able to take afternoons off and sneak out to the beach or idle alone in our backyard. I had started this memoir and didn't feel the need to micromanage the place, although I still filled in when they needed a pair of hands to dice an onion or wait a table.

All was not perfect in paradise, though. Emily, our houseguest/manager, had found herself a new boyfriend, an older surfer dude from Hawaii, who had suddenly moved in with us. A good-looking professional beach bum, he offered me one of his hand-carved, signed surfboards in lieu of room and board.

The front of the house had never made a clear commitment to waiter service. Often the staff would hang back behind the inner counter, watching the customers seat themselves. This was particularly irritating to my business head and pocketbook. At least 25 percent of the potential customers walked up, took a peek, and left. When I hosted, I closed the deal, immediately offering the customers a choice of tables and a warm welcome. I was no shill host. I was a real closer, filling the front street-side bistro tables first. Unfortunately, none of the staff took this aggressive seating posture, a byproduct I believe of Scott's arrogance and Tracey's fear of self-promotion.

The staff, being young and related to the owners, wasn't always reliable. Gray's crew disappeared to surf when the tide was in, Arden and Nico disappeared when a blitz hit the beach (fishing poles in the closet), and Sky hung out back with his crew.

One afternoon, after I'd filled all the front tables in five minutes, Arden complained, "You're not helping. The waiters are assigned tables. When you fill the front first, it creates a lopsided arrangement, which confuses us. Go home and write the Great American Novel." His comments hurt, particularly because he was wrong. I may not have worked in this business, but as a longtime customer, I know the policy of filling front tables first was the twelfth commandment. Other restaurants had a policy of shifting staff to deal with typical early evening discrepancies. Why couldn't we?

There were never any meetings (at least when I was around) where the entire staff could review policy and discuss problems. People were on different chaotic schedules, coming and going as each saw fit. If that TV restaurant-makeover guy ever interviewed them, he would have had a field day.

Emily was in charge of the schedule, but there was no way she would listen to me. She was my boss now and took great pride in treating me like a servant when I voluntarily bused the tables. She sat in the corner like a pompous prom queen, pointing out my errors of service: "Look, you missed one. Go back and sweep again. That table is still dirty. Use a clean rag next time." There was something wrong with this picture, but I couldn't complain to Tracey about her protégé. All I could do was not help, which wasn't in my nature. Sometimes, I wondered if Tracey secretly instructed Emily to punish me.

The kitchen was offering coffee and pastries for breakfast, but the staff refused to serve eggs. That required awaking before noon. The bar often ran short of kegs on busy weekends, and boxes of Belgium Rogue simply disappeared. I had my suspicions as to who the culprits were, but Tracey accepted the kegs having legs as part of doing business. Fortunately, the staff didn't like wine, which was more expensive to replace. If Leslie learned of our leakage, she would have laughed us out of town.

Nico was experimenting with duck confit as a new entrée. He smoked the duck overnight in brine and herbs. It was a spectacular dish, cold over salad, or composted into the taco. One afternoon, a woman and child walked in for lunch and stared at the menu with a quizzical face. After a few minutes of confusion, she turned to me and said, "Excuse me, sir. What's this duck confetti?" She must have been related to the couple that thought ceviche was a Mexican beer and a Lamburgini, a fast car.

Frantic, Tracey called me in New York City the next day. "A large family came for lunch. After they had consumed the entire meal, the woman complained that she'd just found a three-inch nail in her taco. Not a bone splinter or a tack, mind you; she actually produced a large nail. Nico made the taco himself and called them liars."

"They probably carry the nail from place to place," I suggested.

"They threatened to contact the board of health. Naturally, I offered the meal as complimentary, but then they wanted more. They threatened legal action."

"Did anyone bite into the nail?"

"How am I supposed to know?"

"It sounds like a scam. I often get patients who complain that they broke a tooth during a meal, but it's usually a preexisting condition."

"They sure had me convinced."

"The schemers taste blood. Restaurant sharks."

"I'm going to call the board of health and notify them in advance," she said.

"I'd hold off on notifying the health department that you're serving nails."

No one called the health department and the incident was soon forgotten, but it's amazing how many crooks latch into the food business. Another restaurant owner told me about an incident where a customer consumed an entire lobster, and then called over the waiter to complain that it was undercooked. The kitchen offered a second serving, which she consumed, but complained it was overcooked. She loved the third lobster, but she couldn't pay the check because she had American Express and they only accepted Visa.

Chapter 33

Skishing

Arden and Nico had gone to nursery school together in Battery Park City. Nico's father, a famous photographer for *National Geographic*, had moved the family to Antigua and later to Colorado. When he was about twelve, Nico's grandparents rented a summerhouse in Montauk, where the two dock rats ran into one another casting for squid one night with flashlights and umbrella rigs; their friendship blossomed as they hauled.

They were both one with the water. Over the years, their fish love had migrated from surfcasting, where one dons waiters and casts from the flat shore using ten-foot poles (only for the old men and Googens), to rock hanging, where they cast from pervious perches beneath the lighthouse, to extreme surfcasting, where they place spikes on their boots and cast out from submerged boulders, to skishing, a daredevil, deep-water Navy Seal sport. Wearing wetsuits, flippers, neoprene gloves, and a large knife for cutting line, they swim offshore, buoyant in the drifting current, casting with live eels for striped bass. If the bass are big enough, they will troll the boys for a Montauk sleigh ride. Unless the fish is a keeper over twenty-eight inches, they are released to fight again.

This season's sport was spear fishing. Swimming out about a hundred feet offshore, they free-dived and waited at the bottom for the large bass to break by. Spear fishing in these cloudy waters was not for the fainthearted, as sharks and schools of razor-sharp teethed blue fish were attracted to the scent of the trailing blood.

Nico and Arden arrived to work in their wetsuits, turned down at the waist, exposing their tan, well-carved bodies. The middle-aged women, who had timed their coffee break, swooned over the unbridled runway models prancing through the kitchen.

One afternoon, Arden, obviously agitated about something, slammed doors and kicked the wall of the house, just like when he was a little kid.

"What happened to you—your trophy fish get away?" I kidded.

"I don't want to talk about it."

"Come on, I'm your father, maybe I can help."

"Leave me alone! I don't want to talk!" he yelled back and slammed the door.

"It's either girl or fish problems. You hooked up with a mermaid? I understand. Your mother's a lifetime member of shixza-dasha, the maternal organization of blonde Shixzas married to Jewish doctors." My stab at humor completely missed.

"I thought Emily was my friend." He grabbed a fishing pole and headed toward the relative safety of crashing waves, unknowable riptides, and killer crosscurrents.

Sky cornered me at the door of the Shack, where I'd gone to investigate.

"I don't know how to handle the situation. The Irish are accusing Arden of stealing their tips. What should I do?" Sky asked.

My initial reaction was to defend his brother. "You can't believe the Irish. They're always accusing someone of stealing something, the English for stealing their country or the leprechauns for stealing their gold." I was a little annoyed by Skylar's attitude, which reeked of competitive sibling rivalry.

I continued my forensic accounting investigation. Arden usually divided the tips after the evening shift and was certainly in a position to do two for me, one for you. The head Irish denied the story and pointed fingers at the "E-girls." After tallying the tips, it was apparent that there was no truth to the rumor, which Emma started and passed to Emily and so on down the line. Arden was upset that Emily, his long-time friend, hadn't defended him in front of the others.

"As best as I can ascertain, Emma started the lie because she's jealous that you and Nico spend so much time together underwater," I explained. "In my opinion, if you ignore it, the whole issue will die soon enough on its own."

"That's bullshit!" Arden complained. "We always invite her fishing. Emma can gut a bass the equal of any man. She's got knife skills. I'm not talking to her ever again."

"Well, maybe she's just not into threesomes. Some girls are funny that way. She'll hook up with a guy but not his fishing buddy," I advised.

"Is that another one of your jokes? Save me from your metaphors."

"Or bring along a double date next time you go surfcasting."

"That's okay, I prefer my girlfriends with polish on their nails instead of fish blood underneath." He grabbed a pole and headed back to his favorite spot under the lighthouse, where he could commune alone with the fish. "People suck!"

"Be careful."

Unfortunately, in a bit of misplaced aggression, Arden took a one-ounce buck tail hook in the kisser, fracturing his front teeth. He was pulling the weighted hook out of the fish's mouth, when it sprang back while skishing. We commuted to my office in NYC, where I laminated his front teeth. His Hollywood smile won't hurt his fishing for jailbait.

My beautiful wife was date bait. Operating in the public eye without a wedding ring, her marital status was anyone's guess. Eligible, good-looking men were constantly circulating the Shack, particularly the horny Europeans. Tracey introduced them to her single girlfriends, but the foolish girls let the keepers slip through their fingers.

"The Italians like their espresso neat, and the French this way." She trained the staff the correct barista technique for each country, but I got this sickening feeling that her knowledge was too intimate. Was it Italians or an Italian? I constantly queried her about upcoming birthdays. She thought I was joking, but I was looking for a Leo.

I still helped out on nights the Shack was jammed or they were short-staffed, volunteering myself and unwitting friends for rollups, rolling a big dubbie-like joint with a paper napkin and disposable fork and knife. Most of our friends were glad to lend a hand, as long as it wasn't too complicated, like running an open tab on the register or scooping ice cream.

Whenever there was a fresh bloom, I'd cut homegrown flowers—white ripe hydrangea, purple butterfly bush, or multicolored snapdragons—

and pot them in unique floral displays. Twice already this season, I'd alternated the flowerpots at the Shack, tending grasses, lavender, and impatiens. Of course, I never brought roses with their falling petals; even an old boy could learn new tricks.

I'd play the host when it suited me, but I was getting increasingly annoyed with certain people who demanded my full attention for the price of a cup of coffee. For instance, a neighbor flagged me down. "Sit with me. I must tell you about my sister who is stealing my estate." I wasn't sympathetic. This woman hadn't worked a day in her life and inherited a forty-million-dollar estate. She only bought a coffee and was a lousy tipper. Maybe I was a shill host, but if I had to put that much mental energy into a witty conversation, the client should at least be copping a real meal. In my dental office, a conversation might be worth a few hundred dollars, so at the Shack, it should be worth more than the price of a tea. I sneaked out the back door.

Sometimes, I screwed up as a host because I forget people's names. I was confused seeing them in a different surrounding. I'm always talking in the health club steam room. The other day, a guy I knew from the gym complained I'd walked right past him without saying hello or offering a welcome. I wasn't being a snob; I just didn't recognize the guy when he had clothes on.

I was constantly trying to educate the staff in the art of yes. Tim scurried back and forth from the kitchen through a sudden rush of customers. He was obviously overextended. A customer requested a slice of tomato for his daughter, and Tim had declined.

"The answer in this business is always 'yes.'" I added a little irritation for effect. "You need to find solutions. There's no problem a smart boy like you can't solve."

"No! 'No' is the answer!" he replied with equal force. "The kitchen said 'no' to half orders." He crossed his arms in defiance.

Surprised by his negativity, as he was usually a mellow kid, I challenged him: "You couldn't grab the customer a couple of slices of tomato?"

"Call one of your sons and tell them to help." He walked off in an angry huff.

It wasn't always easy finding a "yes" when in the weeds. Since none of my useless sons were anywhere to be found, I jumped in and helped, the family enabler, running around busing tables as fast as I could fill them, when two girls asked, "Do you guys make sandwiches?"

It wasn't a trick question, but for a rare moment I was actually stumped for an answer. "What exactly do you mean by a sandwich? Cold cuts?"

"A sandwich. You know, sand with a slice of itch?" They giggled.

Confused, I tried to wiggle a positive spin as my mind ransacked the food possibilities. "We serve soft-shell crab sandwiches. Chicken? Lobster roll?"

None of my responses satisfied them. Later, I related the story to Tracey. "Does a sandwich always have to be flat?" I queried her.

"A sandwich is portable. They probably wanted food to go. We do that."

"I think they needed a pastrami fix. Anyway, they didn't buy my solution."

"Why don't you just let the professional waiters take the orders?" she scolded me.

"You employ professional waiters?"

"Whatever," she countered with irritation.

"No, the correct answer is *where ever*." I mouthed the words, "Try it!"

"Where ever?" she mimed and then sensed the meditative, happy effect of new vocabulary. "Where ever!" She smiled slightly. "Yeah, you're right. I feel better."

We should have tried this word trick out on our neighbors—Killjoy, the Deli Dolls, and Shaggy, who were growing increasingly hostile toward our success. One morning, Tracey and Sky moved some new picnic tables onto the sidewalk so we could rearrange the furniture inside. The table was in front of the Shack for no more than a half hour before one of them called the police. And one day, our overflowing garbage bin was left unlocked, and the seagulls got in overnight and tossed the leftovers all around the parking lot. Admittedly, it was a mess, but the ladies could have called me at home instead of immediately reaching for the police.

"Can't you talk to your employees?" I pleaded with Tracey. "Every time they park out back, the Deli Dolls throw me dirty looks."

"Too bad for them. They're just afraid of new competition."

I'd heard from a third party that the neighbors were conspiring to put my beautiful wife out of business. Confronting one of them in the parking lot, the Deli Doll admitted, "I plan to be here for the long run. I don't think you'll be in business much longer."

I didn't care for her lousy attitude, and I was getting fed up with playing the peacemaker. If a war was coming, I was ready to pick up the sword. "Oh really? Well, I own my piece of the rock; you're just renting," I said.

"Your wife cursed me out over the parking."

"I told you to call me directly if there was a problem and I would fix it."

"I would forgive your wife if she apologized for yelling at me."

Over a stack of fresh cupcakes, I related the conversation to Tracey. "I'm not apologizing. Ever! What have they ever done for us?"

"It's not what they've done; it's about what they haven't done. You don't want to give them any excuse for causing trouble. You can't let it get personal. You have to protect your business. As the new kid in town, you have more to lose."

"You may practice dentistry in fear, but I can't cook like that."

"Yes, I've been successful for thirty years because I practice scared."

"You just keep hammering away at the same point. Don't you think I've tried making peace with the neighbors? I don't know why, but they hate me and there's nothing I can do to change that. They're making me pay my dues. I'll never quit."

"It isn't that they hate you personally, it's the changes that you represent. The Gig Shack and the Surf Lodge are putting Montauk on the culinary map. *Travel and Leisure* magazine just wrote an article about our town and mentioned the Shack as the place to eat global surf cuisine. How great is that?"

I paraphrased the article. *"Hamptons without Hype: Catch the new wave in Montauk—a quintessential beach town that's not just for surfers anymore."*

Chapter 34

Cracking the Code

The Surf Lodge was making money hand over fist. Last night, at least one thousand patrons jam-packed the place for a concert by the band Moby. Hundreds of cars lined both sides of Industrial Road for the eardrum-shattering performance. New owners had turned the once rundown bar by the side of the lake into a hotspot amusement park for the hipster bikinied crowd. The police ticketed all their patrons' cars. The club offered to pay the tickets as the cost of doing business. The war was escalating.

Some concerned citizens of Montauk claimed that the Lodge's heavy sewage usage was full of shit and would spoil the pristine lake. All that human compost went somewhere, and the single latrine wasn't designed to hold that many fannies. Saturday night at 8:30 PM, the health department ordered Stephen Spielberg's family to move during his dinner. The inspector claimed the outside picnic tables were illegal, but I was suspicious the inspector chose the busiest hour of the week to enforce the rule.

We had our own shit to deal with. Our musicians couldn't stick to a plan. It was like doing business with a bunch of yogis. They were supposed to start playing at five o'clock, but by 8:00 PM they were still unpacking instruments. It was already getting dark as the scheduled guitarist quickly multiplied to four. A friend entered their jam, and now there were five. The noise level was way up, and I knew the police would come.

Determined not to let the musicians spoil my evening, I pulled the band's leader aside and issued him a stern warning. "You either keep the noise level low or you're out of here. Do you understand? I don't want to police you guys from the police. You're already starting three hours late. No second chances!"

I hated this part of the evening, the waiting for the police to arrive and shut down the music. I clapped with one ear and one eye turned to the street.

Fortunately, the police were busy investigating real crimes because they didn't appear. I sighed with relief. A few more songs and we'd be safe for another night. I'd read in the *Star* that the supervisor was considering passing the music ordinance. The restaurant lobby and my family's own efforts were paying off. I couldn't wait for the ink to dry, as I was sick of sweating out this nightly music vigil.

An unremarkable young man wearing an unmarked blue shirt patrolled up and down the block. He passed in front of the Shack and peeked in. He appeared to be searching for something, but didn't enter. The outside tables were filled with patrons eating their dinner. He asked one of our Irish waitresses what she was doing.

"I'm serving the table. What does it look like, fella? We're all full up, but if you wait over there, I'll give you a holler," she snapped.

He calmly stood in front of the Bait and Tackle Shop and listened to the music. He started to dance in place, slowly wavering in rhythm. He was a good dancer.

I was a little suspicious. He was too clean cut, but I didn't recognize the uniform.

My family claims that I am fearless, sometimes to the point of embarrassment. I will talk to anyone, the stranger the better. Quick-witted and fast on my feet, I could get a veteran to confess rank and serial number. I investigated. "You like the music?"

He slowly rocked back and forth in time to the beat. "This band sounds pretty good. I'm only an amateur musician, but I know good music when I hear it."

"Maybe you would like to play here sometime?" I didn't think he was a cop, and the music permit issue was old news. He looked official but the embroidered name on his uniform was impossible to read in the dark.

"You would let me do that? Man, I'm down."

"You're a pretty good dancer. Have you ever danced tango?"

"No, but I always wanted to learn." Suddenly, his eyes narrowed and beaded grimly, and his demeanor morphed into the face of a prison guard who had been caught fraternizing with the inmates. "Excuse me."

An older man exited Shaggy's bar. He pulled on his nose and blew a wad of snot onto the street. His facial muscles twitched, and his masseter masticated, as if he snorted too much spice while inside. He appeared agitated and gesticulated angrily. The older man lectured the younger, but I couldn't make out their conversation.

I wondered who they were, but I didn't recognize the uniform. In hindsight, I should have warned Tracey, the band, or our patrons' multi-generational families who were joyfully dancing. Grandfathers danced with granddaughters. It was a lovely moment and the music sounded really good. I didn't have the heart to cancel the music, which was supposedly now legal anyway. It was 9:00 PM, not late, and the sound level was safe. Tourist families were enjoying a special Montauk moment. I was proud to host such a nurturing family event, a real service, as an asset to the community.

The two men exchanged a heated conversation. The older fellow pointed toward the Shack. Eventually, the younger man pulled out a pad of papers and approached me.

"Are you the owner?" he asked me in an officious tone.

I looked around for the real owners. Tracey was in the kitchen tending to her cupcakes, and Sky didn't like this band. "Silent partner. Can I help you?"

"I'm Officer so-and-so from code enforcement, and I'm charging your establishment with a violation, a zoning change of use. The owner will need to appear in court next week to answer all charges." He handed me an official looking document.

"I thought you liked the music."

"This violation isn't about music. You're being charged with operating an illegal restaurant. Your legal zoning is for a retail store. I witnessed illegal waitress service."

"You must be mistaken. The previous owners have been serving food here for thirty years. Are you in the right location?"

"The violation address is printed right on the summons. Talk to the judge."

Thinking like Tracey, I asked the young enforcer. "Would you like a cookie?"

He declined the pastry and left. I took the bad news back into the kitchen and fearfully handed the summons to my beautiful wife, who was slaving over a tray of red velvet cupcakes with luscious white icing. The tray of perfectly formed pastries, neat as rows of huge strawberries with tiny white hats, seemed to be marching into the oven, but my blood pressure had risen and I may not have been seeing so clearly at that moment.

"If only the code enforcer had tried one of your cupcakes, he never would have issued this summons." I attempted to make light of a darkening situation.

"This is horrible. When will they stop? Why didn't you tell me he was out there?"

"I'd never seen a code enforcer before. I didn't know what one looked like."

"But you said you spoke to him first?"

"About the music. He liked the music, and we talked about tango."

"The fucking tango all the time, I hate these musicians. They're more trouble than they're worth. Now what am I going to do. I don't even have a lawyer."

"You'll need a local lawyer," I agreed.

"Ed's a lawyer."

"He's more of a musician."

"He's been behind a bar, and he's got a vested interest in seeing music legalized," she pointed out. "I'll call him."

Ed agreed to represent her in court. I hoped he knew what he was doing. Noise violations and overcrowding weren't as serious as this zoning code violation, which controlled the Shack's ability to operate as a restaurant.

The next afternoon, I caught a woman trying to remove the plastic baggie filled with water and a fake plastic fish, which had hung over the outside doors to keep out flies. It may be a myth, but the water reflects light and confuses the flies.

"You should be ashamed of yourself, young man. Keeping a living creature in bondage." Her jacket had a PETA badge. Now the animal rights activists were after us.

"It's a fake fish. She wards off the flies," I explained calmly.

The woman tore open the baggie and spilled the plastic guppy on the ground. "Well, no matter, it's a bad precedent you're setting for the children."

"You think that's bad, you should check out my chickens."

Finally, I got some good news to report. After weeks of continuous nagging, the editor of the *East Hampton Star* agreed to give us a review. Finally, the restaurant columnist would sample our fare and, without a doubt, praise our pastries, fish tacos, and young staff. That was the moment I had been waiting for.

The reporter called to schedule a review. Tracey, who took the call, related the contents of their unfortunate conversation. "The nerve of the reporter. She said I wanted free publicity and normally she only reviews real restaurants and not luncheonettes." Tracey held her head high.

"You hung up on the *Star's* restaurant reviewer?" I wanted to say she was nuts, but fortunately I swallowed my negative comments before the words escaped.

"She pissed me off, like I'm supposed to beg her."

"Maybe not beg, but at least be helpful. A review is the most powerful tool for branding and self-marketing. A positive write-up in the *Star* is worth a suck up."

"I know that. I don't need her lousy review. I'm busy enough."

The dining room was half-empty. "We'd hoped all season to make it in the *Star*."

"There's always next season." She walked off, leaving me shaking my head in disbelief. Okay, maybe the interviewer had bruised Tracey's delicate ego, but we had all worked very hard for this. The restaurant would never be perfect; staff will come and go. You can't plan and control every detail in this business. We were as ready now as we had ever been. Tracey had an extreme fear of failure and exposure; blowing off the reporter was safer than being exposed to potential negative publicity.

Sitting alone in the corner, feeling sorry for myself, I nursed a warm beer. I was powerless in helping my family succeed. The world, the town, and my family's self-doubts were holding back potential profits. I might as well just pack my bags and get back on the bus. At least in New York I had some control over fate.

Steve, the head Irish, came over for a chat. "Why so blue, boss? Can I buy you another beer? It's a sunny day in the neighborhood."

"Thank you. You know how to make a sad guy smile."

"No problem, boss. Among us Irish, what you've created is legendary. Back home, nobody's dad is as supportive of the family as you. You make me proud."

I blushed, not knowing how to handle a compliment, the second one he had given me about my role as a dad. He swaggered off to talk up a group of Up Island, middle-aged cougars. The women giggled as he commented on their tan lines. Steve, another James Joyce of table talk, had deep pockets of words, especially for the ladies, but I wondered if he was really straight. He was just too smooth.

George, the Dominican dishwasher, arrived for the evening cleanup shift and slapped me a high-five. *"Hola,* Papi chulo. *Esta bien?"* His fingertips were bandaged with duct tape to protect them from the hot water and sharp plates.

"Muy bien. E tu?" I replied in my pig Spanish, proud that he referred to me as the big daddy, the man with the big hat, the godfather.

"My wife, we expect new bambino." He pulled out a picture of his first child who had died in stillbirth. The newborn child was wearing a pretty dress and looked virtually alive. How sad it must have been to lose his child. He hadn't seen his wife in six months.

"Good luck with your new family."

The phone rang, but the staff was too busy to answer. After five rings, I ran over and answered the call for an order. "Six-six-eight the No-More-Gigs Shack."

"This is Ed. Listen, I got some great news. I was down at the town hall this afternoon. They passed the music permit law. Now you won't have to worry about the police. Restaurants can have live music until 10:00 PM. Isn't that great?"

"Brilliant. Now we can play live music for free, but we still can't legally serve food. What good is that?"

Chapter 35

Just Because the Uniform Fits Doesn't Mean You Should Eat It

I'm just a junkyard dog. No matter how hard I got kicked, I kept lapping back for more punishment. My family fired me three times at the Shack that day.

First, Arden scolded me for interfering in his table management. It was the late afternoon window between lunch and dinner, and I aggressively grabbed the early birds.

I warmly greeted the large families of would-be customers, kissing babies, offering teens lessons in backgammon, and explaining to the parents that the food was child friendly, homemade, baked on premises, and the fish so local it was swimming this morning. We didn't take reservations. All the outside picnic tables quickly filled with large parties, and there was now a line forming at the door for the inside ones. I moved these groups so that they didn't block the entrance, seating them in every available spot, although the kitchen was soon a half hour behind service.

Arden complained. "We can't handle these crowds all at once."

"The business is here, and you have empty tables. Where would you like me to put them?" I replied with equal venom. "You should never turn away business!"

"Tell them to wait in the street or walk around the block a few times."

"But the tables are empty. Why not seat them anyway?"

"Because they won't get their food right away. They'll get pissed off and either leave or drop a lousy tip. Give them one of these buzzers. Stop meddling."

"I can't see turning away good business. If the two outside waiters can't handle the rush, redraw the table map so there are three outside waiters. In business, there are no problems, only solutions," I explained.

`"Mom drew up the table map. Unless you're willing to tell her how to run this business, I'd suggest you fill up your diary and leave the front of the house to us."

I surveyed the fully occupied dining room. I'd done a good job playing host even if my son didn't appreciate my help. I proceeded to the back kitchen and asked Nico if he could use my help in the kitchen. The line cook's orders were already backed up.

"That would be great. Please prep two dozen pineapples, a watermelon, and dice these peppers." He pointed out how he wanted the produce prepped, the order of importance, and where he wanted it stored. Nico and I had good communication, and I was comfortable working under his command.

Tracey carried a tray of unfinished pastries. She and Nico didn't even acknowledge each other. There was an unspoken miscommunication building between them. It was about his girlfriend Emma, whom Tracey and the staff already hated.

I found myself a clean, unoccupied board, tied a fresh white apron neatly around my laundered clothes, sharpened my knife blade like a professional, and attacked the fruit with vengeance. Although not a perfectionist, I was fast, whipping out paper-thin slices of pineapple in record speed. Okay, some might still have had a bit of brown rim retained on an edge, but I was into quantity, not quality. I moved onto the watermelon and knocked out three storage boxes in the time it would have taken Javier to do one. Next came the burnt red peppers. I delicately pealed the charred skin from the fruit and julienned the flesh. Getting the hang of kitchen prep wasn't all that different from doing dental surgery, like when I extracted a wisdom tooth, dissecting the flesh from its sulcular attachment. I had fun, at least until I hit the mango and orange slices. As hard as I tried, I couldn't properly peal a mango or spinelessly section a citrus. Nico demonstrated his technique, but the orange slices kept coming out with too many white fibers attached and little usable fruit, and the mangos, which were overripe, melted between my fingers.

When Tracey surveyed the fruit of my accomplishment, her face showed clear displeasure with the boxes of neatly stacked pineapples, watermelons, and peppers, which had saved the kitchen hours of last-minute stress. Then her eyes targeted the fucking mangos. Her face pinched into a really unpleasant frown.

"You've mangled my mangos!" She held up a slice of the less than perfectly scalloped fruit in her fingertips and wiggled it in the air as if it were a wayward worm that had been discovered in an apple. "What's this?"

"Okay, maybe I need a little more practice."

"Go practice in someone else's kitchen." She threw the mango in the garbage.

Nico noticed our marital confrontation and shot her an understanding glance. He and Tracey had to work with each other every day. It was easier to choose a scapegoat to mutually blame their conflict on. Tracey had learned much from Doctor Gross's school of conflict resolution. When two people don't agree, it's easier to blame it on a third party. Unfortunately, I was that party. My new job was "scapegoat."

"But, I was still trimming those," I pleaded for my fallen fruit.

"I'm not running a cooking school."

No one on the kitchen staff was older than twenty-three. She was running a cooking school, and I had been repeatedly held back. Still wearing the apron, I quit the kitchen, made myself an espresso, and hovered out front, hoping to enjoy the sunset.

Regally standing at the restaurant's entrance, wearing the status symbol uniform of the head chef, a clean white apron, I surveyed the tables to assess our success. I'd seen Pierre, from that restaurant in Bridgehampton, pulling the same stunt. With head high, I professionally scanned the tables to assure that my kingdom was well-run, counting heads and scouting tail. How many customers were eating fish, meat, or vegetables? The overjoyed patrons pointed me out to their children. A new member of the celebrity chef club, royalty had its rewards. Women love a man in a uniform.

It was a warm summer evening. Crowds of tourists were strolling around the town après-surf, shopping for knickknacks, surf souvenirs, and Montauk T-shirts. A gaggle of pretty young things crossed the street, scouting out a dinner destination. From the middle of the street, I willed them aboard my boat. I set my hook on the leader of the pack, the girl with the shortest skirt and the longest legs, bobbing a line of psychic bait. Slowly, she was drawn into my net and her friends followed. The fish got cold feet, stopped mid-street, and surveyed the competition across the street. Fearing that I was losing them, I leaned into the catch and enticed with all my psychic powers. My third eye reeled the trolling trollops. They willingly swallowed our menu.

"Ladies, can I get you a table?" Displaying the power of the uniform.

They were duly impressed to have been landed personally by the head chef. Conferring among themselves, they giggled conspiratorially and chose the corner table.

"A waiter will be right with you," I spoke like an artist.

Sky delivered a tray of cold beers to an adjacent table, as I landed the ladies aboard a seat. With a hint of disdain, he asked, "What are you doing, Dad?"

"Oh, the apron? I'd forgotten to take it off."

"But why are you wearing it in public? You aren't the chef."

"I'm the shill chef now." I untied the apron and dropped it in his hand. "You should try it on sometime. It's a great way to pick up girls."

The Jitney bus drove by, enticing my escapism. I contemplated excuses for an early exit to the weekend, a barometer of my happiness, the time and place I chose to depart. If the weekend marriage and the sun were shining, I extended my return to the Tuesday morning schedule. If it was raining high pressure and Tracey was married to the restaurant, I often left Monday night.

Welcome to the slowly unwrapping world of the weekend husband. We aren't that complicated. We are just fed up with living alone all week, and when we come home to play, our wives avoid us, blame us, or hide out with the children. We consider ourselves excellent husbands. Our mixed-up wives don't appreciate a good thing when they see it, like April, the fiery wife in the novel *Revolutionary Road*. She was never satisfied with her husband, but she had no explanation for the problem. It was all a latent amalgam of discontent. In our generation, the fights are subtler, none of the slam, bam, thank you ma'am of our fathers.

Tracey claimed I acted passive-aggressive by mangling the mangos. I considered her attitude always aggressive. At least I was passive sometimes and allowed her to vent, because if we both acted aggressive all the time, there would be no time for gifts.

According to Man-talk, gifts are what keep a marriage going. The Dalai Lama, Confucius, and the fortune cookie all say: "A woman who keeps her husband in the doghouse will soon find him in the cathouse."

Was that where my marriage was headed? I needed to stop the decomposition and quickly. Where there is a will, there is a way.

I contemplated my gifts as I sat alone in the back of the bus headed to NYC. Feeling something itchy, I picked a hard-skinned bug from out of my armpit. The engorged deer tick bled slightly as I crushed the critter in my palm. Was it my blood?

How long had it been living in my flesh?

Chapter 36

The Last Tango in Montauk

As I waited at the train station for the Argentine tango teacher to arrive, I fretted over my decision to proceed with the Montauk milonga. Neither my wife nor the town was happy with my plan, but I had drawn my line in the sand. If the supervisor wanted to cross it and arrest me, at least I'd go down dancing.

Everything had been prearranged. I'd rented a room, all meals were provided complimentary of the Shack, and I'd offered to escort Mr. Tango to and from the beach. I placed flyers around town announcing the big date. He and his girlfriend had performed around the world, and we were lucky to have them. It was unfortunate that Americans aren't more supportive of dance. This couple, the Alex Rodriquez all-stars in their own country, could barely afford the price of a train ticket in mine.

Six strangers escorted them down the plank. The dancers gave me a big hug. "Doc, there's been a slight change of plan." He introduced me to his friends. "My students will be staying with us for the weekend. I hope you don't mind." They quickly dumped their bags in the back of my car.

"But the bedroom is only big enough for one couple."

"They can sleep anywhere. It doesn't matter. It's all good."

"It's not my house. The owner won't be happy."

They piled in the car. It was impossible to fit all nine people at once, so I taxied in multiple shifts. I delivered the uninvited guests to their cottage. "Could you take us to the beach now? Anyone want lunch?" Doing business with tanguero was like doing business with artists, yogis, and musicians. No one wore watches, paid bills, or stuck to schedules.

Sunday afternoon, Sky cleared all the inside tables and created a dance floor. He surveyed his work. "Are you sure you want to go through with this, Dad? Where are the customers going to sit?" He shot me a disapproving glance.

"Let them eat cake. They can eat standing while they watch."

"At least the bar is still open. I'll work there."

"It's too late to back out now, and Mom didn't actually say no."

"You wore her down with nagging. She only agreed as a gift to you."

"Well, then let that be a little lesson for you."

"You aren't worried about the police?"

"Are you kidding? We won! We finally have a music permit. What can Killjoy do? Tango permits don't exist." I moved the last table to the side. Suddenly, I felt dizzy and weak in the knees. The restaurant was spinning around me. I sat down in a flop and breathed labored breath. The lines in the checkerboard floor floated.

"Are you all right? You look mighty pale to host a party, Dad."

"I am kind of queasy."

"Should I go get Mom?"

"No, please don't tell her. I'm okay now." I stood up slowly and threw a show-must-go-on smile. "She doesn't need an excuse to cancel the tango." Every joint in my body ached. Dancing was nearly impossible. I faked a dancer's poise. I had been feeling weaker and weaker for the past week. I assumed it was exhaustion from my year-round commuting schedule, but I felt like I'd been bit by a vampire and the blood had been drained from the lines. I was working eight days in a week, carrying the stress of my office and the Shack without a day's rest in between. Also, I'd been chauffeuring these needy tango dancers around all weekend.

I had called my physician to get the blood test results after being bitten by that tick. I tested positive for Lyme disease. He diagnosed that I was suffering from Barbiosis, a rare form. My antibody exposure levels were low, so I might have had the disease for some time. I'd already begun the prescribed dosage of antibiotics and was hoping they would kick in before the dancers arrived. There was little risk of long-term illness, but at that moment I could hardly move.

The show went on without my performance. About fifty dancers arrived. Most were complete novices with two left feet. The available talent of trained tango dancers in this fishing town was miniscule, so the evening basically progressed into a beginner lesson and quick performance by the professionals. It turned out to be a good thing that they brought their own students from NYC, because otherwise, the milonga dance party would have been a complete flop. Tracey and I did a few dances together, but my heart wasn't in it. Somehow, my misguided vision of dancers in bikinis and high heels got lost in translation. The pictures I'd seen from Europe, huge crowds tango dancing on the beach in Ibiza, Capri, and Mykonos, were completely lost on the fishermen and surfers.

The tango teacher reprimanded one of the couples. "You are holding your woman like she is a slippery fish. Grab her like this." He demonstrated the correct position.

Most of the women ended up dancing together, as their guys escaped to the bar and got drunk. I did my best to dance with the partner-less broads.

A few hours later, I dropped the tango dancers at the train station and declined their offer to return the next week. I didn't have the strength to continue.

When I returned home, Tracey was already dressed for bed. "Well, that was a lot of fun. I hope you planned another date. I had a great time, and the customers ate and drank a lot more than I'd expected. I actually made some money on the night. Did you notice how many tourists came by to watch? Congratulations."

"Yeah, free show. Great."

"After all your planning, was it all you expected?"

"I'm glad I did it once, but it will be the last tango in Montauk. It will never be as good as the first time. Alfonso was right; this town isn't ready for tango."

"Oh, don't go being so negative again. The crowd loved it and wants them back."

"No! I can't do it again. Thanks but no thanks."

"Nice attitude." She rolled over and fell asleep promptly, offering a cold shoulder.

I should have told her about the Lyme disease, but the fact was that I was worn out. She probably wouldn't believe my diagnosis anyway. Tracey never got sick, and she claimed that this disease was for hypochondriacs. What was the point of seeking her sympathy? I was on the medication and there wasn't anything she could do. She had enough stress without my medical complaints.

The next morning, I accompanied Tracey and her lawyer, Ed, to the town courthouse. There was already a long lineup of young Hispanic males waiting for justice. Eventually, the judge, a middle-aged female, called our case.

Ed and Tracey stood up before the docket. Tracey was wearing her court dress, a one-piece Burberry, comfortable and stylish. She had had last-minute clothing trauma. She'd planned to wear the Prada black and white stripes but on second thought considered it too jail-birdie. Ed wore his usual outfit, a long shirt overlaying pants.

The district attorney read out a list of the town's complaints against the Gig Shack. From the serious tone of her accusations, we sounded like a horrible threat to the community instead of the asset we'd always imagined we were. The details of this proceeding were recorded by a local, public service television station, but I'll replay the events as I remember them, although this may not be a completely accurate retelling of the legal story, as my blood pressure had risen so high it clogged my hearing. She accused us of numerous "code violations, illegal renovations, and mostly unwanted waiters." The district attorney acted like our guilt was self-evident.

The judge's demeanor, kind and sympathetic toward the illegal immigrants that preceded our case, reddened with indignation at our kitchen crime confidential. "How do you plead?" she demanded as if the case was already closed.

Ed hemmed and laughed for a few minutes, cleared his throat five times, and finally replied, "This is a complete misrepresentation of the facts. We are here to answer the noise violation. This is the first I'm hearing of these criminal complaints."

"Who are you?" the judge queried.

"I'm the lawyer representing the accused." He pointed to my beautiful wife.

"Why are you dressed like a musician? In my court, lawyers wear a suit."

Bumbling, Ed nervously dropped his pen and picked it up. "I apologize, Your Honor. This was all such short notice. Next time, I'll dress for the occasion."

"You need advance notice to wear a suit to court? Tell your client to come forward. Miss, are you the owner of this Geek Shack?"

The accused thieves and child abusers giggled at the judge's joke.

Tracey crawled out from behind Ed's shadow. Meekly smiling, she replied mouse-like, "Gig Shack, Your Honor. It's called the Gig Shack."

"Well, I'll be damned if I know what a Geek Shack is, but from the list of complaints, it appears you're an ice cream parlor operating illegally as a restaurant. This is very, very serious. The code officer stated he witnessed illegal waitress service and that you also serve alcohol. Is that true? Speak up!"

"Yes and no, Your Honor," my gorgeous wife whispered in reply.

"That wasn't a multiple choice question."

"Your Honor, if I can interject," Ed spoke.

"Counselor, I'm speaking to your client."

"But, but ..." Ed stumbled.

"I have sworn statements from the police and code enforcement. I will give you three weeks to prepare a reply to these charges. In the meantime, I will instruct the state to rescind your alcohol license." This judge was serious.

Ed stuttered, "Bu ... bu ... but, Your Honor, that's not fair. It's the height of the season. You can't rescind the license now. You'll destroy the business."

"That is not my concern. The law's the law."

"Montauk's resort season is so short. You're taking away the best part."

"Your client should have considered the penalty before committing the crime."

"I don't believe she committed any crime; the zoning is unclear."

"Then you better get to work preparing your rebuttal."

"I can't prepare a rebuttal on such short notice."

The judge slammed down her gravel. "Counselor, our next date will be September the 10th and you better be wearing a three-piece suit and one of those pieces a tie."

Chapter 37

Roadkill

"I felt like a deer in headlights when Scott first abandoned me, now I'm just roadkill," Tracey wept as we left the courthouse. "The judge hates me."

"She doesn't hate you. She's just a cog in the wheel of justice. Unfortunately, she doesn't understand your beautiful community and culinary artistic creation. Her world is inhabited by intoxicated drivers, petty thieves, and wife beaters."

"Well, she stole my liquor license fast enough, without even so much as a warning. I feel like I've been kicked in the stomach." Tracey dropped to her knees.

"You're right. The judge could have issued a warning instead of immediately filing a complaint to the state, especially since they're wrong in their interpretation of rules regarding your zoning." I helped her back to her feet. "One of your competitors is out to get you. Who do you think it is?"

"I'd bet Shaggy. He's just jealous. He's got connections. Maybe the state will ignore the judge, or maybe Shaggy and the judge have history?"

"High school sweethearts? Maybe you need to find a better lawyer, someone who's more connected with the local process, or who specializes in restaurant law."

"You're right. Ed was in over his head." Her voice trailed off.

"His entire case and attire were poorly prepared for court."

"Let's ask around. There must be another lawyer in this town that's passed the bar without staying for a drink or three," Tracey said.

The next day we got more bad news. A certified letter from the state arrived advising that the alcohol license had been revoked. To make matters worse, the new town permit for music only applied to restaurants. Since our Certificate of Occupancy was preexisting, nonconforming, retail with a food variance or legal limbo land, the town denied us the right to hold live musical events. Even though we had been the spearhead in the campaign to legalize a restaurant's right to hold music, we were now denied that right. Music was permitted at all the other restaurants but ours.

Tracey's instincts, ingrained from years of teaching yoga—physical, energetic practice and thinking in the moment—weren't helping to deal with this implosion. Our relationship was so volatile that against my most basic instinct of self-preservation, I spoke the unthinkable. In a fit of mutual drunken incrimination, I accused her of turning into her worst nightmare, a "Leslie." I might have sooner asked for a divorce.

A feminist once advised self-employed women to become like the men they would want to marry, but put a comedic spin on it. What part of the conflict between marriage and a wife's work don't we understand? Where the bride says, "I do"?

The qualities Tracey had learned from teaching yoga should have been useful when facing the difficulty of small business survival, but her patience wasn't covering the mortgage. She needed good marketing skills and strategic staffing, not her strongest points. She had totally forgotten financial planning. She was suffocating on profit-loss and choking me off in the process.

It wasn't always that way. In our old days, her smile lit up a room and always looked like laughter to me. Once upon a time, I had cast a shadow that my wife was always willing to shade, no matter the time of day or location on this planet. There was no whatever, only whenever. When we first married, my white chalk drew a sine curve, a symbol of love, upon her blank slate. She had changed; she was angry at the world, at the town, at the staff, at the boys, and most of all, she seemed to be perpetually angry with me. Why? What the fuck did I do to make her so angry?

I searched my sad wife's eyes for signs of shadowy behavior, a crack in her marble. What a bust. I couldn't take my eyes off of her cleavage.

The problems she faced in the restaurant didn't explain her annoyance. I wasn't the enemy. I thought I was the pedestal. Why would the bust kick out her own pedestal unless she had another to take its place? Should I take a blue pill?

She shot me a stiffened lower lip, as if she didn't care for the tone of our conversation, but we hadn't spoken to each other in days. She said, "Shish! Silence is golden," but I thought silence was still silence.

My world changed when Scott arrived with his arrogant, lopsided sneer reminiscent of Doctor House, that menacing bite, angular carnivorous dentition, and five o'clock shadow. His coming and going were the cause of all bad things.

Snap out of it, boy—what was the point in blame? I'd made my bed, and there was no benefit to wearing it out on my sleeve. Bury the dirty linen, keep busy, there were only a few days left. Be a yogi and make lists of uncompleted chores. On second thought, I'm no vegetarian, I need blood. I planned a new strategy.

We'd lost another battle, but not the war. The supervisor and his conspirators had tried to put us out of business. Their attack didn't make much sense, since we could still sell ice cream and food. Tearfully, we laid off some of the waitress staff and busboys. The customers could clean their own tables.

Taking a seat in front of the Shack, I watched a family of three wrestle with a wobbly table. I made a mental note to fix the uneven patio in the off-season, but that family's restaurant anxiety disorder had just begun, their burlesque behavior, a sideshow.

"Would you leave the damn table alone?" The wife screamed at her frustrated husband, who couldn't find a stable location. If only he would replace the stabilizing wood shims that he'd moved from below the table when he first sat down. Why do some people automatically move the tables? Why can't they just take a spot and leave our world order alone? The trouble with some restaurant customers is the need to display their obsessive-compulsive disorders in public. "You're a moron," the wife announced.

The wife's compulsion was her need to make public statements. I hate that, when one spouse berates the other in public. She waved her arms wildly to get the attention of our staff. "You always embarrass me in restaurants," she continued to denounce her husband. "Waiter! Waiter! Would somebody help us? Damn it."

There were no more waiters. I could have fixed their problem in a jiffy, but then I'd have lost out on this vaudevillian comedic routine.

Eventually, Sky came over and jostled a shill into a satisfactory spot under the table.

"Thank you, young man," the wife said.

The daughter had a genetic ordering compulsion. She was constantly playing with her hair as she moved the salt and peppershakers around the table. She put them in one corner, and the father moved them back. What a pair, fathers and daughters, mothers and sons. The father and daughter both checked the cleanliness of their eating area and gingerly wiped away water stains as if they were dog poop. They were obsessed with self-harm and would most likely hurt others. The mother was just oblivious.

I, the professional bystander, could have warned Tracey in advance that this group would be difficult to satisfy, but then I'd be interfering again and I'd been repeatedly scolded for meddling. I sat quietly and watched the public theatre unfold in three acts.

First, the father and daughter obsessed over their food order, changing their plan multiple times. Their indecisiveness on the menu spread to a complaint about dirt on the disposable silverware. The silverware was actually plastic and had never been used. Sky kindly replaced the fork and knife. They started stuffing their faces. They seemed truly happy for the first time since they had sat, when suddenly, the wife jumped up and grabbed at her throat. Her cheeks reddened and swelled with too big a bite of burger. She obviously couldn't breathe. Wearing the painted faces of a Greek tragedy, the family watched in mid-bovine mastication as their mother choked to death on our chow.

This would be our end. I imagined that evil forces had planted these geeks to choke on the food and sue us for all we were worth.

Sailing in from my corner table, I, the superhero husband, swooped my arms around the chest of the choking victim, interlocked two fists over the curvature of her D-cupped breasts, and performed an operatic Heimlich maneuver. The wayward morsel popped out of her throat and landed in a plop on the sidewalk.

"You saved my life." She thanked me for the emergency intervention.

"You're welcome." My superhero interventions continued as I washed my car with the hose from the parking lot. I waxed the car early in the morning because I was afraid that the Deli Dolls would complain about my parking. It was illegal to wash your car in public, as the soap might contaminate the well water. I used a tiny cap full of soap and a lot of rags. I didn't see how I contaminated anything, but our neighbors were relentless. They called the EPA the other day to complain about a leak from our cooking oil canister. Why couldn't our neighbors just call us instead of leaking the leaks to the feds?

While I was washing my car, one of the deli's female cooks fell out the back door of their kitchen and collapsed into a full-blown seizure. She was screaming Bloody Mary's, Hail Mary's in Spanish, holding her stomach with convulsions of pain, as if giving birth. She didn't look pregnant. She was cursing in an untranslatable wailing Spanish and riveting around in the dirt. Was she epileptic?

The Deli Dolls dumbly watched their employee's spasm. They stood over her and did absolutely nothing to help. I pushed them away and took charge of the situation. "I'm a doctor!" I'm not a local doctor, so maybe it didn't count in their limited world book. "What is she saying? Do any of you speak her dialect?" No one responded, so I diagnosed the problem as we waited for the EMT. "This is no epileptic seizure."

After checking vital signs, I whispered, *"No mas!"* Gently, I rubbed her forehead and spoke softly, guiding her into a safer prone position. *"No mas, esta bien?"* I rubbed her neck and continued speaking softly. She started to relax under my strong healing hands. The spasms soon disappeared. She breathed heavily but without terror. Her eyes thanked me, and a small smile of comfort creased her lips. She was okay. Satisfied that she wasn't an epileptic but more likely suffered a panic attack, I informed the Deli Dolls, "She'll be okay now." I handed the rescued employee to the newly arrived EMT technicians.

The Dolls stared at me with open, incredulous mouths, but maybe my Good Samaritan intervention had a positive effect on our neighborly relations. One can only hope that good deeds will be rewarded in this town and bad punished, although to date, the opposite had been my experience. They never thanked me.

Since I was on this roll of Good Samaritan role, I strolled by the souvenir shop, hoping my good karma would rub off on the other neighbors. Killer Jr. was standing in front of their store catching some rays. I struck up a conversation.

"What are your plans for college?" The kid was a straight-A student.

"I'm still a junior, but I would like to go to an out-of-state school," he replied.

"My son Gray is thinking of a hospitality degree. He really likes cooking, but he wants a four-year education. What are your future plans? I've put three kids into college, maybe I can help out." I was confident that my conversation, if only for a moment, was warming the divide between our families. This was the essence of conflict resolution.

He was about to confess his life plans when a fat, hairy arm reached out from inside the store's door and grabbed the poor kid by the back of his neck. The anonymous fist yanked the boy off the ground, pulled him into the store, and the front door shut tight. I never saw the owner of that arm, but I assumed it was his father, who disapproved of my conversing with his son. This stage left happened so suddenly that I didn't even have a chance to address my neighbor.

It's too bad the old man couldn't bury his hatred and fear of change. Didn't he realize that he had already won? We hadn't hosted live music in weeks, which was his stated goal. Maybe he just had a social disorder, Toilette's Syndrome, a sewage management disease, and didn't want anyone living or working near him. I vowed to force him to answer this question one day. What kind of business would he prefer next door? If he didn't want us, whom would he prefer?

Chapter 38

Opening a B&B

"Since the town claims we're a retail store with a food variance, whatever the fuck that means, I suggest we change our use to a B&B, a Bait and Barbeque shop. It would be the sweetest revenge against our neighbor. Hit him in his pocketbook, like he tries to hit us," I explained to Tracey and Arden, who looked at me as if I'd dropped off the East End. "We wouldn't be selling any live worms or frozen porgies with our lunch, but custom rods and reels by Arden's friend at Van Stall. Exclusively bass and blues and maybe a custom tied fly corner. Can you imagine a wall of hand-painted tackle? Art lure. Arden could advertise fishing expeditions around the world, which you claim is your long-term plan. I think it's brilliant! You studied social networking in college. Can't you create a fishing and food blog? You and Nico should have all your casting buddies bragging about this up and down the bicoastal, or take it to Antigua. It's fucking one of a kind."

Arden shook his head. "Dad, do you know how much work it is to run a tackle store? Fly rods would never fly, and I wouldn't want to take business from Freddie's, another tackle store in town. They're good people and need the income."

"That's mighty gracious of you, but he carries all kinds of tackle, inshore, offshore, and around shore. You would specialize in limited-edition bait."

"It wouldn't be right. Who's going to work it? What do you know about tackle?"

"That's your gig. Imagine a wall of multicolored, hand-painted fish decoys and ten-foot bamboo poles hanging in the rafters. Fish art. You arm the casters, guide them to the special spots, and smoke their catch of bass and blues when they return. Bait and Barbeque, what could be more glamorous than that, hook 'em and cook 'em?"

"You're just dreaming, Dad."

Tracey didn't say boo during the conversation, and I took her silence as a rejection of my inspiration. Eventually, she broke down and voiced an opinion. "I don't want to lose the interior tables, even if the town claims they're illegal. I'd rather leave the space empty than start another line. We're not set up for retail, other than shirts."

"But according to their screwy rules, that's the only legal use of the space. We do retail inside, maybe sell your custom-made dresses or sarongs, keep the main counter open, and sell food on the side. It's a perfect solution and entirely profitable."

"No, I want to be a real restaurant." Tracey sighed.

"The supervisor is testing us to see if we have the will to stick this out. Did you know that there's a hundred-year-old rule in East Hampton that prohibits outsiders from conducting business in this town? Only actual landowners can sell their wares. It just goes to show that nothing has ever changed," I said.

"If we can't have waitress service, the staff loses a lot of income from lower tips. I'd have to try and compensate them with higher wages. It'll change the whole nature of the food experience. I'm not interested in fast food."

"I sell the food." Arden patted himself on the back. "The rest of the staff just takes orders. They may serve the food, but as a waiter, I'm the only one who really sells it. Mom's right. If you take away the table service, we won't make any money."

"Don't you get it?" I said. "The supervisor isn't giving you a choice."

"Then I want to fight the town for a change of use to be a real restaurant." Tracey folded her arms. "Whatever it costs will be an investment in the value of the property."

"Who knows how much that could cost? Besides the legal fees, we would need to buy invisible parking and added sewage. The rules for becoming a restaurant are prohibitively expensive. They require one parking spot for three seats, plus one for each employee. Your allowance is for sixty seats, and the preexisting variance is for only ten cars. You do the math. At $10,000 per spot, you would need to sell a lot of tacos, and it's not as if you actually own a piece of land, a reserved parking spot, for all that money."

"It's just money," my poor wife explained economically.

"Even if you did pay them off, the present sewage system is near capacity for your space. You can't add enough wells to qualify as a restaurant."

"We'll drill down deeper, get the water guys to do a test boring, or we buy an acre of pristine farmland in East Hampton and barter it for a sewage allowance. How many millions could that cost? Think air rights. Sewage rights."

"You're too close to the sea, already," I said. "There's no way you can expand the present system. The only possibility is that the town installs a central sewage system, which they've been talking about for years, but have no money to pay for, or to use some of the extra capacity of your neighbors. Maybe I could make them an offer they can't refuse. Shaggy's already over capacity, his system stinks and needs constant pumping, but the Deli Dolls have that lot out back. They only rent, so if I make them an offer, they have nothing to lose. The souvenir store must have plenty of extra sewage capacity too."

"Good luck," said Arden. "We're already on his shit list."

"Yeah, I know, but what difference is a little shit more or less. I'll talk to them and the town about the central system. Shit! It will be my newest quest."

I called the owner of the unused slip of land behind the deli, which would serve as an excellent location for added sewage. "I'd like to make you an attractive offer."

"It's not for sale, for any price. Don't bother me again." He drove a hard bargain.

"Well, if not a sale, how about renting it so I can add more sewage. That's a win-win solution for everybody. You get a couple of bucks and keep the property."

"No, the ladies control it in their lease. You would need their permission, and I'm not selling it unless they agree. Don't bother me again."

Not one to take no for an answer, a quality my wife both respects and loathes, I called the Deli Dolls and made them an offer they couldn't refuse. I hoped my saving the life of their employee had earned me some brownie points. Boy, was I naïve. "I'll sub-rent the unused lot. It's free money for you." I offered a wasted breath.

"No! You will be shut down any day now, anyway."

Annoyed with her conspiratorial tone, I said, "Well, I own my property, little darling, while you're just a lowly tenant farmer." I withheld my anger and made a joke of her nasty comment. "Maybe you would prefer a bordello next door, cherry pie?"

"We're not interested! At any price."

It just didn't make any sense to my business mind that the Deli Dolls would turn down free money, unless it was more important to them that we failed. Why should they care if we transformed into a restaurant? Our initial success as a restaurant was good for their business. After eating at the Shack, our customers often went to the deli to purchase cigarettes and disposables. In this small town, everyone knew everyone's business. They must have been involved in the conspiracy to shut us down, but their recalcitrance didn't appear a negotiating tactic to raise the price. They didn't care about money. They just feared change and wanted us to fail at any price.

"They all want to shut me down." Tracey frowned fearfully. "Even Shaggy is pissed off I made such a success of his failure and that I'm taking away all his business."

"Let's put all our heads together and find solutions. Every time a door closes, another one opens in its place."

"My competitors are spreading false rumors of violations. They're such liars. We need to quickly find solutions to the loss of the liquor license." Tracey pulled all the staff by their shirttails for an impromptu meeting. "Any suggestions?"

"The fish market has been doing BYOB for fifteen years," said Arden. "That's not a legal restaurant and it doesn't have a license."

"Yeah, they're always packed. People like to bring their own bottle. They can afford better wine," added Emily. "You could charge a corkage fee."

"No corkage fees." The boss waved off that suggestion.

"Yeah, but what about beer? Customers aren't going to come in with a six-pack."

"Is BYOB even legal?" Tracey gestured her confusion.

"I've never heard of anyone being arrested for allowing a customer to bring their own bottle, but they might already have a liquor license," said Arden.

"Well, if anyone was going to be arrested for illegal BYOB in this town, it would probably be me," Tracey joked halfheartedly. "They hate me."

"If the town objects, then we won't allow it. A lot of places allow BYOB. I'm sure they would issue a warning first. Our customers are on vacation. They need a little booze with their food. Otherwise, our duck confetti is cooked. The deli should give us kickbacks of free bottles of beer for all the business I'm sending to them," I told Tracey.

"Let's just hope they stay open late enough to service our customers. Did you notice that the deli is now closing an hour earlier? I'll bet they're doing that just to screw me, so that my customers have to go all the way to the supermarket," Tracey spat in the wind. "I'm afraid to do anything now. All of my fucking competitors are watching."

"You're paranoid," I said.

"Paranoid? You think I'm getting paranoid? Who do you think complains to the police?" She wailed her fists in a fury against the wall and my comment.

I absorbed the brunt of her rant like a good Teflon-coated husband, but then she scratched beneath the surface. I could see her left hook coming, but I couldn't duck quickly enough to cover my hurt. She hit me below the belt.

"You're no better than them. You're always so damn negative; your whole family's that way." She clawed the air in my face. "I'm paranoid— the nerve of you!"

"You wanted to own a piece of paradise. Behind every apple is a snake."

"Whatever! I've had enough of this conversation." Tracey slammed the chair under the table and retreated to the safety of cupcakes waiting to be glazed.

Left alone at the table out front, I stared empty-hearted at the Milky Way. Of late, I was always alone, in the city and out here on weekends. All she did was work. She was dealing with the code enforcement issue by overcompensating, working multiple shifts, and never taking time to go to the beach. If she had any free time, she came home and fell asleep instantly.

Tracey and I loved each other, and more importantly, we actually liked each other, but a mutually undiagnosed anger burned as she was scorched by the town's heat. Why couldn't we get along better? Simple conversations seemed to self-combust. Which came first, the sperm or the egg? Who knew as we both accused the other of being the aggressor. This would pass, I kept reminding myself; the off-season marriage would return. Take a breath and count the days. The man must keep the passion burning.

Marriage therapy was put on hold as we made adjustments in the operations to cope with the town's new rules. The outside bar needed site plan approval, but we didn't remove it because we hoped the supervisor would change his mind. Sky draped it with a large multicolored flag. We installed more picnic tables and placed them in the original bar area and inside the main room. "Picnic tables don't count as seating," I advised.

"Are you sure? Where is that written?" asked Tracey. "Did you make that up?"

"It's not in writing. That's why it's called a loophole. The zoning inspector implied that picnic tables didn't count toward your seating allowance. You could have Sky and Mac Cool paint the tabletops and resell them as art. That way you still qualify as a retail store but the customers are sitting on the art. Brilliant, don't you think?"

"That's stupid, customers sitting on the art? Leave the tables alone, please."

I didn't listen to her instruction. I would be leaving for New York in a few hours, and the unused space was irritating to me. The season was so short. We needed to fill the space immediately. I was her chief and only investor. In her absence, I made an executive decision and directed the staff to move three picnic tables inside. We moved the furniture around and played with the arrangement until we were satisfied that it fit fire code and allowed easy passage. Just like that, we had eighteen free indoor seats.

When she returned from her surf break, she stared open-mouthed at the new arrangement. "What's going on here?"

"Looks good, don't you think?" I admired my handy work. "An executive decision. It's not meant to be a coup or anything, you're still the boss, but I wanted to try it out and see how the new furniture looked."

"Humph!" She frowned and walked off.

"She secretly loves it," I told Sky. "This is a perfect solution. She doesn't have to make a decision, and she has me to blame if the supervisor objects."

"When are you going to learn, Dad? Maybe you should go back to New York and let Mom make her own decisions."

From across the room, I saw Tracey scanning my experimental picnic table arrangement. She didn't appear to love what I had done; in fact, if looks could kill …

Maybe Sky was right. Why was I bothering to micromanage her affairs? Maybe all I was creating was fresh anger to lubricate my separation from the weekend marriage, the weekly transformation to my other life. It's like the child deciding he hates his father so he can more easily make the jump from the safety of the family nest.

That night, a group of Sky's friends, local fishermen, dragger boys, showed up for dinner. They carried a red plastic basket and gleefully tossed about seventy pounds of live lobster on the kitchen floor. The frisky crustaceans skated to the corners of the room, like a hood of young hoodlums when spotted by the cops.

"Shack money," one of the fishermen announced. "A crustacean for a crust of bread, a belly of beer, and your famous Gig Shack ribs, please."

"We netted out fifty thousand pounds of whiting and squid. This by-catch is our Shack money, a little extra cash to tie us over after a few days at sea. Some dumbass lobsterman's baskets got caught in the dragger's nets. They should have known better where to place their baskets. They were on our piece of bottom. Almost ruined us. We had to cut the suckers out of the net, took out a piece the size of a car. Only right we should have kept these critters as a bonus," another boasted.

"A bunch of no good up-coasters, if you ask me, probably from Rhode Island or Massachusetts. Screw them for parking their cages on our turf."

The first laughed. "Some kid's college tuition at five thousand a basket. The cages were broke; we had to throw them aside."

"Ah, fuck them. They should fish their own water. Now, where's my Bud? I got three days of thirst that needs quenching," demanded the hungry lad.

"I got some bad news for you, boys," I said, trying to lasso the wayward lobsters and throw them back into the pot. "The town took away our liquor license. You're all welcome to have dinner, but you'll have to wolf them down dry."

"They hate us Montauk boys. It's time we succeed. Now where are we going to eat? We love the food at the Shack." The fisherman frowned.

"They call us the Lost Boys? One day we'll show those rich Hampton bastards."

I offered the lost and now-found boys back their by-catch of lobster.

"You can keep them. They were free anyway," they said, riding off in search of a quicker, profounder high. "We're off to do a little time travel."

As they walked out the back door, Leslie walked in. "I'm closing after Labor Day," she announced. "I'm fed up with this business. The owners of the marina want me to stay open till November to cater to the occasional charter. I should wake up at seven to flip one egg. It's just not worth it. What's in the basket?"

"Don't put all your eggs in one basket."

"If that's a joke, stick to teeth. Where did you get the lobsters?"

"The Lost Boys' lobsters."

"Speaking of which, have you seen my son? He hasn't been to work in days."

"I'm having enough trouble keeping track of my own."

"You just have to leave them alone to fight their own demons. They'll grow out of it. There's isn't anything as a parent you can do anyway."

"That's not the way I was raised. I can't sit still and watch my son or your son self-destruct when my hand might help them through a crisis."

"What are you, some kind of self-elected guardian angel?"

"I prefer fireman. A volunteer, I rescue stray cats and kids down from trees."

"Volunteer fireman? You'll do anything to become a local. Man, are you ever clueless." She wandered out front in search of Tracey.

Ignoring Leslie's ungracious opinion of my net worth, I checked my horoscope in the *Post*. It advised, "Gemini, keep doing whatever you are doing. There is no right answer." I love the sports column and the horoscopes in the *New York Post*, which are written for real weekend fathers like me.

Family life was full of problems, no matter what I did to make the world right. I couldn't choose the cards, but play the deck as best I could. The restaurant wasn't the real trouble. I would find happiness and distinguish myself in my reactions to trouble.

Chapter 39

The Meal Ticket

Some restaurants change staff regularly. We changed nations. First we hired the local American kids for front of house, and then the Polish girls. As the summer progressed, the Irish students came, partied their brains out, and left us with legendary memories. As we approached the last weekend of the summer, we were shuffling for any available help. The customers were still here, but every seasonal business in town was chasing after the same employees. A nice group of Eastern Europeans, Czechs, and Slovakians had transferred their hours from another gig to work the checkout at our Shack. They were sweet, gorgeous, and spoke moderately good English. More importantly, their college schedule back home didn't begin till late September.

"Now that we have staff, I want to stay open until the end," Tracey said. "Even without alcohol, we're so busy. If the weather holds, I predict our best sales ever. We'll lose some profit not selling alcohol, but there seems to be quicker turnover."

The One Hundred Days of Hampton Restaurant Hell was suddenly extended another thirty-one days. What was an off-season husband to do? The business employed our three sons, and they were genuinely happy to work a little longer. I was just the pedestal. If my wife's beautiful bust was shaken by a bad wind and started to tumble off its axis, what could I do? The pedestal couldn't play the juggler, leaning a little to the left or bending through the right in an attempt to stabilize the bust or catch her if she fell. The pedestal must stand still, stay solid, and allow the weight to right itself.

"Montauk turns into a ghost town after the summer ends," I shuttered.

"Why must you always be so negative? September has the best weather, and the ocean is still warm. There's also the seasonal migration of fishermen and surfers. I'm not too worried," she said. "Oh, did I tell you? The Surf Lodge offered me a contract to bake and deliver breakfast pastries. Their French manager just loves my croissants. We may not count as a real restaurant, but we can still cook good food."

"Congratulations."

"Since I'll be up at 6:30 baking their pastries, I might as well be open for breakfast. I could flip some eggs. Also, I purchased a glass enclosed pastry counter, which should come tomorrow. Without alcohol and music, we're losing our evening crowd. I need to adjust the product. The new girls are willing to help with the early shift."

"That's a well-thought adaptation to the restrictions."

"I'm not going to reinvent the wheel at this point."

Coming out of the kitchen after working a double shift, Gray was tailed by his groupies—local young ladies, red-haired, freckled, and wearing short skirts. The Pied Piper of pastry, he was their rock star. They loved to watch him cook. "I've decided to switch to a culinary major in college," he announced. "I really like this business."

"But you were my last hope to be a dentist," I pleaded.

"I don't like blood. One good thing about having a family food business is that at least you know where your parents are," he joked.

"You're funny, Gray. Well, one good thing about a family business is that at least I know where my money is being spent," I countered.

"Speaking of which, Gray, I need your help to prepare that wedding cake," said Tracey. "It's my first one, three tiers for $500. A five-year-old's fancy, black-tie birthday party in Bridgehampton, investment banker—good deal, don't you think?"

"Your red velvet wedding cake, white icing over blood-colored cake, is wasted on kids. You should do a black wedding, with those plastic bride and grooms, but instead of dancing, the bride could be holding a knife in the groom's back." I laughed at her creation. "The price seems a bit low for the amount of work. Professional cakes are expensive. Loaves and Fishes in Bridgehampton charges $100 for a pound of lobster salad. The bride's a banker. She can afford $2000 for your work of art."

"You're going gothic on me again." Tracey showed teeth, but not in a smile. "Why must you always be so critical?" She took my last hope to be a dentist and pulled him back into the kitchen. "Call us if you need a ride." I was alone again.

My heart exploded with anger toward my wife. She sure knew how to touch my button: a sticky, icky feeling of abandonment, creeping up my spine. Why's she so thin-skinned? I was just kidding about the plastic wedding props, although I truly felt she'd undervalued the cake. It cost her more to make it. I'm the fucking meal ticket for this family. She didn't even offer me a food stamp of acknowledgment. I worked all week, and when I came out here, she didn't have the time of day for me. Residual blood pressure pounded in my ears, delaying any chance of recovery from tick fever.

I appreciated that Tracey had different spatial needs than I. That's why she hated to tango. We were opposites: she's an Aries, while I'm a Gemini. We were considered a good match. The cold bird, she sought freedom to fly. I'm a teddy bear, who wanted to be squeezed. It's almost as if we switched gender roles. When I complained to her that I was tired of always being alone, it just pushed her further away. I was addicted to her attention. I couldn't get enough of it. If marriage was my vice, I needed to kick this habit or find another to replace it.

Another couple called it quits that day because the wife was fed up with taking care of the husband, whom she claimed acted like a third child.

According to Thich Nhat Hahn, the famous Buddhist Zen master, "People deal too much in the negative, with what is wrong. Why not try and see positive things, to just touch things and make them bloom." Tracey had created this beautiful cocoon, but I felt empty, left out. At that moment, I made a personal quest to focus on the positive and negate the negative, or the no-toothache-today experience. Hahn said, "The foundation of happiness is mindfulness. The basic condition for being happy is our consciousness of being happy. If we are not aware that we are happy, we are not really happy. When we have a toothache, we know that not having a toothache is a wonderful thing. But when we do have a toothache, we are still not happy. A non-toothache is very pleasant." As a successful dentist, I vowed to practice not having a toothache, or in this case, a heartache.

Tracey claimed I was always angry with her, but from my perspective, my anger was merely a defense against her anger. It didn't make much sense. If my goal was happiness, I was going about it wrongly. I needed to appreciate the good things in my life instead of focusing on what was missing. It wasn't that hard. The will. I'd instructed Tracey in the will to make her business succeed. I needed to will myself to happiness!

Still, it was getting harder and harder to deal with Tracey's perceived aggression. Monday was the out-going night in our weekend marriage. I tended to raise the aggression on the out-going to lubricate my grief on separation. Tracey was cold on Friday's in-comings as she hesitated to lubricate my welcome back into her bed.

Monday night's exit dinner with Emily, what was I thinking? "So what does your boyfriend do for a living?" It was a rhetorical question. I knew her boyfriend was a freeloader who was just taking advantage of my good nature, but I was trying to make dinner conversation and become more comfortable with some guy who had moved into my home without so much as a thank you. "What are his future plans?"

"It's so easy for you as a doctor to ask what other people do," Tracey reprimanded me in public. "Not everyone defines themselves by their occupation, like dentists and lawyers. You don't have to answer his question, Emily. He's being inappropriate to ask it," she referred to me condescendingly, as if I lacked all social skills.

From my position, Tracey's tone of voice was overly aggressive and she had embarrassed me. She was publicly attacking me, and I was fed up with playing the male praying mantis that muffled all responses for sexual self-preservation. Her attitude trolled an immediate negative response. "I'm not attacking Emily. She's welcome to stay in our home, but I feel I have a right to learn more about this guy who moved into my home through the back door. For all anyone knows, he might be a serial murderer."

"I told them he could live here while Emily works in the restaurant," Tracey said with extreme vigilance. She was counterattacking, and the battle drew fresh blood.

"Well, no one ever asked my opinion," I gestured through my hands.

"You hardly live here, and my employees need housing. It wasn't up to you."

"That's great. What am I? Chopped liver?" My counter-counterattack had now embarrassed her before her friend and employee, so she swung for the jugular.

"I am fed up with your constant aggression. You either need to get a lid on it or get on that bus!" Tracey slammed down her wine glass and walked out of the room.

Emily and I looked at each other with equal embarrassment: she, because she had been the source of our fight, and me, because I didn't see a solution to the hole I'd dug. Tracey's response was over-the-top and outside the normal boundary of our marital conflict. Once in the station, that divorce train was hard to un-track. There should be an anonymous organization for restaurant spouses.

Before I departed back to NYC, I patrolled out front on the sidewalk, searching for a few straggler tourists to fill the front of house, a last-minute gift. Tracey saw me standing at the doorway and complained, "Why are you lurking there?"

Her words hurt more than all the other miscommunications to date. I got on the bus and vowed I wouldn't speak to her for a week. Maybe I'd even find some excuse to stay in the city next weekend. The season wasn't nearly over, and I was a train wreck.

A dangerous game had developed with my life and my wife. I used her as a muse for my memoir in a game of Russian relationship roulette. Sometimes, I was unsure of my real motives. I could have ignored Tracey's original comment or explained to her that she had embarrassed me, but instead I attacked, as if my aggression would force her to acquiesce. Who was the bully and who the abused in this relationship? Aggression had accomplished only one thing: more anger. We were like the Palestinians and Israelis, who constantly upped the bloody ante. This behavior didn't work for countries, and it was a complete failure in marriage. I needed to be nicer to my wife.

Chapter 40

Blooms Day

The migratory frigate bird stood on one leg, perched in an elegant yoga posture, an impossible pose, right wing wrapped full around waist, her tight, black mantle painted against the sandy matt of a Montauk beach. It was strange to view a frigate this far north, let alone one landed. I've spotted wayward whales, triggerfish, and even pelicans, but never this solitary traveler. When aloft, she is the most beautiful flyer, looping to the sea to scoop dinner down her gullet.

From the fringe of sight, a man-sized teddy bear strolled across the dunes, whipping his arms to and fro as he bounced merrily along the beach. The stuffed man-mammal stopped behind the bird and curiously inspected her position. The bear attempted to imitate the posture of the elegant one-legged bird. But try as he might, he kept falling. In a vaudevillian gesture, he shook the sand from his well-worn fur and inexpertly bent into an imitation of Claw to Big Paw posture.

The bird appeared oblivious to the bear's invitation. The bear crept slowly along the sand and stealthily snuck up on her. She jumped away. "Leave me be!"

The fun-loving teddy stood in frustration in front of the frigate. He jumped up and down in an attempt to gain some recognition, but the bird held the one-legged posture, ignoring him. "I'm sleeping," she shuttered.

The exothermic bear placed two paws around her waist. "Can we go now?"

The cold bird squirmed free from the bear's grasp. "Whatever you want. I don't want to make any more decisions. I'm freezing."

"If we go, will it be we, just you with me?"

"So many questions, like what should I wear? My bikini's missing a triangle."

"Brazilian, three triangles? A and B for the breast, C to cover your crotch. Whatever happened to D? If the words fit, you should at least wear them," he pantomimed.

Rolling her frigate eyes, she said, "P doesn't come close to covering your head."

"I've tried to tailor my teddy talk to your delicate constitution, but my sexual wordplay always seems to cause you to fly off your handle." The teddy bear grabbed the frigate bird by the waist and violently forged a tango embrace. Suddenly, they were dancing tango inside a miniature version of the Gig Shack. Marching around the room, they paused in front of the gelato counter, paw to wing, chest to chest, in a studied pose.

Inside the child's music box, the waltzing bird and bear toys were now accompanied by another couple; a small-town beach miniaturized milonga was in the making, as the supervisor held the local judge in an awkward embrace. They all swirled steadily through a tango number and danced atop the tables. Magically, they completed the number without leaving the confines of that petite rectangular dance floor. The judge and supervisor's smiles were frozen in rapture, the two arms of local justice, joined as one, locked lip-to-lip in an unsteady tango embrace.

Drama queens. Epic night sweat. Happiness the absence of anger. Anger the happiness of absence. Darwin's law of self-preservation, everyone does what makes them happy? Dysfunction. Disruption. Disrupt. Drink to forget. Forget to drink. *Composto de Erva*—mate hangover. Hung over, or hard on a morning geyser.

"Wake up, Lewis, you're so warm." Tracey pushed me away.

"Fuck you! Fuck you!" Killjoy jumped between the dancing couples. His head was impaled on the multi-legged body of a hermit crab. His claws clattered chatter, a soliloquy of unintelligible epitaphs. "Fuck you." With black stalked eyes twirling from his brow, he made a sudden dash for the door but was blocked by Shaggy and the Deli Dolls, who were dressed up in revealing outfits for Carnival. "No dancing. No dancing. Fuck you! Fuck you …" Killjoy's claws jawed away, eyes rotated 360 degrees.

"Wake up! What are you screaming about?" Tracey shook me until the foggy memory of animals dancing, teddy bears, frigate birds, and hermit crabs drifted into history. "You were cursing in your sleep?"

The ghostlike images, so vivid just moments earlier, quickly faded. Why couldn't I remember my dreams? If they are forgotten, did they even occur? Sleep was another state of rapture, like the exaltation of the spirit, an expensive perfume, a rare drug, being sexually transported, or an epiphany. Rapture and happiness were the fleeting goal.

"I need to bake the doughnuts. Will you be all right?" Tracey worried.

"A silly nightmare. I'll meet you for lunch." Forgetting last week's fight.

While Tracey readied for Labor Day, I steadied my unconscious mind by undoing the laundry, displacing the dishwasher, and weeding the garden. The weeding was an endless occupation, like sweeping sand off the sidewalk on the beach, my first real job, or correcting the endless rampages of dental decay, my present profession. I loved to weed and never considered mulching red cedar bark that looks like clay and kills all life. Compost equals cultivation. I didn't grow plants. I grew dirt. This week's weed was the next flower's skeleton. James Joyce said fat men with big mouths make the best fertilizer.

Around noon, I strolled through town to meet Tracey at the Shack. Passing Kirk Park, I spied a lump of clothing piled under a bench. On closer inspection, the disheveled pile was a young man's bedding. "Mac, Mac Cool. Are you okay?" Rolling him face upward, I listened to his breath. "Come on, man. What are you doing? You sleep out here all night?" He reeked of old beer and new vomit. Removing his stained shirt, I rinsed it under a nearby hose and washed the sleep from his eyes. He was a smelly mess.

"I'm okay. I'm okay, doc." He sang an Irish ditty. "Leave me be." He got up slowly and smiled like an old drunk. "We Lost Boys of Montauk. We'll fight for liberty." He spat out a wad of dried throat phlegm. "We'll fight for liberty. With heart and hand to burst the galling chain ..." He coughed up bloody sputum this time. "We'll ..." He coughed so hard he couldn't breathe and rolled back onto the ground.

I smacked him on the back to clear the airway. "Mac, what are you doing? You promised you'd take better care of yourself. Now look at you. Sleeping it off in the park. Does your mother know where you are?" I offered him a draught from my plastic water bottle and helped him stand wobbly to his feet.

"I'll call her, doc. No worries, old bloke." He rummaged his pockets, but he'd lost his phone somewhere in the night, and standing straight upright was still an issue.

"You can borrow mine. Make the call. Come with me for breakfast at the Shack. We can talk on the way." I neatened his attire. "So what happened to you last night?"

A homeless earwig squatted on his earlobe. The slithering black bug escaped with gray matter from somewhere deep inside his head and jumped to the ground.

He spoke nervously. "Last night, I finally met the real Lost Boys of Montauk. I've been to the other side. I did it, doc, transmuted. Time traveled. Shagged karma from past life. Seen the other side of the universe. What a fucking awesome sight!" He squealed with delight and did a little Irish dance. "Been to the edge and back. I've been to the edge and back. Doc, I've been to the edge!" He slapped his thighs.

"Mac, the Montauk Project is just a local tale to explain those abandoned bunkers. There were never any Lost Boys, or aliens, or secret government cover-ups."

"I swear I've seen them. Hiked the Walking Dunes through Talk House's Trail, past Elisha's cemetery, the Tarworks, and Devil's Crater. That's where they be hiding all these years, in Hither Woods, near the Split Rock and Indian's Jump. Living right under our noses, a regular Buonaraba. The Lost Boys found. Lord of the Flies, Promised Land, and all that. They're living by the Code of Fuse Box, no cyber-junkie shit, I swear."

"Mac Cool. What drug are you on?"

"Joyce was right. Them cokeheads, old sons of bitches blocked the truth all these years. Not wanting change." His eyes were bugging out like a hyperthyroid.

"I'm a doctor. I know about drugs. I can help you." I reached out.

"I swear. Super Spottum. Clean as a whistle." He showed a fleshy forearm. "The Lost Boys told me who the conspirators were. The Montauk Mafia trying to close the Gig Shack." His hands shook so hard he had to hold onto himself to prevent elevating.

"Mac. You're wacko. You're speaking like a crazy kid."

"Them Fake Feinians I'd wager! Nazi sympathizers planted here for the next war. A secret rear guard." Shaking uncontrollably, now he spoke with the full brogue on. "The Freeholders blew Montauk's one chance for independence. Doomed the secession and King James Dongan Patent of 1686. Duped the real Friends of Erin into believing in a cause, a covenant, then by and by took a paid pass from the Count of East Hampton, another sorrowful year of servitude and slavery thumped by the supervisor's heavy yoke, our fight for liberty betrayed by those cowards. Left Danny Boy, the local dentist, to hang by his gutta percha." Mac Cool stared off into the gaze of a stoking summer sun. He was sweating. A white powder shadowed his nose.

"Mac, you need professional help. Please come with me." I reached out again.

He swatted my hand away. "You're no better than the other old bloomers." The cut of his pupils hurt more than the actual words. "Show cause and be free."

"Mac Cool, reliving James Joyce's novel about a man's search for immortality is killing you. Close that book already and return to your suburban roots. There will be no epiphany at the end of your odyssey, only sadness. Give up this fantasy world, this portrait of an artist as a young man. Acting like an Iris bull, although a common affliction of youth in general, is no more rampant in the artistic souls of Montauk than the make-believers across the pond. It is irksome for the rest of us. You must abandon this imitation of an imaginary literary character. Put on a bathing suit and drop the knickers. You are a flesh-and-blood American kid, not some cartoon character, dressed in natty tweeds and cardigan, as if you were right off the boat from Cork Town. You aren't even Irish. Your vocabulary was stolen from a Victorian novel. Your life is a nostalgic narcissism; at most, you're a just a common graffitist pretending to be a real artist." I'd said more than I'd intended or truly believed. It was his life to win or lose.

His eyes parboiled and reddened with anger. "Take a mulligan, old man! Speak for yourself. Off with you." His hands drew into coiled fists.

"Mac, I'm just trying to help."

He threw a weak, telegraphed swing at my head, which I easily parlayed, pushing him past me into the ground. He cried from my feet. "Wild goose chaser. You wouldn't know happiness if it hit you." He picked himself off the ground and wiped the sand off. "I'd hoped you understood my art, but you're just mummer at the end of his rainbow."

"Come on, Mac. I am your friend."

"Chill-lax, old man, your journey is done. Mine has just begun."

"It doesn't have to end like this."

"Yes. It does, I'm a chapter in need of an ending. You said so yourself. Too many drugs spoil the brew." With tears in his eyes, he retreated on his beloved skateboard toward Lake Montauk, slowly at first, but as I attempted to follow, he sped up, further and further away into his looking glass.

With a burst of speed I'd long forgotten, I blocked his exit down the paved road. "I'm pretty fast for an old guy?"

Pulling up his skateboard into his right arm, he parlayed my blocking maneuver with a counter-cross and sped on foot back into the park.

I followed close on his heels.

Cornered, he climbed into the cradle of a tree and called down, "If we never meet again, have mercy on my soul." He meowed. "You can't get me. You can't get me." He stuck out his tongue with defiance. "You can't help me."

For a man who claims to be volunteer fireman, I was not a very good climber. I am actually quite afraid of heights. I jumped up and down and swatted air.

"Give up and leave me be." He climbed higher. "You can't reach me!"

Grabbing hold of the lowest branch, I swung one foot up and then another, until with complete desperation I righted myself in the lower cradle of the tree.

Astonished at my audacity, Mac climbed higher out on a limb.

"I'm hopeless. Can't you see? I'm hopeless."

He avoided my lunging grasp and crawled out on a narrower branch high above, which bent under his weight.

"Just give me your hand. It's never too late." I made a final lunge.

As the branch above me broke, he ping-ponged from one tree limb, off another, until his shirt caught an edge and he was within my grasp. I caught his fall, grabbing his wrist before he hit ground. His skateboard hit a rock below and broke in two.

Chapter 41

Labor Day

Leslie was in a really pissed off mood. "I'm closing the Bones for good. I'm suing my fucking lying landlord, my Italian macho drug addict chef, and any other fucking male who tries to get in my way." She counted customer heads at our outdoor tables.

I ducked for cover before the crosshairs of her suing shotgun honed in on me.

"Have you seen my errant son? He hasn't been home in days."

I had mixed emotions whether I should inform her of Mac's emotional state. My allegiance to him was as a friend, but she was a fellow parent and had every right to expect my full support. "I saw him this morning. Didn't he call? He misplaced his phone. He was on his way to the skate park last I saw. Would you like me to drive around?"

"No. When I catch him, his butt's going to be grounded for life."

"Well, he was acting a bit strange, but he's okay. I think."

"Acting strange is his natural state. I've forgotten what a normal son looks like. I'll go by the park, but if you see him again, tell him to get his ass home and pack up his things. I'm closing my Montauk operations and relocating."

"I'm sorry to hear that. You worked so hard all summer. We hardly had any time to hang out together. I want you to know that you have a wonderful, smart son. Mac and I got to know each other a little. You should be very proud of him."

"Yeah, whatever. Say good-bye to your wife. I'm out of here at the end of the week. I need to take a long trip and let all the bullshit of this business die away."

Tracey and I met with our new real estate attorney at his fancy office. A local fellow, he had once worked for the town, but now he played the private side. He wasn't particularly confident that we had a

249

legal leg to stand on, but since Tracey was so expert at standing on one leg and we already owned the building and had three sons who could eventually grow into ownership, we decided to proceed with an appeal of the building department's decision that we were a retail space which could only serve food over the counter. The lawyer wouldn't speak until we whet his lips a little.

"Think of it as an investment in real estate," Tracey advised as I swallowed hard on my signing over a five-thousand-dollar retainer on a probable lost cause.

The attorney quickly pocketed the check and proceeded to review the mountain of paperwork from thirty years of attempts by previous owners to upgrade our little Shack into a full restaurant. Historically, the names of our three present neighbors kept popping up in opposition to any change. When he'd finished, his face twisted into an angular frown and his gaze narrowed on me. "So where were you born?"

His question took me by surprise. I'd just invested a week's worth of sweat and dentistry into his new corvette and all he cared about was where I was born?

"I'm from the Bronx and he's an Up Island," Tracey spoke first.

"Whom do you know?" he asked, referring to the local hierarchy.

"We know the youth of Montauk," Tracey said proudly.

"Maybe their parents are somebody?" I added.

"I doubt it. Not the group of youth we know."

"Oh yeah, our home is the local lost and found."

"Well, that won't help much, but there may be another angle," the lawyer advised. "If I can prove that the original intent of the pre-1980 variance was to allow you to operate as a restaurant, for all intents and purposes, given the parking and sewage allowance, then we may have a chance. I've scheduled a hearing in a few weeks. In the meantime, I'll inform the judge of our appeal. Just keep your nose clean and make peace with the neighbors. Maybe this time they will be too old to object."

Tracey was confident that the meeting went well. I had my reservations, but I didn't voice them; she had enough on her plate just trying to get open for dinner.

"If I can just survive Labor Day weekend, then I'll go in with you to NYC on Tuesday. I have a meeting with another lawyer who specializes in liquor licenses."

"Where are you going to meet this liquor lawyer?" I asked.

"In a bar behind Madison Square Garden. He has an office at the back of the bar."

"Why doesn't that surprise me? Where else would a liquored lawyer work?"

She laughed at my joke. Well, maybe not a belly laugh, but at least she cracked a smile. Her thin skin toward perceived criticism was thickening. "He passed the bar, but he never left. He's serving lime with his time."

Swallowing a lump of pride, I strolled over to Killjoy's with a peace offering tray of goodies—gelato sandwiches in multiple flavors. I needed his sewage capacity. Killjoy was behind the counter counting out one-ounce lead weights as if they were gold coins. I heard the miser cast the tin soldiers in his basement, a total violation of EPA rules, and that he had been doing it for so long the town wouldn't prosecute his alchemy.

"How you doing today, neighbor?" From his entrance, I offered the tray.

Barely looking up from his pile of lead coins, he barked. "What do you want?"

"I got a question for you. There's always going to be a business here. If you don't like us, what kind of business would you like to see?"

"Fuck you."

"Mr. Killjoy, I'm trying to make peace. I'm courteous, why the cursing?"

"Cause your fucking bitch wife cursed me and the deli girls."

He was a good one to complain about other people cursing, but I sucked up his direct insult. "Okay, I apologize on my wife's behalf."

"That isn't good enough. You're only trying to make nice to get at my sewage. Well, shit on you and shit on your whole family." He had me there. He'd out-shitted me again. Some little birdie had already informed him that we were sewage deficient.

I needed his crapolla, so I retreated with my ass still intact between my legs. I was the persistent type, and his constant cursing had become music to my ears, like the bark of a little dog or a rooster's crow. One day I'd have a chance at a word-worthy revenge.

The Gig Shack was packed for dinner when I returned. Labor Day weekend approached, the last party of the summer, and the tourists had jammed every available seat. The tables had finally turned. We were so popular that I sent our overflow to Shaggy's place, which was only half-full.

Tracy Feith, a popular fashionista, was waiting for a table with three supermodels in tow. I played the shill maître d' to the hilt. He was a regular customer and I really wanted to show off those female super-bodies, but there was at least an hour wait.

"Mr. Feith, I'll do my best, but you see how crowded it is."

"That's okay. We'll wait." He motioned to the girls. "I really like your place."

One of the stunningly beautiful amazons added, "You have the best food in town! Those fish tacos, spicy empanadas, and nickel/dime bags of smoked ribs ... yum." The way she licked her lips with a flicker of tongue made my heart flutter.

"Have you tried the Surf Dogs? An Argentine sausage with chimichurri sauce on a homemade bun." I advised them on new menu items and pictured those lips sucking down a well-done smoked sausage. "I recommend the peanut butter smoothie too."

"Your food is Shack Therapy."

"Thanks, Tracy. It's nice to know I didn't mortgage the marriage for nothing."

A little while later, a young girl of about ten years came up to me.

"Mister, are you the owner of 668?" She held out a finger-licked empty plate.

I looked around for another family member, but none was in immediate sight. "I guess I am. How can I help you, little girl?"

"You make the best cheese quesadilla I've ever eaten. Please promise me you will never close. My tummy loves you."

"Tell your tummy to thank the town board."

What could I say? It was just one of those perfect nights in the restaurant business when everything ran according to plan. The staff and our sons worked hard but efficiently. Tracey was the queen of the show, and all our customers left with a smile.

Around 11:00 PM, we were getting ready to close the kitchen. A few customers were finishing their dinner at outside tables. A policeman walked in and asked for the owner. This was becoming a regular occurrence, and when I pulled Tracey away from her baking, she was in no mood to play with this youngster in a uniform.

"Here are your cookies!" Annoyed with the constant harassment by the supervisor, she took her whole tray of freshly baked chocolate chip cookies and dumped them on the counter. "Take your pick—or for that matter, take them all. I don't care anymore." She nastily flipped a couple of cookies in the cop's direction.

The cop didn't appreciate her flippant attitude. "Do you have a liquor license, miss?" His eyes scanned the room for some unknown offense.

"You know perfectly well I don't have a license anymore. Your boss stole it."

He looked around the joint at the fire department seating allowance signs. At least it was past the witching hour and we weren't over the limit, but he was licking his lips and smiling like a Cheshire cat who'd just swallowed a canary when he left.

"What was all that about?" she asked me with concern.

"A wakeup call?" Maybe she should have been less flippant. You win more friends with honey, but the arch of this story was already predestined.

The next morning, when we opened the doors for breakfast, another cop served Tracey with papers, a warrant for her arrest. She was being charged with operating an illegal bottle club. The charges claimed that the cop from last night had witnessed a couple out front drinking from one open bottle of beer during their dinner.

Tracey queried all of the employees who'd worked the previous night to determine whether anyone had seen this open bottle, but no one had. I'd been out front at times during the evening and didn't see any alcohol either. Tracey had baked in the kitchen all evening; how could she be held responsible? If the customer snuck in a bottle of beer, why was it the owner's responsibility to police them? Shouldn't the cop arrest the customer with the open bottle? Had the supervisor set up this sting because our C of O was retail and not a restaurant?

I visited the Fish Market. It wasn't a legal restaurant either, but the owner, a local blueblood, advertised BYOB for years. Everyone in town knew his customers brought their own wine and beer. He even offered free corkscrews and ice buckets. In front of his shop was a new sign notifying customers that there was no liquor allowed on the premises. After fifteen years of committing this heinous crime, the authorities had issued him a simple warning, but in my wife's case, they arrested her for the first errant Bud. To date, I'd discounted the notion that there was a conspiracy in this town to put my beautiful wife out of business, but it had become increasingly obvious that the Montauk Beach Billy's and the Beverly Beach Billy's of East Hampton were in cahoots.

There were endless examples of the supervisor's capricious enforcement. A nearby pizzeria was allowed to serve beer on premises even though their Certificate of Occupancy was for a bank, and that famously decadent bar and cocaine hotspot on Route 27 had a liquor license even though it was legally a car mechanic's shop. These restaurants had been allowed to operate illegally for years, but we had been open one season and were subjected to constant harassment by the cops and their courts. There was something terribly, terribly wrong with this judicial picture.

Tracey had another meeting in court with that judge, the one who had started the whole downhill judicial process. Our new lawyer explained the case was put on hold due to our request for an appeal of the zoning ruling. He also explained to the judge that the building department had misinterpreted the zoning laws and that we were entirely legal to be a restaurant. "A complete miscarriage of justice!" he quoted.

The judge couldn't give a damn for his legal maneuvering and rolled her eyes. "Yeah, yeah, you really think so, counselor." To our complete astonishment, she claimed that we were "verboten" and should be closed immediately if not sooner, due to undisclosed heinous offenses, even though we'd never once been accused of any infractions. "Your client is an egregious offender." Where had the judge gotten this misinformation? Someone high up really had it in for my beautiful wife.

"She hates me." Tracey cried buckets of tears.

"The judge did look peeved that she would have to wait for the appeal before she could slam you with her gravel."

"I can't wait for the season to end. I am so done."

"If we can hold a long-term view, a five-year plan, you're just working out the kinks until the boys mature in their roles."

We got back to the Shack in time for the Friday afternoon set-up of Labor Day weekend. Tracey immediately dived into her safety net of baking scones, croissants, cakes, pies, and cookies. She was in her element, a sort of cookie cocoon. I kept busy folding the rollups, napkins around the fake silverware, and feeding the staff tip jar.

The dishwasher was late, so I soaked my arms in suds and serviced the pots and pans. It was busy work, but it kept me near my beautiful baking wife. She threw me a sliver of a thank you smile, not much, but it was enough for my pedestal to stand tall.

An inexpert dishwasher, at one point I confused the temperatures of the three-sink hand-washing system and blocked contaminants in the grease trap. Not wanting to ask for help and bother my wife, I drained all three sinks at once, which created a minor flood. I cleaned up the mess before she noticed, spoke privately to Nico about technique, and cleared my plate before Gorge and the evening staff appeared.

"Papi chulo, please, you are big, important man. What you doing? Gringo no do Gorge's job." The dishwasher pulled the last dish out of my hand and removed my apron. "You hurt my feelings." He made a sour puss.

"Okay, Gorge. This ship is yours." I plunked the dishrag in his hand and went out front looking for another job to keep me busy but out of everyone's way. By this point in the season, I had a large inventory of jobs I could fill, an expert in none but competent at a few. I mashed a spud, cut heads off of live crabs, and filled the ketchup bottles to capacity. Remember, in real life I am a doctor. I could handle any emergency.

Emma full-backed up to my face. She had that same tenacious look in her eye when we'd first met and she started a campfire in an Antiguan thunderstorm. This time her tenacity was directed at me. With closed fists, she screamed at me, "I quit!"

Why me? "You can't quit," I pleaded. "It's Labor Day weekend. Please stay a few more days." Actually, Tracey would have been glad to get rid of her. None of the staff liked her. We only tolerated her all summer to keep Nico happy.

"I don't care if you beg me to stay or offer me a raise. I quit!"

I hadn't considered offering a raise to an employee we wanted to leave, and I certainly wasn't about to grovel. Maybe she thought she had us over the barrel. We needed every hand on deck to get through the last weekend. "Why are you quitting?"

"No one here likes me. They make fish eyes when I walk by. I can see them snickering behind my back." She squinted paranoia in both directions.

"Nonsense. We love you." I could visualize Tracey and Emily rolling fish eyes, but I needed to consider Nico's take on the matter. We couldn't afford to lose him too. "Wait here. I have a good-bye present for you." I didn't actually have anything for her, but it froze her steps. In the meantime, I cornered Nico in the kitchen, who knew more about the history of this discontent than he'd let on to. I backed him into the stove.

"Should I just let the pink elephant in the room quit?" I demanded, half-joking by using the Disney metaphor for the person we needed to talk about.

He threw me a shark eye and exploded into a litany of stored grievances. "That's a nasty comment. She is still my girlfriend. Why are you calling her an elephant? What did she ever do to you? You were the last person I expected to take sides. Everyone in the Shack has treated her so poorly. They hate her. It's enough to make me quit too. Fishing season starts in Antigua soon; maybe I should leave now."

Suddenly I realized I'd inadvertently stepped into a warm pile of shit that I had no reason walking near. This was a lose-loser for me. I scanned the kitchen for a signal from Tracey, who was conveniently nowhere. Thinking on my feet, I pulled Nico over to the computer and Googled Disney's pink elephant metaphor. When he was satisfied that I hadn't offended the love of his life, he calmed down.

"It's for the best if she leaves now," he agreed. "I'm going to have to work 24/7 through the next two weekends, and she has to get ready to go to school in Maine."

"Okay, then we are all agreed. I'll go say good-bye."

Emma was standing out front with hands on hips and a prissy pout on her face.

I offered her a strong handshake and my winning smile. "Thank you for a good season. If you ever need a letter of recommendation or anything."

"That's it? Where's my bonus check? My good-bye present."

"But you quit. I don't normally give a bonus to a quitter."

"I'm a quitter?" Her hands fisted again, and her forehead reddened. She was not a cougar I'd ever want to be caged with, so I reached into my pocket and slapped four crisp Grants into her hand. It was chump change to be rid of that ball buster once and for all.

Dealing with Emma completely wore me out, so I went home, poured a stiff Scotch, then another, and maybe a hat trick. Tracey came home sometime later on her moped, equally exhausted. We both passed out immediately, but were awoken at sunrise by the phone. I took the call from Leslie, who proceeded to tell me the saddest story I'd ever heard. Mac Cool had died accidentally in the middle of the night. Leslie found him unconscious on the floor. He was dead.

Her story was every parent's worst nightmare. The hospital had made repeated attempts to resuscitate him, but in the end, he had taken life too far out to the edge. He had traveled to the nether, nether world, a home no child can return from.

"I feel like I let him down. I failed as his guardian," I explained to my family as we all cried that morning with grief. "I'd seen him a few days before he died. He said he wanted to take life to the limit. If only I'd held him tighter in that tree."

"He had a long history of being in treatment and on antidepressants. His psychiatrist should be held responsible," said Tracey.

"You don't understand. He told me he'd met up with the Lost Boys that night. I should have known he was unstable. Something about him had suddenly changed."

"The Lost Boys?"

"The myth about two brothers who fell into the Montauk Project time travel generator and were never seen again. Mac Cool was experimenting in time travel. We need to go to Camp Hero and find him. Maybe he's stuck in another dimension."

"You're a doctor. You don't really believe in such nonsense? What would you have you done anyway, have him institutionalized?

Who knows what drug he'd swallowed or how much alcohol he consumed."

"I guess you're right. There is nothing left but grief."

"It was an accident."

"Yeah. It was just an accident."

Mac Cool was a hip cat that crawled too far out on the tree limb of life. He got scared and jumped. If only he had held on a little until a fireman rescued him.

I blamed myself. I was a shill fireman, not the kind of hero you want to save a child or a cat in a real fire. Obsessed with my own affairs, deluded by my own epiphany, I'd stood idle while this young man died. In frustration with my own incompetence, I wailed fists against my face and head in a display of self-flagellation. The self-abuse didn't hurt as much as the loss of Mac Cool.

Chapter 42

Change of Use

We survived Labor Day weekend with a skeleton crew and the whole family, including yours truly, working two shifts. If the season had been that busy all along, or if Montauk stayed open longer, Tracey would have made money hand over fist. Unfortunately, with the beginning of a new school year, the town quickly depopulated. September had the most perfect weather, crisp and clear. A few farmers and fishermen remained, and the homeowners, who rent their houses out during the summer, returned.

"Do you think I should stay open through the fall?" The praying mantis wife eyed my skull. She licked my earlobe. Was that a sign of affection or a pre-dinner tasting? Would she kiss me before she lopped my head off? "There are still plenty of people in town. I don't want to close yet."

"Whatever." I chose self-preservation.

"That's exactly what I was thinking." She patted me on the head. "Let's keep the boys busy and wait until things really get slow. Dr. Lonely can survive a little longer in NYC on his own, can't you? It's going to take weeks to clean up and shut down."

"Gross! Gross will be next year's brilliant!"

Tracey and I went home and watched an old black and white movie, *Mildred Pierce*. Mildred opened a successful restaurant and then split from her husband. She gave all her money to her useless daughter and the ex was left hanging curtains. "I loved that." Tracey praised the actress, who seemed a bit cold-blooded and distant to me.

Next we watched the cooking channel. Paula Dean, that white-haired female chef from New Orleans, explained how she dumped her husband when she had started a restaurant with her two sons. The nonverbal message was coming in loud and clear.

"I need to think of a new plan for next year. If we don't get back our liquor license or waitress service, we'll need to become a high-end deli," Tracey said.

"How do you feel about that?" I asked.

"I want to be a real restaurant. There are five delis in this town within a one-block radius, all serving the same two inches of crappy bologna and greasy fried chicken. I could be a gourmet food shop, a mini Dean and Deluca, but I'd have to change the wooden counters, add displays, and remove the interior seating. The change from hard ice cream to a front gelato counter is a must; my wrists hurt from a season of scooping from frozen containers. It's just that I don't want to spend the money and make a commitment yet. We'll only open from Thursday to Sunday. We all need a rest."

"Without alcohol, the indoor seating wasn't very profitable. People sit around for hours drinking one cup of coffee and using your free Wi-Fi. Maybe Starbucks can afford that product, but they're based on volume. You might as well go retail."

"I have the off-season to fight it out."

Tracey and the boys had countless meetings about the future of the Shack. Arden pushed for the high-end Italian product and even offered to work in Little Italy to learn the ropes and sausages. Skylar wanted to keep the product intact until all the litigation was completed, but we had no idea how long that could take. Gray sort of compromised between the two plans. I kept my mouth shut and just enjoyed the process of watching my family work together. I had finally become an expert witness.

Half of the town's population under the age of twenty-one attended Mac Cool's funeral, a testament to his popularity. Many spoke privately of his artistic and poetic aspirations. When you push yourself to the edge of consciousness, it's best not to be alone. Everyone was clueless why he died, except me.

I had my theories, but Tracey held me back from voicing them when the funeral director asked if anyone had last words. "You're not his father," she said.

"He should be honored. There's no blame."

The casket was lowered into the ground. We all tossed a rock onto the wooden coffin, as was the custom. In a break from tradition, his skateboard, signed by well-wishers, and some of his graffiti artifacts were placed above the coffin. Everyone was invited to place an object of remembrance. I tossed in a thick copy of the annotated *Ulysses*, by James Joyce. Inside I'd written: "Check out the funeral scene, chapter six."

Mac Cool's funeral left us all a bit shaken, Tracey perhaps more than most. She could not voice her inner sadness, other than the obvious, another mother's loss, but a deeper fear was welling within, the fear that has existed since the dawn of time. Would a child step into the void when the mother wasn't watching?

"I'm moving back to New York," Arden pronounced. "I'm only working in the Shack next year if I can run the place my way." We were all in the car after the funeral.

"Does that mean you're kicking me out?" asked Sky. "Who put you in charge?" Years of acrimony and sibling rivalry welled upward.

"You're content hanging out with your buddies and playing music. The Shack needs a new direction."

"Again. Who put you in charge?" Sky volleyed back with more vehemence. He was protecting his piece of turf by pushing his brother away.

"This is not about you and me but the future of the Shack. I'm not planning on spending the rest of my life there anyway. I'm just trying to help— then you, Gray, and Mom can have it." Backed into a corner, Arden quickly retreated.

They both looked to Tracey for a solution, whose head had fallen into her lap with mental and emotional exhaustion. Then they turned to me for direction. This was a Sophie's Choice I had no interest in solving, so I turned to Gray for an answer.

"Now, now, big brothers." He put a hand on each shoulder. "We're all a little stressed. Take a chill pill, smoke a joint, and we'll figure the future out tomorrow."

Satisfied with Dr. Gray's economical, face-saving solution, the family dropped me off at the train to NYC for my week of work and proceeded back out to Montauk. A few days later, Sky called me at my office.

"Is Mom in New York with you?" he inquired, as if one could lose one's mother like an old watch or a new penny. "She hasn't been home for a few days, I think."

"You don't know if your mother is okay? Where are your brothers?" The alarm in my voice could be heard over the whirl of a nearby dental drill.

"Arden and Gray went offshore on a tuna fishing expedition to the canyon. They're due home tonight. I've been up island with friends, but it doesn't look like she's been home. The Shack's only open on weekends now, you know."

"I doubt she went deep sea fishing. She gets seasick in a bathtub."

"I'll keep trying her phone, but you know it's never charged."

"Yeah, why does she have a cell phone if she never answers it? I'll be out later on tonight's Jitney, but call me if you hear from her."

I shut down a hot root canal without fully reaming the chamber and cancelled my last two appointments. The bus ride out seemed slower than I'd remembered, and my frantic calls to her phone went unanswered, but she polices her calls, and if by chance she didn't want to talk to anyone, she just wouldn't answer.

A perfect storm was brewing for sinking my beautiful wife's ship. Not the fishing boat variety the boys were on, I was sure she wasn't out there, but the simultaneous collision of events: Mac Cool's funeral, the stress of closing the Shack, the supervisor's continuous harassment, and now the competition between brothers. The fall is the season for change, and she wasn't very good with transitions.

Arden picked me up from the bus station. "Any word?" I asked.

"We checked all the sweet spots and called her friends. Nada."

"You don't seem too concerned," I noted.

"She probably just needed a break. She'll reappear when she's ready."

He acted as if he knew something but wasn't telling. I couldn't stay home alone, so I made the rounds around town, checking all the beaches and hotspots. For some reason, I decided to check her mother's house, on Old Montauk Highway, about a mile away from ours. There were no cars in the driveway or lights on in the house. I was about to give up when I spotted a faint light coming from a corner bedroom. Inspecting closer, there was Tracey, alone in bed, reading a worn copy of James Joyce's *Ulysses*. She tore the pages from the thick volume as she finished them.

It was ironic that she should have chosen this classic story to read. Individually and as a family, we had been on a hundred-day journey into uncharted waters. Crisis after crisis had taught us much about the business and about ourselves. Tracey's epiphany was living in the moment, and mine was the acceptance of happiness. Bust needs pedestal and vice versa. Writing this story was a testament to my family's strength.

"What are you doing?" I slammed the door. "Don't you realize how upset we all were that you disappeared? Where have you been?"

"I've been here all along." She slowly closed the remaining pages of the book. "I needed a break from all you boys." The floor was littered with torn pages.

"Why? What did I do?"

"You didn't do anything. I wanted them to take charge."

"Without telling anyone? That's just brilliant. The only one you punished was me. They went fishing and didn't even know you had gone."

"I guess you're right. I'm really sorry. There's no benefit in running away unless people know you already left." She looked so sad and vulnerable alone in the dark that I didn't have the heart to chastise her further. "Next time, I'll leave them a note." I put my arm around her and held her tight to my chest until we both fell asleep.

The next morning, Tracey returned to work and her baking as if nothing had happened. None of the boys mentioned her absence either. I was sitting out in front of the Shack having an excellent double espresso and freshly baked croissant with homemade jam, when a young girl from the neighborhood came by and asked for a job.

"Please, I'll do any job you have. I just wa … wa … want to work at the Gig Shack. You guys are so hip." She was a nice girl, but unfortunately, she was slightly learning disabled and had a speech impediment. No other business and certainly no restaurant, which deals in customer service, would bother training or hiring her. There were social service agencies for the disabled, and frankly, I was fed up with taking care of the community when, to date, the local community, or at least the supervisor, had done everything to fuck us. Fair was fair, I'd thought.

"I'm sorry. We're not hiring," I told her, but Tracey overheard our conversation.

"Nonsense, there's always some kind of work for a sweetie. Would you be willing to work for free food and tips?" she asked the young lady.

"Would I? You bet your bo ... bo ... bottom do ... do ... dollar. When can I start?" The girl beamed from eyetooth to eyetooth, right through her braces.

So Tracey spent her entire afternoon training our new employee silverware-rollup techniques and ketchup-cup filling. Tracey was the queen of patience. The girl came back every afternoon and was disappointed when there were no more napkins. What she lacked in linen skills, she made up with desire.

While I was outside, a local guy came to my table and offered me cash if I would mention him in my memoir. It was a stab at immortality. The hardware and liquor stores were spreading the word that I was writing a memoir about opening a restaurant in Montauk. You wouldn't believe how empowering it was to hold a pen over people's heads. Once locals knew I was loaded with a six-pack of words, they ran for cover. Or else, strangers who wouldn't have given me the time of day were coming by to say hello. Of course, I never took anyone's money. Much.

Not that I was above taking or offering a bribe if it would promote the efforts of my family, but the cash offer got me to thinking about why I was really writing this memoir and how it would fit into my own personal epiphany. There was the obvious quest for revenge against the beach bullies. I had little confidence in the present administration, and there had been a clear case of conspiracy.

I also had a political agenda to upscale the town and promote a more business-friendly environment. In my vision, Montauk would be the green tourist destination of the East Coast, promoting maritime non-automobile transportation. Taking advantage of its natural resources—excellent train and bus service to New York City, nearby airports, and deep-water harbors—alternative modes of commuting would be sought, so a visiting family could enjoy a week at the beach without any need for a car. High-speed passenger ferries would connect the Montauk docks to New England. A free downtown bus carrying surfboards on its side would lope from the train, to the dock, to the beach, and back into town. A central sewage system would replace the outdated drains.

Having absorbed a litany of complaints as the vent for my family and the commercial neighbors for the past season, I desperately needed an outlet to express my own feelings. Writing this story was my release valve from the pressure cooker, a self-psychoanalysis. A testament to my family's struggle and a safe place to hide when everyone was working at the Shack and I'd already been fired three times in one day. Although patched and worn, my Teflon skin was now ready to rant and roll.

Around that time, Emily's boyfriend disappeared, which wasn't a loss as I was about to kick him out of our house. We had offered him work at the Shack and catering gigs, but he always had some excuse for not working, which was that he was a professional surfing bum. He had offered us one of his hand-carved surfboards as a gift for allowing him to live rent-free for three months. That was very civilized of him. The custom-made board sat in the corner of our kitchen but disappeared when he did. I guess we had just rented his gift. What a lowlife. The real problem was that Emily had bought tickets for them to spend the off-season in Morocco. Her bags were already packed, but the boyfriend hightailed his ass out of town before she awoke. She eventually found the piece of shit, dragged his sorry ass all over Africa, but he dumped her with his bad debt and a broken board somewhere between Casablanca and Timbuktu.

"What's love got to do with it?" I explained to Tracey that I had heard in the beginning of the summer that the guy used women.

"If you knew all along, why didn't you tell her?"

"I wanted to, but you told me to mind my own business."

"I never told you that. I thought you were Emily's friend too."

Tell me if I'm crazy, but isn't this déjà vu from earlier in the story? Anyway, by this point in the season, I was sick of talking about Emily's love life or lack thereof. I'd introduced the woman to lots of nice guys, and she'd fallen for the worst.

"The liquor lawyer called from a bar," Tracey said. "The state refuses to reissue my alcohol license unless the town says our C of O is legal. As a retail establishment, I am not allowed to sell or serve alcohol. The town can't prove an illegal case of BYOB. I never knew this guy had a beer. I wasn't even there. I want a jury trial." Her voice rose, and the mere thought of time served made her eyes twitch.

"Okay, slow down. Let's find solutions, a positive spin. You're not illegal, but you are retail. You could sell beer by the case."

"I don't want to sell beer to go."

"I'm just trying to make a square beer keg fit a round hole."

"I don't like that solution. What else you got up that sleeve."

I pulled up my sleeve and showed skin. "I got a million of them. I know for a fact that there are many other local food establishments that are not legal restaurants but have alcohol licenses. You need to provide your lawyer with a list. He could then show that the town acted capriciously in their enforcement of the rules."

"Capricious enforcement? Do you just make these things up?"

"You contact the building department for a list. Your lawyer would charge thousands; just think of the money you'd save by doing it yourself."

"Thank you for delegating another job for me, boss."

Even though she had asked for advice, our conversation quickly deteriorated into another "you are telling me what to do." Tracey came from a family of artists. She could paint a beautiful picture, but it was difficult for her to sell it. Where she saw walls, I saw doors. How could I open doors without doing it for her?

The dining room counters were imported from a Buenos Aires flea market. The place screamed tango. Maybe we couldn't dance legally inside, so I pulled her through the closed door and out in front onto the sidewalk. My right arm caressed her back as my left hand encouraged a tango embrace. "Let's commit an act of civil disobedience." We turned up the music and danced for an hour under the beam of a foggy street lamp, right there on the public street. The supervisor's phone must have been ringing off the hook to report our act of guerilla tango.

Chapter 43

A Family Restaurant

Nico departed for warmer waters a week after Labor Day, abandoning Gray as head chef of the ship. Though barely sprouting whiskers, Gray took to his new position with a keen hunger and the cutting edge of a seasoned veteran. The family psychologist had found his life calling. "All of you get out. This kitchen is mine!"

Coping with the reduced schedule and staff, he chopped the menu to fit the limited fall business, which had tapered to a drizzle. He reorganized the walk-in refrigerator and freezer and retrained the remaining hands to operate under his vision.

"The first thing is to get rid of breakfast. We don't have the staff for three meals, and Mom's not willing to serve an egg sandwich," he said.

"But you're only open Thursday through Monday now. There's a waiting line down the block for breakfast," I said. "Breakfast is a no-brainer."

"It has never been our meal, and I'm not working fifty hours straight."

"Okay, chef, it's your kitchen," I agreed without much of a fight, but you don't turn away business. Frying a few eggs would have been easy, and the off-season, morning prep crew often stood around doing nothing as there wasn't that much turnover of food, but I'd learned by now that my opinion wasn't worth a hill of beans, and to be honest, I'd lost interest in trying. Who says you can't teach an old dog not to bark?

"Dad, are you representing?" He plunked a worn 668 hat on my head. "I need someone to pick up three cases of lobsters from the dock." He handed me a pile of money. The child offering the father money was an ironic turn of enabling. I pocketed the cash and his list of fish products and headed to the market. The scenic ride to the dock was an escape from the empty dining room.

As I entered through the dock's back door, marked Private—Commercial Clients Only, the bustling crew of fishmongers froze in silence and stared at me with a mixture of disbelief and annoyance. Who the hell was I to enter uninvited this forbidden sanctuary? As an unknown face, they assumed I'd entered through the wrong door and was a mere pedestrian ogling their catch for a quick photo shoot. After a few toothless, dirty sneers, they resumed their fish hauling and cursing as if I were invisible.

The large, sterile shed was filled to the brim with crates of fresh fish and feisty crustaceans that had been long lined, dragged, baited, netted, scraped, harvested, and raised from seed from well-lit inland waters to the dark deep seas. The hides of decapitated tuna and swordfish glistened with an effervescent rainbow of colors, and porgy eyes beamed back at me with crystal clarity. Along the far wall was some biologist's joke, a bizarre collection of environmentally challenged lobster shells. A recent blight had attacked the species causing strange and unsightly deformations in their claws and tails. Although the parasite was harmless to humans, the disease had done a job on the poor bottom dwellers' love life.

"Restaurant owners only?" The foreman interrupted my uninvited inspection by placing a white sheet over the rogue's gallery.

"Six-six-eight," I meekly assured the weather-beaten crewman that I belonged in the room. He was dressed in yellow, blood-soaked overalls, and his hair was spotted with fish scales and unknown gizzards. He sheathed his sharp fillet knife in its scabbard.

"Oh, Gray sent you? Good kid. Why didn't you say so sooner?" The head monger smiled conspiratorially and ordered his assistants to gather our pre-arranged haul of mussels, clams, and flounder. "Thanks for the business. You were one of our best accounts by the end of summer." I signed the receipt and departed to my car.

A group of tourists surrounded the trunk of my car and salivated over the crawling critters. "Which restaurant are you from, mister? We love lobster. Man, that is so glamorous, having your own restaurant in the Hamptons."

Feeling like a rock star, I gave them directions to my Shack, but declined their request for special reservations. "First come, first serve, but ask for me and I'm sure my kids will offer you the best seat in the house."

I don't know why we refused reservations in the off-season. Add that to the list along with table management, lousy marketing, and where's the bacon.

When I got back to the Shack, Arden was dissecting a huge codfish for home use. He'd battled the monster onboard in hand-to-hook combat. He had fought the beast for hours, lured from the abyss, the canyons off the continental shelf. Expertly sharpening his thin-bladed knife, he lectured on the anatomy of the giant fish as he filleted perfect loins of toothsome flesh. His fingers delicately worked along the animal's spine, tethering tendon from muscle. With the precision of a sushi master, he massaged the marble from the meat. "Parasitic worms." He picked off the nearly invisible splinters.

Gray allowed me to pinch hit as he was short of staff. He surveyed my pile of mangled mango bits. "Listen, Dad, I'm going to teach you the proper technique to skin a mango for the salsa. When you're done with these boxes, I'll need help cleaning the steamed lobster too." He sharpened my blade through three cycles of machining and then attacked the oval fruit. With the hands of a surgeon, he parlayed two thick slivers of red and orange meat before coring the remaining pit. It was a neat job and conserved much more meat with less effort than my untrained hacking had done.

Utilizing my new knife skills, I made quick work of dozens of mangos. A recent expert with the paring tool, I skinned fruit to the brim of the large container. Next came the raw red peppers. I trimmed both ends and discarded the seeds, then unfolded the remaining fiber and smashed it flat. The scrolled vegetable made for an easy dice.

The kitchen was a beehive of activity, and we each had our assigned interwoven responsibilities. There was cursing and yelling when we were in the weeds, but no one threw pots or broke dishes. Shucks.

In the meantime, Gray smothered schools of live lobsters headfirst into cauldrons of salted, boiling water. After ten minutes, the shells turned all shades of pink, and he dumped the steamers into buckets of ice to cool the flesh. "Tails and claws." He tore heads from bodies and with a wooden mallet smashed open the shells and picked out perfect white morsels of meat.

In my inexpert hands, the mashing mallet made quite a mess. The kitchen floor and my face were soon covered with bits of broken shell and salty juice. It was a good thing I was wearing protective glasses.

From my lobster lobotomy, I looked up through a cloud of crusty film growing on the lens. Tracey was coming toward me. She was smiling and carrying a large tray of devil's food and carrot cupcakes right from the oven. "Hot tray," she warned all in her way and safely stored them in a case. Turning back toward me, she surveyed my mess.

I expected a quick rebuke and the thumbs, strike three, you are out sign. How many strikes had I earned today? Instead, she smiled more broadly and kissed me tenderly on the cheek. "You are a good man, husband."

There is no finer compliment a wife can give her husband.

Sky came back from the bar area. "Does anyone know the past tense of break dancing?" He checked our eyes for an answer to his charade. "Broke dancing? Dancing broke? If you guys are done with your dance break, we got hungry customers to feed."

This was the moment we had slaved for, the whole family working together in that back kitchen. The boys were finally taking ownership of their individual product. We had a well-knit family restaurant on the brink of turning a profit. This was as good as life can get. We were working our asses off, and I was finally part of the team.

The owner of the hardware store was out front, waiting for his espresso and cupcake. "How's it going, mayor?"

"No, you should be the mayor."

"No, doc. You should be the mayor. You got people skills."

"Yeah, but you're a made man. You were born here."

The owner of the liquor store walked in with the same order. "How's it going, mayor?" He slapped his buddy on the back.

"We should all be the mayor of Montauk, as if that job actually existed," I said.

"If that job existed, who would want it?" answered the owner of the Vine.

"I already got enough headaches," added the owner of all things hard.

"Well, if I was the mayor, the first thing I'd do would be to secede from East Hampton. They don't love us the same way we love them," I pronounced.

"You got our vote."

In another clear act of civil disobedience, that evening we hired Seamus, the Golden Voice of Ireland. We hoped the supervisor had more important things to worry about, like balancing the faltering budget, than our season-ending party. The one-man band took to our tiny stage and romanced the chords of his guitar with a soulful blend of rock and Irish ditties. The ladies swooned with his tunes, and the local Irish came out from under their rock or wherever it was they were hiding all summer.

One group strolled over from Shaggy's place. They were well lubricated, but all the gears weren't meshing. In fact, they could hardly stand in one place without falling over one another or into the other customers. For a while, I accepted this drunken display with humor, but then the aggressive physical interaction nearly escalated into a mosh pit of bouncing human bodies. The other customers were shooting them dirty looks, and the tension was rising. In the view of the drunken few, running into other people may be a way to communicate, but I got nervous that it could get out of hand, so I pushed the chief culprit, a young lady, aside with a gentle shove toward the door.

By my own admission, I made a lousy bouncer. "This is a family place." I had no tolerance for an ugly display. As gently as could, I escorted the lady off the property. "You need to leave now. The regular customers are complaining," I whispered.

She was quite strong for a small woman. "Get your fucking hands off of me!" She threw a faint swing at my chest, grabbed my shirt by the lapels, and pulled me tight toward her. "Don't tell me what to do!" She dug her nails into my chest. "I'm going to smash you in your fucking mouth."

I hadn't expected such a sudden violent reaction, being a bit of a virgin when it comes to alcoholic behavior, so I raised my hands in an act of submission and to make it clear to her comrades that I hadn't touched the bitch.

Suddenly, I was surrounded by two of her goons. They didn't throw any punches, but the three of them were definitely leaning on me. It took all my strength to keep from getting crushed. They were deep in my body space. I didn't see any alternatives but to violently push them away. I ripped my arms side to side, like a basketball center fighting to hold his rebound. It didn't do much good; as I pushed one away, another took their place. The drunks were closing in fast.

Honestly, I was a little scared. These goons were so drunk that they hardly felt my shoves and I expected the situation to get out of hand. Clenching a fist in self-defense, I tried one last feint. "Look, there's Billy Joel!" I shouted and pointed toward our bar.

The three Beach Bullies turned toward the fake celebrity sighting, leaving me a window to escape their clutches. "Where's Billy? Where's our Billy?"

"Here's Billy!" I pulled out my club and smashed the three of them over the head and into submission. Actually, that isn't what happened. Sky noticed his father's predicament and peacefully escorted the drunks back to their bottle.

A bit shaken by the altercation, I found a quiet seat in the corner, took a deep drag from a hidden flask, and vowed to never play bouncer again.

Toward the end of Seamus's third set, Sky finally got up his nerve and jammed with the great singer. Sky strummed a mean lead guitar. It was a magical moment as we all cheered my son's debut. It was too bad he'd waited till the end of the season before he took the stage. One day, maybe he'll perform at the Montauk Music Festival.

Columbus Day weekend was the final party of the season. The town rescheduled the fireworks that had been rained out the past July 4th. Tracey fretted about whether she would lose money being open. When I showed up that night, she was already yelling at the staff. Her arms were elbow deep in the suds as she angrily washed the dishes.

"Why do I have to do everything around here?"

"Can I help?" I made a lukewarm offer to wash.

"I baked all those cupcakes, and no one's coming to eat them. Who was I kidding? I should have closed a month ago."

"Call all our friends for a last supper. You might as well enjoy your last weekend. You'll be missing the action in the off-season."

She thought over my advice. "You're right, give me the phone." She dropped the dirty pot. "We have all winter to clean, let's have a party."

A big smile crossed her lips. "Husband, you never cease to amaze. You are the yang to my ying. Let's party!"

All negative thoughts about the wife's business loss disappeared. Marriage is a lot like football. You lose touchdowns and recover fumbles. That cartoon about the post-coitus praying mantis couple came back to mind. In the picture, the female turned to her decapitated partner in bed. "Was it as good for you as it was for me?"

"I will toast to that." I pulled out the private stash of champagne, and we clicked glasses. "Just imagine the parties we could have had if the town hadn't taken away our liquor license and table service. You would have been the hit of the season."

Tracey knocked back the dregs with one gulp. "I am done. I am so done."

Arden came running in with that week's issue of the *East Hampton Star*.

"We're in the *Star*. We're in the *Star*!" We all gathered around and nervously read the half-page column:

> *The Gig Is to Relax: Some people like to relax here in the summertime and some people like to frantically relax. Frantically relaxing is sports galore, parties galore, benefits, shopping galore, and making sure you get into the newest, coolest restaurant of the season. 668 is a fun, funky place for people who know how to relax.*

The article offered a three-star review of the food, the service, and Tracey.

> *The owners were about to sit down for dinner when the wife-mom popped up from her chair and insisted that we wait until the butter cream had come to room temperature before we try it. She then personally grated sea salt onto our cupcake. Yes, she is a pastry chef. And she cares.*

We had more good news. The newspaper reported that the supervisor would resign from office and that he was accused of illegally using government funds for political gain. Jay was right all along. The supervisor had criminally abused the office for two terms by running a big political Ponzi scheme. The news of our tormentor's ouster was a fitting vindication for our one hundred days of hell.

In a final act of civil disobedience against that regime, Jay invited Brian, a blind guitarist, to jam at the Shack. The band was spectacular. As the night sky lit awesome fireworks over Umbrella Beach, Brian performed an electronic rift straight from Jimmy Hendricks and in tune with the overhead explosions.

Spare me a moment for the supernatural, but I have a weird story to tell.

The next morning, I hiked alone into the deserted fortress of the Montauk Project, a complex of abandoned buildings housed on the easternmost tip of Long Island. I walked along the coastline, past the ranch, the stone house, the Beards and Warhol Estate. Sneaking up from the beach, I climbed the steep, undefended cliff and crossed the moat of ancient moorland, sylvan Oak and Holly. A few steps off the sheer rock face, the broken tar remains of a WWII military road queried. Sand blown off the beach and onto this road had not been disturbed in many years. The park was completely surrounded by barbed wire, and over the broken-down entrance, a threatening sign read, No Trespassing. In the distance, the dilapidated radar tower, one of the tallest buildings in the Hamptons, loomed like an evil force. Wind cried through the monolithic radar's grate.

Climbing over the fence, my pant leg momentarily caught the wire, and I struggled to break free from this invisible hand. With desperation and a heightened sense of fear, I tore the cloth and dropped to the other side. I followed the path for a little while until I spotted smoke rising from the chimney of the park ranger station to the left. A military looking vehicle idled alongside, a checkpoint blocking the entrance to the main road. Avoiding the guards was vital to my inspection.

Camouflaged by the deep underbrush, I trucked through the woods the other way until discovering a small, unoccupied, one-story white building. I snuck inside. Fire and water had destroyed the ceiling, which hung over the shiny red vinyl seating, partially burnt, with stuffing tossed about. This had been the recreation hall, the PX. One pin still stood upright at the end of the defunct bowling alley. Empty bottles of beer were thrown around the floor, as if the crew manning this station had been summoned to an emergency in the midst of throwing a final strike. The world had stopped here once, if only for a moment, the building badly damaged, attacked by an extraterrestrial beast.

The other buildings demonstrated a similar, false impression of decay. A ghost town, the residents seemed to have all vanished at once into thin air. Bedding lay neatly tucked in rows of empty bunk beds, a prison waiting for the return of its inmates. Dishes and glasses were still stacked on the tables, as if some unknowable force had transported the previous occupants during dinnertime.

The derelict church was really a gymnasium. Nothing functioned as it appeared.

I'd long heard rumors of occult, alien interventions, a Nazi rear guard for the Fifth Reich, and adventures in synchronicity. Had our government conducted psychological warfare experiments in the 1950s? Whom can one believe? Was this the exact spot where the Lost Boys had vaporized, rebels rejected by the mother ship? If not, why was the supervisor still maintaining the site? Why the barbed wire and high security? Who was he keeping out? What failed experiment was he keeping in? There was a sinister sense to this preservation, as if the feds were fearful that any alteration of the time warp might alter time itself. Suddenly, the conspiracy theory seemed plausible.

Stealthily, I snuck into the main radar building. The walls were electromagnetically shielded, but the padlocked, double steel garage door was suspiciously open. Wind hummed through broken windows with a vital energy, as if the building was alive with secrets. A steady thumping caressed my feet, but it may have been my heart surging to my toes. I took a deep breath to slow my pulse and reassess my observation.

The inside of the monolithic concrete bunker housed a motley assortment of unusual machines, designed by some mad scientists on LSD, with hundreds of diodes, transmitters, and capacitors. Most of the cathode tubes were broken, but the esoteric crystals' actual function was unlike any machine or computer I'd ever witnessed. I was as likely to recognize a time machine in this cluttered, metallic morgue, as pick out Jimmy Buffet from a lineup of out-to-sea surfboarders.

Intrigued by the derelict machines, I touched the face of an ugly green capacitor. The oxidized copper skin, kissed by a sliver of sunlight, was unusually warm. Suddenly, the reflective glow invaded my touch and sent a wave of anxiety up my spine. I felt ill, as if this evil looking contraption had parasitically suckered into my mind. Neurons tingled up the base of my neck, and my skin spiked with goose bumps. My consciousness wavered with repressed memories and past life regressions: a child suckling from a single breast, a large toothy canine standing on my chest, a child hanging by the laundry room rafters while its blind mother passes repeatedly hauling wash. My only urge was to escape from the mental vice of that sorrowful place.

Gathering my wits, I tore my hand free from the mind-machine connection. Fleeing, I tripped over an object lying on the morgue's floor. I couldn't believe my eyes. It was impossible. This wasn't right. The horror. The most horrible horoscope of them all. The perceived object was Mac Cool's skateboard, the one that shattered in his fall from the tree, the same board I had placed in his grave.

Chapter 44

Zone In/Zone Out

The restaurant closed for the season after Columbus Day. Small-town boredom and tumbleweed pickups blew into town, chasing out the high-end Humvee and the Surf Lodge's meat market cruisers. Main Street returned to its deserted off-season roots, a stunningly beautiful, depopulated ghost town. The surf shops ran end-of-season sales on winter wetsuits, and the bass register went on a blitz.

Arden returned to college for his last semester, and Gray enrolled in the French Culinary Institute, leaving Sky and a ragtag group to clean up the kitchen mess.

"Maybe I should quit this fight already and accept that I'm just another deli?"

"Is that what you want to do?" I asked Tracey.

"No, but I've sunk every penny we have. It is the righteous fight."

"A good card player knows when to hold and when to fold."

"I'm really nervous. My zoning hearing is coming up next week. The town already sent out notices to all the neighbors. If Killjoy and his conspirators block the application, like they've done for thirty years, I'm screwed."

"You should contact all your friends. Send an e-mail blast asking for their support. Whatever happened to the quest list of addresses I collected all summer? Emily was supposed to create a database of customers."

"Nothing happened with it. I hate asking people for help."

"They're not strangers. They're your friends and loyal customers. It's in their interest to see you survive. Why not ask? You could drown the dissenters in positive energy." My frustration with Tracey's fear of self-promotion was apparent.

"If it's such a good idea, why don't you do it yourself?"

I was quite capable of giving her advice, but I had no interest in doing the laundry myself. It was her show and if she didn't care enough to do the dirty work, or wasn't willing to adapt to the hard water, then the clothes could stay dirty. It irked me that as the silent partner, I had to remain silent, but my job was to be the witness and the banker.

"Husband. You are like an ox tethered to a cart, carrying all our possessions. You will continue to bull your way forward through the world, no matter what we say."

"Thank you for the compliment." Although, I'm sure it wasn't meant as such. It was ironic she considered me the bull, when all I ever wanted was to be my wife's hero.

Ignoring her straight arm, I envisioned next week's zoning meeting and considered Machiavelli's strategy for dividing and conquering enemies. Our neighbors never liked one another and only gathered as one in opposition to us. Now that their leader, the supervisor, had been dethroned, I needed to find the weak link in their fortress. I pictured pulling old Shaggy into the back room and threatening him with a lawsuit for selling us the building with a forged or at least questionable liquor license. If the Deli Dolls showed their faces, I would threaten to turn the Shack into another deli and undercut their prices. Killjoy was the real problem and probably the only one likely to show. What was his weakness?

Over the phone, I told Arden my secret plan for disrupting the enemy triumvirate. "If Killjoy shows at the meeting, I'm going to inform him that Shaggy is going around town saying nasty things behind his back. Who is his real enemy?"

"Dad, you're going out of your mind. Didn't you always advise that it was bad business for the owner to allow things to get personal?"

"Yeah, but Killjoy started it. He made it personal first."

"What are you really going to accomplish? He'll only end up hating you more than he does already. The guy did have grounds for being angry. Go drill some teeth."

I knew he was right, but I couldn't overcome my anger. I stayed awake at night dreaming of cutting Killjoy's head off the body of a six-legged crab, a soft-shell BLT sandwich, light on the mayo, heavy on sweet revenge.

"I'm going to come out next weekend for the hearing."

"Yeah, that would be nice." I pictured Killjoy's decapitated body.

"I'll drop by Killjoy's and talk him up, fisherman to fisherman, but if he doesn't take the bait, I'll blog the bastard's name. You forget, I'm a salty dog when I want to be."

"Maybe I should park my car in front of his driveway so he can't get out?"

"Dad. Let me deal with him. Bye."

Hanging up the phone, my mind reeled with conspiracy theories. Our lawyer's argument was that since the town had given us a liquor license already, they couldn't now take it away, or the finders-keepers theory. His point seemed a bit naïve, but he was a bar specialist. It made more sense to me that the town had enforced capriciously.

I explained my theory to Tracey over dinner. "They allow other non-restaurant zoned establishments to serve alcohol. How can they prosecute only us? I think the supervisor was behind the conspiracy to close the Shack."

"Where do you come up with these theories?" asked Tracey.

"Mac Cool told me before he died. The Lost Boys confessed everything."

"I love you, dear. You are the smartest man I know, but I'd look twice in the mirror before I listened to the conspiracy theories of lost boys or girls."

"Well, who do you suspect?"

"It's just the system. Once the gears get moving, the wheel of justice has to grind out the truth. This is my last chance to set that wheel on a new course." With a sense of foreboding, she asked, "What are you planning to say in front of the zoning board?"

"It's a secret. If I tell you now, you won't let me come."

We met numerous times with the lawyer to map out a strategy. The week leading up to the zoning board hearing was one of the most stressful to date. I give Tracey some credit; although a nervous wreck, she swallowed her artist's pride and contacted everyone who was around and the original owners of the Shack, who agreed to testify that they had always operated the place as a restaurant.

A few days before the hearing, our lawyer got a letter from the Deli Dolls saying that they would not object to our application if we agreed to prevent our employees from parking in the lot. "Legally unjustified, but expedient, one down."

"Maybe I'll make Shaggy an offer he can't refuse. I know he won't help, I just don't want him to show up and sabotage your chances." A new strategy played in my mind to break up the triumvirate.

"Don't call Shaggy, it would just motivate his evil impulses," Tracey requested.

"Okay, maybe he'll just make like an old duck and fly south for the winter."

The weather the day of the hearing was awful. The rain fell so hard it washed away the asphalt border on our driveway. It was an inauspicious sign, but they say you can't control the weather or the zoning. We salted the old courthouse in East Hampton with our supporters. The room overflowed with goodwill and well-wishers buzzing that the people's voice would finally be heard. We were confident that we had a good case.

A graveling hush crushed the common cheer as Killjoy and his wife entered the courthouse through the back door. The whole audience turned and stared, shooting them dirty looks and evil eyes. The Killjoys sat alone in the back corner, acutely aware that they had entered enemy territory. He had confronted previous owners of the Shack and always prevailed, but never had he faced such a backlash from the community. He bit at his lip, and his wife fidgeted with discomfort.

Would Shaggy show up next? I imagined strolling over to Killjoy's corner and finally hitting them with the line, "So you want war? Let the best family win." It was a stupid comment best left unspoken, but at the time, I wasn't thinking straight. My heart raced and leaped in my throat. I tried controlling my anger with yoga breath, but I was losing control. My chest tightened. I was stuck to the bench and couldn't get up.

Arden approached the Killjoys, shook their hands, and wished them well, even though they hadn't returned his previous calls for reconciliation. Boy that kid had balls. He could sell shoes to a man with no feet. He shot Killjoy his Doctor Gross patented lumineer smile, a perfect set of pearly white porcelain, a nice gesture considering the circumstances, but completely wasted on that Beach Billy, whose ability to change was as glacial as Montauk stone. Concerned now, Killjoy scanned the court for backup.

The zoning board was comprised of five volunteer members, but was effectively controlled by the zoning board chairman. An older gentleman, he had sat on that same seat for over three decades and was instrumental in passing the original zoning for the Shack and preventing any changes since. He didn't appear happy to see the same issue resurface after all these years, and he approached our meeting with a stern frown.

Disheartened that our adversaries controlled all the branches of government, I anticipated a quick retreat. The war would soon be lost.

Disgusted, I turned to the back of the courtroom to see if the opposition had arrived. There seemed to be some faint sign of recognition between Killjoy and the chairman of the board. Maybe they went to high school together.

Our lawyer presented his opening argument to the board. "With all due respect to your years of service and commitment to the goodwill of our community." He was ass kissing and cowered before them. "It is apparent that there has been an injustice and misunderstanding of the original 1980 decision. When the zoning board approved the original variance for parking and sewage, it effectively approved the change of use."

The chairman didn't even give our attorney a chance to conclude his legal brief. "There were no mistakes made here!" His voice slammed like a judge's gravel. "This property was only granted to be an ice cream parlor, not a restaurant, and that is the end of the story." His mind was closed to debate. "If previous owners operated it as an illegal restaurant, then they lied to us and the State Liquor Authority. We're not here to police if someone tries to pull the wool over our eyes. You are wasting your time."

Tracey's worried eyes met mine and cried like a Gulag widow. Our last-ditch case appeared hopeless, the chairman's mind preconceived. He had made his decision about our zoning thirty years ago and now defended his vested opinion. Any debate was probably a foregone conclusion.

In the far reaches of the courtroom, Killjoy smirked with premonition.

Our lawyer presented the rest of his legal argument. He had obviously done extensive research into the town zoning codes, the history of the Shack, and knew all the loopholes better than the actual board. His confidence quickly won over the crowd, which murmured that our case was a slam-dunk.

I wasn't so sure. My blood pressure thumped so high that for a brief moment the whole room spun counterclockwise. I can't be sure what happened next, but I thought the chairman announced, "Counselor, if that's the best you got, I'm not convinced. I've never been out there, but it was never supposed to be a restaurant." He motioned for the lawyer to take a seat. "You're wasting my time. Is there anyone else who wants to speak?"

I wanted to allow Tracey to speak first, and anyway, if I had stood up at that moment, I probably would have passed out. I felt seasick, groggy, like a third mate caught in a winter swell. I looked around the room to see who would go first.

Killjoy's wife jumped up to the microphone, representing the opposition.

"There are parking and sewage limits which should prohibit any change of use." She had good points. I made a mental note to address those issues when it was my turn.

A long line of our supporters took the stage next and voiced their opinion that the Shack had the best food in town, was reasonably priced, and that we were asset to the community. They thought it was unbelievable that in these tough financial times, the town would close a business that paid taxes and shepherded the local youth.

The mother of the girl with disabilities appeared even though we hadn't contacted her. The mother lectured the board that Tracey's was the only business in town willing to hire her daughter and teach her a trade. The woman made a heartfelt case, and for the first time, it appeared that the chair of the board was softening his stern stance.

Tracey took the stand next. It was her assignment to explain the economics of the business. Although she was shaking like a leaf on the drive over, she looked surprisingly calm and collected in front of the microphone, and maybe a little bit flirtatious with the old guy. She looked drop-dead gorgeous in her Zoning Appeal uniform, meat and potato, brindled brown linen that matched her hair color, nothing too fancy. In a clear and concise statement, she educated the board that a restaurant job put more money in the waiter's pocket and the local economy than if they operated as a take out.

There was definitely a change in the board's attitude. They smiled approval that they were dealing with a loving and nurturing woman, instead of the usual fly by night.

Before Tracey had even sat down, Killjoy, huffing and puffing, reclaimed the stand. He angrily pointed an accusatory finger at me. "That guy! You know what he did? He blocked my driveway once." That's all he said and took a seat.

The spectators all looked toward one another with a "what was that?" If blocking his driveway once was the best argument he could come up with for closing our business, then he really was finished. Someone in the crowd murmured, "What a bozo."

Replying to Killjoy's challenge was my opportunity to take the stand. I've been in courts of law before, on both sides of the aisle, but never was I more nervous. My ears rang with the beat of my heart as I took the stage. The mental notes I'd made while waiting were already argued, and I didn't want to appear redundant. "I'm the silent partner." It was meant as a joke, but the board wasn't smiling. "Papi chulo? The sugar daddy?" They still didn't get my stab at humor, so I addressed the competition instead. "Mr. Killjoy has complained about every owner of the Shack since its inception. I ask him, what kind of business would you like next to you?"

Killjoy would have spat in my face if he had been within range.

I turned back to the board members, who appeared annoyed that I was on a personal vendetta, and changed tactics. "The board has a moral and legal obligation to provide a clear and manageable zoning. We cannot operate as a preexisting, nonconforming whatever. Most of our business is pedestrians from the hotels, and the sixty seats are already granted. We are not asking for any additional allowance. Regarding the sewage, restaurants' usage requires less than a fast turnover takeout, and presently we are operating at a third of capacity. I surveyed my neighbor's interest in sewage because downtown needs a central system before the next big hurricane hits. Everyone is supportive of central sewage except him." I addressed my enemy.

Licking my chops, I continued, "Now, let me get to the heart of the matter." My voice raised two octaves, and I pointed an accusatory finger at the board's blank faces. If I couldn't convince them, at least I'd confuse them. "When I purchased the building, I did my due diligence and hired your town building engineer. He told me at that time that there was no difference between selling ice cream and other food products. That is your town code. I relied on your employee's advice. You are committing contractual jeopardy. You can't selectively enforce the rules. That would be criminal. I demand justice."

The audience broke out in applause. "You tell them, pops!"

The board members communed concern with one another but didn't interrupt. I considered threatening further legal action but withheld my last bullet for a later date.

"Furthermore!" Unconsciously, my voice raised two more octaves. "There has been a blatant, illegal, capricious enforcement by your code enforcers. There are numerous other establishments that are zoned as banks or even gas stations, which you continue to allow operating as restaurants. I demand a consistent rule of law. I demand justice and an end to the unwarranted harassment!" The crowd cheered wildly.

The board's mouth hung open in horror. They weren't expecting Nathan Hale's, "Give me a legal C of O or give me death." What was supposed to be a mundane hearing had turned into an indictment of all the misdeeds of the present administration. Mac Cool would have been proud of my performance. I hoped my little wife wouldn't hang me.

Killjoy and his wife vacated the courtroom though the back door, the same way they had come in. Our supporters took the stand, and one by one, each voice was greeted with wild applause. Finally, our last witness, Arden, reached the podium.

Dressed in a natty, New York suit, he captivated the board members' attention. Mainly he spoke about the food experience in a restaurant setting versus takeout and how the Shack had presented the local youth with artistic and culinary inspiration.

The board excused themselves to an adjacent hidden room, while the audience of well-wishers sat with bated breath waiting for the decision. Turning toward one another, we postulated the outcome from the changes in each board member's expression. Some of us saw facial sympathy where others saw only annoyance. Tracey and I bit nails and exchanged anxious glances with our supporters. Eventually, the hung jury reappeared. The courtroom was so still you could feel the vibration of a silenced cell phone.

The chair thanked us all for our attendance and the show of community activism.

The actual timing and mechanics of the decision are not important. The main point is we had won! Against all odds and the old boy conspiracy, the zoning appeals board accepted the merits of our argument and determined that the 1980 variance did allow for a restaurant use of the space. The squeaky wheel of justice had squeaked in reverse.

We had won! We were finally a legal restaurant!

After a huge cheer, our supporters returned to our house for a post zoning-board hearing hangover. The wine and cheeses flowed. With loaded knapsacks, we headed off to the beach for an end-of-the-year bonfire. The boys and I dug a pit and gathered driftwood from the dunes. The sticks caught an updraft, and the flames exploded against the darkness. Flickers of torchlight shadowed figures on the water. Overhead, the Milky Way gleamed. Sky pulled out a handmade guitar and sang a few tunes. Brilliant!

A few days later, I had a happiness epiphany while swimming in the Olympic-sized, saltwater pool. After thirty minute-laps, I saw my reflection in the ripples of shimmering pool light. Tripping on endorphins, the ripples spoke like lips echoing an inner voice. The secret to happiness was appreciating all the good things in life and negating the missing. We play the cards we are dealt. Owning the Shack was an investment in marriage, parenting, and community, all the blessings that Tracey and the Dalai Lama preached but I chose to negate. I'd heard this theory many times before, but now it made complete somatic sense. I felt the happiness down to my toes. By practicing the single tango life part-time in the city, I had the best of all worlds. It had been the best of times.

Breinigsville, PA USA
23 May 2010
238526BV00001B/4/P